BARNACLE BRAT

(a dark comedy for grown-ups)

Adrian Baldwin

Body text set in Georgia

A CIP catalogue record for this title is available from the British
Library.

For James Alan Baldwin (1934-2012)

Acknowledgements and a Warning

Firstly, the warning: As it says on the cover, this is a novel aimed at *grown-ups*. The story is *not* for youngsters. Why? Because some of my characters use Adult Language; often foul, blasphemous, or sexually charged – on several occasions, *all three*. I didn't necessarily *want* them to but sometimes they insisted. That's characters for you! Some of them can be a right bunch of ****ers.

Okay, now I've got that out of the way, the acknowledgements:

Kane Baldwin.

Despite my regular nit-picky interrogations on all matters key-cutting, shoe-repairs, trophy-engraving and the like, he kept his humour and patience throughout.

I'd also like to gratefully recognise the help of two of my early-readers:

Sandra Baldwin and Bronwen Brooks.

Their feedback and ability to spot typos was invaluable. If *you* should find any errors, glaring or otherwise, that slipped through the net, they are all mine.

                                                                A.B.

BARNACLE BRAT
(a dark comedy for grown-ups)

'When there is absolutely nothing left to do,
you HAVE to pull the trigger.'

PROLOGUE

The bit where nobody knows what's going on

WHAT THE—

Leon Blank awoke to find himself hanging upside-down, seatbelt cutting into his shoulder like a knife. He coughed and a shudder of pain shot through his chest and lit up his neck. One ear encountered a high-frequency hum. His eyes, dazzled by light, could take nothing in.

Until a few minutes ago, 'Betty', a vintage Volkswagen Beetle, had been Lester and Veronica's pride and joy; now, she was a creaking, overturned, twisted metal shell – a write-off beset by fumes and threads of pallid smoke.

As his vision adjusted, Leon caught sight of a section of face in the rear-view mirror. A familiar blue eye, now smoke-smudged and puffy, blinked back. Wiping the eye, he aligned the reflection, squinted, and recoiled sharply.

This is what he saw:

His parents; in the back, also suspended in seatbelts.

Despite their situation, the tethered sexagenarians appeared as great bats, experiencing nothing more traumatic than a preflight nap. A single thought poked its silly head out of the dusty cellar that was Leon's fuddled mind: *Sixty-year-olds look much older upside-down.* He immediately berated himself for thinking so. Then, as if synchronised, their eyes blinked open. They looked akin to startled Victorian chimney-sweeps.

'*Oh fuck!*' blurted Leon.

Veronica gave him a familiar scowl. 'Language, Leon.'

Leon shouted over the hum in his ear: '*What?*'

'Language.'

'*Oh, right! Sorry, Ma!*'

'And there's no need to yell.'

'What the fuck happened?' asked Lester, checking his hearing-aid was in place as he looked around.

'*Lester, please!*' yelled Veronica.

1

What the fuck happened? An appropriate question, and exactly what Leon was thinking. Encumbered by a stiffening, crooked neck, he explored on eyes alone.

To the front, immediately behind gnarled dashboard and cracked windscreen, Leon identified crumpled bonnet and a snatch of iron railings bridged by stone wall. By his head he discerned a section of pavement wet with rain, and beyond, to his right, colouring the edge of his peripheral vision, a Royal Mail letterbox, shining like a bale-fire, about as red as red can be, everything illuminated, as it was, by Betty's headlights reflecting off the wall.

Kneading his stony neck, he turned off the lights, slowly worked his head to the side, and saw that it was night. A black sky hung like an inky void under the inverted world outside. Suspended above the nothingness, street lights investigated rain-soaked road, their reflections attempting hopeless gatherings against the muddling downpour. Leon watched, spellbound, as the heavy rain poured 'upward', drenching the surrounding palette of sodium-orange and slug-grey. He had always been fascinated by rain, especially *hard* rain – the look of it, the sounds it made – but this upside-down rain was something else.

As it dawned on Leon that he couldn't feel his legs, and he worried that this might be a bad sign, a coughing fit seized him. The convulsions rattled his lungs, scorched dry by vapours, and sent a whole new wave of suffering through his neck and chest.

When the pain subsided, he noticed the high-pitched whine in his ear had dropped to a low drone. Over the still-running engine he heard a thunderous pitter-patter above his feet: rainstorm pelting the vehicle's underside. The deluge almost hissed as it splashed all around.

Putting the worsening heavy weather to one side for a moment, Leon's mind tried to take stock. He reviewed the topsy-turvy perspective and clear evidence of a road traffic accident but for some reason his brain wouldn't process them into anything that made sense. His *Now* was an *After* with no awareness of a *Before*.

Leon acquiesced to his mental disorientation, accepted it as easily as the physically absurd situation he'd found

2

himself in. Anyone who knew him well would probably not be surprised; he had a well-established, not-so-rare personality trait: he would regularly become sidetracked, often by trivialities – sometimes getting involved to the point of obsession – and this occasionally resulted in disconnects from 'serious matters'.

But why *tell* you when we could just as easily *show* you? Here's an example:

Once, when walking to school (Leon must have been about twelve) his shoes developed a faint squeak; both of them – at the same time! Leon thought this far too improbable to be mere coincidence and the incident really freaked him out. He spent hours crawling around the kitchen floor, shoes on hands, ears low to the tiles, attempting to place the precise location (somewhere in or around the heel area) of the offending squeaks. Is that strange behaviour? Yes, okay, a little, but listen to this: on the following day, Leon learned that his chemistry teacher, Mr Fitton, had become the seventh victim of the so-called *Head Honcho*, a serial killer whose 'signature' was to leave his victims' heads in one place, limbed torsos in another; both in plain view but usually many miles apart. An Aberdeenshire lady out dawn-walking her dog discovered the chemistry teacher's severed head on *The Wallace Monument* in a see-through plastic bag suspended from William Wallace's extended hand.

Mr Fitton was still wearing his bifocals.

The limbed torso was found early the same morning by cleaning staff, in a passport photo booth at Watford Gap services on the M1. Someone, presumably the killer, had taken time to pose the body and insert four pounds. A strip of neck-and-shoulders photos remained untouched in the dispensing slot. Cardboard signs bearing various messages had always been left draped around the torsos' stubby necks and this case was no different.

Mr Fitton's sign read: **HOW DO I LOOK? I CAN'T SEE A THING WITHOUT MY GLASSES.**

A senior police officer insisted they *were* doing everything possible but admitted they remained baffled by the murderer's motives, sick sense of humour, and speed of transit (suggestions of *two* serial killers working in tandem were pooh-poohed). When Leon heard news of the gruesome discoveries, during morning assembly, he never flinched – his mind was on his shoes. He did think about it later. How it was a shame for 'Fitz' and the Fitton family. But he also told himself *'These things happen'* and quickly got back to scrabbling about on all fours to further investigate *The Great Shoe-Quacks Mystery* (he didn't actually name it thus, but he could have done).

Leon had been this way for as long as his parents could remember. They had never regarded it as a problem, though. And for Leon, it was just 'normal'. *His* normal: easily deflected from the moment at hand to a moment in his head.

CALL ME ARCHIE

Even now, dangling in an upturned car, Leon remained partly detached. An acceptance of the apparent inevitability of dire circumstance, a gentle disconnection from his discomfort, his parents' pendulous restraint, and the preposterous nature of their collective situation – none of these surprised him.

What *did* surprise him was the deep voice from his left:

'Don't worry, Leon, old chap. We'll have you out of here in a jiffy.'

Leon worked his stiff neck far enough to see.

Fettered inelegantly under the passenger seat, detained by tangled seatbelt, hung a ventriloquist's doll: four-foot-tall (give or take), rosy cheeks, thick eyebrows, kiss-curl of hair pressed flat against polished wooden brow, and a fancy smoking jacket over silk pyjamas.

'Who the fuck are you?' Leon asked, calm as you like.

'*Leon!*' Leon heard his mother bark.

The dummy's jaw slid open to reveal a toothy grin. 'Lord Archibald.' He made it sound like a formal announcement.

'*Lord Archibald?*' Leon echoed.

' 'Tis so. We spoke earlier. Dost thou not remember?' Lord Archibald's big eyes clacked as they blinked.

'What the hell are you talking about?'

4

'And do call me Archie, dear boy. All my friends do.' Lord Archibald projected his voice as if he were a stage-actor delivering Shakespeare; booming and dramatic, the manner massively at odds with his diminutive frame. Leon couldn't help it; he laughed.

'What's he laughing at?' Lester wafted his liver-spotted hands at a pall of smoke hanging between him and the passenger seat. 'Leon, who are you talking to?'

Veronica's handbag had come to rest on the upholstered car roof, directly below her head. Rummaging, she said: 'It'll be his imaginary friend again.'

Leon did his best to address the dummy face on. 'Don't listen to mum, she gets confused.' He threw 'Twenty-three now, Ma!' over his shoulder then readdressed Lord Archibald: 'I haven't had an imaginary friend since I was six.'

'*Fifteen*,' corrected mother, bringing a compact to her face. 'Oh, look at the state of me,' she wailed. 'My make-up's all over the shop. No, don't look at me, Lester. Not till I've put some lippy on.' A hand plunged back into the bag.

'I was ten at most,' Leon persisted. 'Thirteen, tops.'

Lord Archibald wasn't listening. He was foraging the outer pockets of his smoking jacket. Lester wasn't listening either; he was watching Veronica, aided by her mirror, apply a circle of pink to her lips.

'His name was Mr Pickles,' Leon went on.

'*Who* was?' Archie boomed.

'The make-believe friend I had when I was—' Leon's eyes met his mother's in the rear-view mirror and he settled on 'when I was younger' before explaining further: 'He was a three-foot-tall marionette. Bit lanky, awkward, and kind of funny looking. Said he liked girls but found it hard to talk to them. I remember he got depressed on a regular basis.'

'Fascinating,' Archie said unconvincingly, his attention focused on exploration. Unable to find what he sought in the smoking jacket's outer pockets, he switched inside.

'Yeah, I'm not sure he was good for me growing up. Really, I mean, what kid needs a *depressed* imaginary friend? I used to tell him stories to try and cheer him up. Other times, I'd put on music, make him dance . . .'

'Wait.' Archie paused his search. 'You made your depressed imaginary friend . . . do an imaginary dance . . . by moving his imaginary strings?'

'How else?' asked Leon. 'I made him talk, too.'

'Bit creepy,' said Archie, not moving his mouth.

'*Creepy?* It's not creepy. Most kids make their imaginary friends talk. Anyway, what about you?'

'What about me?' Lord Archibald expanded already-bulbous eyes.

'Well, it may have escaped your notice, but you are . . . how shall I put this . . . *a dummy.*'

Archie's hands now shifted to pyjama-trouser pockets, patted them stiffly. 'I prefer the term "Mannequin" myself.'

'Whatever. You can't talk without help.'

Archie shook his head. 'You silly boy, do you see anyone helping me?' His eyes flicked side to side then returned to Leon. He waited, wide-eyed, staring. 'Well, do ya, punk?'

'No, but— hang on . . . "*Punk*"?'

'Aha!' the dummy's bottom jaw shifted, established a satisfied smile. A Swiss Army knife was presented for inspection. 'Say hello to my little friend.'

Leon could accept just about anything so long as he wasn't in obvious and immediate life-threatening danger. Even hanging downside-up in a wrecked car seemed kind of benign – had Betty been stuck on railroad tracks, an express train hurtling towards her, it would have been different – but threats of physical violence, be they real or perceived, always freaked him out. And in a battle between Flight and Fight, with Leon, Flight always won. So, true to form, the sight of a knife, no matter how Swiss or useful or unopened, only a metre from his jugular, sent him into a mild panic that kick-started a continuous click-click-clicking on his seatbelt release-button.

'Good idea, but you won't escape that way,' said Archie. 'Not until I've unleashed Excalibur.' He flourished the puny (still unopened) knife as if it were a sword.

Leon thought the dummy's technique less King Arthur more D'Artagnan but this was no time for quibbling. Bottom line: Archie looked mental – menacingly so.

'Mum, Dad, try your seatbelts! Try them *now*!'

For a while, Betty's interior reverberated to the sound of much seatbelt release-switch pressing but Lester's efforts on Veronica's switch (she was busy loading a mascara brush) and his own, proved fruitless – as did Leon's.

'Told you,' Archie said. 'The mechanisms are all buckled. Let us have no more of this frivolous time-wasting.'

'Don't listen to him, Dad. Keep trying.'

'I *am* trying, son.' To Veronica he said: 'Sorry, who is it I'm not listening to?'

Veronica didn't reply – she was glooping her lashes.

'For 'tis blade time!' announced Lord Archibald dramatically – before anti-climatically setting about systematically prying open the Swiss Army knife attachments in search of the actual *knife* part. No mean feat for wooden fingers. First out: tweezers, then a corkscrew followed by a can opener, bottle opener, flat-head screwdriver, Phillips screwdriver, and magnifying-glass; a nail file, scissors, ballpoint pen, fish-scaler, pliers, a miniature saw, and a cheese fork.

Archie sighed, defeated. 'Damn the Swiss and their love of cheese!' he boomed.

'What's up?' Leon asked. 'Can't find your sword?'

'You may scoff but how am I supposed to cut you free without a blade?' Archie submitted the teeny two-tine utensil. '*With this cheese fork?*'

NOT EASY BEING A DUMMY

"*Cut you free.*" Welcome words which would have pacified Leon had he not already been calmed by the plodding procession of diminutive-accessory openings (all sense of imminent blade-peril had subsided with the magnifying-glass, all attempts at escape by way of seatbelt release-button abandoned at the fish-scaler).

'A Swiss army knife without a knife,' said Leon. 'Surely, that's an oversight.'

'I remember now,' said Archie jerking his hand as if to click fingers. 'It fell out when I used it to remove a splinter.'

'*Fell out?* What kind of cheap— hang on . . . *a splinter?* Are you winding me up?'

7

'Not to worry, old boy.' Archie folded away all but the miniature saw blade. 'I'm sure this will do the trick.'

Leon looked doubtful.

The dummy shaped to place the serrated saw edge under Leon's seatbelt. 'No, them first,' Leon said, nodding towards his parents. The nod made him wince.

'Really? Well, okay, but remember our deal,' Archie said.

'Deal? What deal?'

'One moment, please.' Lord Archibald turned, as best he could upside-down, to face Veronica (who was attempting to do something with her hair despite gravity mocking her efforts by pulling every greying strand away from her head). Reaching out his tiny tool, Archie kicked and wriggled within his loose harness like a trapped spider-monkey. 'Balderdash; short by inches!'

'Mind my dress,' said Veronica. Then she landed in a heap on the car's roof lining (Lester's dogged seatbelt-popping had paid off). Leon thought the colourful expletive she let out understandable given the situation.

Veronica whimpered as bits of smashed rear window cut into her back.

'You okay, Vee?' asked Lester, still clicking his own seatbelt release-button.

'Oh, yes. Never better. I nearly landed on Betty's roof lining but luckily, all these pieces of broken glass were here to break my fall.'

Lester said, 'See, persistence pays, Leon. Persistence pays.' And, if proof were needed, Lester's own seatbelt now popped. He landed face-down on top of Veronica.

'*Bloody hell, Lester, you dozy great twat!*'

A little surprising but again excusable, thought Leon.

'Sorry, Vee,' said Lester.

Old hands now moved into action: Veronica braced her palms under Lester's broad shoulders as he raised his considerable weight from her slender frame. Fragments of glass cut into Lester's knees and hands but he didn't complain. Leon, one hand on his neck, strained to clock their scrunching and scraping. 'Are you okay?' he asked.

To Leon, Archie said, 'Oh do keep still.' He'd slipped the little saw under the shoulder strap of Leon's seatbelt and

8

was working it back and forth. The exertion made his hanging wee body swing to and fro. After just a few strokes, a bunch of damaged wires dropped out of a hole in the dashboard. As one, Leon and Archie emitted an involuntary yelp. Some wires, the broken and bare ones, crackled with current. 'Okay, the trick is to remain calm, old boy. Simply remain calm.' Looking far from calm, Archie went into overdrive. 'Look at me,' he said, jaw and eyelids clacking as he pumped the saw, 'see how calm I am? I'm very calm!'

'Yes, you look calm. But then you're made of varnished wood, two substances renowned for their fire-resistant properties.'

The clacking and sawing stopped simultaneously and suddenly. Leon sought an explanation; Lord Archibald held up what remained of the saw. The blade had snapped.

'Curse the heavens!' the dummy boomed.

'Hey, if we *do* get out of this alive,' Leon said, 'remind me to buy one of those things. They really are amazing.'

Archie blasted 'Why have you forsaken me!' through the passenger door's missing window, shook a fist at the sky and yelled: '*FAAATHERRRRRRRR!*'

The yell went on for several seconds.

This guy is *seriously* bonkers, thought Leon.

The dummy's head rotated, owl-like.

'Seriously bonkers am I? Then scoff no longer as I remind you that my trusty army knife has scissors, remember.' The broken saw stub was eased into the knife handle then, after a quick fiddle, another attachment coaxed out and presented to Leon with a 'Ta-da!'

Leon eyed the attachment. 'Tweezers?'

'Sorry, not that one. These things all look alike in the handle.' After yet more fumbling and a scream of 'They should be colour-coded!' Archie plucked out another tool.

'A bottle opener. Perfect.' Leon stretched out a hand. 'Why don't you let me do it?'

Archie jerked the knife away. 'No, 'tis mine!'

'But I have opposable thumbs, look.'

Leon presented his thumbs to Archie's face; flexed and wiggled them (which are pretty much the same thing) then immediately wished he hadn't. He felt it akin to tap-dancing around a legless wheelchair-user singing, '*Hey, Stumpy, look at me!*'

Archie's glare hardened.

The anatomically-superior thumbs retreated to neutral territory as Leon attempted to segue into connected but immaterial reflection: 'Is it *opposable* or *apposable*? Not sure now. I think it might be both.'

'Nobody toucheth my army knife, knave.'

'Are you sure? Might be easier for me; not having hands made of pine.'

'Oak.'

'*Whatever*, it must be tricky.'

Leon adopted the demeanour of an automaton: wielding stiffened hands as if they were long wooden spoons, randomly prodding the environment, at one with Archie's disability. 'Not much better than spades, are they, really?'

The dummy's stare was fierce and unblinking.

Leon, back-pedalling: 'In a way.' (Nothing, not even a flutter.) 'In a *good* way.'

In a good *way? What am I saying? And why do I seem hell-bent on offending our best, possibly only, chance of getting out of here. Apologise immediately!*

'No offence, Archie—'

Good.

'—But it is a bit like watching a donkey trying to tie a shoelace.'

Oh brilliant. Well saved, Leon.

'You know, because of the whole *hoof* thing.'

What?!

'Not that I'm comparing your hands to hoofs. Is it *hoofs* or *hooves*?'

Not helping. Abort, abort. Fast as possible.

'Forget that; doesn't matter. Hey, look! Your knife's monogrammed.'

Good spot; keep it going.

'I hadn't noticed that before. "L.A." How cool is that? *You* talk now.'

Nice.

Lord Archibald's manner brightened immediately. 'Oh yes, thank you, dear boy; how kind.' A wooden fingertip passed affectionately over the knife's fancy lettering. 'One could be forgiven for thinking the initials signify *Los Angeles* but of course—'

'So how's it going with the scissors?'

'Crikey, the scissors! I'd almost forgotten. I do apologise. But fear not, for if I'm not mistaken, and I don't think I am, it should be,' Archie's fingers ran over the closed attachments, 'this one. Yes, I'm certain.'

'Good. Good. Thing is, I don't know if you can tell, what with you being a dummy—'

'Mannequin.'

'But the air in here is packed with fumes. One little spark and—' Leon was interrupted by the sound of metal piercing wood.

'Why is it,' Archie said, jabbing himself in the forehead with the flat-head screwdriver, 'that one can never (stab!) find (stab!) what one (stab!) is looking for!'

Leon reached across to prevent further damage.

'Come on, we'll be fine. Just keep looking.'

'Yes, of course,' Archie said. 'Forgive me, dear boy.'

After folding the screwdriver away, he scanned the knife back and forth over his eyeballs, scrutinising the handle for a hint of scissor. 'What was that about a little spark?'

Leon considered the self-inflicted slot-shaped hole now residing in the middle of Lord Archibald's kiss-curl.

'Nothing,' Leon said. 'No spark. Move on.'

'Not worried the wiring might suddenly burst into flames, are we?'

'*Actually*, yes.'

Archie chortled, heartily. 'Honestly, you're such a big girl's blouse.'

'Excuse me?'

'Don't you think if the wires were going to ignite they'd have done so by—'

Before he could say 'now', two of the wires kissed, fizzed, sparkled and ignited a small but keen fire in the dashboard.

'You were saying?'

'Fire! Fire!' the dummy screamed, his head wobbling around aimlessly. '*Do something, boy! DO SOMETHING!*'

CHAPTER ONE

The bit where things start moving

SCARY CLOWN AND SUPER CREEP – BUT FIRST: POPPY

Manchester's 'Metrolink' light-rail overground tram system services the Metropolis and its suburbs, shuffling people, in, out, and around the city, every day bar Christmas day.

It was aboard one of these trams that Poppy first noticed the young man sitting at the other end of the congested carriage: she looked up from her novel and was immediately drawn to the distant look in his soft, oh-so-blue eyes. Was he, too, looking for true love and wondering if his soul-mate was ever going to show up? Was he dreaming of bumping into her on a far-off sandy shore one hot musky afternoon? Did he picture instant, deep affinity, undeniable adoration, and all-consuming attraction? Could he feel cool, playful waves licking at their sun-kissed limbs? Had Blue Eyes, like her, not had sex for six months? Okay, *ten* months, *dammit!*

(There was no way Poppy could have known, but it had been a lot longer than that for Blue Eyes – *a lot longer!*)

Poppy Winters: an unconventional-looking girl, early twenties, with an individual clothing style and distinctive asymmetrical white Bob flashed with a bold copper-coloured streak; an arty, quirky young woman, free-spirited and free-wheeling, who, although avant-garde in a fashion-sense – from her vintage 1940s Irish Tweed green-and-olive checked overcoat to her monochromatic four-inch-heel ankle boots – had a long-standing love affair with good old-fashioned Romances. And she was definitely open to the idea of one for herself.

The seats near Blue Eyes were taken and the close-encounter-zone around him stuffed with passengers but Poppy had a plan: once the standing had thinned at St. Peter's Square, she would walk by, casually, as the tram made its turn into Piccadilly Gardens, and with perfect timing *accidentally* fall into his lap (managing to hook an arm around his neck without elbowing his face would be a bonus).

Okay, so it wasn't a sharp bend, and the tram, even if it hit a green light at Mosley Street, wouldn't be going much faster than two lovers strolling through Stamford Park, but Poppy was sure she could make the 'mishap' look reasonably convincing; enough, anyway, for it not to appear overly ridiculous and in no way make her look like a predatory slapper and/or potential bunny-boiler.

Besides, Blue Eyes wouldn't mind. His soul-mate landing in his lap; what could be better? She would gaze into his soul, flutter the lashes around her sweet green eyes, say 'Oops' and laugh a little – perhaps coquettishly. Then, after taking her time 'struggling' to her feet (she'd play this bit by ear but it would take as many failed attempts as she felt she could get away with), she would, by way of an apology, insist on buying him a lunch-time cappuccino at the city-centre café of his choice – and no, she wouldn't take 'no' for an answer; it was the least she could do after violating his lap (at least twice, perhaps even three or four times) with her bottom.

Poppy thought her bum her best feature and hoped Blue Eyes would be able to gain an accurate sense of its awesome pertness despite the thickness of her coat. She might have tried to flash him a little cleavage, but until men were more honest about preferring small-to-medium-sized boobs rather than all those big ugly knockers she continually spotted bouncing their way around the city (*the tramps!*) and she actually had some cleavage to show, she would continue to rely on her delightful goddess-like derrière.

The plan was good; foolproof. And not long to go. For now, she would just watch from afar. It's romantic, she told herself, beautiful, even – and in no way weird; definitely not. There's a big difference between staring and admiring. And what I'm doing is definitely admiring. Just look at him, still with that faraway look in those sexy blue eyes. Poppy sighed, softly. I think your luck might be about to change, Poppy, dear-heart, she mused. And you know what blue plus green means, don't you? Yes. Our children will have turquoise eyes! Nice.

Poppy smiled without thinking and immediately knew the names of their adorable offspring: Emily, Sebastian, Ruby, and Charlotte. Danté, should there be a second boy.

POGO

Leon hadn't noticed Poppy Winters; not because the morning rush-hour tram was teeming with travellers, commuters, and early-start shoppers, but because he was focused on the heavyset clown seated directly in front. The one that had taken – unjustifiably, Leon believed – the wall-mounted 'Priority' seat: a single seat meant primarily for those less-abled.

The clown was sleeping, head tilted slightly forward, feet up on the seat beside Leon. The massively over-sized shoes swayed in keeping with the movement of the carriage; the bulbous toecaps beating a rhythm against Leon's arm. As Leon was sitting by the window, he was effectively corralled. If he wanted to get out, he would have to step over the clown's legs, and he didn't fancy doing that. This clown looked evil, even asleep.

Leon was immediately reminded of Pogo, clown alter ego of serial murderer John Wayne Gacy. (Leon had seen *To Catch a Killer*: a film about Gacy's life and infamous killing spree. He'd found it disturbing, freaky, and fascinating-in-a-bad-way. Pretty much how he felt about clowns in general.) Leon didn't remember elongated shoes but everything else looked correct: chalk-white face ruptured by big blue triangles around the eyes; large red-paint mouth fixed in an inane grin (shaped like a hanging bat stretching its wings); the costume: red and white stripes on one side, solid red on the other, pom-poms for buttons; pointy hat (also with pom-poms); and frilly ruff-collar and cuffs. Yes, it was Pogo; he was sure of it.

But where had Pogo come from? Leon hadn't seen him board. Big guy, dressed like a clown; how could he have missed that? He ran a suspicious eye over the snoozing bozo, clocking tiny details often missed on a first sweep:

14

the thin strand of drool extending from one corner of his constant grin; the grubby white gloves; the enormous cluster of helium-filled balloons; the I'm Pogo badge—

Leon took a big shoe-knock as the tram snaked through close bends. Jesus, they really are huge, he thought. They must take ages to polish. Imagine having to resole the fuckers!

Just then, Pogo snarled. Spit spluttered from his angry lips as he began muttering aggressively in his sleep – something dark and malevolent; the voice deep and demonic (this wasn't *The Exorcist* exactly but there were a number of '*Mother-Fuckers*' and '*Cock-Suckers*' in there; and one '*Donkey-Blower*' – though Leon might have misheard that one). Leon flinched as a gloved fist shot out. The balloons bounced over the tram's ceiling lights, separated momentarily, then reassembled as the hand, just inches from Leon's startled mug, pointed an accusing finger . . .

'*You*,' Pogo spat. '*You little shit!*'

After Leon had gone cross-eyed trying to focus on the fingertip, the glove withdrew (the balloons bumping back over the lights) and returned to Pogo's lap. Then the vile sputum-heavy sleep-muttering continued.

Now normally, at awkward, potentially upsetting, or possibly hazardous moments like this, Leon would 'detach', treat the situation lightly, make inappropriate jokes, or think about something completely different. But this time he did nothing. He was mentally stuck, and worse, felt like he was about to freak out. Why though? Getting worked up was generally reserved for trivial but frustratingly annoying matters, like shoe-quacks; or for times when he was clearly in *imminent* life-threatening danger, and that didn't seem to be the case here. Not unless Pogo suddenly awakened, pulled out a carnival strength-test mallet, stepped right up, and hammered Leon's terrified head deep into his chest cavity (*K'TANG!*). So, why wasn't he detaching like he usually did? For some reason the 'ability' escaped him.

So what *should* I do? Leon wondered.

With a favourable result in mind (getting to work, on time, in one piece, with minimum, preferably zero, clown engagement) he weighed up the likely odds of success for the three conventional options.

Freeze:

Initially okay so long as Pogo didn't wake. But Leon couldn't remain inactive indefinitely; he'd miss his stop, be late for work and made to endure another of Reg's *How Lateness Lets Our Customers Down* lectures. Besides, Pogo was bound to wake at some point. *Then what?*

Flight:

Was it physically possible? Even if his legs didn't feel like lead – *and they did* – Leon would still (a) have to step over Pogo's baggy-trousers, (b) need to avoid the big, swaying shoes, and (c) have to take care not to get entangled in balloon strings whilst performing (a) and (b).

No, it was too perilous. Leon sensed his legs would be *too* leaden, *too* unwieldy. Flight could only end in disaster. One sudden movement from the tram and Leon would be riding the clown, cowgirl-style. Pogo might not like that. Or he could love it, which might be worse. Before Leon knew it, he'd be stripped naked, forced into a wooden barrel and rodgered senseless through the bung hole. No, thank you.

Fight:

Again, the leady legs thing, but putting that to one side: he could get the first punch in, maybe knock out the clown. Yeah, right. BAM! Say goodnight to the circus, Pogo. Who was he kidding? He'd never biffed anyone in his life. Biffing takes timing, technique, nerve, power. For all he knew, his untested punch might prove to have as much strength as an undernourished daddy-longlegs – one of the nerdy, limp-wristed ones. No, he didn't have the physique for fighting. Operating his computer mouse to machinegun virtual zombies into red mist was one thing, using the hand as an actual weapon to wallop an actual clown, quite another.

He could picture it now:

He would thump Pogo in the hooter, the nose would make a loud *parp* noise, Pogo's eyes would blink open all annoyed, and Leon would be hilariously and embarrassingly beaten to death with a squeaky clown shoe (this would take several minutes). Once the beating, squeaking and resultant high-pitched yelping had died down, a bunch of Pogo's mates would enter the scene. After dwarfs had poured buckets of cold custard over the bloody corpse, Munchkins, accompanied by a Mariachi band, would sing '*Ding dong the bitch is dead*' as Oompa-Loompas, Smurfs and carnival midgets celebrated by taking a group whizz on the deceased.

Leon didn't fancy that scenario one bit: a farcical-looking clown laughing hysterically behind a whole bunch of 'little people' all acting like obnoxious jackasses? All that, yet *he'd* be the one made to look like a fool. He'd never live it down. He would have to move away – forever.

What to do? All options appeared equally unappealing and impractical.

The voices in his head argued back and forth: one for this option, one for that, one for the other. *Run! No, don't do anything. Punch the fucker!* (Leon had always heard voices inside his head. Didn't everyone? Wasn't that: just *thinking*?)

But he couldn't just sit there, he decided. *Action* was necessary. He had to *do* something; simply *had to*. And goddammit, he would – right now – he would ruddy well get out his notebook!

MORE POPPY

Oh look, we have the same notebook, Poppy observed, her inner voice excited. That has to be a sign. What are the chances of us both having a black A5 spiral-bound notebook? I'm definitely going to write a poem about this later; something about him, about his kind eyes and unusual aura.

The young man at the end of the carriage was a little odd, in a way she couldn't put her finger on, but that was good, she liked 'Different'. A far cry from the dullards who usually crowded the tram, she believed this one had the potential to be heroic. Yes, she definitely liked what she saw. Her instincts were positively glowing. The artist in her soaked up the visual image, the colours, light, composition; the inner-poet took a snapshot of senses, feelings, and emotions. She would call on these later, probably in her coffee break at Razors Edge, the hairdressers where she worked as a stylist. No time now, she might get 'into it' and miss her stop, or more importantly, the turn. Wordsworth's daffodils didn't wilt in the two years it took him to record them for posterity; she could wait a couple of hours.

As she had another 'soak' – appreciated the scene's mood, textures and perspective – she felt the poetic cogs on the creative side of her brain start twitching. There was an automatic rhyme for carriage, which she instantly rejected as far too obvious and way too square, but what rhymed with dullards? Plenty for tram: clam, cram, exam, flimflam, I am, jam, lamb, scram, swam, wham bam, thank you, Ma'am. *Wham bam, thank you, Ma'am?* Oh no, that wouldn't do, that wouldn't do at all. A girl doesn't wait ten months and then—*Jesus, where are we!* She checked outside. *Phew!* They were approaching Cornbrook.

'Cornbrook, Ladies and Gentlemen,' a computerised female voice announced over the public address system. 'This station is Cornbrook.'

The woman sitting next to Poppy rose, moved towards the doors. Alarm bells rang in Poppy's head. What if Blue Eyes gets off here? Her genius plan would be scuppered. She looked down the carriage, stiffening as the tram settled against the platform. *Stay on, stay on, stay on, stay on— Oh my God, I sound like Mrs Doyle.*

The doors shooshed open and a few passengers stepped out. Leon was not one of them; so far, so good. Additional passengers boarded. The doors hissed shut.

'This is the Piccadilly service,' said the public address system. 'Next stop Deansgate-Castlefield.'

Just two more stops before the turn, our 'chance' encounter, and the start of a bright new future together. We will be like swans, my love – but without the hissing and honking – paired for life, like French Angelfish or Turtle Doves. Yes, Poppy was sure this was going to work.

(Some say that sensitive 'artistic' types have acute inner voices – one pessimistic, one optimistic – and they do constant battle, back and forth, in a far more exaggerated way than experienced by 'normal', less creative souls. This may be why so many artists, musicians, writers, and the like, swing between hopefulness and depression. Make of this what you will.)

Anyway, Poppy's optimistic voice had spoken; now, just moments after leaving Cornbrook, it was time for a little balance: *Turtle Doves? What am I talking about?* He's going to get off at Deansgate. *I just know it. Loads of people get off at Deansgate. He's bound to. Yep, I'm certain. Deansgate . . . definitely Deansgate; either Deansgate or St. Peter's Square; one or the other.*

Then, a bit of back and forth thinking: No, he won't, not if it's our destiny to be together. *Destiny?* Balls to that; sometimes destiny needs a little assistance. Right, like *I* can change destiny. Why did I even make a plan? I should *never* have made a plan. I'm not a planner. I'm a creature of spontaneity. Courage, girl, courage! Yes . . . I should go over there right now and say hello . . . and then what? . . . I don't know . . . be spontaneous. Okay, I will!

Just then, as Poppy was transferring weight from her awesomely pert bottom to the soles of her killer ankle boots, a sweaty lard-arsed blob clutching a family-size box of assorted Krispy Kreme doughnuts under massive tits, flopped into the empty seat beside her; his beady black eyes bearing down on her as he wedged her in good and tight.

So tight, Poppy almost squealed.

NOTED ODDITIES

Leon was feeling better for having acted so positively. He had slipped off his *Left 4 Dead* backpack, taking great care not to elbow a clown shoe, eased out his A5 notebook (a thick one he kept short story ideas in), turned to the back and quietly added Pogo's name to his list: a log he kept.

Leon had noticed *unusual* things, things other people might miss, for as long as he could remember, but during the last few days he'd detected a definite increase in the weirdness (and frequency) of the sightings. *Like what*, you ask? Well, I'll tell you: yesterday he experienced a tomato singing 'I will survive' (it managed the bit about *Going now, and walking out the door* before Leon shut the fridge door), witnessed a fully kitted-out Astronaut in the Chinese

Takeaway (Two Wongs), and later, retiring for the night, glanced a foot-long fire ant scurry under his bed (it wasn't there when he checked).

This morning: he heard a voice in his pillow (it instructed him to *Wake Up*, even though he felt sure he was already awake); discovered his toothbrush in the toilet (he suspected Richard of foul-play; perhaps a petty retaliation for some perceived slight); and then, as he'd approached the tram station, he discovered Chicken-Man.

Leon didn't like the look of the man/chicken hybrid. The reaction was instant; something about the costume. But mostly, his confrontational manner: up in everybody's faces, deliberately obstructing their progress.

Chicken-Man was about five-foot-six, had a fluffy yellow body with floppy wing-arms, orange legs culminating in splayed-toed chicken-feet, a big yellow head topped with an orange comb, and a florid human face poking out of a hole underneath a brown beak. He was accosting as many people who entered, exited, or passed the station entrance as he could, despite being ignored by all. On occasion, he would attempt to jovially peck the heads of small children, only for parents to pull, carry, or wheel away their kids, double-time. Leon wondered how long it would be before the bothersome creature got his arse kicked. Not that Leon wished violence upon Chicken-Man. But it would be so much easier to slip by if a little pullet-bashing was taking place. Though Leon abhorred confrontations, he thought taking *advantage of one* to *avoid one* seemed reasonable. They equalled each other out. That was Karma.

From a safe distance, Leon had watched a five minute succession of buttonholing and cold-shoulders, then finally managed to slip by when Chicken-Man became distracted by two large, unaccompanied dogs taking an unhealthy interest in his egg-dispenser.

Jesus H. Christ!

Leon jumped as Pogo suddenly blurted a tirade of foul-mouthed abuse. The gist, as far as Leon could ascertain, seemed to involve the insertion of unknown objects into places where they couldn't possibly be accommodated. Not without assistance, masses of lubricant, and a large supply of morphine. Leon wiped a glob of clown slobber from his cheek as another surge of slaver oozed over Pogo's chin, made grey/white streaks then drooled down into the ruffled collar. Leon loathed everything about clowns but this one was particularly repugnant.

Eyes back on the log, quietly turning pages, Leon came to the conclusion that the previous sightings had been interesting, entertaining, *amusing* even. Not *unnerving*. Okay, Chicken-Man was a little unsettling, but he wasn't full-on scary – and not potentially dangerous as Leon was now starting to think of Pogo. There was something undeniably and exceptionally disturbing about this dozing, dribbling, sleep-blathering clown. He looked likely to snap awake at any moment and in rousing take a stripy baseball bat to whoever was nearest: proximity bludgeoning (Leon hadn't been able to spot any evidence of baseball bat secretion but reliable conclusions are difficult to make as clown trousers are notoriously loose).

As Leon quietly returned the notebook to his backpack, during the stop at Deansgate-Castlefield, the clown's babbling got louder and more frenzied – still incomprehensible, but clearly vicious. What was he so riled about? Had there been a fancy-dress bash on somewhere last night and Pogo missed it? Is that why he sounded so incensed? Or was he on his way to a children's birthday party and hated kids? Jeez, could this foul-mouthed fermenting ball of anger really be a children's entertainer? One too many tweaks of his nose (despite hushed warnings: '*Do that once more, Princess, and the next time your parents see that freckly little face, it'll be on the side of a milk-carton*') or an accidental bursting of a balloon-animal, and surely he'd blow a fuse.

Leon pictured the scene:

Pogo, bellowing like a mad bull, charges around the patio, scattering ring-leaders and persistent offenders like rag-dolls to all corners of the garden as onlookers wet their party frocks and crap their best trousers. Some children run screaming into the house. At the kitchen breakfast-bar, enjoying a natter and an afternoon white wine, mothers wonder how many more times they'll have to tell their kids to 'Keep it down out there!' And lying in a heap against the back fence, the main culprit tries to avoid looking into the clown's eyes, looming right above his own.

'Go on, birthday boy, tug my pants again. I fucking dare you. What's that, Timmy? Speak up! Your arm's broken? Oh, dear. And you want Momma? Well, boo hoo, fuck face, and guess what. When she gets here, I'm gonna stick my hand down her dress. Yeah, that's right, you big cry baby, I'm gonna cop a feel of mommie's tits. How about that?'

Oh this party clown, 'children's entertainer', whatever he was, was evil; Leon just knew it. He needed to move, needed to move *now* – and stealthily like a night-time cat-burglar or POW scaling a perimeter fence under the nose of an inattentive guard.

Backpack clutched to his chest, Leon rose silently to his feet, steadied on a hanging grab-handle and, as if stepping over a laser-tripwire, slowly arched one foot over the clown.

As the foot landed lightly on the other side, Pogo opened an eye.

CHUMLEE

Poppy felt like her lungs had collapsed. Doubted she'd ever talk again. Hadn't been this winded since Lynne Horton had punched her in the breadbasket after finding a cheeky limerick she'd written about Lynne's reputation for dishing out blow-jobs willy-nilly round the back of the school gym to any Sixth-Former that so much as looked at her.

This is what Poppy wrote:

There is a fifth-former called Lynne,
Who gives blow-jobs round the back of the gym.
She'll finger your bum,
To help make you cum,
Then give you a big sticky grin.

What Poppy wanted, besides to breathe again, was to do that slight body-shift people make to let adjacent passengers know they require release, but she was locked in so tight it was impossible. No problem; eyes alone should be enough. She put them on her captor hoping to convey the simple message: *Move it, Jabba!* The tiny, sunken eyes that blinked back might have made her jump, or gasp, had either been physically possible.

'Wanna doughnut?' the big blob asked.

Poppy nodded towards the exit.

Pudgy fingers produced a custard-oozing Chocolate doughnut, brought it to her face. Perhaps nodding was a bad move. 'Thanks but I'm watching my figure,' she said. Being crushed made her voice low and husky.

'Mind if I watch it, too?' Blobby chortled.

What a joke; he'd hardly taken his beady eyes off what remained visible of her size-8 since he'd body-slammed it up against the window. 'If you let me out,' she rasped, 'you'll see a lot more of it.' *Okay, that didn't sound right.*

'I can see plenty already,' said Blobby, gawping down her front. He might have been thirty, or fifteen – hard to tell. The over-sized face now went on the move, opened up. His itty-bitty teeth were worn and gappy but together they seized like a shark; one attack severed half the doughnut (held before Poppy's face, the doughnut had appeared huge; against the blob's giant knobbly-potato head, it looked miniscule).

What did he say: 'Can see plenty'? Poppy couldn't see how. Only her head was on show, wasn't it? Everything else lost under – well, *him.* So what was he looking at? She followed the trajectory of his stare: her coat had lost its uppermost button, the lapels were splayed open (on account of the blob's ample gut pushing from underneath) and her shirt, having popped two top buttons, was gaping. And, nestling inside: a pair of small/medium breasts compressed so tightly as to appear voluminous and heavenly. Oh my God, she thought, I have a cleavage. Yes, indeedy! Proper jugs. Check those bad boys out.

The blob *was* checking, his eyes almost on stalks.

Poppy simultaneously felt revulsion and pride; on top of amazement – the clasp of her front-fastening bra holding out like that under so much pressure? Incredible! *Impressive!*

Snaffling the last of the gooey Chocolate Custard, Blobby chomped noisily, riveted to the voluptuous spectacle. Okay, enough, Poppy thought. They'd both admired the bad boys and their uplifting squeeze long enough.

'Hey! You!' Poppy croaked.

'What?' grunted Blobby, finally looking Poppy in the face.

'What's your name?'

'Chumlee.'

'*Really?*'

'Yeah – why wouldn't it be?'

Poppy would have shrugged had it been physically possible. 'Chumlee it is,' she wheezed. 'Well, Chumlee, how do you fancy letting me out?'

'Sure,' said Chumlee reaching in and flicking open the bra clasp, quick as you like. One handed. And in *one* go. Fat fingers, who'd have thought?

'Yeah, thanks. But I kind of meant *me*, not *them*.'

'Oh, right, sorry about that,' Chumlee said, looking far too pleased with himself. 'You might not believe this, but that was my first time with a front-loader.'

'That *is* hard to believe, Chumlee. What are you, a watchmaker? Locksmith? Wait, don't tell me – a nano-technician.' Poppy hoped she hadn't sounded *overly* sarcastic. No, hang on; she *did* hope she'd sounded overly—

'Personal Trainer.'

Poppy laughed (as best she could given the restrictions on her diaphragm). 'Good one.' But Chumlee's chubby head wasn't laughing. 'Oh, you're serious.'

'It's a family business.'

'Course it is.' Poppy was starting to sound like an asthmatic. Why, she wondered, do the nutters always sit next to me?

Chumlee's eyes had wandered south again and showed no sign of returning. 'So,' Poppy rasped, 'is it your week off, or are things just a bit quiet at the moment?'

'Want me to try and refasten it?' Chumlee sucked sugary residue from his fingers in fevered anticipation. 'Might take two hands.'

'No, it's fine, really. I can put them away later. But if you *could* get up for a second,' *you crazy tub of—*

'You've got a really sexy voice . . . sort of husky.'

'Yeah, I get that a lot; especially when I haven't inhaled for a while. And now, I really do need to get out.'

'No, you don't.'

'Excuse me?'

'You don't get off till Piccadilly Gardens,' said Chumlee spraying crumbs.

'How the hell do you know where I—'

'Seen you before – lots of times.' Half an Apple/ Cinnamon surrendered to Chumlee's teeny gnashers. 'You *always* get off there.'

Stunned silence for a moment then Poppy said:

'Are you the stalker who keeps emailing me photos of his tiny genitals?'

'No, but if you give me your address . . .'

'I have all I need, thanks.'

'Wanna come back to my house? If we went halves on a taxi—'

'Are you serious?'

'Normally, I don't like to jump straight in.' The Apple/Cinnamon's surviving half now joined the half-eaten first half. 'I like to take my time; woo a girl – make her laugh.'

Undo her bra . . . hold her captive.

'To be honest,' Chumlee spoke around a loose ball of mush, 'I prefer it when *they* make a move on *me*.'

Yeah, that must happen a lot.

'But a lot of girls just turn out to be *deceitful prick-teasing bitches!*'

'I know. What *are* some of us like? We can be a funny bunch.' Poppy laughed, mostly to calm her captor, and it seemed to work:

Chumlee cooled, smiled. 'But I thought as you're giving me positive signals . . .'

'Positive signals?'

'You're sitting there with your tits out.'

'Fair point, go on.'

'Yeah, so I thought I'd ask you straight out – about the house. We'd be alone. Both my pare— I mean, *housemates*, are out. I could eat Häagen-Dazs off your body, if you'd like.' Chumlee was now perspiring profusely. 'Hey, maybe you could do me at the same time. Is that even possible?'

'How old are you, Chumlee?'

'Old enough.'

'Well, full marks for trying but I think we're done here. Now, I don't want to be rude but I really do need to breathe soon.'

'*I* do. I *love* to be rude.' A fresh doughnut – Strawberry Gloss – rose to Chumlee's sugar-frosted lips. 'And I do have certain skills.'

'Oh, God, no . . . please don't.'

Dough-studded oxen tongue pushed its way into the shockingly-pink hole and Poppy's sense of confinement grew tenfold as Chumlee worked the doughnut backwards and forwards at speed over his chubby tongue.

'Am I meant to be the doughnut?' Poppy asked.

Still tonguing, Chumlee grunted in the affirmative.

'Thought so; quick tip for you, Chum: *That* does *not* look sexy. It looks *revolting*. Now, if you don't mind . . .'

Behind the doughnut, a sound transpired that would have been pure nectar to Lynne Horton back in the day: a long resonating '*Mmmm*'.

'Okay, that's it. Move it, Lard Arse!'

The tongue flicked lizard-like inside the rosy hole.

'And I didn't mean the tongue.'

'Thcream if you want me to go fathter.'

'*Oh sweet Jesus.*'

The *Mmmm*ing got louder. People were looking. Poppy's mind fizzed: surely this can't be happening. Wedged in by an elephant-arsed sex-pest and oh no, *Blue Eyes is getting off the tram!* Wait; make that *diving* off the tram. Well, that's something you don't see every day.

The doors clunked shut. Poppy tried to free her arms but only succeeded in jiggling her boobs around.

'*MMMMMM . . .*'

'*Taxi!*'

CHAPTER TWO

The bit where it gets Quiet:
The Lull before the Coming Storms

KEYS-N-STUFF: SEEMA AND REG

Leon was still thinking, two hours later, despite scuffed knees and a grazed elbow, about how impressive his dive from the tram had been. *Moved so fast, I bet the dozy clown never even saw me.* As he re-imagined the incident for the umpteenth time that morning (working in a few improvements: a tidy new tuck-roll-and-up landing, *no* damage to his backpack, *not* winded, plus high scorecards and enthusiastic applause from those awaiting the Bury tram) something cannon-balled into the side of his head.

Eyes made owlish by safety-goggles, he glanced around and found the mischievous culprit, waving.

Seema Khan: thirtyish, healthy size-14 British Asian of Bangladeshi roots with eyes and hair as black as Indian Ink. She ran the dry-cleaning section with time and smiles for everyone; even Reg – unless he was in one of his moods.

A few words about Keys-n-Stuff:

Like every branch of Keys-n-Stuff (a national company with over two-hundred outlets), this shop offered various services: key-cutting; dry-cleaning; engraving; jewellery- watch- and shoe repairs. A see-through counter housed shoe-care products and engravable items: polishes, insoles, laces, pet tags, lighters, hip flasks, that kind of thing. Walls displayed house- business- and memorial signs. A glass-fronted cabinet held enough cups and trophies to make even Manchester United envious. By the key-cutting machine (where Leon had been cutting a cylinder key until he was so rudely interrupted), a large board paraded a cornucopia of shiny key blanks – thousands of them, row upon row of every conceivable size and type.

Having raised goggles, Leon looked down, past his mucky, maroon bib-apron.

At his feet lay the 'cannonball' – a rolled-up sock.

His eyes resurfaced to find Seema now grinning from ear to ear; her teeth as white as the whites of her eyes.

'Now don't be doing anything silly, Leon. Reg will be back in a moment. It wouldn't do to—'

Leon rushed over, hands outstretched, ready to tickle.

Squealing, Seema turned about, and dragging Leon in her wake, tried to disappear headfirst into a rack of cleaned clothes. As her upper body, quivering with laughter, attempted to escape between clear-plastic garment-bags, Leon pulled back on her hips. Together they spawned a bizarre tickling/giggling pushmi-pullyu.

'Leon!' yapped a small familiar voice from the doorway.

Late forties, bald (apart from a clump of wiry grey hair over each ear), Reg stood only five-foot-two in elevated heels but always wore his clean, brown, warehouse-style coat with self-important pride. Bustling up to the counter, he whipped off his wire-framed glasses as if he couldn't believe what he was seeing.

'Honestly,' said Reg, 'I leave the shop for five minutes.'

Leon's boss had an extremely soft tone; barely audible, in fact. Even when he got angry and raised his voice, his utterances still retained a feathery, *female* quality. For some reason, this contrast – ineffectual indignation – could get Leon laughing, if he wasn't careful.

'Seema, what on Earth are you doing in there?' Reg demanded to know. 'What *are* you two up to?'

As usual, his enquiries carried all the gusto of a fairy fart transported by a light summer breeze.

Suppressing a smile and trying to look as blameless as possible, Leon sidled away, back to the key-cutting machine. Reg waited, furiously polishing his glasses with a hankie, as Seema, top half still lost in dry-cleaning, looked for a semi-believable exit-strategy.

A little history: Seema had put in a good word for Leon when he'd been looking for a temporary job after leaving school, whilst he decided what he *really* wanted to do. The post was meant to last a few weeks, couple of months, tops, but he'd been there ever since. From the start, despite Reg's officious nature, or perhaps because of it, the pair indulged, whenever possible, in playful one-upmanship between themselves. Good-natured sparring was the highlight of their working days. And so, Leon had been tempted to say 'Yes, what *are* you doing in there, Seema?' but as he and Seema had always had a real soft-spot for each other, he decided he couldn't just leave her stewing like that.

'Keep looking, Seema,' Leon said, his intonation more suggestive than encouraging. 'I'm sure you'll find it.'

'*What?* Oh yes, good idea. Thanks.'

Seema's bottom moved, a reaction to some unseen upper body movement, then the other end said: '*Aha!*'

She backed out of the garment-bags, straightened up, and turned, holding aloft an empty coat hanger.

'Oh hi, Reg; didn't hear you come in. Hey, remember that hanger I thought I'd lost? You might not; it was last week. Anyway, panic over – here it is.'

'Really?' said Reg. 'An errant coat hanger?'

Seema waved the evidence: undeniable proof.

Reg remounted his spectacles, a stiff finger nudging them into place. 'Well, thank goodness you found it, Seema.'

'Leon helped. *Was* helping. *Had been* helping.'

'I see. So what I witnessed was just Leon helping you look for the said coat hanger?'

Seema nodded. 'Thanks, Leon.'

'No problem,' said Leon, winking to her as he lowered his goggles. The key-cutting machine buzzed noisily as he resumed cutting the cylinder key.

'Okay, so that's that all sorted,' Seema said, raising her voice above the machine. 'Now, how about I make us all a nice cup of tea?' She headed for the utility room (kitchen/ rest room/storage area) at the back of the shop.

'Listen, I'm not as green as I am cabbage looking.'

Out of view, Seema shouted 'Sorry, what was that, Reg?' over the noise of tap filling kettle.

'I said: *I'm not as green as I am cabbage looking.*'

No response. Just the sound of Leon blowing metal dust off the newly cut key accompanied by the clatter of mugs and spoons and the drone of a noisy kettle.

Reg shook his head. 'She's not even listening.'

'I don't think she can hear you, Reg.'

'Oh she can hear me. She just doesn't *want* to hear me.'

'Pardon?'

'I said, *She*— oh yes, very clever; very droll.'

Rounding the counter like a scolded orangutan, Reg *accidentally* bumped into Leon. Not hard, but enough to underline managerial displeasure.

'It's about time you grew up,' he quipped.

Leon smiled covertly. That's *so* Reg, he thought.

(Reg did lighten up occasionally, but he spent so much time worrying about surprise visits from his Area Manager, that he was always fussing – especially when it came to his 'No larking around' rule and keeping the shop ship-shape and spotless. His overbearingness was constant; relentless to the point of being comical. Add this to his general nature and it's easy to see why Leon and Seema could never take their boss seriously. Reg knew about all their little giggles and elbows, but for the life of him could not figure out what they found so funny all the time. He wasn't an amusing man. Not in the least. So what was their problem? Reg put it down to childishness and an inability to take life – and work – seriously. Silly, silly staff.)

'All this larking around like kids whenever I'm out of the shop.'

'Sorry, boss.'

'Well, it's got to stop.' Reg grabbed pliers and a Rockport shoe. 'Honestly, sometimes I feel like I'm just talking to myself. How many more times do I have to tell you both?'

Leon didn't answer. He was 'finishing' the key; working it against the key-cutting machine's spinning nylon brush.

As Reg ripped away the Rockport's worn heel, he kept a watchful eye on Leon's work. The light finishing process removes any residual roughness from the key and should take only seconds, but Leon's mind had been drifting more than usual of late, and Reg really needed him to stay focused; they had a lot to do today.

Why, only last week, he'd witnessed Leon drift away right in front of a customer. The lady had asked for a duplicate mortice key to be cut; a manual but straight-forward process that should take no more than a minute.

Leon said he'd do it immediately if she'd like to wait. She would. As she waited at the counter, Leon placed her original key in the key-cutting machine, placed an uncut key alongside, hit the power switch, and began to match-cut. Twenty-one seconds in – Reg was timing – and Leon had 'gone'. After ten seconds of inactivity, Reg could stand it no longer and *Ahem*-coughed. Leon came back like he'd never been away, picked up seamlessly from where he'd left off, finished the key, and served the customer.

'What?' he'd asked, as he spotted Reg's shaking head.

Blank by name, blank by nature, Reg had been thinking.

'Okay, Leon – that should be smooth enough now.'

Turning off the machine, Leon held up the new key, side-by-side with the original, and compared.

'And check it properly. We had *two* returns last week.'

Two? Listen to him. I must have cut over two hundred keys last week: mortice keys, latch keys, safety keys, car keys, caravan keys, padlock keys—

'Is it okay?' Reg asked. (Leon nodded.) 'Good. Engrave Mrs Hadley's hip flask next, please; she could be here anytime. Then replace the dodgy eyelets on Mr Worrall's boots; he's picking them up at four. Oh, and don't forget the tan Moccasins still need resoling and polishing. And after that, perhaps you could make a start on—'

'Tea's up,' Seema interrupted. She placed a tray of mugs on the counter. 'Except, we're out of tea, so I made coffee.'

'There you go, Reg,' she said passing the BECAUSE I'M THE BOSS mug, 'hot and strong, just like you.'

Reg tutted; shook his head, but inside, he was beaming.

'And here's yours, Leon.' She whispered into Leon's ear: 'Wet and frothy, just like you.'

'Char Wallah,' Leon whispered back.

Seema laughed at that. 'Oh by the way, Reg, is it okay if I leave a little early tonight? I have to pick up my sister's new sari for the wedding; only about ten minutes or so. Thanks. How's the coffee?'

'Not tonight, Seema.' Reg blew on his beverage. 'I'm calling a staff meeting.'

'What a shame,' said Leon. 'After you made coffee, too.'

31

'Come on, Reg. It's only twenty minutes.'

Leon chipped in again: 'Thought you said *ten*.'

'Quiet, Mowgli, the adults are talking.' Seema put herself between Leon and Reg, made her eyes doe-like . . .

'I can do extra tomorrow.'

Reg shook his head, sipped his drink.

'Oh great,' said Seema. She knew they were in for another of Reg's *'Thirty-years-I've-worked-in-this-shop'* lectures (they always started that way).

'Don't listen to her, boss. She's just upset because we've run out of sugar.'

'I am not. I told you, I'm on a diet – for the wedding. Oh, Reg, do we really have to have the lecture— I mean "staff meeting", *tonight?*'

'Come on, Seema, it'll be fun,' Leon said. 'Remember the last one on company rules and regulations? Don't tell me that wasn't interesting; that eighty-four minutes flew by. So, what's the topic tonight, boss: Head Office guidelines on customer satisfaction; standards of best practise?'

'Maybe,' Reg peered over his glasses, 'we should have a special one just for you, on the potential dangers of sarcasm on the shop floor.'

'Ha! In your face.' Seema all but did a little dance.

'So, it's not about Seema's unprofessional giggling?'

'Hey! I do not. No more than you.'

'No, it's not about Seema's giggling – or yours, Leon. We're going to have a refresher course on the health and safety issues that can arise from larking about in the workplace. And we'll keep having them until the message gets through.' Reg eyed them both. 'Right?'

'*Right*,' drawled Leon and Seema in unison.

'Good. Now I need to phone Head Office, order more stock. Can I leave you two to run the shop for five minutes?' (The staff nodded.) 'Good.' Reg carried his mug to the door of the back room, turned, said, 'Well, get your skates on, please, there's lots to do,' then disappeared.

Seema made like she was going to hit Leon with the coat hanger and he accidentally let out a squeal which surprised both of them. He would certainly have been ribbed about it had Seema not been preoccupied with disappointment.

'Can't believe he won't let me pick up the sari,' she said.
'That's your fault.'
'*My* fault? You threw a sock at me.'
'Oh shut up, Man-Child.'
'Hey! "*Mowgli*" was bad enough, but "*Man-Child*"?'

Seema tromped back to the dry-cleaning section, grumbling under her breath. There, she shifted clothes from one rack to another then shifted them back again, clanging coat hangers with each shove.

Leon knew to leave her alone for a while.

They'd likely laugh about it later.

THE KEY TO POPPY'S HEART

In the afternoon, Leon, assigned to polishing the contents of the trophy cabinet after being ten minutes late back from lunch (for the second time that week), and labouring under the weight of knowing that Reg would now keep him at work until gone six, did his best to ignore the furious *thump-thump-thump* of Reg's hammer on a Combat boot.

Not only was Reg still miffed about Leon's lunchtime punctuality (Leon claimed he'd had to jump in and give CPR and mouth-to-mouth to a Chinese woman who collapsed in the sandwich shop), he was still deeply miffed about *this morning's* tardiness. And he *seriously* doubted *that* defence, too: that Leon had suffered a heavy nosebleed after being bitten by a crazy squirrel, then, later, having returned home to change his shirt, was forced to await the arrival of a replacement tram driver due to the original driver experiencing a severe case of spontaneous combustion that rendered her unable to operate the controls and therefore incapable of continuing – being, as she was, reduced to a pile of ashes.

Leon said Scene of Crime Officers were quick to arrive but vacuuming the remains took a good ten minutes; apparently, she'd left a window open and had blown all over the cab. He also explained how one particularly chatty SOCO told passengers not to be unnerved; although they might not have previously witnessed this definitely natural occurrence, it actually happened all the time – so much so that it probably wouldn't even be reported by newspapers, radio or TV.

Reg hadn't believed this far-fetched series of events any more than Leon's previous outlandish excuses but without making exhaustive phone calls to Metrolink or Greater Manchester Police there was no quick way to disprove the squirrel/nosebleed/combustion story. So Reg had told Leon to make up that time by taking an *extremely-short* lunch. But no – he'd been *late again!* How many times was that in the last few months?

Reg knew exactly.

And now *this*: a neglected customer.

The boss had spotted the customer as soon as the door opened. His hammering slowed as the customer waited at the counter, almost within touching distance of Leon's back. Reg's unblinking piggy eyes peered over their wire-framed lenses. They would peer until he felt Leon had had long enough – and that wasn't long. Then he'd let him have it. Boy, would he let him have it.

Leon was on automatic-pilot: hands busy but the mind elsewhere. Last night, a vicious and bloody catfight between two skin-tight PVC-coated red-devils had spilled out of a stretched limo at the top of Leon's road. The initial pair was followed by several more PVC-coated demons, similarly topped with flashing Satanic horns. Some attempted physical separation; the rest encouraged one or other of the primary devils to '*Lamp the fucking bitch!*' as a singular, uncommonly-tall Princess of Darkness, pitched in with a plastic pitchfork.

(Leon presumed the hellcats had been heading into the city to kick off a pre-fuelled hen-party when one of the primary devils had said something adjudged deeply derogatory by the other.)

The fight had lasted over ten minutes and Leon had the misfortune to observe every unsavoury girl-on-girl second (he'd seen quite a few bitch-brawls over the years but this one was *spectacular*). That was the *real* reason he'd been late this morning: reviewing the incident had made him walk straight past the shop. And questions remained unanswered even now: *What could have been said to start such a fight? Were they all friends again this morning? Wonder if that tall one is single.*

Reg had maintained the slow hammering so as not to tip Leon off; it was for the boy's own good and certainly not because he took a tyrannical pleasure in bringing his junior to heel. Almost there, just a couple more seconds, then the amount of time a customer might reasonably be expected to wait would have *more* than expired.

Seema could sense these moments, and she sensed one now. As Reg focused on Leon, *she* focused on *Reg*. She pictured it thusly: Reg was an orb-spider, hunkering down, patiently eyeing up his prey: Leon; who she saw as an innocent moth. But she, Seema Khan, no lover of spiders, was a hummingbird, and hummingbirds are more than happy to eat insignificant orb-spiders for breakfast. She was a master of timing, and timing was *everything* in spider-bashing. She would not fly to the rescue until she'd watched the boss exhibit *every* involuntary reflex reaction (dead giveaways to Seema's experienced eye) listed in what she had come to think of as *The Spider Chronicles*:

Reg's eyes tightened, the brow furrowed.

Check, check.

The jaw set.

Check.

Fingers squeezed whatever tool was in use.

The blubbery lips stiffened.

Check. Check.

(And yes, Seema is aware that spiders don't actually do any of the actions mentioned, thank you – especially the bit about angrily gripping shoe-repair tools. *Does it matter?* No offence but such interjections are unnecessary, a touch impolite, and can spoil the build-up of suspense. Fine, we'll say no more about it. Let's just move on, shall we?)

Wetted by beefy tongue, the lardy lips pulled back – a breath was drawn in.

Check! Check! Check! That was it! The spider was about to strike.

'Leon, customer!' announced Seema in her sweetest tone. The proclamation carried all the joy of a heartfelt Merry Christmas well-wishing.

Thanking her (he knew an *orb-buster* when he heard one) Leon turned to face the customer. To Poppy he said, 'Sorry about that. What can I do for you?'

Poppy handed over a front door key and a smile.

Seema got back to work (pressing a pair of pants), humming quietly, comfortable with the certainty that Reg, having jerked his head round and whipped off his glasses (in one rapid motion), would now be staring, pink-faced and frosty-eyed. He didn't like to have his thunder thwarted did Reg. *Thunder? Ha!* Seema giggled at the thought; giggled again when she heard the boss take out his frustration on the Combat boot with his hammer.

By now Leon had picked an appropriate blank from the wall display, locked *it* and the original in place on the key-cutting machine, and activated the power. Already ringing with the clouts and clobbers of Reg's noisy cobbling, the air positively buzzed. Slipping on goggles, Leon grabbed the cutter handle, looked to Poppy and asked, 'Just one?'

'Yes, please,' she replied, her smile never breaking. 'You never know . . .' (*God, it's loud in here.*) Poppy found her voice rising: 'It could be–'

Leon turned the handle and the machine *shrieked* and *squealed* as it cut into the blank.

'–the key to my heart.'

Unfortunately for Poppy, her words were lost under the cacophonous grinding noises so she settled for just watching Blue Eyes work; that and checking out his bottom every few seconds. Nothing wrong with that. Looking didn't make her a slut. Her sisters probably only said that because *they* were no longer free to check out guys' butts now all three were '*sooo* happily married'. Heck, if it hadn't been a possible Health and Safety issue she'd have leaned over the counter and given his cute little bum a cheeky squeeze right there and then – trollop or no trollop. Sometimes nice guys need a slight hint – a helping hand, as it were.

Poppy knew that the young man behind the counter, like so many men, whatever their age, Leon would most likely be hopeless at reading those precious-few hard-to-spot teeny-weeny telltale signs: the abundant smiling, the major eye contact, the excessive laughing, the gesture mirroring, the head tilting, the hair tossing, the hair flicking, the neck stroking, the lip nibbling, the lip licking, the let-me-think pouting, the giggling, the arm-touching, the blushing (the shy ones), the lolly-sucking (the brazen ones), the banana-throating (the *really* brazen ones) – okay, maybe they'd twig the last two but normally each hint, every intimation, all clues, would slip unceremoniously under the radar.

Men hardly ever pick up on the signals girls give out. Not until much later, when they will dismiss them, most likely as wishful thinking. How strange that these indicators of interest should be too subtle for guys when they are so glaringly face-slappingly transparent to other women. Men are stupid in this regard. Poppy knows this. The Asian woman will know this. All women know this.

And Poppy knew the challenge she faced – one faced by all *non*-scrubbers, especially those favoured with less-noticeable, cuter, more unobtrusive tits – how to find a way to ask a guy out without appearing obvious or desperate or slutty. Or better still, to get *him* to make the move so they absolutely, definitely, in no way could ever be said to look (to the guy or fellow females) like a complete and utter tart.

Seema eyed the uncustomarily pretty woman at the counter entirely certain that her interest lay beyond duplicate keys – and to far more than just Leon's bottom. She'd witnessed these performances before, from time to time. Seema could hear the wheels revolving.

Poppy's 'wheels' were indeed turning; around a choice: would Leon – she'd made a mental note of the name; liked it – be more interested in the Hallé (a Rachmaninov concert was coming up) or a trip to Manchester Art Gallery. Which to suggest? She wasn't sure. Should she propose both? No, that might look needy. As her deliberations went on, she noticed the friendly-looking woman behind the dry-cleaning counter give her a reassuring, sagacious smile. Yeah, *she* gets the picture, thought Poppy. Poppy smiled back. An understanding. *Sisters.*

Seema was thinking: Good for you, girl. You go for it. *Go on*, ask him out. He could use a good date. But break his heart, lady, and I will break your face.

CHAPTER THREE

Homeward Bound
(The bit where we start using proper Chapter Titles)

TRAM AGAIN, TRAM AGAIN

As another working day – a working day much like any other working day – slipped further behind, Leon's mind stayed focused on Wayne, the name he'd just written in his notebook; then struck out; then rewrote – only to wonder, now, if he should strike out again.

Wayne.

Odd?

Yes – but odd *enough?*

Wayne, hands in anorak pockets, had been moving up and down the aisle of the half-full tram for the last few minutes, stopping to address anyone who caught his eye; currently, a pony-tailed woman talking into a mobile.

'Hello, what's *your* name? *My* name's Wayne,' Wayne interjected. 'Who are you talking to? That's a nice phone. I've got a phone but I lost it. It was in my *sweat* pants.' (He emphasised '*sweat*' as though it were important for some reason.) 'Somebody stole my *sweat* pants – in the park.'

The woman blinked but carried on talking to whoever was on the other end. 'You shouldn't be telling me that when I'm on the tram.' Lowering her voice and face nearer to her lap, she added: 'Yes, you *are* a naughty boy, a *very* naughty boy.' She tried to arrest a giggle. 'Honestly, what are you like?' The giggle escaped, became a dirty laugh.

Undeterred, Wayne moved on, checking faces – so many faces; each ignoring his presence.

Leon couldn't see much of Wayne's face; the drawstring hood of his puffy orange anorak was tied so tight, the resultant aperture left only a tiny moon of a face; features bunched together jousting for space. The little moon gravitated over to a full-sized face atop a hotdog.

'Hello, what's *your* name? *My* name's Wayne. Is that a hot dog? I like hot dog. I can't eat mustard though – it makes me sweat. Do you like ketchup? Why haven't you got ketchup?' Then, pointing: 'Is that onions?'

The man, almost cross-eyed with focusing on his frankfurter, never flinched, and after a couple more bites, the moon passed over, sailed away towards a cluster of passengers standing in the relatively open area offered between tram doors.

Leon watched Wayne deftly navigate between a brace of dental-nurses, around a woman burdened with shopping, and back through two overtly gay men who bitched loud and camp about how Mr Foofoo would not be going back to Woofters. *Ever!* (Leon assumed the little guy with the sparkly collar, pink I ♥ MY 2 DADDIES vest and bandaged ear was Mr Foofoo: the Shih Tzu currently sulking quietly within the muscular tattooed arm of the shorter, T-shirted man.) The taller, Versace and Viton guy said, 'I know. He's usually *so* the life and soul of the party. Aren't you, Precious? Yes, you are. And now look at him, poor thing.'

Leon hoped Mr Foofoo would soon be feeling fabulous and strutting around like a rooster in a diamante trouser suit and sailor hat, if that's how he rolled. And he hoped something else: that Wayne was wearing something under his coat. All Leon could see below the anorak's knee-length hem was a pair of mottled bare legs – their chunky pink calves and sockless ankles pitching in to push around a pair of well-worn Hi-Tec trainers.

The Hi-Tecs shuffled over to what Leon calculated to be an Auditor or Banker – fancy suit, quiff – studying the Financial Times on an iPad.

'Hello, *my* name's Wayne. What's *yours*? Is that a book reader? Doesn't it hurt your eyes? Why don't you just buy a book? I like a book. It's on a shelf at home. I borrowed it from Trevor up the stairs.'

The opportunity for a potentially frivolous question: 'Did Trevor up the stairs loan *the book* or *the shelf*?' was overlooked as Quiff gazed beyond the scrap yard bridged by the tramway, to Victorian warehouses recently converted into highly-prized ultra-modern apartments.

'What are *you* reading? The one I'm reading is about Jack the Ripper. It's called *Jack the Ripper*. It's a bit scary. He had a knife and he *did* use it.'

The suited one brought his eyes back to the e-FT.

'Ever done a prossy?' asked the tiny moon face.

Quiff did not react. Not so much as a single glance. Unsurprising; the cold shoulder is a commonplace system for commotion-free commuting in cities.

Now some might consider '*Ever done a prossy?*' a strange question to ask a total stranger but Leon felt sure Wayne meant 'done' as in 'boned' rather than 'butchered'. (Didn't he?) Either way, Leon considered the enquiry 'odd' enough to keep Wayne listed.

'There is a brothel in Urmston,' Wayne told the indifferent Banker slash Auditor. 'It's called a massage parlour and Mandy's Megastars. Everybody knows about it. Do you know about it?'

Quiff tapped a Markets Data icon. A wealth of equities, currencies, commodities, capital markets and other banking bollocks scrolled this way and that.

'What are you into? They might do Domination. But probably not Knife Play. Knifes make people nervous.' (Wayne didn't say *knives*.) 'Do knifes make *you* nervous?'

Leon thought Wayne might be a Care-in-the-Community, but harmless enough, probably. Not the sort to suddenly turn violent. He looked more likely to be the *victim* of violence – past, present, and future. Leon wondered why Quiff didn't keep one eye on his inquisitor, though – just in case. Just in case Wayne's clenched paw suddenly produced a butcher's knife from one of those well-warmed anorak pockets and ambushed his complacent sun-bronzed neck.

All too easily, Leon pictured the scene: Wayne's pounce; the first slash, deep sting, and initial feeling of minty cool freshness about the neck; Quiff's surprise; then attacker and attacked screaming like electrocuted baboons as the blade repeatedly flashes under the ceiling lights; open jugular letting arterial-spray up windows and over ceiling; blood raining down on panicked bystanders – mayhem and cries as the tram hits the M60 tunnel; the once-indifferent slipping and sliding in an attempt to put distance between their whimpering souls and the tooled-up orange anorak.

Carriage carnage.

Wide-eyed, Quiff stares up, clutching wet slice. Mouth agape, he gurgles and gasps as haemoglobin pours down his sleeve, colours his tailored shirt cuff, coats his luxury watch, and streams between his manicured fingernails. A sense of warm liquidity around the lap and inner thighs coincides with a pre-recorded announcement from *Gabrielle* (the name Leon had given to the woman who generously donated her honey-toned voice to the public address system). 'Ladies and gentlemen,' she purrs. 'The next stop will be Stretford – Stretford, the next stop.'

The Banker's shoes enter the station blood-filled and twitching. (Leon had noticed them earlier: leather Brogues: size 12s, laced, polished brown leather uppers decorated with punches and serrations, classic toe, Goodyear welted leather soles – quality.) Doors sigh open, people spill out. Howling, they run platform and scramble stairs as, fitting over, bleeding done, the now ex-Banker slumps motionless inside his suit (Armani: nice; now soaked in two or three of your own bodily fluids: not so nice).

'Anybody know what station this is?' Wayne asks.

'Stretford, cloth ears.' Even when she's insulting, Gabrielle sounds sexy – maybe more so.

Stooping over Quiff the stiff, Wayne scouts for station signage. Only Leon spies the cheeky mercenary, a young man with a monkey-like face and 'Ian Brown' Adidas trainers, who briefly risks all – he reaches in, between blooded anorak and *ex*-Banker, angling for free technology. The dead hand does not give up its cargo easily, though, and a spatter of on-screen splatter squeaks against Quiff's lifeless fingertips as the electronic Financial Times, scrolling under the pressure, is pried out.

Wayne, scanning each side: 'Doesn't look like Stretford.'

'Well, it is,' insists Gabrielle. 'Now let's get this show on the road. Someone on here needs to get home and have a shower. And I don't mean me. Right, mind the doors.'

The doors whisper to a close behind the liberated iPad and its departing new owner.

NO, *THIS* IS STRETFORD

'Ladies and gentlemen, the next stop will be Stretford,' announced the PA system; Gabrielle's voice, smoothly serene. 'Stretford, the next stop.'

Leon gave the exterior his gaze. There it was: Stretford. No doubt about it; Stretford House, a 23-storey tower block, confirmed as much. He had been woolgathering anew.

Looking at the tower always reminded Leon of one of his favourite films: Billy Liar. (Because they were made in the same period: the mid-Sixties.) He smiled to himself as he heard Mrs Fisher's voice ask: *Daydreaming again, Billy?*

Leon watched Quiff, packing his iPad into a leather Messenger bag, step his Brogues to the nearest door. Adidas trainers followed suit. The tram eased to a stop. Leon felt a cold breeze as the doors huffed open. Out went Brogues and Adidas trainers. In came sensible low heels carrying a mousy-haired girl, high pull-on boots, a pair of Hush-Puppies, ratty Moccasins and lace-up green pumps.

'Hello, what's your name? My name's—'

'Piss off,' said the hybrid in the high pull-on boots taking a seat. (At first glance the make-up, wig, and low-cut dress suggested *Transvestite*, but hefty, hairless mammaries upheld *Transgender*. Each to their own and all that but this was not convincing: six-foot-three, scrum-half shoulders, Desperate Dan jaw, big hands; basically, a docker in a frock – either that or a munger[1] on a grand and pitiable scale.

Wayne's little moon face, stunned for a second, moved on, seeking better fortune. Leon sympathised. The bare legs and puffy coat shuffled Wayne's cinched features back to the pony-tailed woman: still on the phone, listening.

'Hello, what's your name? My name's Wayne. Is this the way to Bury? I think I might have got a wrong tram. Where do *you* live? That's a nice mobile. Who are you talking to? I've got a mobile but I lost it. It was in my *sweat* pants.'

---

[1] Munger: Noun. British informal, derogatory. An unattractive person, especially a woman. Combination of Minger and Munter. Yikes.

'Dave, listen. I promise you won't have to go to A-and-E,' Pony-tail said. 'Just leave it switched off, and for God's sake don't move.'

'Somebody stole my *sweat* pants—'

'Yes, I'm getting off the tram now. Be there in five minutes.' Pony-tail stood, breezed past the orange anorak and made for the doors.

Wayne shuffled on, compelled within to engage without.

The owner of the Hush-Puppies: fifty-odd with mad, frizzy hair and a pronounced overbite; had taken the seat next to Leon. Leon watched as the man now removed a large pad from a scuffed leather satchel. He opened the pad (staff paper lined with staves) on his knee and immediately began humming and crooning in a low register, pencilling musical notes and symbols as he did so. He erased a few, quickly added more, then – presumably reading them back – moved his wild mane in slow circles, as if hearing the composed melody play in his head, happily lost inside it, oblivious, it appeared, to his fellow passengers.

Leon felt an envy – the non-begrudging kind – worm into his soul.

The PA system crackled. Gabrielle's voice, serenely smooth: 'Ladies and gentlemen, the next stop will be Dane Road – Dane Road, the next stop.'

Wayne said, 'Hello, what's your name? My name's—'

'*Wayne!*' barked a face with a blob of mustard on its nose. 'Yes, I know! Now fuck off, will ya?'

WHAT WAS IT RICHARD SAID?

That was a bit unnecessary.

Yeah – hot-dog man had looked so polite, too.

Leon had got into an exchange with himself walking the canal towpath (he'd taken the longer, scenic route home). Some people can be so ill-mannered, he reflected. Scratch that thin veneer of day-to-day lukewarm toleration for their fellow traveller and underneath they're just ignorant, belligerent twerps. What was it Richard said?

People – who needs 'em?

No. Something like that, though.

A narrowboat, puttering alongside at four miles an hour, went unnoticed. (Aboard, a row about where fault lay: the navigator's map-reading skills or the left the helmsman had taken at Chester. 'This is *not* god-damn Birming-ham, Pam,' carped Helmsman. 'I know! *I* told *you* that over an hour ago, Chuck,' yelled Pam from below deck. Americans.)

People are idiots?

No, not that one; it was more like . . .

People are only nice when they want something?

'Hello?' shouted Helmsman.

People are rarely as they seem?

'Hey! Excuse me!' Chuck applied time-honoured voice-amplification procedure: a hand round the mouth: 'AHOY! You there!'

Yes, that was it! *People are rarely as they seem.* Richard talking sense for once; a nice change from the *usual* foul-mouthed outbursts.

'Hey, buddy! Can you tell me which canal we're on?'

Leon now turned away from the towpath – a short walk led to concrete steps. As he climbed, he more-easily recalled one of Richard's scathing declarations regarding the proletariat:

Idiots shovelling shit in government sweat shops for a few grains of chicken feed.

'Did you see that?' Chuck asked. 'He totally blanked me.'

'Don't blame *him*,' muttered Pam.

Spineless gullible rodents. I don't know who's worse–

'Ignorant cocksucker!' shrieked Chuck, unleashing, in decreasing order of mass, a broadside of screwed-up leaflets: Knowing your Narrowboat, How to Operate Canal Locks, then Things to Do and See in Birmingham.

–the ones who remain silent; or the ones who are sycophantically polite.

Leon didn't think any of that held water. Surely it wasn't true. Not in all cases. And wasn't it kind of offensive?

Not speaking up for yourself, that's fucking offensive; offensive . . . and fucking weird.

If you asked Leon, *Richard* was the weird one. And Leon knew exactly what the self-diagnosed agoraphobic would be doing right now.

AND SO HE WAS

Richard was behind a pair of huge, military-style field-glasses, spying at a window – could be any window in the house – binoculars sweeping, waiting for any half-decent-looking female to present herself within the considerable range of his 'Big-Eye' lenses. Innocently walking, close to the house or at the end of the street, minding her own business in a garden or car, going about regular routines at home, Richard would find her; all of her – all of them.

Bathrooms and bedrooms were especially favoured – they held tantalising promise. And sometimes they paid off handsomely. Yes, Richard loved bedrooms and bathrooms.

And Kelly Buxton.

Sometimes she went about braless.

Exactly as Leon had pictured him, Richard wore a tired, untied dressing gown over stained Che Guevara T-shirt and grubby pyjama bottoms (Leon suspected even Seema wouldn't be able to remove the splotches and stains from these garments). The fatigued ensemble was completed by threadbare slippers that propelled Richard around the house, from window to window, constantly relocating his eagerness to find unsuspecting targets for 'observation'. He wasn't prying – not even peeping. Of course not; as he had often told Leon, he was 'merely observing'.

Leon couldn't discern the difference.

WITHNAIL & I

A few doors from home, Leon bumped into his paternal grandparents at their front gate.

'Hey, look who's in.'

'Actually, we're on our way out. Sorry.'

Although Leon called round often, his grandparents always seemed to be out. Leon suspected they hid. He thought Bill and Norma, both in their eighties – but physically well – might be a little bit bonkers.

'Who was that tart you were talking to up there?' asked Bill, nodding up the street as he hitched his trousers over his pot belly.

'Tart? No, that's just Peggy. You remember Peggy. She lives across the road.'

'The one with all the kids?' spat Bill.

'That's the one.'

'Got enough of them,' said Norma, patting one of the many rollers in her hair.

'Has to be at least eight of the little bastards,' said Bill.

'And every one a different shade,' added Norma.

'Must be a *right* tart,' decided Bill.

'Asylum seeker,' said Norma. 'On benefits, I heard.'

'Yeah, I heard that, too,' said Leon. 'Apparently she did a moonlight flit from Longsight about ten years ago; slipped over the border late at night.'

'Hey, you couldn't lend us a tenner could you, Leon?' asked Norma. 'Things are a bit tight; you understand.'

'Pensions are a disgrace,' hissed Bill.

Leon heard this from his grandparents almost every time he saw them. On auto-pilot he took out his wallet: a folded, black fabric affair – he didn't mind, suspected they didn't have much – pulled apart the Velcro and looked inside. 'I've only got twenties,' he said.

'That'll do.' Grabbing a twenty, Norma planted a lipstick kiss on his cheek. 'Still not changed your – *wallet* – I see.'

Bill winked at Norma; knew what she meant by *wallet*.

'Better make it forty,' he said, seizing an extra twenty.

'So where are you going?' asked Leon.

'Duh – it's Friday – *bingo* night.' Each waved a celebratory twenty.

'Do you know, I've never been; maybe I should—'

'Get real, Leon,' said Bill. 'It's not for kids.'

'*Kids?*'

Bill and Norma had already started to walk away.

Half a minute later, Bill called: 'Hey, Leon! Found yourself a nice girl yet?'

Cackling heartily, Norma slapped Bill's shoulder.

The pair wandered away snickering enthusiastically.

Leon closed the front door; hung up his backpack, then, turning, nearly bumped into Richard, who had just raced down the stairs, cigarette locked between his lips, binoculars in hand (Richard always hurried when switching windows lest he miss something). Grunting gruff greetings they paused for a second, face to face – there was a passing resemblance, though Richard looked considerably older – before Richard disappeared into the front room.

After he'd checked the answering machine – no messages – and picked up the morning post, mostly junk mail and circulars, Leon followed.

Richard had already taken up position in the large bay window (a window offering 180 degrees of panoramic view). 'Well I hope you've had a better day than mine,' he grumbled, binoculars sweeping the area, 'I haven't seen a thing.'

Leon brushed aside a bunch of DVDs with dodgy handwritten titles and flopped down on the sofa. He perused the back of Richard's dressing-gown and pyjama legs (Leon had long since given up asking when Richard was going to get dressed. As he never went out, Richard didn't see any point). Nothing had changed, apart from the left slipper: a new cigarette burn by the Biryani stain.

'Not so much as a sniff,' Richard added, breaking wind without breaking sweep.

'Do you have to do that?'

'Don't blame me for having an empty stomach. It's not my fault there's no food in.'

'There's food in.'

'Call that food? I can't eat that bollocks you eat.'

'Salad and fruit is not bollocks.'

'You're not becoming a vegetarian, are you?'

'No. There's fish in there. And chicken—'

'*White* meat! That's no good. I require *red*. Lots of it. Hamburgers and steak and pork pies and— Jesus! Is this prick-teaser ever going to show?'

Watching the open dressing-gown flap back and forth in keeping with the to and fro of the binoculars, Leon thought Richard looked like an actor press-ganged from a Noel Coward play to perform the role of a slovenly midshipman, sent aloft, from his sick-bed, to the crow's nest, to keep vigil until land was spotted (although, he should, if we're being historically accurate, really be using a telescope).

Discovering an island inhabited by naked caramel-skinned beauties with an insatiable yearning for lanky, pale horn-dogs would have suited Richard perfectly – especially if the island somehow existed *indoors*; perhaps contained within some kind of glass-enclosed bio dome.

'Richard . . . as a supposed agoraphobic—'

'What? There's no *suppose* about it.'

'Could you live in a glass-enclosed bio dome? Would that be classed as indoors?'

'Do pipe down, Leon; can't you see I'm busy?' Richard's right hand dropped from the binoculars, dipped into pyjama bottoms. 'Come on, Kelly. Let's be seeing you.' Rearranging his crotch, he added: 'Come to Daddy.'

Leon pulled a face which would have complemented the word *Urgh, Ew,* or *Yuck*, perfectly. How he'd love to have the lazy lecher thrown overboard and keelhauled, then flogged with a cat-o'-nine-tails. *Have this man stretched over a cannon and given two dozen lashes, Mr Christian.*

Richard let out another fart; this one long and instantly foul.

'Do you have to be down here?' said Leon.

'I was here first. If you don't like it, fuck off.'

'Why don't you try upstairs? Maybe you'll have more luck there.'

'I've *been* up there, been up there for hours – got nothing. Not a whiff. I'm hoping a change of scenery will change my luck. Besides, I like the personal, up-close feeling this window offers.'

'*This window?* Those binoculars could see the hairs on a gnat's chuff from three miles away.'

'I know, so imagine the view I get when Kelly walks past. Especially if it's one of her *unfettered* days – the angle from here is perfect. Christ, I hope today's a Braless.'

Richard's right hand had not returned aloft. Leon hoped the midshipman wasn't rummaging below decks or fiddling with his rudder. First sign of a rising mizzenmast and he was jumping ship. *Maybe that's why he hasn't got a telescope; too unwieldy to use with one hand.*

'Don't you need to keep both hands on binoculars – you know, to keep them steady?'

48

'The problem is there's no discernible pattern to her comings and goings. Her shifts are constantly changing. Sometimes she works mornings, sometimes afternoons, other times, nights. It's the same with the no-bra days – no pattern. I tell you, Leon, it's a nightmare.'

'Maybe you should keep a log.'

'What and be like you? That *would* be sad. I might be depraved but I'm not pathetic.'

'You kind of are.'

'And what's *your* latest sighting, then?' Richard gurned his face, adopted a high, mocking voice: '*Ooh, I'm not sure. I'll have to check my sad little logbook.*'

'Don't take the piss, Richard. I think I've been losing sleep over these things.'

'You *think* you've been losing sleep? Don't you know?'

'It might just be *time* I've been losing. You know, when I'm thinking about them. I'm not sure. It's confusing.'

Richard made a *Pfft* sound – from his mouth this time.

'It's not just that. A couple of the more recent ones have felt . . .'

'What?'

'I don't know – *dangerous.*'

Richard tutted sighed and scoffed all at the same time.

'And they've been getting progressively more frequent.'

'Really?' said Richard sounding totally disinterested.

'Yes. So will they *keep* getting more frequent?'

Leon exited the room.

'You know, *more and more and more?*' he called from the hall. 'And what happens then? It can't just carry on. Things reach critical mass. Something has got to give.'

'What a drama queen,' muttered Richard.

'Come again?' asked Leon, returning with his notebook.

'Nothing.'

'Could have sworn I heard something.'

'Oh, I said: Tell me about the last thing seen.'

Leon doubted this but answered: 'A one-armed wrestler. Saw him by the allotments. I had to take a detour.'

'He can't be much of a grappler with one arm.'

'He might be good with his legs.'

'*Good with his legs?* I've told you, they're not *real.*'

'What, all of them?'

'Some might be – *maybe* – but the rest are just in your head.'

'They *seem* real.'

Richard aimed the field-glasses towards the sofa, to where Leon, reseated, was penning an addition to his log.

'Jesus! You should see the size of your head through these fuckers.'

Leon looked up, forced on an exaggerated smile then returned to the page.

'*Pogo?*' squawked Richard, spying the entry. 'That's a clown's name.'

'You don't say.'

'Those bastards really freak me out. Hair, make-up, intolerable antics, ridiculous fucking clothes . . .'

'Yeah, yeah, you've told me.'

'Stupid honking noses . . .'

'This isn't about you,' muttered Leon.

'Big squeaky shoes. *Buckets of fucking confetti!* What's that all about?' Richard returned his attention to the street. 'The fuckers should be shot at birth.'

'They're not *born* clowns, Richard.'

Leon glimpsed a momentary image of a pointy-hatted red-nosed baby-clown shot from mother's Tunnel-of-Love as if from a cannon through a cloud of glitter and confetti to splash-land in a barrel of custard accompanied by uproarious laughter and applause from a far-too-easily-amused medical team.

'What?'

'I said: They're not *born* clowns. That *would* be freaky.'

'Come on, they freak you out too, don't deny it.'

'I must admit, this one *was* freaky. *Really* freaky. See.' Leon held out a notebook doodle but Richard's eyes remained fixed to the binoculars.

'*Oooh, the one I saw was* reeeally *freaky.*' That high mocking voice again. 'They're *all* freaky. *Freaky fuckers.*'

'When do you ever see a clown? You never leave the house.'

'On TV.' Richard tossed his cigarette end out the window. 'And there's never any warning. There should be warnings. "And for those of you who hate freaky-clown fuckers, please be aware that the next item features at least one freaky-clown fucker, so viewer discretion is advised." '

'Think I'll run a bath,' said Leon rubbing his feet. 'Have a long soak.'

'This is ridiculous. Why aren't there any women on the move?' Richard wheeled around, angry and impatient, stared at Leon, as if he might have the answer.

'Why don't you try at the back? Maybe Mrs Hobbs is doing some laundry.'

'Are you trying to be funny? You know she does laundry on a Tuesday.'

As he re-pocketed his notebook, Leon studied the scruffy snooper. 'You know who you remind me of?'

'How can I possibly know who I remind you of? Oh, this is hopeless; balls to it.' Richard left the window, attended a cabinet and rifled drawers. 'I need a cigarette.'

'Withnail,' Leon continued. 'Richard E. Grant's character. You know, from Bruce Robinson's *Withnail & I*?'

'Bollocks.'

'Would you like me to tell you why?'

'No.'

'You might think it's because you're both unwashed, slovenly, failing, and foul-mouthed.'

'Fuck this for a game of soldiers.'

Richard tipped the contents of the drawers onto the carpet, dropped to his knees. 'You check down the back of the sofa, I'll recheck this lot.'

'But you'd be wrong. It's because, like you, Withnail is filled with indignation over what he sees as life's injustices. He rages against the world, blames others for the adverse consequences of his self-centered lifestyle.'

'Which film magazine did you steal that from?' Richard said, rummaging through carpeted drawer crap: opened letters, take-away menus, spectacle cases, tissue packs, coins, pens, batteries (worn-out ones, indistinguishable from the new), instruction booklets for the TV and DVD player, keys, paper clips, plastic lighters (both full and empty), scissors, elastic bands, sweet-wrappers, old/spent inhalers, crap, crap, and more crap.

'I didn't steal them. They're *my* words. Some of us do actually have a vocabulary beyond *Bollocks, Fuck* and *Balls*.'

'Utter bollocks.'

Leon looked lost for a moment. 'Where was I?'

'*Self-centered lifestyle.*'

'Oh yes. And like you, he is arrogant, self-serving, self-indulgent, and, it has to be said – a coward.'

'Are you going to check the sofa or not?'

'Although to be fair to Withnail, at least *he* left the house on occasion.'

'Leon, please! I can't do anything without my smokes.'

'You don't do anything anyway.'

'How dare you!' Richard blasted wide, offended eyes towards his accuser.

Leon's only reply was a cursory shrug.

Spotting a pack of Marlboro Reds behind a cushion, Richard dove at the sofa.

Leon knew the pack was empty as soon as it was picked up.

Richard's frustrated face thawed into a wretched, pitiful grin: 'You'll have to go to the shops.'

Leon pursed his lips, shook his head.

'You *have* to.'

'What I *have* to do – is get in a hot bath and rest my aching feet.'

'I'll run a bath while you're gone. Have it ready for when you get back. Would Sir prefer oil or bubbles?'

'Forget it.'

'Leon, if you don't get me some smokes, right now, I'll die, I know I will.'

'Don't be so dramatic.'

Richard took on the expression a child might adopt if it was lost and hungry and in desperate need of assistance: woeful, pathetic, miserable – but Leon wasn't buying it.

'If you want them, go and get them.'

'How am I supposed to go? You know I can't go, you sadistic fucker!'

'Well, I'm not going,' said Leon with a defiant stare.

CHAPTER FOUR

Run, Leon, Run

THE PRECINCT

For thirty minutes, Nobby and Svetlana had witnessed Leon browsing the DVD section of the shop, a modest-sized Spar convenience store, muttering gripes such as: 'No, *you'll* have to go' and 'You know *I* can't go, you sadistic fucker' and 'Leon, if you don't get me some smokes, right now, I'll die, I know I will' before he'd finally approached, placed an empty DVD case on the counter, and requested a pack of Marlboro Reds.

Nobby the Newsagent, whose paunch strained shirt- and trouser buttons in equal measure, had supplied a pack and a price as Svetlana and her cleavage rummaged below counter for the correct disc.

'While you're down there, Svetlana,' Nobby said, grinning at Leon. (To picture Nobby, imagine a loathsome progeny spawned from Mrs Toad and Piers Morgan. If what you see is odious, vile, slimy, and nauseatingly repellent; a creature more suited to fly-blown swamp than convenience store, then you have him.)

Performing the very opposite of going down, Nobby's mail-order bride and her low-cut top had come back up, a DVD grasped between long Soviet-crimson fingernails.

Ah, Svetlana. What to make of her?

Leon thought her beautiful, of course; but *too* beautiful. Intense beauty overpowered him – always had. Beauty possessed the power to render him effectively speechless, or worse, turn him into a blithering blatherer. (Only very recently, having grown accustomed to Svetlana's acute prettiness, had Leon been able to manage any proper sentences in her company. The Russian turned up two months ago, already wed to Nobby. To this day, no-one knows how the loathsome toad pulled it off.) Why *did* Beauty, Leon wondered, turn him into a blathering blitherer? Unimaginative idiot-men never seemed to be affected in the same way. Was it because *he* was sensitive and creative? Because he more manifestly appreciated the accuracy – the truthfulness – of what existed around him? Did he see more clearly than they?

Now, refusing to ponder on this any further, he surveyed his surroundings as reflected in the café window:

Parallel rows of shops, seemingly squaring off, shaded and scowling under stilted canopies, challenged each other across an expanse of grey paving slabs. Little contravened the uniformity of the plain: an occasional bench and its consort, a full waste-bin; a smattering of oblong concrete planters (flowerbeds once, now handy places to store fag ends and crushed beer cans); and, here and there, omitted slabs sprouted metal tree-protectors with incumbent broken tree – thin trunk snapped to a jagged point at roughly the same height as the top ring of its unjustly-named defender. Pissing posts for passing mongrels.

Upholding the tradition, a free-roaming dog moved from one to another, sniffing and splash-peeing. A couple of skateboarders performed 'grinds' along one of the planter's long edges. At either end of the expanse, space existed for two extra shops but the 1970s architect (an obvious supporter of the architectural style known as Brutalism) had wisely omitted these to allow ingress and egress into his solidified vision: an urban block of striking angular geometrics and roughly-hewn concrete. A row of black bollards toothed the gaps, one at each end of the hard rectangle known locally as The Precinct.

In the north passageway, a gang of kids repeatedly kicked a football against a broken NO SKATEBOARDING, NO BICYCLES, NO BALL GAMES sign. In the south, a ring of teens coalesced, compared resources, then clubbed together – to buy fags and/or cheap cider, Leon supposed.

Within this mecca for trouble an unhealthy number of shops no longer traded. Locked up and abandoned long ago. Of those that persisted, early evening brought down many a graffitied shutter: urban canvases to elaborate performances of art – or acts of defacement and vandalism, depending on your point of view; either way, if nothing else, the tags and sprays injected a splash of colour to this otherwise lacklustre landscape. Unshuttered, and exposed to the early evening, besides the Spar: Big Chicken Fast Food; Bargain Booze; Ladbrokes; Kath's Kaff; and, off in one corner, an L-shaped amusement arcade: Midas Well.

Inside the doorway, endless electronic *bloops* and *bleeps* reverberating hither and thither, a thin white dude and a mixed-race beauty with honey-coloured skin and thick corkscrew hair played pinball, both holding the other and one flipper each. As they played, the dude pulled her in tight; the girl threw back her head, laughed heartily. Leon thought she *looked* wonderful – and doubtless with a warm-hearted nature to match. Why didn't *he* have a girl like that? Leon felt a wave of envy – the begrudging type.

You'll never have a girl like that, you inadequate little ponce. Now stop daydreaming and bring me my nicotine!

No! Not that scumbag again. Leon didn't want to think about *It*. (Just the thought of the reprobate's name made him feel like he needed a bath.) Nonetheless, and in spite of himself, Leon formed a mental picture: visualised the freak rummaging through ashtrays and bins, picking at gaps between patio paving-stones, ferreting for semi-reusable fag-ends, all the while cursing the loss of spying-time due to Leon's overdue return. Well, hard luck, Leon thought. The lazy bastard will have to wait. He had something to do first. Why else would he be staring in at the café window?

Kath's Kaff: smells of dreariness and deep fat fryers. A place of ruptured sausages, billowing eggs, plastic menu board and laminated tablecloths, rattling coffee machines, industrial-strength tea, timeworn ketchup-squirters and original decor: half-tiled walls, old advertising posters. And skirting the windows: crusty waist-high 'decorative' net-curtain beyond which odious faces twitched in idle chat.

(Leon had wondered if 'Kath' actually existed but concluded it was unlikely; he'd eaten there many times and never heard anyone speak of her.)

Anyway, that didn't matter right now; he wasn't searching for the elusive Kath – he was scouting for Jenny, a new waitress. Not *new* exactly, she'd been working there a while, off and on, but each time Leon saw her, he felt like he had the first time: 'accelerated' – more *awake*. Around her, he invariably experienced curious flutters and fancied she felt the same. If he spotted her now, he would definitely go in (he never went in otherwise). And one of these days, perhaps today, he *would* ask her all about herself.

Did she have a second job? Is that why she worked so infrequently? Which part of Ireland was she from? (Her beautiful lilting accent, fluid and uplifting, could swing from vulnerable to threatening over the course of a sentence. Leon always struggled not to picture a tall Celtic fairy-pixie brandishing a knotty Shillelagh; bewitching but possibly schizophrenic.) Did she attend college? If so, what was she studying?

Really? Interesting choice. What made you choose that? And what do you like to do when you're not working? Oh, cool, me too (unless it's something girly, like shopping or visiting a spa). Do you ever go to the cinema? Favourite films? Most treasured books? And would you please, let me see what you look like with your hair down?

Hang on – activity!

Heaped plates of Double-Egg-and-Chips preceded a waitress from the kitchen.

Nope. Not Jenny.

Disappointment and the sight of grease-glistening food punched Leon in the gut; a double whammy – one taking away his appetite, one making him bilious. His belly rumbled regardless and it occurred to him that he hadn't eaten for over seven hours.

Was Jenny in there? Her presence didn't look promising but she could be busy in the kitchen (there existed a serving hatch but its smallness supplied only a limited view).

He chose to give it five more minutes.

Okay, so if she did show, what would he order? There could be no repetition of the embarrassing beef lasagne incident. Trying to make out you'd ordered this dish thinking it would be the *vegetarian* type (after he'd learned Jenny was a Veggie) is so easily defeated by the simple question: 'Why did you eat it, then?' Leon had gone the colour of the ketchup he'd dolloped all over it. She'd been very nice, said it was fine, she wasn't militant about it. Even so, he would not be making the same mistake. *A mushroom omelette, perhaps*; as good as anything else and it came with extra merit points in the shape of a side salad: three lettuce bits and a quarter of tomato. He would eat slow and appreciate the 'show' (he liked how Jenny sashayed and sauntered, naturally and without affectation, gliding effortlessly between tables, like, he felt, a gazelle on Vaseline) and, afterwards, if feeling sufficiently confident – this required a minimum of two separate smiles and at least one unnecessary glance in his direction – he'd stretch out their 'time together' with a dessert or slice of cake followed by a cup of tea . . . and then, who knows.

He would have to guard against getting stuck with the 'wrong' waitress: Olive; the one that resembled a warthog sucking a lemon; the one currently lurching a plate of thinly-buttered bread towards Mr and Mrs Double-Egg-and-Chips; the one that moved like a troll on uneven stilts. But that ogre-infested bridge (built upon the dual pressures of order-book tapping and a stream of *Come on, you're not Gordon bleedin' Ramsey, what the fuck's it gonna be?* expressions) would be crossed if and when Leon came to it. And *last* time he'd sworn *next* time would be different.

After witnessing several bouts of frustrated, violent egg-prodding (with only one yolk in four being runny and therefore chip-dip-worthy) and using up four minutes of the extra five allotted to observing the café interior, Leon became aware of two buxom middle-aged women on the other side of the glass, at the table nearest the window. Had the sun been high they'd be sitting in his shadow. His looming presence had suspended their All-Day-Breakfasts.

One, on an operation to administer brown sauce, had stopped mid-squirt; the other, equally inert, held a forked sausage just inches from her gaping mouth. So stationary were they that the scene looked like a photograph. Or rather, a postcard; one of those saucy sea-side affairs normally populated with the bums, boobs and crude innuendo of half-naked minxes, seedy office lechers and horny but incompetent newly-weds. Leon wondered what category he might be looking at – 'unintentionally-lewd housewives', perhaps – and what the caption could be.

57

How about:
'Check you out, Nora – squeezing in a second sausage.'
'I know, Mavis. And I've just had a big black pudding and a mouthful of juice.'
Urgh, gross! Leon sensed he'd gone too far. Frankly, it was the kind of thing he'd expect Richard to produce. Even the rudest of saucy postcards wouldn't stoop to such blatantly offensive and vulgar smuttiness. And it appeared to Leon that 'Nora' and 'Mavis' were of similar mind. Their stare hadn't wavered. *Quick, think of something else. Can't stand here all day, they'll think I'm bonkers. It only needs to be* slightly *rude and* marginally *funny.*

Mavis, big arms, slothful, raised a quizzical eyebrow at her friend. Nora, hypersensitive and thin-necked, blinked behind her sausage.

Something about needing a good fork? No, that's rubbish. Errr . . .

' 'Ere, Mavis; you seen the way that waitress is walking?'
'Yes, I bet she's had 'er browns hashed.'
No, no! What does that even mean? Think of something else!

Mavis turned now, full face to Leon: a challenge of sorts.

Nora, lowering sausage, inched cautious eyes sideways.

Shit, we're losing them. Abort, abort. They could turn hostile.

Leon had thought creating comical risqué double-entendres would be easy but he'd failed to generate anything Greasy-Spoon-related that was even vaguely amusing – dubious, yes; salacious, yes; humorous, no.

Hang on. What was he worried about? He didn't want to write saucy postcards, anyway. How did he get saddled with that? He realised he'd once again strayed off-course into unchartered irrelevance (Leon was never sure if this was him thinking 'inside' or 'outside' existent events). No matter; no longer self-compelled to create bawdy, unnecessary postcard captions, and content to be 'back in the room', deliverance brought out a relieved smile.

Nora and Mavis did not reciprocate.

They feared the young man staring in at the window might be bonkers.

HEY, BLANK, YOU MONG!

'What have we told you about staring?' hollered a voice to the rear. 'People don't like it.'

'Yeah, fuck off, Retard,' squawked a second voice, as shrill as the first was deep – and just as Manc[2].

Leon turned towards the advice. Saw Danny and Carl, two young men about his own age, sitting atop a nearby bench, arses propped on the backrest, Nikes planted on the seat. Below them, a black Staffordshire Bull Terrier, currently secured to the bench by two metres of heavy-duty chain, strained to make Leon's acquaintance.

'Sic 'im, Butch, sic 'im,' teased Danny, as the dog challenged the extent of his restraint, growling in frustration at the stubbornly non-diminishing space.

Leon felt reasonably confident the heavyweight chain would hold, but then envisaged: (a) Butch defeating the bench's inertia and fixings, (b) Butch dragging the seat and its riders across the concrete like a dog-sled on ice and (c) Butch chewing off one of his kneecaps as the clientele of Kath's Kaff looked on, surprised and unnerved, but not wishing to get involved.

Perhaps it's time I was moving, Leon thought.

Danny, the leader, was big – *very* big. Imagine a cross between a Silverback and a bulldozer; kind of slow-moving, but not as dull-witted as you might think. The self-appointed hard-man of this parish had a face like a jellied ham and sported major bling: chains, dog-tags, watch, rings, ear-rings, bracelets, two gold teeth, and 'iced-out grillz' (hip-hop style fake-diamond encrusted braces).

Carl, a cold, sly, sickly-looking sidekick with an eye on the top rung, habitual baseball-cap-wearer, and owner of the unfortunately-high voice, was currently dropping thin fries into his ratty, chewing mouth.

---

[2] Manc: Noun. Short for Mancunian, yes; an inhabitant of Manchester (surely you knew that) but also a *dialect*: often thick, nasally, with over-enunciated vowels. *Proper Manchester* is pronounced as *Propa Manchesta* . . . a much-celebrated accent; except in Liverpool, of course, but who are Scousers to criticise accents?

(Together, the nefarious pair supplied whatever pharmaceuticals the area required: tranquillisers, poppers, painkillers, cannabis, cocaine, LSD, heroin, ecstasy, crystal meth, PCP, khat, amphetamines, magic mushrooms, GHB, nitrous oxide . . . or, how about, for that awkward first date: Viagra with a side order of Rohypnol or ketamine?)

From anecdotal accounts (and the exchanges he'd been unable to avoid witnessing first hand), Leon knew the pair well enough to generate a wide berth whenever possible.

According to Moss, Leon's best and possibly *only* true friend, outsiders had tried to muscle in on their turf several times. The intruders had soon disappeared, though – two, quite literally. Danny, thought by some to be indestructible, had once been grenaded, and shot on no less than four separate occasions – once in the head. Yet, here he was, still going strong, and showing no signs of imminent death.

Carl claims *he* was once stabbed (in the arm, stomach, or leg, depending on who you ask; the location and circumstances of the alleged knifing seem to change every time he tells the story) but has never, Leon overheard on the Metro, been able to produce a scar. Leon remembered thinking: I can understand what might drive someone to want to do away with such a despicable creature, but why would they want to get that close? *Now, a sniper rifle . . .*

'Oy! Didn't you hear us, Fuckwit?' enquired Carl through a mouthful of partially-chewed potato.

Leon blinked at them as if he'd just woken up.

Danny chose this moment to raise his Kappa T-shirt and reveal a gun tucked into tracksuit bottoms.

Carl pointed, mimed shooting Leon in the face.

Butch, also no stranger to acts of intimidation, now beefed up his own performance. Front paws bouncing, hind quarters scraping at the concrete, he snarled canine contempt. Leon noted the studded leather collar stretching into the shape of a fat teardrop. This dog was all muscle, teeth, and anger. He would bite poor Mr Foofoo's tear-stained head clean off whilst doing him in the ass then eat his still-warm guts as a post-coital snack. Weird the things you think of when you're unsettled, Leon thought. And now I really should be going. (Leon classed himself as a *dog-*

person but that meant *normal, friendly, docile, man's best friend* dogs. Not vicious devil's-spawn hell-hound mutts.)

Giving the dangerous trio a wide berth, Leon walked around the bench as if a tacit exclusion zone were in place, the Bull Terrier following his progress like a jittery Geiger-counter needle. As Leon curved the perimeter, aimed indirectly for the relative safety of beyond, he was struck on his back and neck by a barrage of fries. Despite his instincts – or perhaps because of them – he stopped.

A heavily-loaded silence reigned briefly then yielded to Carl's voice: 'Hey, Ichabod! What the fuck are you waiting for?' To Danny, Carl added: 'Oh man, we should've took out that posh bastard ages ago, bro.'

Leon noticed a chip had come to rest on his shoulder. Good chip throw, he couldn't help thinking. Why can't I throw like that?

Danny grasped the steel-link leash, retreated the Staffy (which fought every inch), freed the looped chain from the bench, and let him back out. Butch, pulling his master's arm straight as he sought to take full advantage of the extra allowance, spoke into the slightly-shortened but from his point of view still disappointingly large divide. The blast sounded like: 'RAAAWAARWRARWARRARARWARARA!'

Carl again, with menace: 'Better keep moving, Fuckwit.'

Again with the 'fuckwit'! Leon flicked the chip from his shoulder. He turned slowly; faced the hard-man, the rat-faced one, and Butch, likely Foofoo defiler.

Danny elbowed his stooge and Carl stood, ready for confrontation, resetting his cap in excited anticipation.

Bouncing on the balls of his feet, arms held in an ape-like position, he addressed the top of Danny's huge head:

'Man, is he for real?' he squeaked. 'Must be trippin', Blood. No way is he frontin' me.' (Carl does so enjoy his street talk.) 'The fuck you staring at, you bent cunt?'

Butch, frenzied now, was reeled in again. Danny held the barking mutt by the collar as if set to unleash him at any second. All three watched as Leon broke the boundary of the separation area he normally imposed on himself.

'Oh, this is going to be fucking hilarious,' Danny said, feeling no immediate need for actual motion.

As Carl stepped down from the bench, puffing out a less than impressive chest, Leon moved ahead in what seemed like slow-motion: he slipped off his backpack; commenced to run (at funeral pace); reached over his shoulder; pulled out a glinting samurai sword (the backpack hit the ground) and with a lag befitting stretched time, howled: 'Baaaaaan-zaaaaaaaaaaaaaaaai!'

Instantly upon them, Leon decapitated Carl with the first swish – the liberated body fell forward, spilling what remained of his fish supper. Before Danny could say '*What the fuck?*' the second swing cleaved his meaty bonce clean off – razor-sharp katana right through his MADE IN MANCHESTER tattoo. The head rolled away, splashing through maroon spray issuing from Carl's neck. The whole event was over in a flash.

'How's that for *fucking hilarious*, Danny?' asked Leon, surveying the scene. 'Like it, do you, when someone goes all Kurosawa on your arse?' He took a step back to avoid whoever's blood that was creeping towards his Converse shoes. 'Oh, and it's "We should've *taken* out that posh bastard" not "*took* out", Carl, you imbecile.'

As Leon walked away, the geyser of blood that had been gushing several feet into the air from Danny's neck finally settled down. The scene had been pure Monty Python. Leon wondered if Peckinpah had ever seen the 'Salad Days' sketch and if so— Leon stopped; something behind him was coming his way. He knew immediately what it was: Butch, dragging Danny's massive headless torso in his wake. The Bull Terrier yelped as Leon, spinning on a heel, sliced the gleaming blade clean through the dog's middle.

In one easy move, Leon expertly returned the sword to its sheath, Samurai style, then leisurely strolled back to his pack, picked it up and shrugged it on. 'Yeah, you better keep moving, Fuckwit!' he heard over his shoulder.

As Leon headed for the exit, Danny shouted a postscript: 'Tell your boyfriend we've got that special stuff he likes!'

'Tell him yourself, Meat Head,' Leon muttered.

Having stretched the distance to the edge of the precinct, Leon turned, brushed the chip from his shoulder, and shouted: '*And he's not my boyfriend . . . you halfwit!*'

CHAPTER FIVE

From Precinct to Church Street

HOSPITAL TEA

He'd run most of the way, unsure if Butch had been on his tail. The cries of 'Go, Butch! Sic 'im! Sic 'im!' were probably a ruse but he hadn't waited to find out.

Now, hands on knees and finally getting his breath back, Leon straightened up . . . across the road stood the deeply-red Royal Mail letterbox. He was on Lower Church Street, scene of the crash. Nothing bizarre in that – he walked by here at least twice most days. Even the weird feeling this place always gave him had grown to feel familiar. The *usual unusualness*, as he had come to regard it.

He would normally just ignore the feeling and walk on. But today, this time, he suddenly felt *really* unusual – more unusual than ever before. He became lightheaded, giddy, the breathlessness returned with a vengeance, and a mad tingling invaded his hands, feet, and lips.

'Well this is new,' he said, resuming the head-down hands-on-knees position.

'Oh thank goodness,' said a small voice. 'Down here.'

Leon spotted a blot of chewing gum on the pavement, thought it looked like the face of a pale, wiry wraith. The tiny eyes blinked up at him. Here we go, Leon thought, another one for the Odd Log. This is getting to be—

'Help me,' pleaded the squashed gum.

'*Help you?*'

'I'm stuck.'

'*Stuck?*' A nervous laughter developed in Leon's throat. He teetered and the gummy face braced for a possible trampling. On jelly legs, Leon tottered to a car parked at the kerb and steadied himself against it, leaning like a drunken sailor. As he concentrated on not panicking and not fainting, a scene played out in his head:

Lester: 'So come on, son. What have we learned?'

'Er . . .' Leon was extremely familiar with the routine. His dad must have asked him *'What have we learned?'* a gazillion times since he was a kid. But come up with an answer? He couldn't even recall—

'Any accident you can walk away from is a good one,' said Lester in the tone adopted by those obliged to explain. 'Okay, technically, you didn't *walk*; firefighters cut you free and paramedics *carted* you off. But you know what I mean.'

'Come away from there, Lester,' Veronica said, returning with cups of vending-machine tea. 'What nonsense are you telling him now?'

'Nothing, I was just saying how he—'

'A brave soldier, that's what he is.' Veronica took up a position before the priority chair, compelling Lester to relocate to visitor seat two, away from the bed-head.

Leon, a small boat adrift on a fog-covered loch, heard a distant voice say: 'A *very* brave soldier.' The words echoed softly, kissed him lightly on the cheek, as if the speaker were an angel. He might or might not have replied: *'Don't say that, Ma, I'm not ten.'*

'The doctors said you're going to be fine, just fine,' continued Veronica. 'You're a bit banged up but it could have been a lot worse.'

'Exactly, and don't worry if you get a few ill-effects: confusion, headaches, anxiety . . .'

'Lester.'

'Nausea, vomiting, seizures, hair loss . . .'

'Lester!'

'They're all perfectly normal symptoms after a trauma to the head *Ow-ow-ow bloody hell!*' Lester was on his feet pulling tea-splashed trouser away from his thigh. *'What was that for?'*

'Sorry, Lester. What am I like? Wasn't too hot, was it?'

'No, no, only slightly scalding,' said Lester, flapping the steaming fabric.

'Don't listen to your father, son,' Veronica set down what remained of her tea, tucked Leon's already tight blankets, 'they didn't say – what he said – and they certainly didn't mention *hair loss*. They might have said that to *him*. No, the doctors said *concussion – mild* concussion.'

64

'They said *traumatic brain injury.*'

'*No!*' Veronica wheeled on Lester. '*They didn't.*'

'Vee, he's been in a coma for—'

'Right, that's more than enough from you. You can drink your tea in the corridor. Go on. Come back when you're ready to talk sense. And may God forgive you.'

Veronica crossed herself.

'*Why?* What did I say?'

'You know what you said.' Veronica locked her arms in a tight fold. Leon had seen mother aim this pose at father (and himself) many times over the years; the posture always made him want to giggle. Here she was, desperately trying to appear firm and resolute but just looking so – well, lovable.

'I don't, Vee. I'm trying to think. What *did* I say? Why don't you remind me?'

'Okay then, I will . . .'

Lester sipped his tea.

'You said . . .'

'Yes?'

'Something about his hair? No, wait – the other thing.'

Lester raised an eyebrow, waited.

Veronica's face went blank. 'No, it's gone.'

'Doesn't matter, Vee. Hey, don't forget your tea. I just bought it for you, fresh from the vending machine.'

'*Aw*, thanks, love.'

'You're welcome. Now, why don't we have a quiet minute? Let Leon clear his head. He's got a lot to take in.'

The moments that followed were fleeting, fuzzy, and familiar all at once: hushed shapes and hazy movements.

Leon sensed flowers being arranged and slow, paternal pacing; the smell of antiseptic, paper, and tiny lemons . . .

Unclear vision explored its limited scope: plain walls and featureless ceiling bathed in too bright white light, like being in a dazzling heavenly mist. A batch of shadowy faces leaned in, conferred, nodded, pulled back into obscurity . . .

Fingertips perceived smooth, clean linen.

After an indeterminate spell, there came another face – pretty this one, even out of focus. What was she checking? A trace of unscented deodorant was all that was left behind.

Leon discerned his leaden head, propped at an angle, would not budge. A neck brace? Was this a recollection or happening *now*? Time was blurring, sense of place growing more irregular. Vague ocular definition gently succumbed to a gradually pervasive fog that in some way felt welcoming and recognisable. He went into it easy . . .

And above the quiet, steady sound of his own breathing, a gentle barrage of noise: hospital hubbub: an autoclave sterilising, squeaky corridor-footsteps, medical teams chatting, doors on the move, telephones ringing, staff being paged, lost visitors redirected, lift pings, wheels rolling . . .

Veronica quietly informing Lester that he'd wet his pants.

WATCH THAT MAN

Leon suddenly found himself taking the tail-end of a belly-laugh towards the gutter (the car he'd been leaning on was now heading towards the rise of the hill). Fortunately, his legs solidified; he caught his balance and regained the pavement.

'Out the way, Nobhead,' shouted a cautionary bicycle rider.

'Okay, first of all,' Leon retorted, 'you shouldn't be on the pavement. And second, little girls shouldn't be using language like that. What are you, about ten?'

'Fuck off, Paedo!' was the dainty cyclist's considered response.

Charming, thought Leon.

'And don't fucking follow me or I'll call the fucking cops!' A pink mobile phone was held aloft, proof she wasn't bluffing.

Leon wasn't about to turn back and take the long way home. Not when there was a perfectly good short-cut at the top of the hill. No, he would wait – wait until the young accuser was out of sight. He watched her toil away at the pedals, taking forever. It would be easier, he decided, and quicker, to get off and push. And the language!

Fuck off, Paedo! And don't fucking follow me or I'll call the fucking cops! Shocking really. Some might advocate a spanking, put the snotty brat over a knee and tan its hide until it wailed like a steam train, but Leon would never contemplate such action. Not because he was never smacked as a child, and not because he believed corporal punishment didn't work, but because he knew any such action might give a certain degree of credence to her outrageously unfounded claims. Allegations that could look bad on paper – if transcribed into a written statement at a police station, for instance (you might get away with leatherings in some places, rural areas for example, but *city* cops would be tough on child-beaters, Leon supposed).

And how prejudicial would a jury be when they heard the victim was still too distraught to attend? As they wheeled her tiny pink bike into the hushed courtroom, they would become unanimous, if they weren't already, in wanting the sick-fuck perpetrator hanged or castrated, or both – perhaps at the same time. And who could blame them? Imagine explaining to your fellow inmates, once the screws had 'accidentally' let slip that you were not actually in for a string of armed bank heists as you'd claimed.

That could be *very* tricky. Even covered in an ugly mass of hastily applied felt-tip tattoos and sporting a freshly-shaved head, Leon knew he could never look hard enough to deter even the tamest, most open-minded, most forgiving of prisoners from vigilante acts of violence upon his person – perhaps, ironically, upon *his* bottom.

But wait, she'd gone. Questionable hypothetical beatings or buggerings were moot. The little princess was up the hill and away. Foul-mouthed so and so; honestly, youngsters today; in your face and venomous – bloody kids.

Jeez, I sound like an old man. I sound like Bill!

As happenstance sometimes dictates, Leon now spotted another old man – a *very* old man – over the road: a skinny individual with piercing raven-like eyes, thin nose, high forehead, and dusty suit. Eighties? Nineties? No way to be certain. He was standing beside the letterbox, cap in hand, looking over. The man had hillbilly teeth, chimpanzee ears and a chronic blink. He pushed a strand of dyed-black hair behind one ear, nearly smiled. Or was it a sneer? Leon wasn't sure. He aimed a thumb uphill . . .

67

'I don't know if you heard.'

The old man nodded.

'I hope you don't think . . . y' know . . . what *she* said.'

The old man coughed and batted away Leon's concern. 'Kids,' he said, rolling his pitch-dark eyes.

'Exactly. I'm only twenty-four. It's hardly the age of someone who'd . . . I mean, they're usually older, aren't they? Men who . . . A *lot* older.'

The old man rotated his cap, chomped his chops in the way only old people can. He didn't look well.

'Not as old as *you*, obviously; I'm not suggesting . . .'

The old man batted this away too. 'I wouldn't worry about it.'

As Leon took a turn at nodding, he imagined for some reason that the man whiffed of furniture, tobacco, and peppermint.

'She probably just needs a good span—'

'I have to go now,' Leon interrupted, already taking a first step.

'No problem,' the old man said, 'surprised to see you here at all, to be frank.' He beat a chalky shoulder and discharged dust motes caught the light of the low sun.

Floating, they cavorted, Leon thought, like the spirits of insects, glowing with beauty and colour. There can be a surreal, overwhelming magnificence in simple, seemingly mundane occurrences, if you look close enough. Not everyone sees this splendour (sadly, voyeurs of utter banality, as beauty, are rare).

Leon would like to have stayed, watched the aesthetic elegance of the tiny particles as they hovered and danced in the fading rouged remnants of the sunlit air, but the spreading drop in temperature urged him homeward.

After ten paces Leon glanced back.

'You've got some mettle, lad,' the old man called, 'I'll give you that.'

The twisted splendour of St. Mary's crooked spire pulled nearer. Each time Leon had checked, every ten paces, all counted aloud, the old man had remained standing by the letterbox, lifeless, staring.

'Eight, nine, ten,' tallied Leon. Still the old man hadn't moved. Surely that couldn't be normal. 'One, two . . .'

The roof of the oft-repaired bus shelter by the church entrance advanced into view; almost at the top.

'Nine, ten.' *Still bloody staring!* At least, Leon believed so; the old man was a fair distance off now – hard to be sure. Arms wide, Leon sent a signal: *What? What is it?* (No response.) Can ancient eyes see this far? – Probably not.

Irritation turned to compassion.

The old man cut a gaunt, sad figure all on his own. *Painfully* alone, felt Leon. As if he had family but they couldn't be with him. Moved away, Leon decided; emigrated to Spain – no, Canada. The elderly gent had been posting a letter to them. *Dusty*, as he now became, didn't have any friends. Dusty had outlived all his old pals.

After a few more paces and some final characterisation, the hill plateaued; the road continuing into the distance.

On the right, on the other side of the road, lay the church and bus stop – on the left, the short-cut home. As Leon took the left, onto the pedestrian footpath, he looked back over the brow.

'*What the* . . .'

Well, Dusty wasn't staring now. He'd vanished! But how does a decrepit codger suddenly disappear like that? He surely couldn't have run to the Metro station, ducked inside. He hardly looked capable of motion, let alone the necessary speed. Perhaps he was hiding behind the letterbox, this childish old man. Compassion turned back to irritation. Leon resolved to wait – wait until the silly old fool poked his head out.

Five minutes later and Dusty hadn't reappeared.

Leon decided to give it five more.

After less than two, Leon shouted: 'I know you're there, Dus— old man! Why don't you just come out and show yourself? Come on, joke's over!' (The letterbox failed to grow a head.) 'Well okay, but know this: the joke's on you!'

Leon wondered if he should walk back down, that would certainly put an embarrassing end to the old fart's infantile antics. No, definitely not; his feet had had enough for one day. Yes, it was only a hundred metres or so – downhill –

but the return slog would be *uphill*. *Again!* Plan B? Hide behind the bus shelter, keep vigil from there?

No, he couldn't see that working. And if anyone saw him they might think he was demented or something. Have him taken away by people in uniforms or white coats.

Maybe wait an hour? There was no way a pensioner, a clearly senile one, could maintain such a puerile game for *that* long. Could he? The sun was towing the day away; old bones would surely be feeling the growing nip in the air – had to be. But what if the silly galoot did wait out the next hour? He'd be able to slip away undetected under the cover of night. No, there was only one thing for it.

Back at the bottom of the hill, Leon was quickly able to confirm – after twice walking around the letterbox – that the old man was definitely not hiding. Unlikely as it seemed, Dusty must, Leon determined, have legged it to the Metro station when he, Leon, wasn't paying attention.

Daft old sod wants to grow up, he thought. Dusty clearly *had* been there because he'd left a small bouquet of flowers resting at the foot of the letterbox.

Casting his eyes back up the hill, Leon decided to take a break; a breather in preparation for re-climbing the north face of Upper Church Street. He removed his backpack, sat on the pavement, leaned against the stone wall that surrounded St. Mary's extensive graveyard, and rested his eyes on the letterbox – the redder-than-red letterbox . . . *the redder-than-red letterbox . . .*

THE REDDER-THAN-RED LETTERBOX

'Fire! Fire!' the dummy screamed, turning his wobbly head to face Leon. '*Do something, boy! DO SOMETHING!*'

'Do something? What would you suggest?'

'You're the one with the lungs . . . *blow!*'

Now, upside-down blowing might not be the easiest thing in the world, especially if you were asthmatic as a child, but Leon gave it his all – blew until he got dizzy. A hooker with forty years experience and lungs the size of beach-balls couldn't have blown harder.

Sadly, all his blowing didn't help. If anything, it fanned the fire. As Leon rested momentarily, hoping to catch a second wind, he noticed Lord Archibald had fallen motionless, the only flicker of life a tiny blaze reflecting in each varnished eye as he watched the flames lick around the dashboard breach.

'Well, don't just sit there like a gormless dummy,' Leon wheezed.

Lord Archibald snapped to. 'Yes, yes, the scissors, I'm looking, I'm looking.' The Swiss Army knife underwent a burst of close scrutiny then the eyes swivelled back to Leon.

'Why have you stopped blowing, you beastly boy? Keep blowing! Imagine it's a birthday cake.'

'*A birthday cake?* How is this like a fucking—'

'*Leon, please!*' snapped Veronica from below.

'Sorry, Ma.' Digging deep, Leon returned to huffing and puffing. The sound was high, hoarse and painful. Imagine a narrow-hipped first-time mother straining to naturally birth balloon-headed twins – without an epidural. Leon sounded worse. And the dashboard fire persisted.

'Aha!' the dummy exclaimed. 'Oh no, that's not it,' he added, returning an unhelpful magnifying-glass to the body of the knife. 'Sorry.'

'Jesus H. Christ,' Leon rasped. *What an annoying little fu—*

'*Leon!*' Veronica, a staunch Catholic, had always made her view clear: blasphemy was even worse than swearing.

'Alright, alright, let's not panic,' said Lord Archibald. 'Panic never helped anyone. What was it Kipling said . . . "If you can keep your head when all about you are losing theirs—" Argh! My fucking head's on fire!'

Said Leon, 'I'm fairly sure the next line is "If you can trust yourself when all men doubt you . . ."'

'NO, NO, MY FUCKING HEAD'S ON FIRE!'

Lord Archibald was correct – his fucking head *was* on fire. A fist-sized glob of something thick and gelatinous, and definitely ablaze, had shot from the dashboard breach and stuck to his nose. He flapped and screamed as the flaming gooey clump slid down, passed between his crossed eyes, over the kiss-curl, rolled under his painted hair and settled at the crown. Blue flames lapped his big wooden noggin as if it were being flambéed.

(Leon thought the dummy's upside-down head atop a burning blob reminiscent of a miniature hot-air balloon with the basket on fire.)

'*DO SOMETHING, YOU LITTLE SHIT!*' shrieked the panicked head.

There came then a loud hiss.

Archie, quiet now, turned slowly, deliberately, to Leon.

A steady trickle of golden liquid journeyed over his chin, ran down his face, and traversed his hair. The gooey globule, steaming but no longer alight, fell away. The dashboard fire sizzled a moment then it, too, went out.

'Sorry about that,' said Leon, re-zipping.

Lord Archibald shivered his head. Drips flew from ears, nose and hair. 'Did you just urinate on me?'

'Not directly.'

'Then why do I appear to be covered in—'

'Backsplash. I think you might have caught some backsplash.'

'*Some*? Look at me.'

'Is it *back-splash* or *splash-back*?'

'It's dripping off my nose.' Archie was right, it was.

'No need to thank me.'

'*Thank* you?'

'Look at it this way, at least the fire's out.'

'But you pissed on me. You *actually* pissed on me.'

Leon leaned slightly, whispered behind his hand: 'You know, I have it on good authority that some people would pay good money—'

'Not to *you* they wouldn't. If they'd really wanted Golden Showers they'd have gone to a massage parlour – that one in Urmston, probably. Do you know it?'

'Are dummies allowed—?'

'*Mannequin! MANNEQUIN!*'

Leon went cockeyed trying to focus on the Army Knife suddenly at his face. 'See you've found the scissors.'

'These things,' Archie said, demonstrating the scissors' snipping action close to the tip of Leon's nose, 'will cut through anything.'

Leon deployed what he hoped would be soothing politeness: 'Take it easy, Archie. You don't mind if I call you Archie, do you? You said it was okay.'

'And I do mean *anything*.' Archie's eyes flicked towards Leon's zip.

'*Mum?*' Mild panic now in Leon's voice. '*Dad?*'

Archie chuckled, shoulders bobbing ten to the dozen.

'Lord Archibald, *please . . .*'

'Lighten up, old bean, I am but joshing. Honestly, thou art such a drama queen.' Smiling, he presented the micro-scissors to Leon's seatbelt.

'Drama queen! Did you just say *drama queen?*'

'Told you.'

Leon noted the increased frailty in Veronica's voice as he climbed on his soap-box: 'I am *not* a drama queen,' he protested, sounding dangerously like John Merrick.

(He'd had this accusation levelled at him in the past, several times, and had never been able to understand why. The 'drama queen' allegation was one of the few things that could make his blood boil. He *wasn't* a drama queen. He was sure of it. They were *all* wrong.)

Lord Archibald began a series of diminutive snips.

'Fine, fine, you're not a drama queen. Perish the—'

'Argh!'

'What, *now?*'

Leon's fingers dipped, resurfaced; confirming the dummy had drawn blood – a tiny bead, anyway.

A fingertip was held out.

'What, *that*? – That wouldn't feed a flea.'

'*Wouldn't feed—* Listen, Archie, or Lord Archibald, or whatever your fricking name is – my parents and I are trapped in an upside-down possibly-about-to-explode Volkswagen Beetle and our only hope of salvation appears to be an ill-equipped dummy armed with the surgical skills of a cack-handed horse-butcher suffering from rheumatoid arthritis and Parkinson's!'

'Now, now,' Archie chortled. 'That kind of defeatist attitude never helped anyone. Remember Mr Pickles, Leon. What would Mr Pickles say?'

'Oh, I don't know, he'd probably tell you to take that useless Army knife of yours, open all its attachments, and shove it where the sun don't shine.'

'Up your arse.' Veronica's voice was now so weak, Leon barely caught it.

'No, I can't believe Mr Pickles would say that, Mrs Blank. Surely, he'd tell Leon to think *happy* thoughts.'

'*Happy thoughts?*' scoffed Leon. 'What – like the rain's eased off?'

'Has it?' Archie peered outside. 'Oh, yes. Do you know, I hadn't even noticed. Methinks the morrow—'

'Jeez! Enough with the Shakespeare, already.'

Leon was feeling deeply peculiar, and not a little queasy.

Was it the blowing? Blood settling in his head? Could the capsule's haze be poisonous? Was he being slowly poisoned by carbon monoxide? (He'd been unable to turn off the engine; the key had jammed in the ignition.)

He felt sure the exhaust pipes, or whatever they were called – Leon knew nothing about cars – *must* be damaged, probably leaking noxious vapours in every direction.

Can exhaust gases only kill in enclosed spaces? Did a couple of shattered windows negate Betty as an enclosed space? He wasn't sure.

Deciding that fumes or exhaust gases or whatever they were, were only lethal if you breathed them in, Leon sealed his lips and pinched his nose.

'What *are* you doing?' Archie asked.

Leon shook his head.

Archie sniffed the air, nervously. 'Can you smell petrol?'

Leon thought it odd that ventriloquist dummies could smell, yet couldn't blow. Under normal circumstances he'd have mused on it further, but worried about how long he could hold his breath, he abandoned the notion in favour of a sudden brainwave: a search for door furnishings.

'Now what?' asked Archie; watching Leon's fingertips pad around the door upholstery.

Leon's cinched lips shaped a smile. A handle had been located; he was already rotating the mechanism. The door was badly out of shape but somehow, the window rolled halfway-down; or, from an outside perspective, halfway-up.

Leon squeezed his head out and expelled any bad air that might be lingering within his lungs in exchange for a long, deep gulp of fresh cool oxygen.

The cold rush intoxicated, made him feel high – a laid-back, woozy, who-cares-about-imminent-death-anyway kind of elation. As if someone had shot him full of morphine. He felt drowsiness bordering on rapture. All thoughts of toxic vapours evaporated.

'Hang on,' Archie said, 'wasn't that window broken?'

Leon flexed an addled grin. 'Methinks someone needs a new monocle.'

'Could have sworn . . .'

Leon knuckled Archie's noggin. ' 'Tis the woodworm, I'll wager.' A peg-legged drunken sailor of a laugh ventured on deck.

Lord Archibald looked far from amused but continued snipping. 'What do they make these accursed seatbelts from – carbon-fibre laced with bollocking Kevlar?'

'What's up, Archie?' Leon tittered. 'Nano-nippers not quite up to the job?'

As Archie let out a frustrated groan, Leon's woozy snickering hit the rocks. A sudden wave of exhaustion cleared the decks; Captain Chuckles was washed overboard, lost at sea; Leon floundered in the doldrums; the gunner's daughter kissed the brass monkey's loose cannon for the last time (I may have made that one up) and everything was three sheets to the wind. Yes, the good ship *Stretched Metaphor* was gently sinking. Blissful euphoria became a wilted smile and slumping eyelids.

'Come on, Leon, show a leg. You need to stay awake. Talk to me.'

'What about?' Leon's tone was indicative of 'Piss off.'

'Anything,' suggested Lord Archibald snipping on pluckily. When Leon said nothing, the dummy discharged a big old nudge.

'Hmm?'

'Tell me what you're going to do after this unfortunate accident.'

'Don't know,' Leon drawled. He sensed a fog rolling in.

'Will you finish your story?'

'Yes – maybe – if I can.' Leon made the face of the sleeping. 'Now, shush.'

Lord Archibald yelped, loud and abruptly. The wiring fire was back, instantly bigger and bolder than before; a dashboard inferno – the heat, brutal and pervading.

'Mmm, toasty.' Leon's voice was low and aimless. Unsure if he was drifting toward sleep or unconsciousness, but unconcerned either way, he felt oddly at peace.

'Wake me up when you're done,' he whispered.

A monsoon-heavy cloudburst fell all around. Had that just started? Leon wondered, wearily, if he was slipping in and out of consciousness. How would he know? Had a little time passed, or a lot? Did it matter? What was the question again? Through the drowsiness he thought he divined a tension in the air: the gathering charge of a coming storm.

There came now a loud crack, deep inside Betty's guts. With a whoosh, burning viscous oil squirted flamethrower-style over Lord Archibald, igniting his pyjamas and smoking jacket almost instantaneously. The Swiss Army knife flew from Archie's unconvincing grasp as his arms flapped wildly at the overwhelming flames and he emitted a long, high scream. Exactly what Leon would have expected from a fast-burning ventriloquist dummy. The scene put him in mind, absentmindedly, of a careless vampire caught in midday sun. Then Archie's head fell off with a sharp metallic twang. The wooden noggin landed on Betty's roof, crunched into a glass-strewn puddle of flaming gunk.

'*FUCK! FUCK! FUCK!*' cawed the head.

'Happy thoughts,' murmured Leon, his voice the light flutter of distant moth wings.

'Piss on him,' Veronica may have suggested. If heard correctly, she wasn't sounding at all like herself. Leon put it down to—

He couldn't think of a word for fumes . . . Why wouldn't his brain do what he wanted? Was he *thinking – actually* thinking – or only *dreaming*? A picture formed in his delirious mind's eye: himself, barely conscious on a high, narrow ledge; the world below, missing. Not a thing to see.

Faintly recognisable odours persisted: melting resin, propellant, baking timber. But sounds: crackling varnish;

slowing cries of 'oh fuck' and 'fuck no'; rainfall and the rumble of approaching thunder – they were gradually ebbing away.

Floating in the ether, Leon missed his mother's admonishments: several 'fucks' and not a word about it? That couldn't be right.

Lester had gone quiet, too.

Leon hoped they were okay.

YOUNG GUNS AT THE BUS STOP

Leon found Moss, his best friend but in no way boyfriend, waiting in the bus shelter at the top of Church Street – or Upper Church Street if you want to be overzealous about it (the council had placed street-name signs at the top and bottom of the hill but no-one knew exactly where Upper Church Street ended and Lower Church Street began. Except nit-picking Reg, he might know).

Anyone who knew or saw Moss would probably describe him as a stoner. He clearly smoked far too much weed (well, duh) so the label was fair. His general demeanour was so profoundly laid back it made his lazy eye, despite being as bloodshot as its 'good' neighbour, seem positively energetic.

Both eyes scrunched as thin lips, set inside a fuzzy blonde beard, pulled on a skinny joint held between pale fingers. Smoke came out slow, trailed up through straggles of blond hair poking out from under a knitted Inca hat.

'Alright, Moss?'

Moss rose slowly and they hugged like old friends do.

'Going to see Uncle Ronnie?'

'If the bus ever comes, man; every twenty minutes they're supposed be. Pretty sure I've been here longer than that.'

'I know. You didn't have that beard when you got here.'

'No, I did, man.'

'Course you did. What was I thinking?'

'Oh yeah, right, sorry, man; got you now.' Moss laughed then re-parked his butt on the bus shelter seat, had another drag – a long one. 'Or is it every *forty* minutes?'

As he exhaled, blue-grey smoke rose into the now biting air. Evening was truly about them.

'How are the shoes doing?' Leon asked, casting his trained eye over Moss's North Face Haydens. (Grippy, eco-friendly casual moccasin-style footwear with a rubber sole engineered from partially recycled products, cotton canvas lining, and laces crafted from natural materials. Leon knew them well; he'd restitched the nubuck and suede leather upper of both shoes a few weeks earlier.)

'Yeah, good, man. It's getting cold, though.' Moss's breath confirmed his point. 'Hope this bus turns up soon.'

Leon nodded, watched his best friend take yet another drag.

The sign above the entrance of the Odeon Cinema (built during the early Thirties in 'Egyptian' style and originally called The Pyramid) boasts of a Matinee double-feature: WYATT EARP and GUNFIGHTER'S MOON; the former starring Kevin Costner, the latter, Lance Henrickson.

Two boys burst through the main cinema doors – *saloon doors* in their minds – firing pretend six-shooters and Winchesters at each other. The young bloods are Moss and Leon, nine years old and full of bounce and vinegar.

'*Peeoww! Peeoww! Peeoww!*' yells little Leon as make-believe death puts Moss in the proverbial dirt. Leon blows on his 'Colt 45s' then replaces the spent cartridges with fresh bullets from his fictitious belt.

But Moss isn't dead. He looks up and pleads, 'Please don't shoot me again, Wyatt.'

'Then you get the hell out of Dodge,' Leon says in his best cowboy drawl before spinning the fanciful handguns into invisible holsters.

Leon thought for a moment he could hear the sound of a reel spinning; the last piece of film, not fully inside the spool, clacking around inside his head.

He found himself looking at the now empty bus stop, hands resting on the heels of imaginary childhood pistols.

Moss had got out of Dodge.

Leon turned to discover his friend taking a seat inside a Number 93. The bus had finally arrived. He waved as it pulled away and Moss raised a lazy hand.

The bus hadn't quite vanished from sight when Leon felt a prod in his back. Twisting delivered a familiar combo.

'Wow,' said Leon. 'Nan, Granddad; don't see you for ages then twice in one day – thought you'd gone to bingo.'

'We did,' replied Norma, the misfortune in her frown matched only by her partner's.

'No luck, then?'

'*Mecca Max?*' said Bill. 'More like *Mega Twats.*'

Not wishing to learn the specifics of a Mecca Max, Leon assumed for brevity's sake that it was a big win and it had eluded them.

'That's forty quid we won't get back,' Bill added.

'You blew *all forty* on bingo?' asked Leon.

'No, no, not all of it,' insisted Norma.

Bill again: 'Some went on the slots—*Ow!*'

Norma, having just elbowed Bill's tummy, said: 'We *have* got some left.' Then, smiling dolefully, she added: 'Not much – but *some.*'

'Right,' said Leon. 'So where are you off to now?'

'Precinct,' hissed Bill rubbing his jarred gut. 'Get a few nibbles for tomorrow's—*OW!*'

'*Nibbles?* What, are you having a party or something?'

'Nah,' said Norma. 'Just a few friends round; Saturday evening cards.' She tutted, clicked her head back as if to underline how boring it would probably be.

'Maybe I could—'

'Just oldsters playing a few hands,' advised Norma.

'Yeah, you'd be bored shitless,' wheezed Bill.

'Right, come on,' said Norma, not really moving, 'we'd better get these nibbles before I freeze my tits off.' She pulled gently on Bill's sleeve and added, wistfully: 'And while we've still got a few coppers left.'

Before Leon could think to stop, out came the wallet. Bill and Norma nudged each other like excited school kids.

'What do you need,' asked Leon. 'Five? Ten?'

'Twenty should be fine,' said Norma, helping herself.

'Better make it forty,' coughed Bill, also dipping. 'We can get a few drinks in then. You don't mind, do you, Leon? Pensions are a disgrace.'

Yes, so you keep telling me, thought Leon, simulating a non-beleaguered countenance.

Bill passed the second note to Norma who folded the two together into a tight stamp-sized square.

The wallet curled up for the night, feeling ravaged and a good deal poorer than it had started the day, then slunk off, back to Leon's pocket to lick its wounds.

Well this turned out to be an expensive day; eighty quid to Nan and Granddad – the Spar on top . . .

'Good job somebody's got a good job, eh, Leon?' said Norma.

'Yep,' said Leon with little enthusiasm.

'So why the long face?' inquired Bill. Then, under his breath, to Norma: 'He's gone again.'

'You alright, son?' asked Norma.

'I suppose so – why?'

'You seem preoccupied.' Norma put a hand on Leon's shoulder. 'If you need someone to talk to, you know you can always call on us.'

'Aw, thanks, Nan,' said Leon, looking away as his grandmother pulled down the neck of her thick jumper to stuff the flattened twenties inside her bra.

'I'll call round later, shall I?'

'Bit late now, lad.' Bill had edged several feet away and was encouraging Norma to do the same.

'Okay, what about tomorrow?' asked Leon.

'Not tomorrow, Leon,' said Norma trailing Bill. 'We'll be getting things ready for our cards night.'

'No problem; how about Sunday?'

'Yeah, no, we've got that thing,' said Bill looking to Norma.

'Yeah, we've got that thing,' agreed Norma.

By now, the elderly pair had put several yards of Church Street between themselves and their grandson.

'Okay,' shouted Leon, 'some other time, then!'

'Yeah, definitely!' yelled Bill.

'You know we're there for you, Leon!' hollered Norma.

CHAPTER SIX

At home with the Blanks

RICHARD'S PIT

Leon held out the carton of Marlboros.

'Not now, Leon. Can't you see I'm busy? It's Kelly, and we just hit the jackpot, big time. No bra.'

'So what happened to *I'll die if I don't get a fag*?'

'Jesus, you're a big Mary sometimes. Just throw them on the bed.' Richard was engaged in the business of excitedly aiming a Handycam out the window. The digital camcorder appeared whenever a pretty girl (or not so pretty so long as Richard decreed her body 'agreeable') walked up, down, or across the street (he could spot them a mile off; because of the binoculars – also mail order). Right now, it was Kelly's turn. *Again.* A few extra recorded minutes of bra-less magnificence to add to the swelling collection; magic to be watched back later. So far, over fifty recorded minutes of Kelly and her unfettered breasts: snatched moments, a minute here, a minute there, edited together (alongside slow-motion replays) into one long joggle-fest. Richard claimed Kelly's bouncing boobs had a 'bewitching jiggle', said he could watch them for hours. And he did; over and over, up and down and up and down, bobbing away.

'That's it, my lovely,' said Richard, his breathing now heavy. 'Keep that speed just right.'

'What *are* you like?'

'Fuck off – you love it, too. Don't pretend you don't.'

Richard's free hand slid under Che Guevara, tweaked a nipple. Leon averted his eyes, looked around the room.

Not a big bedroom, boxy in fact, but made to look even smaller because of all the stuff crammed inside. The place looked like a ransacked storeroom; a deserted lock-up facility visited by earth-tremors and abandoned by disappointed looters; its floor and shelves strewn with boxes of junk, piles of books and magazines, bric-a-brac, pieces of furniture, things that should arguably have been thrown away long ago. And buried within, nestling beside an unfolded camping chair whose sole purpose in life, it seemed, was to support a brimming ashtray, Richard's pit: a green folding camp-bed topped with soiled pillow and dishevelled sleeping bag pocked with cigarette burns and suspicious splotches.

And underneath the camp-bed, secreted beneath an old army blanket, a tatty suitcase – home for the material form of Richard's 'interests': a copy of the classic *Lesbian Lavatory Lust* on VHS tape, more dubiously-titled homemade DVDs, a near-empty bottle of baby oil, a table-tennis bat (don't ask), a plug-in hard-drive containing the ever-expanding footage of Kelly in motion, and several copies of *Slinky, Stag,* and *Parade*: 1960s 'Pin-Up' Magazines uncovered during a comprehensive late-night exploration of the attic. (Leon refused to accept Richard's proposal that the magazines must have been acquired by Lester, probably when he was a teenager.) As porn stashes go, Richard's was, in truth, a slightly dismal, pitiful collection. But then, as Leon mused: There's probably something inherently lugubrious about *all* porn stashes.

'There she goes – Kelly the magnificent,' Richard said, straining to eke out a final glimpse through the branches of the large maple tree at the end of the street. Her arse wasn't as mesmerising as her tits but it still had to be watched, obviously. 'God, I wish I could follow her.'

'Why don't you, then?'

Richard's glance said: '*You know why, you little shit.*'

'You can leave the house when you want to,' Leon insisted.

'Bollocks. You don't know what you're talking about.'

Richard kept eyes on the maple, no doubt hoping Kelly might have forgotten something and upon realising make an immediate return.

Leon sat on the camp-bed, directed his thoughts at Richard's back. I know you can leave the house, you big fraud. I've seen you in the back garden at night watching Mrs Hobbs . . . I'm sure she'd start closing her curtains if she knew *you* were skulking about with your binoculars.

82

'It's true that I might be able to manage a couple of minutes outside, if sedated. But if I was to take the poison Dr Popperwell dishes out, I'd have to spend a week in bed.'

No change there then.

'I'm convinced the pills he prescribes are meant for animals – *large* animals. He's most-likely not a doctor at all. The demented Taffy's probably a quack; an unemployed cattle vet masquerading under forged qualifications.'

'Hey have you heard the one about the gay agoraphobic? He had a hard time coming out of the closet. Get it?'

'What are you trying to say?'

'Nothing, it's just a joke.'

'Agoraphobia is no laughing matter, matey. No laughing matter at all. I get dizzy just thinking about outdoors.'

Except when you're in the garden.

'Christ, I'm getting light-headed again. Why did you have to make me think about outside?'

'I didn't.'

'Out of the way, I need to lie down before I have a full-blown panic attack.'

And he did – lie down that is – on the camp-bed; sank his head into the tainted pillow, flipped out the camcorder's view-screen and reviewed the latest recording.

Leon studied him. *Agoraphobic?* What bollocks, he thought. It's nothing more than an excuse – a subterfuge to lie in bed all day or loll around the house ogling tits. The guy's so full of shit he's unbelievable. Panic attacks, my arse. Next, he'll be re-spouting that crap about the gentle rhythm—

'The gentle rhythm of Kelly's mammaries calms me.'

Staggering.

Without looking up from the view-screen, Richard added: 'I find tits help ease my stress levels.'

Leon thought: You're not fooling anybody. The only thing getting stressed around here is me. Oh, and the front of your pants, I see. Thanks for that. You really are quite the debauched pig, aren't you? You're almost as disgusting as your grubby pillow. God, I hope those blotches are drool stains and not—

'What are you staring at? Don't give *me* the evil eye.'

'I wasn't; don't get paranoid. I was thinking about something else entirely.' *But now that you mention it; look at you.* Leon eyed the sluggish wastrel. *I've never known anyone so lazy – lazy and depraved.*

'I know exactly what you're thinking – you're thinking I'm lazy. But I'm not lazy, I'm just not well.'

'Actually, I was thinking lazy and depraved.'

'*Depraved?*'

'Some might say perverted.'

'Oh grow up, Leon. They're just normal healthy interests; nothing wrong with having a passion for something. You should get one.'

'I have passion,' Leon said.

Whatever label might be applied: passion or perversion, diversion or deviation, recreation or aberration, Richard had had enough for now.

'It's no good, I can't watch any more. I've got one of my headaches, thanks to you.'

He stowed the camcorder on the chair, plumped the stodgy pillow (akin to fluffing a bag of damp cement) then replaced his head.

'Did you hear me? I said: *I have passion.*'

'What? Those shitty little stories you keep trying to write? Do me a favour. Now make yourself useful and draw the curtains; they'll be firing up that fucker any minute and I feel a bastard migraine coming on.' He slid out the pillow, placed it over his face and grumbled through the wodge of suppurating foam: 'Why do they always put them right outside people's houses?'

'Oh dear, what a shame – perhaps I can get it moved. I'll phone the council's street-lighting department first thing in the morning. Is there anything else you need in the meantime? How about something to put you to sleep? Two dozen Xanax pills and a glass of warm propofol, perhaps?'

'No, nothing; just close the curtains and get out. And don't forget to leave the smokes.'

Leon flipped the Marlboros onto Richard's chest, landing them plum centre of Che's stoic face, and waited.

Guevara has been credited with several famous quotes (go ahead, Google them, we'll wait). Richard said nothing.

'What was that?' Leon cupped an ear. 'Thanks, Leon? Much appreciated, Leon? Can we settle up later, Leon? Of course we can. Oh, you're welcome, Richard. Don't worry about it. You get some sleep.'

Richard remained silent.

Leon stepped quietly to the camp-bed and leaned over, palms hovering just inches above the yucky, blemished pillow; sorely tempted to smother the life out of the—

'Why are you still here?' asked Richard through the pillow. 'Go on, get out!'

SUMMER 1966 GIVES WAY TO AUTUMN 1963

He should have moved out ages ago!

Traditionally, and historically, the Blanks (a majority of them, anyway) had always put themselves out, especially to help family, but this was *too* much. Swanning around like he owns the place. Anyone would think this was *his* house.

Leon didn't want to brood but found it hard not to; couldn't help thinking of *It* as an unwelcome guest: the uninvited, unwanted, brazen relative who turns up on the doorstep (not for the first time), late at night, bags in hand, claiming nowhere else to go; a bulbous-headed space-cadet, back from outer space, pleading ground-control to clear re-entry. The type who just needs somewhere to stay for the night, a few days at most, whilst their capsule is overhauled after a close encounter with a meteor storm, or some other bullshit. The sort who, having grovelled their way back in, immediately treat the fridge like a free mini-bar, the house like a hotel; a parasite that will drain every last drop of hospitality from their host and find fault as they're doing it; the kind who always outstay their welcome and hang around like the proverbial bad smell; those whose blatant bullshit spews forth effortlessly and without limit.

Why am I still here? Why are you still here! Ungrateful, free-loading, blood-sucking wanker!

'Fancy a cup of tea, Leon?' Veronica, teapot poised over a large mug, smiled warmly from the kitchen counter.

'Yes, please.' Leon slumped into a chair at the table.

'Cheer up, lad, might never happen,' said Lester.

'Like your dad's films,' said Veronica, rolling her eyes.

'Nearly there, Vee.' Lester was loading an 8mm film spool onto an old movie projector; threading a snake of frames through various sprockets, teeth, guides, and gates.

'He's been saying that for hours,' said Veronica, placing Lester's tea by the projector. 'Would you like one, Leon? It's fresh brewed.' She presented a smile, warm as the last.

Leon nodded. 'Please.'

As Veronica went back to the counter, Leon and Lester exchanged a warm, knowing look. Both knew her short-term memory was broken. Their unspoken pact ignored the number of times she asked the same questions; repeated the same things; forgot that which had been discussed only a moment before.

Leon smiled. 'At least you got yours,' he said softly.

'Asked for hot chocolate,' Lester whispered.

Veronica returned, took her place at the table.

'Mmm, lovely,' she said after sipping from a bone china cup. 'Sure you wouldn't like one?'

'No, I'm fine, thanks.'

Lester winked at Leon. Once again, the pair had successfully and politely overlooked the enormous goldfish in the room. 'Okay, but you're missing out,' Veronica said, gently placing her cup on its saucer.

'Get ready, everybody.' Lester moved into position, halfway between projector and light switch. (The kitchen light was currently on, the blinds already drawn.) For some reason, he always reached for them at the same time, even though his extended arms could never quite bridge the gap.

Lester hovered for a moment like a strange flightless bird, head equidistant between switches. Then he killed the kitchen light, shifted slightly (both wings still outstretched) and flicked the projector's on/off lever to *on*.

As the machine sprang to life, he took a seat, raised the mug of tea that wasn't hot chocolate and said: 'Here goes.'

Leon smiled at that. For as long as he could remember, his dad had performed the 'Switch-Bird' and said *'Here goes'*. The films varied but the ritual remained the same.

Perhaps this is how Leon developed his love of films? Started years ago, watching family home movies as a kid:

the excitement of sitting in a darkened room, the noisy whir and clicking of the old projector, the warmth of its lamp, and all those recognisable never-ageing faces in emotive, familiar places shining large on the wall; every viewing a way of reliving the past: *Happy times.* He felt this now as he fixed eyes on the projection, one of three bright faces settled to reminisce.

Illuminated images flickered and gambolled upon a square section of kitchen wall but mismatched half-frames produced an unsettled world of ground over sky and good-natured grumbling from the audience – a shaky start.

'Bear with me,' pleaded the projectionist, twiddling.

After a hint of sprocket-bleeding, frames jumped into line, all edges and borders resuming their proper place. 'Thank you,' Lester said, acknowledging the wry applause.

'Here goes,' said Leon playfully.

'Gosh, you sounded just like your father then, Leon,' said Veronica. And she wasn't wrong. Beyond using the same words; they also had *extremely* similar voices – eerily so, sometimes.

A field, distant hills, summer sky, big clouds . . .

'Cornwall, Sixty-six,' Lester announced. 'We'd just got the Lambretta. You'll see her in a minute. Sports edition, two hundred cc's – I fitted all the extras myself: mirrors, horns . . .'

Veronica made a comic show of pretending to yawn – slanted it towards to Leon.

Leon recognised the field, a field he had never seen in real life, and wondered how many times he'd watched this particular spool of home movies (movies plural because Lester had been in the habit of splicing separate films – films sometimes made years apart).

This spool, as always, had no sound but vibrant colours:

Rich greens, paint-box blue, fluffy whites. Panning right, the camera finds a small orange tent and Lester, nineteen, at the peak of fitness, sitting astride a shiny scooter – a Lambretta SX 200 to be exact: blue and white paintwork, impressive array of mirrors and horns, 'LB' decals, and tall aerial topped with an RAF 'target' flag – a thing of beauty and clearly Lester's pride and joy.

'Brand new she was,' Lester said. 'A step up from the old Vespa 125, eh? Can you see her properly?'

What had been sharp, blurred, sharpened, and blurred again (Lester liked to focus-twiddle even if it wasn't strictly necessary). To a chorus of teasing cat-calls, the footage eventually settled on optimum sharpness.

In keeping with the snazzy ride, Movie-Lester is equally stylish, and the key word here is *sharp* – slim-fitting checked shirt (button-down collar), thin tie (knitted), tight trousers (narrow bottoms), and Winkle-picker shoes.

'I've still got that suit, you know, Leon. The jacket's handsome: mohair, two-tone, narrow lapels . . .'

(Leon had long since given up wondering why anyone would take a suit, shirt and tie on holiday, let alone wear them on a hot summer day. But that's what they did. That was Mods.)

'Three buttons, side vents, silk lining . . .'

Veronica had another roll of her eyes. 'You'll be telling us next you've still got your . . . uh . . . doodah.'

'My parka? I have as well; in the wardrobe with the suit – might still have that tie, too.' Lester got all moony. 'Those were the days, son. Even the bloody Rockers couldn't spoil it. And they tried. Yes, those really were the days.'

See, Lester Blank wasn't just a *regular* Mod back in the Sixties – oh no – he reckons he was a 'Face', too; one of the *main* Mods, leading the pack on long runs to the coast and all that. Weekend jaunts from Manchester to the most popular destinations could easily cover five to six hundred miles, round trip. But Lester didn't mind. The long rides were the best part. Especially if you were out front, as Lester claimed he often was. Margate, Brighton, Southend, Bournemouth, Hastings, Clacton; none of these were too far for a 'proper' Mod. Besides, even with this larger-engine scooter, he could still, he boasted, get over ninety miles per gallon – even with his 'bird' on the back.

Leon smiled. He knew what was coming next:

Movie-Lester takes a step forward, eagerly waving-in the unseen camera operator, then the action jump-cuts and, as if by magic, he is replaced by Movie-Veronica. She's waving and smiling and looking so fine: an eighteen-year-old beauty. Her gorgeous copper-coloured hair is cut boyishly-short but there's zero androgyny here – not when she's modelling a figure-hugging lemon-yellow trouser-suit cinched tightly around her skinny waist by a black plastic belt (accessorised with jet-black button-earrings and monochromatic Polka dot canvas tennis shoes). She might have looked ever-so-slightly 'waspish' but there was nothing *irascible* about Veronica; she looked as happy as a honey bear in an apiary and as pretty as a primrose in sunshine – the proverbial picture of health. Any healthier and she would have burst.

Spoilt for great angles, the point-of-view shifts. Intense sunlight catches in the scooter's mirrors. The camera readjusts to a new, glare-free angle and zooms in (Lester loved a good zoom). Veronica sits, side-saddle, posing as if the scooter were a prize on an afternoon game show. Giving her best cheesy smile, she wafts a hand over the controls, demonstrates a slight turn of the handlebars and innocently strokes a mirror.

Having zoomed back out, an out-of-focus hand, giant compared to Veronica, now motions in the foreground, the sense of encouragement conveyed through wave.

Veronica acquiesces, performs a little dance: Mod-style, of course. The big hand returns with a thumbs-up, then, wanting something more, gestures to the Lambretta's leather seat. After a brief, playful refusal, Veronica turns to the scooter, plants her flat shoes, and bends. Placing her hands on the seat, she sticks out her tush and gives it a saucy wiggle: a bit cheeky, but sexy in a classic 'cheesecake pin-up' kind of way. The hand is pleased and lets her know. Yet another zoom removes green field until only arse, tightly bound in lemon cotton, fills the frame.

An absolute peach of an arse, it has to be said; but that was his *mother's* arse up there! Leon didn't want to see that. All the same, he couldn't help smiling.

And Lester is still on it; or *trying* to stay on it. The arse is now in motion, running around the scooter, attempting to escape the attention of the leering lens as it follows close behind, chasing. The only things missing are Benny Hill, a string of additional girls, and the 'Yakety Sax' music.

For this part of the movie, at least if Leon was in attendance, Lester and Veronica would usually fall silent – briefly. And this time was no different. What followed the temporary lull varied: sometimes a giggle or a cough, sometimes a nudge, a sideways glance, a mischievous smile, a playful shake of the head – today, it was a gentle kick under the kitchen table and a grimace from Lester. As ever, the moment passed with the next splice:

Summer '66 gives way to autumn '63 (Lester's splicing wasn't necessarily chronological). A football match: Lester in goal; Sunday League stuff; a pitch of marsh, mire, and mud, interspersed with sporadic tufts of grass – the stubborn, never-say-die type; lots of cold hammy legs running all over the place and no more than fifteen or twenty well-wrapped supporters cheering them on. A willowy teenager wallops the ball, sending it whizzing past a wind-blown sheet of newspaper. Diving full-stretch to his left, Lester's filthy glove tips the ball around the post. Pairs of hands appear from pockets and applaud, silently.

This save, and others, always got Leon thinking about his dad's hopes, plans, and expectations; and how they were all ruined, destroyed in a fleeting moment of misfortune, never to recover.

You see, as a kid, Lester had had a dream: a dream to be a professional footballer. And it hadn't been pie in the sky either because as a teenager he turned out to be good – *really* good – and, at long last, after several seasons of Sunday League football, he was finally spotted by a talent scout and invited for trials with Manchester United (yes, them! Miracles do happen every so often).

The trials – about a week before the Cornwall holiday, so we're talking summer of '66 again – couldn't have gone better (he made a memorable impression, they said: *Most promising young goalkeeper they'd seen in years*) and at the grand old age of nineteen (not like today, where boys are signed before they can tie their own bootlaces) an initial five-year deal was offered subject to contract. As Lester understood it, he was seen as the perfect replacement for Harry Gregg, hero and survivor of the Munich Air Disaster. (Harry had suffered a serious shoulder injury followed by a succession of other injuries and it was clear to all that his remaining games were numbered.) Yes, any day now, that contract would be landing on Lester's mat.

Except, of course, it didn't.

What happened is this:

As Lester scootered through Altrincham – this would have been a few days after returning from Cornwall – everything seemed perfect; the future, the weather, and every light on green. The plan: collect Veronica from catering college, go to her house in Timperley (or rather, her parents' house), indulge in some hopefully not too awkward generation-gap small talk, then have a lovely sit-down meal. Veronica had offered to cook; her intention to get Martin and Pat to finally acknowledge that Lester *was* a lovely person and that he *would* make a fine son-in-law.

Martin and Pat Collins were always affable, but a touch formal – a bit snooty, in truth. They always tried to make Lester feel welcome but it was the 'trying' that made things uncomfortable. Lester knew they'd have preferred their daughter to be with someone less likely to vote Labour and a whole lot more Catholic, like them.

Lester's parents, Bill and Norma, who no-one would ever describe as self-important or la-de-da – an accusation many, including Veronica, had often levelled at Martin and Pat – raised their son to be C-of-E (i.e. absolutely no interest in religion whatsoever) and self-respecting 'working class'; even though Bill's entire career was spent at home following a clerical error which saw the park he was taken on by the local council to keep, closed by the same council one week later – and because no-one seemed to notice, or informed the payroll department, he was diligently paid the not-ungenerous weekly salary right up to his retirement. They even laid on a last-day lap-dancing stripper-gram, which Bill felt only fair, since they'd clearly had a whip-round, to attend and enjoy to the fullest.

For as long as Lester could remember, his parents' motto had always been: Have as much fun as you can and try not to get caught.

Veronica's parents were the opposite. They didn't like the whole scooter-scene thing, either; even if Mods did dress reasonably smart. '*A young lady on a scooter, legs apart at several miles an hour? It just isn't right, child.*'

But what could they do? The kids were in love; had been for years. No, Mr and Mrs Collins would just have to tolerate the situation until their little girl, youngest and most treasured of three daughters, came to her senses; which they hoped would be very soon – Lester and Veronica were to be married in the autumn.

Anyway, the plan: after Martin and Pat had retired for the evening (the pair were early-to-bed early-to-rise types) the love birds would settle down with their latest ciné film. Lester had just had it developed and was looking forward to watching it with his beau. Veronica was enthusiastic, too, on one level, uneasy on another. What if her parents gatecrashed the screening? Perhaps on the off-chance they might spot something untoward, something they could later use to try and finally convince her that Lester was obviously *not* 'suitable' husband (or son-in law) material. Or worse, what if they asked to watch the whole movie?

Lester reminded Veronica how her parents had scoffed when she first mentioned the planned camping trip: '*What? In a* tent – *Are you serious? Why not come with us to the coast, dear?*' (Martin and Pat had often bragged of owning a half-share in a four-berth caravan at – wait for it – Prestatyn. '*Bring Lester if you'd like,*' they'd added without enthusiasm.) After much fretting, Veronica had settled on: *No*, Lester was right. Her parents *wouldn't* ask to watch the film. They never had before.

But, Lordy, what if they *did*?

That's right – this was the footage filmed during last week's holiday – the one with the lemon trouser suit – the one with their precious daughter's teenage arse!

Lester, thinking of that, smiled to himself as he sailed through the lights. He was still smiling when a police van ploughed into the side of the scooter.

The Black Maria had raced through red, unlit and unannounced; no flashing lights, no siren, and no slowing down until it was too late. The impact instantly slammed the right side of Lester's head against the van's windscreen (the wearing of crash helmets was not compulsory in the

Sixties and Mods tended not to bother) and dispatched rider and his transport to the kerb.

At first, the agony in Lester's right leg was like nothing he'd experienced before. As he endeavoured to shut out the pain, a crowd gathered. Mouths flapped but their words were muted. Lester couldn't hear anything over the intense ringing in his right ear. A middle-aged woman pushed her concerned face in close. Lester read her lips: '*Don't move, dear,*' she mouthed. '*Whatever you do, don't move.*' Lester didn't feel much like moving, anyway. His right leg, he would later discover, had a broken femur, shattered patella, busted tibia, and splintered fibula: pretty much the complete set – a full house of wrecked leg bones.

By the time Police Constable Gray's helmet pierced the peering huddle, some five minutes later, Lester was, perhaps due to shock, 'comfortable' with his suffering.

The young policeman – not much more than a lad, really – had run to a nearby call box (the radio in the van was kaput), called for an ambulance, and then phoned his Sergeant. The Sergeant was understanding, told him not to worry, everything would be okay. 'Broken bones heal, lad,' he said, choosing to completely ignore the possibility of internal bleeding, damage to organs, potential brain injury and the like. 'As long as the injured party's *alive* when the ambulance gets there, there's every chance he'll be fine. He might not walk again but— Gray? Are you alright, Gray?'

P.C. Gray was being sick in the call box.

Incidentally, he was sick again later, after he'd driven the badly dented but still-running police van back to the station. Still shaking, he was about to climb out when he spotted something on the windscreen: an imprint; a clear outline of Lester's right ear. Gray threw up without warning through the spokes of the steering wheel. The second memorable impression Lester had made that month.

After three months of traction with his leg in plaster, Lester's bones healed (the Sergeant had been right about that) but his knee, he was told, would most likely be permanently dodgy. 'Funny things, knees,' they said – and the hearing in his right ear? Well, they couldn't be sure. Chances were that it would never fully recover and he would probably need a hearing aid for life. 'What about football?' Lester asked. Yes, no reason why not, as long as he was careful and didn't put too much stress on the knee: back garden kickabouts, knockarounds in the park, that kind of thing; but no, not professional – definitely *not* professional. Even Sunday League would be risky.

And so it was that Manchester United signed Alex Stepney on September 1st, 1966 from Chelsea for a then record fee of £55,000. He was twenty-three, a little older than Lester. And the rest, as they say, is history.

As a footnote, Lester received some money from the Saturday Hospital Fund; enough to cover some, but not all, of the 'easy terms' weekly payments he was making on the scooter – these were the days before big-money insurance pay outs. And, bizarrely, the Eumig projector, strapped to the back of the Lambretta's seat by way of two hooked bungee cords, escaped without a scratch.

LEON'S ROOM

A foot-tall 'Batman' superhero figure stood on Leon's desk, fists on hips, looking out through the open window at the night sky, as though on guard duty. The bedroom housed several action figures, dispersed to various surfaces around the room, each one seemingly keeping vigil over its own sector of boyhood toys, models, and games: junk and paraphernalia to some, personal belongings and pure nostalgia to their owner.

And everything in its right place.

Shelves filled with hundreds of books; all alphabetised.

More shelves lined with DVDs, also alphabetised.

(Leon once attempted to categorise his extensive film collection into genres but was forced to bail after getting bogged down in organisational details. Where should *Edward Scissorhands* reside: Fantasy; Romance; Fantasy/ Romance? *Run Lola Run*: Crime or Art-house? What about *One Flew Over The Cuckoo's Nest* or *American Beauty*: Drama; Dark Comedy; or so-called 'Dramedy'? The whole cross-genre sub-genre problem is a deep chasm, best avoided by those with mild-to-moderate OCD. Thankfully, when *Eraserhead,* a cult-fantasy-horror-sci-fi-drama-art film, threatened to throw him over the precise-placement precipice, Leon sensibly aborted. Having castigated himself for even considering anything other than the neat, orderly pattern of the ever-reliable alphabet, it was with a feeling of relief that he finally filed David Lynch's surreal nightmare vision under E and moved on.)

Adorning the walls: a pin-studded map of Wales, Front of House film-cards, and mini film-posters: *Fistful of Dollars, Midnight Express, Withnail & I, King Kong, The Shining, Raging Bull, Taxi Driver* . . . Classics.

A black and white film, *The Loneliness of the Long Distance Runner,* sound muted, played on a small TV. Leon was sitting in bed making notes in his notebook. He'd had a new idea he hoped might make for an interesting short story – working title: 'Dark Horse.'

'Dark Horse' was to be a black comedy. A story about Roger: a fifty-six-year-old bank clerk, long overlooked for promotion and shortlisted for upcoming redundancies.

Roger (based on Reg) had stumbled upon a plot to rob the bank he worked for but rather than tell the bank or report what he knew to the authorities, he decided to let the gang go ahead with the robbery. Roger's plan: to steal the booty from the robbers (he had overheard where the haul would be stashed until the heat died down).

Roger's plan would not go well.

Leon was trying to think what kind of life-threatening danger could befall Reg – sorry, *Roger* – when a piano started up: loud Honky Tonk music coming from what sounded like a few doors away.

Had Leon been at his grandparents' house he would have witnessed Bill and Norma playing cash strip-poker with four elderly friends, all in various stages of undress and drunkenness.

The living room, hunched over a worn linoleum edged by polished floorboards, had 1940s style furnishings; the major players being a wooden dining table, a crazed leather sofa and an upright piano – lots of wood and browns.

Bill laid down his cards. 'Read 'em and weep; full house, aces over tens. Get 'em off.'

As he collected the sizeable ante, those around the table removed an item of clothing; some, more reluctantly than others. One, in just Y-fronts, seemed *very* hesitant.

'Come on, Alf,' said Norma, dancing naked (apart from a cowgirl hat) by the piano, 'don't be shy. We've all seen it before.' On keyboards, a man who looked over ninety, also out, also naked (other than a baseball cap with 'Redneck' stitched on the front), belted out Country and Western music. Vibrations made a multitude of empty beer bottles atop the piano dance around.

Norma, dancing *The Cowpoker's Do-si-do* (or whatever it was), tipped her hat as Alf idled over to join her near the piano then slapped his wrinkly arse as he bent to select the sheriff's hat from a collection of hats on the sofa (we're not familiar with the rules for themed geriatric strip-Texas-Hold'em evenings but it seems a player only gets a hat when they've lost all their clothes and money and are therefore deemed 'out').

'Yeehaw!' cried Norma, grinding her saggy bottom into the piano player's back as she simultaneously waggled her slack tits at the players still at the table. They cheered her on whilst Bill, ever competitive, dealt the next hand.

This was an orgy waiting to happen but as it's not one we think you'd wish to see, let us quickly depart the scene.

And now, beyond the discordant and annoying Honky Tonk piano, Leon heard something even more disturbing: a shrieking female foghorn that yelled for Darren, over and over. '*Darren!—Darren!—Daarren!—Daaaaaaaaaaaaarren!*

With each bellow, a neighbourhood dog replied with an eerie bark that reverberated between houses and garden walls. This, in turn, set off other dogs. Together they barked and howled as Darren remained at large.

'*Daa—*'

Leon shut the window, returned to the bed, and picked up his notebook.

He listened to the near silence; closed his eyes – and relaxed. Almost had it – the pen was on the paper, poised –

when Richard opened the door. Leon sighed. 'Can't you knock?' he said.

'*Can't you knock?*' replied Richard in a mocking, childish voice. 'Honestly, you're such a child. I just came to thank you for these.'

'Fine, now, if you don't mind, I'm busy.'

Richard lit a cigarette.

Leon wrote: *How? How do I kill him?*

'What are you doing? Had another mental vision?'

'No.'

A buff-coloured cloud hit the ceiling. 'Not attempting another of your pathetic little stories, surely.'

'Trying to,' said Leon without looking up.

'Just look at you, scribbling and dribbling. Who do you think you are – *Stephen King?*' Richard sidled over. 'I don't know why you bother. You won't finish any of them, you never do.'

'And why is that do you think?'

No answer.

Leon looked up, found Richard's head tilted at the most awkward of unnatural angles, rubbernecking. Leon snapped the notebook to his chest.

Richard's eyes instantly shifted, met Leon's challenging gaze. '*Why?* You want to know *why?*' Richard's tone was haughty and superior.

Leon nodded.

'I'll tell you why – because you're incapable of doing anything on your own.'

Time passed with Richard glaring down and Leon staring up, notebook clutched to his ribs. The first move was finally made by Richard: strolling casually, as if he'd intended to all along, to Leon's desk – where he gave it his backside. The Dark Knight wobbled but survived.

As Richard withered his cigarette, billowing smoke across the room, Leon tried to concentrate; though, in truth, he knew he wouldn't get far – he couldn't be genuinely creative with such a negative presence in close attendance. And sure enough, after five minutes of condescending sighs, finger strumming, derisory tuts and sensing every shake of Richard's big, untidy, supercilious head, it could be borne no longer. So Leon raised eyes, ready for confrontation.

But Richard was ahead of him. 'Think I'll go and see if Mrs Hobbs is having her bath. It must be nearly time.' And with that, cigarette gripped between his lips, he moved for the door, tightening his dressing gown belt as he went.

Leon watched Richard's cynical face cross the room, running a channel between smoky ribbons breaking from his nostrils, and waited for the parting shot he knew would come. And when Richard reached the door, it did. He paused, looked back dramatically: 'You'll never finish it,' he predicted. Then he disappeared down the stairs.

The forecast was made with certainty but Leon refused to be phased by *It*. If anything, the prophecy fired up an 'I'll show him' attitude. He put pen to paper in anticipation of 'the Hole' – something Stephen King had referred to in *Misery* – and waited.

(Leon had read the book and watched the DVD many times. The fictional writer, Paul Sheldon, would gaze at the page until he found this *hole*; a well of the subconscious mind that would – once found – issue forth ideas and voices, characters and story.)

And Leon waited, and waited, gazing at the notebook, longing for the hole to appear; the hole which would, once discovered, according to King, open up, effortless and free. Then, after what seemed like only an hour or so, he finally felt himself relaxing, moving deeper and down; slipping; entering the Alpha State: *Writers' Nirvana*; falling into the hole . . . And at that instant *they* arrived. Not the ideas, voices, characters. But police sirens and charging vehicles! – A long, disturbing, wailing tide of them, rushing past. They overpowered the noise-insulating properties of the double-glazed window and sealed up the hole.

Frustrated, Leon gave up. The night was lost. He cast his notebook aside, ejected the DVD (Tom Courtenay had run his race), popped in another, grabbed the remote and drowned out the continuing cacophony of alarms by turning the volume up.

Way up.

Raging Bull had never raged so loudly.

CHAPTER SEVEN

Back to Work

NOT THIS CLOWN AGAIN

A few stops down, the packed tram pulled up to a crowded platform. Leon, standing by the doors, somehow managed to keep his place despite dozens of extra Monday morning commuters squeezing in. As he waited for the doors to close he gazed out, idly, at the freshly vacated platform – and there he was.

Pogo!

His multicoloured balloons bobbed up and down on their network of strings like seal heads on a rough sea as below the surface the clown hurriedly shoved coins into a platform ticket machine. With each coin that dropped, rolled, and registered, the painted face glanced round – to a small 'space' next to Leon.

Not this clown again. He'd really given Leon the willies last time. How much worse would it be with the bozo wide awake? Leon did his best to spread out nonchalantly, to imperceptibly use up the space.

Another coin, another fleeting look – a murderous desire lurked under that red-paint smile; Leon felt it in his bones. He willed the doors to close. *Come on, come on . . .*

Gloved hands rummaged baggy trouser pockets.

What's the fecking hold up? Come on, let's go, let's go— oh shit . . .

The rummaging had stopped. Pogo was grinning at Leon; he'd found what he needed – a final coin.

The ten pence piece was displayed in classic *'Is this your card?'* style.

Oh feck! Fecking feck feck feck . . .

As white gloved fingertips slotted the coin, Leon furtively jabbed the door-button at his side. When nothing happened he tried to employ telekinesis to make the ticket machine reject the coin. Nope, didn't work. Fair enough, it was a long shot. Undeterred by failure he focused the power of his mind into forcing an internal mechanism jam. He could do this. With enough will-power he could *definitely* do this. He focused, scrunched his face, uttered a low hum he hoped no-one would realise was emanating from him, and miracle of miracles, the machine made an unmistakable noise: something internal – a brisk *chika-chika-chika-weeeeeeeeeeeeeeeeeeee* sound – then something dropped:

Pogo's freshly-printed ticket.

The clown aimed a smirk over his shoulder as he reached into the tray. Right, that was it; Leon would have to mentally induce spontaneous human combustion. Burning clown wouldn't be pretty – the screaming, the honking, balloons popping, et cetera – but needs must.

Again, nothing. *Damn.*

Okay, only one option left: he would do a runner, catch a bus, any city-centre-bound bus – walk the last leg if necessary. If he was late, then tough titty, Reg would get over it, eventually. Yes, he would jump off the tram and *Run, Forrest, Run!* He would do it now.

Shit – too late!

Ticket in hand, eyes brimming with intent, Pogo strode towards the tram, his long, comical shoes rising and falling like flippers high-stepped over dry land by an out-of-water frogman.

Leon was rooted, mouth hanging open, brow knit with worry. He wondered why he hadn't simply *detached* like he usually did. There was safety in detachment: he would drift off and the next thing he knew, he'd be somewhere else – like at work. Maybe it wasn't too late? Perhaps he could force it? *Detach! Detach!* he yelled internally. *Detach, you fecker!*

Detachment didn't happen; separation doesn't work that way – *can't* work that way. A disconnection has to be easy, unintentional, unplanned and unforced. Detachment is a docile drift, a subtle slide, not a crude thrust.

What did happen was this: the doors started to close.

Oh thank feck for that! Leon may have shouted aloud (and yes, you're right; he had watched a lot of *Father Ted* over the weekend). That was a close one, he thought, feeling his body relax.

But Pogo had picked up speed, approaching as fast as his ridiculous shoes would allow, balloons flapping behind him. To Leon, he screamed: 'Hold the doors!'

Again, Leon froze to the spot. And he did it well.

'HOLD THE FUCKING DOORS, YOU CU—!'

The doors sighed shut as Pogo reached them – and he was not a happy clown. One glove pounded the window, the other stabbed frantically at the Open-Door-button, as he directed something involving several 'fuckings', a couple of 'cunts' and a whole lot of spittle at Leon. In essence: '*It was your fault! You! You did it!*'

Leon made an expression he hoped would declare: *What? It wasn't my fault. There was nothing I could do. I did try. Perhaps you couldn't see from where you were.*

Keeping pace as best he could with the now moving carriage, Pogo pointed an accusing finger emphatically at Leon, prodded it against the glass for added intensity.

But Leon wasn't about to be intimidated by this buffoon. Not with the tram easing away and the doors tightly sealed. He would be a brave soldier. Show no fear. Be lionhearted. *And would you look at that*: his mobility had returned; his hands were bravely flicking Vs in Pogo's face.

Leon sensed the clown, presently slipping from view, may not have appreciated the Vs – a jarring din rattled through the tram as several hefty kicks clobbered the carriage. Bollocks to him. What were the chances he'd ever see Pogo again? (Slim, right?) Leon flicked a few extra Vs just because he felt like it. He turned from the doors to find a parade of bug-eyed commuters gawking in his direction.

'*What?*' Leon asked.

LIKE TO HEAR A POEM?

'Surprise!' squealed a voice in Leon's ear. Leon jumped and turned to find Poppy beaming at him.

Where the hell did you spring from? he almost blurted. What he actually said was: 'You again.'

'What? I just happened to be on the tram. I haven't been following you or anything weird like that. What kind of girl do you take me for? How dare you?'

'What? . . . No . . . I didn't mean . . . I was just . . .'

'Relax. I'm just kidding,' Poppy grinned.

Leon managed a smile but felt the tenseness in it. Not his usual easy-going—

'It's okay, I won't bite,' said Poppy. 'Not unless you ask me to.' Then she laughed, suddenly and loud. Actually, it was more a snort than a laugh and it surprised Leon; enough to take his eyebrows up a notch.

'Again, kidding,' she said.

Two teenagers rose and weaved nearer the doors. Poppy moved quickly, secured the window seat and waved Leon in. He took the adjoining seat.

'Thanks for cutting my key, by the way.' The key was held aloft. Out came that smile again.

'You're very welcome,' said Leon, questioning why anyone would walk around with a spare key in their hand. Had she been clutching it the whole time? No wonder so many keys are lost.

Poppy pushed the key into an imaginary lock, turned it and swung open an imaginary door.

'Seems to be working okay,' Leon said.

'I'm sure it will,' smiled Poppy.

'*Will?* You haven't tried it yet?'

'No, I forgot.' Poppy snorted again. This was clearly how she laughed. Leon thought it a little unusual but somehow it seemed right – *for her.* She was quirky, different; atypically attractive. Leon liked that about her.

Today's fashion highlights:

A bowler hat at a jaunty angle, a 1950s olive-green day dress dappled with orange-and-yellow flowers; glitter-green toenails peeping out from a pair of 1970s auburn-brown leather peep-toe platform sandals (inspired by 1940s styles: enormous bows, buckled ankle straps, colossal 5.5" heels, chunky soles); and a 1980s grey-and-cream tapestry shoulder bag. The coat was a wool weave, post World War II affair. An ensemble that was eclectic, edgy, effortless (it seemed) and definitely elegant.

Leon didn't have a clue about Poppy's wardrobe – except maybe the shoes – but to him everything appeared to be genuine, vintage clothing. This girl has got style with a capital S, he thought. Why can't I be fashionable? I hope she doesn't think I'm a square.

A square!? What is this, The Jazz Age? Get with it, daddio. Don't you mean a nerd? Or a geek? A dweeb? A weirdo . . .

Poppy gazed at Leon – or more accurately, into his captivating blue eyes – grinning the whole while. Leon smiled back politely. He felt he should say something, even though he spoke last. Or did he? He wasn't sure now he thought about it. Let's see . . . she spoke first – definitely – then . . . oh sod it, best just to go again. Can't just sit here like a lemon . . .

Well, go on then!

Finally he piped up: 'Well, if it *doesn't* work—'

'Would you like to hear a poem?' blurted Poppy. She quickly apologised, emitted a short, donkey-like hee-haw then added: 'Sorry, what were you saying?'

'No, I was just saying: sometimes a bit of roughness can be left in the grooves. It's easily fixed. Just needs a bit more smoothing. If it doesn't work, bring it back.'

'Okay, I will. Thanks.' Did he just ask to see me again? I think he did. And what was that about *smoothing my grooves*? Frisky little devil! Typical guy – bet he's picturing us, right now: him as a struggling artist; me as his muse, being all *Aphrodite at the Waterhole* in his Paris studio. We've been drinking Chateau Degas by the Seine all afternoon and now he's got me posing naked – *again* – on a velvety chaise-longue . . . and he's telling me how beautiful I am and why he positively prefers to paint women with *small-to-medium* size tits. *Poppy, STOP! Focus!* He's probably thinking no such thing. He's probably just admiring the green eye-shadow. How it makes my eyes—

'Are you okay?'

'Yes. Why?'

'I thought you said something about *tits*?'

'*What?* No, I might have said . . . "*it's*" – as in . . . *it's* a spare key – for my neighbour; in case I lock myself out again. Not that I'm always locking myself out. I wouldn't want you thinking that.'

'No, I wasn't thinking that.' I was thinking how amazing your eyes are. Nice voice, too. Sexy smile. Check out her tits. *No!* That's the sort of thing *Richard* would do. Besides, she's looking right at me, she'd be bound to—

'I've only done it once.'

Leon couldn't help himself; a wave of cheekiness swept over him. '*Really* – you've only done it once?'

Poppy administered a non-too-firm backhand slap to Leon's leg. What a saucy monkey. Blue Eyes has a sense of humour, the rascal. Who would have guessed? Playful; mischievous; cute face, but thankfully not *too* handsome – and with a hint of scoundrel. She liked that about him. Looks like he'd be a good kisser too . . .

(Poppy would take *Cute* over *Hot* any day of the week. On the subject of handsomeness: Poppy didn't like men who were blatantly 'Hot'. Her sisters' husbands are so-called 'hot' and they're vain, insensitive, arrogant and dumb. And let's not forget: obnoxious cheating scum. All three had hit on one of the bridesmaids at their *own* weddings. Poppy knows this to be fact because *she was that bridesmaid.* Each time! *The bastards!*)

'So *would* you?'

'Would I what?'

'Like to hear a poem?'

BLOODY CUSTOMERS

Leon had politely declined a poem, explaining that he was on his way to work and would be getting off in a minute.

He didn't mention that he'd just been threatened by a foul-mouthed circus clown and was a little preoccupied.

Poppy said she had several *short* ones but didn't push it when Leon shook his head. He had, after all, said: 'Definitely next time, though.' As if people were constantly reuniting on the Metro.

That was fine with Poppy, she didn't want to appear too keen; hadn't even followed him to the tram doors, though it was her stop, too; didn't want Blue Eyes to think she was shadowing him – didn't want to look like a desperate crazy-bitch stalker. Besides, she already knew where he worked, the station he travelled from, where he shopped, and had narrowed his probable residence down to somewhere near the park on Broad Street. And yes, she might have discovered his actual address if she hadn't bumped into an old friend on Saturday, but that didn't make her a bad person; it's not like she'd ever do anything with that knowledge. She had no intention of ever walking down his street hoping to accidentally bump into him. As she'd thought at the time: she wasn't *that* sad!

Now, creeping towards the end of what had felt like a very long day, Leon chanced a look at the shop clock (he liked to hold off for as long as possible; the longer he could resist, the better his chances of discovering it was nearly home time). There were still more than two hours to go. Time aplenty for his next job: Mr Frampton's tankard.

Leon secured the one-pint tankard in place on the engraving machine's spindle then began typing into the connected laptop. Mr Frampton's requested inscription comprised a message in big letters at the top, the name of his ex-wife (including the strangest 'nickname' Leon had ever heard), an unusual tag, and then, at the bottom, a sequence of numbers.

The pewter tankard, the most expensive in the shop, would, once the engraving was finished, stand testament to luck, loathing and lost love, and look like this:

HA! FUCK YOU!

Mrs Eileen 'Cunt like a Bucket' Piecraft
(Skanky-Arsed Ex-Wife Bitch/Slut from Hell)

4-17-22-35-36-47

Keys-n-Stuff *never* turned away engraving jobs, no matter how offensive or distasteful; crude engravings were still money-earners. As long as they paid in advance, customers could have their personal description however they wanted. Besides, Mr Frampton had originally only requested 'Ha! Fuck you, Eileen!' It was Reg who mined the customer's deep-rooted anger and suggested the verbose, colourful additions.

(During Leon's training, he'd been instructed to always suggest additions and wherever possible to politely recommend alternatives: *'Congratulations and Felicitations'* in lieu of *'Well done'* – *'Wishing you a festive and frolicsome Christmastide'* over *'Happy Xmas'* – *'Cocksucking Trollop'* rather than *'Slag'*. Not that these were better, but because engravings were charged by the character.

'On engravings where the customer wishes to vent their anger, don't be embarrassed by colourful words,' Reg had said. 'The only offensive thing about a four letter word is the tiny fee. In engraving, *"Bollocks"* is worth double an *"Arse"* or a *"Dick"*, for example.' Leon wasn't embarrassed, although the words did sound bizarre coming from Reg's mouth. In time, he would learn that his boss could only ever say such words in an official capacity and *never* used them in ordinary conversation. Not even something mild, like *'Crap'*. 'Why settle for a *Mofo*,' Reg went on, 'when it's *three times* as profitable to have a *Motherf—*' 'Yes, thank you, I understand,' the trainee had tactfully interrupted.)

In truth though, in the eight years he'd been working in the shop, Leon had experienced very little demand for profanity, long or short. And most customers preferred to stick to a minimum of characters to keep costs down: *'Happy B-day'*, *'Congratz'*, *'Soz ur ded'*, and the like.

Although Leon did win brownie points when he, upon hearing who the ex-wife had been having an affair with, persuaded Mr Frampton to go with an extra engraving on the tankard's reverse:

'And Fuck You too, Dave, you Sneaky Low-Life Two-Faced Bollock-Headed Bastard of a Brother!'

Leon had wondered how anyone with such a large win (a reported six million plus) could hold on to being so angry. What would *he* do with such a large amount? Not waste time on *negative* feelings that was for sure. Maybe indulge in twenty-four-seven short story writing? He might get something done, then. Richard would scoff no doubt but so what? Who's he to criticise anyone? He'd probably blow all the money on marathon orgies round at Mandy's Megastars! Actually, no, Richard would probably buy a remote mansion out in Alderley Edge, with a pool, hot tub, and purpose-built sex rooms, and get the girls to move in, Hugh Hefner style, so he could take advantage of their naked jiggling bodies whenever he got a—

As Leon entered the last of Mr Frampton's winning lottery numbers a woman with mad hair, pointy tits and an attitude to match, burst into the shop, much like a jilted wife might gate-crash a hotel room expecting to catch a cheating husband underneath some hussy from work (or wherever). Leon half expected her to shout, '*Aha!*' (or possibly, '*A whore!*') but she didn't. Instead, the woman marched a polythene-covered brown jacket to the counter, held it out like a dirty nappy, and shook it as if to say, *Look!*

'Hello, Mrs Pearson,' smiled Seema.

Mrs Pearson slammed the jacket on the counter. Then, standing stock-still, brought hands to hips in time-honoured *Go on, ask me, I fucking dare you* tradition.

'What seems to be the—'

Mrs Pearson ripped open the polythene to reveal the full hideousness of the brown.

Seema didn't understand; it was shit-coloured when it came in. She only *cleaned* them. There was nothing she could do about—

'How is that dry-cleaned? You tell me.' Mrs Pearson now adopted an arms-folded position. Her lips tried to do the same.

'I'm sorry, Mrs Pearson, I don't—'

'It wasn't there when I brought it in!'

Seema ran her fingers over the jacket, studied it closely.

'Sorry, am I missing something?'

'*There! There!*' Mrs Pearson pointed to an invisible spot somewhere on the lapel. '*What is that?*'

Seema leaned in for closer inspection . . . nothing.

She shifted angles hoping that might reveal something; a microscopic splodge – *anything*.

'May I . . .'

'Be my guest.'

Seema walked the jacket to the window, raised it to the light, squinted, turned it; turned it again. 'I can't see—'

'*What is it? What is it?*' Mrs Pearson was almost singing.

Seema, eyes almost touching the lapel: '*Where*, Mrs Pearson, *where?*'

Argumentative customers: Leon couldn't stand them. Poor Seema, he thought, if she gets any closer to that shitty jacket, she'll be wearing it. He sighed and hit Enter on the laptop. The engraving machine's carbide tip passed over the tankard, slowly scratching out the inscription . . .

$$Y \; O \; U \quad A \; R \; E \quad F \; U \; C \; K \; E \; D \; !$$

Staring at the message, Leon felt a sudden wave of the bluest despondency pervade his being. His hands shook, his head hurt, and he felt sure, had he tried to speak, that his voice would stick inside his throat. Not that anybody was listening. Feeling empty and tired, and altogether not great at all, he sank onto his stool.

'YOU ARE FUCKED!' The message resonated inside his skull. He wasn't sure why, but for some reason the words felt true. He *was* fucked.

Overcome, he leaned on the counter, fingers rubbing temples. He saw Seema burrow her face into the turd-coloured jacket and Mrs Pearson jab away at an atom of gravy, or whatever it was. The image no longer seemed funny, only ridiculous. He heard Reg, in the back, chanting an all too familiar monologue – an order: a long tedious list of soles and heels in a wearisome range of sizes and thicknesses and materials.

Not for the first time, Leon took stock: the meaningless trophies; banal engravings; endless shoe repairs; constant key-cutting; Reg and the lack of recognition for a job well done, lectures for the slightest mistake and reprimands for any occasional expression of humour. Okay, so he had the odd laugh with Seema, but was that enough? – *Hardly*. The job was routine, boring, and required zero imagination. His head was full of strange, wonderful ideas but they couldn't be utilised or enjoyed *here*. *Here*, his imagination inconvenienced, got him into trouble.

Frustration and a sudden deep despair invaded Leon's core. His face slumped into his hands – hands full of tiny cuts and scars. He felt worthless and invisible, and that no-one would recall him. He didn't want to be here; not at all. And he'd known it for some time.

This is *not* what he should be doing. What the fuck had he been thinking? And to think, Reg had told him if he worked hard he could have a job here for life! *Jesus!*

JESUS! Oh shit . . . 'YOU ARE FUCKED!'?

Shouldn't that read . . .

Leon checked, double checked and triple checked.

Phew! He hadn't mistyped. The inscription wasn't mocking his life or writing off his future. The tankard had *not* been incorrectly and irreversibly engraved.

There it was on screen, paper, and most importantly, metal; faithfully etched — the inscription, as requested, undeniably exclaimed:

HA! FUCK YOU!

But the relief was short-lived. Although the words passed no judgement, the curse was still insulting: a spit in the face. And the fact that it was aimed at Mrs Frampton, not him, did nothing to pull Leon out of the lowness he was under. He continued to feel like shit – about himself, the present, and his future.

And for the next few minutes the blues persisted. (This sudden bout of despondency wasn't new. He'd had spasmodic patches of downheartedness before.)

'Is everything alright over there, Leon?'

The utility room had sprouted a head.

'We don't have to charge you for another spoiled engraving, do we?' Reg laughed, but he was serious.

Leon studied Mr Frampton's tankard: '4-17-22-35-36-77'. Weird, he reflected, how winning lottery numbers always look so obvious after the event.

Reg hadn't finished: 'Wouldn't like to have to see *another* tankard coming out of your wages.'

'Seventy-seven,' mumbled Leon. '*Seventy*-seven? Oh for fuck's sake.'

The boss emerged, went up on tip-toes. '*Especially* one of those expensive pewter ones.'

But Reg's focus was irresistibly shifting.

Leon's head sank, found the counter.

'*Please*, just shoot me now.'

Reg scoured the dry-cleaning racks.

'Leon . . . where's Seema?'

Seema was with Mrs Pearson, round the corner, in a street where Mrs Pearson said the light was better.

LESTER BLANK

Leon's dad's lottery numbers had never come up; a couple of small wins for matching three numbers was all.

Lester had always said he didn't care about money, though – and better still, he'd been 'lucky in love'. Said meeting Veronica was better than any lottery win.

That may have been true (and a tad cheesy) but even so, Leon often felt sorry for his dad; not because of the lottery, Lester was right, money wasn't important – but because of what happened to Lester's adolescent aspirations: the scooter accident in the summer of 1966 that had wrecked his knee and with it, any chance of a promising career in professional football.

Yes, we already know about that, I hear you complain. *Why don't you just get on with it and tell us what happened next, for feck's sake?* (Honestly, you and your questions. And kindly watch the language!)

Well, suffice to say, Lester lost his place as a plumber's apprentice – he could no longer, for example, kneel easily to a radiator or u-bend– and *if* he *did* manage, and *if* he *could* stay down long enough to finish the job, it would take *forever* to get back to his feet. (Imagine Douglas Bader, bless him, in plumber's overalls on your kitchen floor, spanner in one hand, roll of sealant tape in the other, hopelessly and despairingly attempting to scramble up your kitchen sink unit. Such clownish buffoonery looks neither pretty nor professional.)

And so, long story short, Lester ended up as a car park attendant, employed by the council to endure night-shifts on a grey acre of asphalt on the outskirts of the city.

Not Lester's ideal job but he made the most of it and performed his duties with diligence whilst trying at all times to retain a sense of humour – even with the most obnoxious of customers. Like it was his fault when their precious cars acquired scratches they claimed definitely weren't present *before* they'd parked.

Leon heard their voices as if he were there:

'*No*, we *didn't*, you fascist twat! Who the fuck reads signs when they're parking?' (As with many car parks, this one was covered in gaily-coloured ALL PARKING AT OWN RISK notices.) 'And *yes*, perhaps we *could* have read them *after* we'd parked but it's a bit late then, isn't it, Hitler? What are you, some kind of retard! Anyway, I'm not arguing with a lackey. Give me your ID number. I know someone at the council. I'll have your job before the end of the week.'

'Ah, but could you conduct the commission as convivially as I?'

'Could *what*?'

Lester, offering a Biro: 'Would you like a pen?'

Leon almost smiled at the thought of that – but desolation and hopelessness prevailed.

Lester had always acknowledged attending car park, if one wasn't careful, could indeed be soul-destroying.

'But I, son,' Leon recalled Lester once saying, as his dad donned a coat and checked the evening sky through kitchen window, 'am shaped of sterner stuff.' Then, after sitting for a final cuppa before leaving, Lester had further reassured Leon that he'd discovered he actually *liked* working nights.

'Crabby customers aside, it's all cabin, coffee, and the Classics – and the occasional car, of course. Oh, and customary cyclical check-ups, but they're only casual.'

(In case you're wondering, Lester established he appreciated stretched alliterations whilst reading J. K. Rowling's *Harry Potter* books, and once in a while, thereafter, would work to wangle one in. Takes all sorts.)

'And I'd presumed I'd be paid on a par with paltry or pitiful but praise be to shift-allowance, my pay proved to be prodigiously more than piddling.' (Okay, enough already! We wouldn't want you thinking Lester was like that all the time. He couldn't afford to be; when he pushed it, he risked being playfully slapped upside the head by Veronica. She found word-wizardry amusing for only so long.)

Leon remembered how excited Lester had sounded when he'd finished reading *The Half-Blood Prince:*

'Another great Potter, Leon. I don't know why you won't read them.'

'Because I'm not ten.'

'Neither am I but I still enjoy the fantasy. You don't know how to suspend belief, that's your problem.'

'What? Course I do. I read all the time. Proper books, too; not all that boy-wizards and crap.'

Veronica, a light slap to the back of Leon's head: 'Language, Leon.'

'Well, I love them. It's going to be agony waiting for the next one.'

'I could let you have one of mine . . . *Breakfast of Champions . . . Catch 22*?'

'No, thanks, I'll just go back to doing my crosswords.'

'He can get hours of entertainment from those.'

Leon liked to think that's where his father accrued his occasionally impressive diction; from the crosswords – as opposed to the Potters.

'And one of these days he'll finish one.'

'Yeah, thanks for that, Vee.' Then, after a sip of tea: 'No, I know what I'll do; I'll *reread* the six so far – in order – from the beginning.'

Leon shook his head.

'Someone remind me to grab *The Philosopher's Stone* on my way out.'

'Remember to grab *The Philosopher's Stone* on your way out, Lester.'

'I didn't mean now, Vee. I meant— never mind. Actually, would *you* mind nipping upstairs for it, Leon? There's a good lad. Bookshelf, by the bed.' Lester smiled wryly: 'Modern classics section.'

'*Modern classics section?* You own six books.'

'It'll be the one on the left.'

Picture Leon sighing. *Harry Potter*? '*Classics*'? *Really*? Why couldn't Lester read something 'grown-up' like Vonnegut or David Mitchell, like *he* did? And surely his dad could have found a better job. Anything would have been more fulfilling than overseeing empty vehicles. No, Leon had never been convinced by Lester's *being-happy-with-one's-lot* spiel. Always thought his dad was just putting on a brave face.

Now, as he blew metal dust traces from the completed tankard, Leon could hardly remember a time when he hadn't felt sorry for Lester and the whole job thing. More than once he'd said: 'Who knows, dad, you might have been a coach or manager by now, with a hatful of medals, a knighthood, a stand named after you . . .'

'Alright, lad, don't keep going on about it.'

Leon recollected a strong arm around his shoulders, apologising, and then: 'It's okay, son, really – stop beating yourself up about it.' A paternal squeeze, a fatherly smile and: 'Honestly, it's not a bad life being a car park attendant – even on the graveyard shift.'

Veronica, a comforting hand on Lester's broad shoulder: 'Besides, it was all he could find with his knackered knee.'

Lester, joking, not for the first time: 'Hey, they don't let just anyone in, you know. You *have* to have a limp if you want to be a *proper* car park attendant. Think about it, when was the last time you saw a car park attendant without one?'

Lester always laughed heartily at that. Leon never could.

As Leon removed Mr Frampton's tankard from the engraving machine, the blue funk indicated no inclination to decamp and depart, compounded now as it was by renewed anchor-weighted guilt. How could he have been so snobby about Lester's choice of reading material? What did it matter that his dad liked J. K. Rowling? – So many do.

When the seventh Potter materialised, Leon would buy him a first edition. Get it signed, if possible. And he would never again mention the subject of playing-professional-football; it wasn't helping anyone. What else? Yes – tonight, he would surprise his parents with Chinese takeaway. Their anniversary wouldn't be for another three or four weeks yet but what the hell.

Finally, for the first time in what felt like ages, Leon's face managed a full on smile. This lasted a full four seconds then some kind of panic or dread set in. He felt an icy claw poke his sphincter (or duodenum, or colon – something in that area, anyway – and definitely not in a fun way). A question arose: Was he reviewing remarks his parents had *actually* made? Or was he only projecting the kind of utterances they *might* say?

(Leon could picture a scene so vividly in his mind, that later, when he recalled it, no less vividly, he was never a hundred percent certain if he was remembering something that had really happened or just revisiting how he'd pictured it.)

Was not being sure either way an early indication he was already going the way of his mother?

Veronica's short-term memory-span had been in steady decline since the millennium and last year saw many of her vocalisations begin to include references to 'whatsits' and 'thingamabobs' and 'doodahs' and whatnot. Worse, and more painful to witness, a lot of promising sentences just slipped away, unfinished.

Leon cogitated on his own mind and/or memory playing occasional tricks, and how, of late, they'd grown worse – *confusingly* worse. Not for the first time, Befuddlement belly-flopped into his blues. Grumbling to himself, he polished the tankard with far more vigour than necessary.

Lowness *and* Befuddlement: either can make for a desperate bedfellow but lay down with both and it can be a herculean task to rise again. Sensing this, perhaps, Leon decided he needed to stop thinking so much; the whole thinking thing was messing with his head, getting him down. *Enough already!* He slapped his face; which surprisingly, came as some surprise. '*Ow!*'

He looked about the shop. No witnesses – *again, phew. But note to self: That hurts more than you'd think. Don't do it again.*

Setting the tankard to one side, Leon vowed to get busy, concentrate on the next job in hand: Mrs Anderson's Riding Boot. He blocked out the ongoing dry-cleaning debate (Seema and Mrs Pearson now outside the shop, imploring passers-by to support opposing opinions on stain-evaluation), ignored Reg's continuing mantra for materials, and set to work. After removing the old zip, he lightly glued a new zip in place, arranged the boot on the stitching machine, and began sewing the two together; a slow, gentle process requiring care and serenity.

As Leon's hands meticulously progressed the boot under the stitching needle, a task they'd done countless times, his relaxed and therefore unguarded mind once again found itself free to roam – and so it did: wondered again, rather glumly, if *'unluckiness'* might be genetic, after all. He'd once read about the so-called 'unlucky gene' on the Internet, worried his father might have it (and maybe passed it on). As far as Leon was concerned, he, Leon, had never been a *lucky* person, and Lester: well, he'd never had any luck either – not that Leon could discern.

(Yes, yes, the whole meeting-Veronica thing but shut up, we're talking about Leon's *perception* of his dad in general, here.)

Once the zip was sewn down one side, Leon's hands instinctively turned the boot ninety degrees, stitched the zip base then turned another ninety degrees. As his fingers worked the boot, sewing the second side, Leon's mind wandered back to last night – when he'd also been thinking about his dad.

The scene went something like this:

Cold heavy angled rain thrashes incessantly against every exterior facet of the kiosk. Works in conjunction with sweeping winds to drive leaves and litter across the car park. Apocalyptic clouds, black and burdensome, prowl the pre-dawn sky. A weak autumn moon haunts backstage. The result: a miserable setting enduring exactly the kind of climate Leon might have imagined for a sad, dark story.

With only weather and the occasional vehicle for company, a car-park kiosk at night might be considered one of the deadest places on Earth, but a roomy tomb this is not. Inside, a few contents: thin desk; one wooden chair (of the stiff, uncompromising variety); a solitary low-wattage bulb; a single-bar electric heater (meant to be two-bar but half the workforce steadfastly refuse to participate); and a notice board – of which Lester has utilised a small corner to accommodate three photographs: a holiday snap of Veronica, himself and a young Leon camping in Wales; a signed picture of Alex Stepney; and the Lambretta SX 200 scooter, immortalised on a 1960s black and white Polaroid.

Despite meagre furnishings and windows to three sides, the interior feels cramped. Especially when occupied, as the kiosk is, by a lone attendant, almost 24-7-364. (We'd have to deduct something for barrier operations, infrequent rounds, and, periodically, smoking staff's smoking.) Kiosk cramping is particularly noticeable at the changing of attendants: the booth coercing an intimate dance of shuffling anoraks, booted feet, and jockeying umbrellas.

Lester hadn't bothered with a brolly tonight; it was far too windy for one to be of any practical use. He'd limped his grey uniform to the humdrum car park holding on a hat. His shift started at ten. It was raining then, and it's raining now, six hours later.

✶ ✶ ✶

He sits alone, Lester, under forty watts, browsing a well-thumbed vintage football programme, turning the pages at a velocity compatible with the vocation . . . slow.

Finally reaching the back page (team listings), he places the programme on the table – then pours himself a cup from a Thermos flask. Blowing steaming coffee, he casts an accusing eye at the isolated bar of heat.

With lips and cup united, and typical, dreadful timing, full-beam headlights illuminate the notice board. Lester swivels his head, squints through rain-lashed glass. No doubt about it: a vehicle wants in. Reluctantly, he gives up his cup, zips up his jacket, and turns up his collar – then hobbles out, into the deluge.

The car park is close to empty, just a handful of cars; overhead, a leaden sky, oppressive and turbulent. City lights half a mile back do what they can to brighten the scene but somehow a pretty backdrop only succeeds in making things look worse here: this lonesome place, dull to start with; and a remorseless downpour seemingly determined to wash away any trace of residual colour, no matter how stubborn.

Turning his countenance against driving rain, Lester raises barrier, and shivering, watches the Range Rover roll by without so much as a word from the driver. Would it hurt to honk? Too much trouble to toot? A nod would be nice; *any* genus of grateful gesture. How about a sympathetic smile? Just a wink or wee wave would be welcome; not to mention, well-mannered. And why is it that people tip others on a basic wage (porter, waitress, taxi driver, stripper) but *never* a car park attendant?

Funny that.

As Lester strains, struggling to lower the aluminium pole (they never seize up when it's warm and dry, only when it's wet and cold), his eyes move to the warm(ish) interior of the kiosk.

Leon might have written: *Lester has the air of a broken man.*

By the time he's back inside, the coffee is down to kiosk temperature. 'What a waste,' Lester says, sliding open a window and draining the cup.

Fresh one poured, he reoccupies the chair.

Sipping sweet, hot Java, Lester's eyes rest on the familiar faces staring back from the notice board:

Boy Leon.

Youthful Veronica.

Alex Stepney, retired age thirty-six.

Headlights sweep the notice board – another car pulling up to the barrier . . . a hard, impatient toot.

Lester runs a hand through his seriously thinning hair.

'You know it should have been me, don't you, Alex?' he says with a wistful smile.

Another toot: longer; louder.

'Course you do.'

Setting down the cup, Lester sighs, 'Oh well, onwards and upwards,' and heads outside, back into the rain.

117

CHAPTER EIGHT

Poetry in Motion

MISTY AND FAR AWAY

Leon was no longer thinking about his luckless dad, at least, not consciously. As he'd waited amongst the crowd on the platform, he decided he didn't want to end up like Lester: doing a job that wasn't his *true* calling. Leon was unsure what his true calling *was*, but knew it wasn't cutting keys, repairing shoes or engraving other people's trophies.

Work had been really shit today – and there had been that whole previous confrontation-on-the-tram affair – but, for the present at least, he'd decided to clear his head and put all that behind him. Right now, all he wanted to think about was a potentially interesting notion he'd had on the journey back; an idea for a new short story. And he hoped the 'scenic' route home, along the canal, would be conducive to formulating a more *detailed* plot.

After descending the wooden steps adjacent to the Metrolink station he turned right and at a slow, leisurely pace walked the towpath on the south side of the precinct.

By the time he'd followed the curve of the waterway (turning north towards the allotments) and passed a lone, fishless angler who paid him no heed, Leon had a rough outline of two or three main characters, the initial set-up, and an idea for the catalyst: a key moment which sparks the narrative into life. He didn't know presently how it would end but that was okay; the denouement could occur to him – and hopefully *would* – at any time. For now he just wanted to come up with what happened next, *after* the catalyst moment: where the story would go . . .

As he was brainstorming options, Poppy jumped out from behind a bridge pillar.

'Surprise!' she exclaimed, arms wide.

Leon nearly backed into the canal. For a second he thought it was that fucking clown again.

'Oops, careful there, Leon,' said Poppy, gently pulling him back by the elbow.

'Jeez, I wish you'd stop doing that.'

'Sorry.' She gave him a disarming smile.

'What were you doing under there, anyway?'

'Being creative.' Poppy revealed her notebook. 'I sometimes like to try different locations for my writing.'

'Okay,' said Leon, thinking it sounded completely reasonable and yet marginally weird at the same time. *You like that big green bow in her hair though, don't you?* I do, actually. She— *Tell her then!* No! She might think it's a declaration of love or something. *And you don't know if she's a bunny boiler or not?* Exactly. Plus, it might sound a bit girly.

'So,' said Poppy after a brief silence. 'Ready to hear one of my poems now? You did promise.'

'Did I?' asked Leon. *Just because you say 'next time' doesn't mean—*

Poppy gave him a look. Think of a puppy or a kitten widening its eyes, head slightly tilted.

'Just kidding. I'd love to hear one.'

'Are you sure? If you don't want to . . .'

'No, I do. Definitely.'

'Okay.' Poppy flicked a page or two. 'Oh, this is a nice one. It's called "If I'd Walked to Piccadilly Gardens".'

She cleared her throat, and for reasons known only to her (Leon assumed it was for dramatic effect), held out her free hand. And off she went, the hand hovering in mid-air, reciting more from the heart than the page:

'Did you kiss me with your silent eyes,
'Misty and far away?
'Then imagine me rising,
'And sauntering your way.

'If I'd walked to Piccadilly Gardens,
'And timed my fall just right,
'Might you have caught me,
'And held on really tight?'

Poppy spoke in one of those semi-serious poem-recital voices; not pretentious, but emotional and impassioned. Ignoring the notebook (which begged the question: why, if she knew all the words, was the book even out?) her eyes – wide and serious – remained fixed on Leon. She was *really* getting into it:

'Would I have taken you to a gallery?
'Could you have enticed me over me a meal?
'Then what stage brought our first kiss,
'And did it seal the deal?

'Could I have been the girl for you?
'Would you have become my chap?
'If I'd walked to Piccadilly Gardens,
'And landed in your lap.'

'I wasn't sure about *chap* . . . but anyway . . .'

'Might we have twinned our souls together,
'Shared each other's dreams?
'If I hadn't been wedged by Chumlee,
'And his box of Krispy Kremes.'

There were many more stanzas but eventually, after leaving a long enough pause for the words to resonate – to settle – Poppy asked the time-honoured question:
'What do you think?'
Leon wasn't sure what he thought but no matter, Poppy kept talking (and turning pages): 'At least my stuff rhymes, right? Not like all this *modern verse* crap. I prefer the metre of the more traditional form, don't you?'
'Well . . .'
'Oh, you'll like this,' Poppy enthused, flattening a page. 'It's a bit cheeky but what the hell.'

AND ON SHE WENT

Leon was beginning to regret taking the scenic route home.

He'd enjoyed Poppy's company and the first dozen or so poems (hadn't they agreed on *one*?) but the long recital was wearing him down. The verses had been funny in places, especially the limericks, but the girl had been performing virtually non-stop since the surprise ambush that almost propelled him into the canal; Poppy lagging behind by two or three steps, Leon compelled to match *her* pace if he wasn't to stray beyond what politeness dictated the required listening distance to be. Twenty-seven-and-a-half minutes of back-to-back poetry and still going strong. And the work had gravitated towards the steamy:

'He ran; she swam; they crashed into the foaming.
'His strong arms. Her soft body.
'Young bronzed limbs roaming.

'Waves of bliss; bodies kiss; two rolling in the swells.
'He whispers:"I love you".
' "I love you, too!" she yells.'

The reciter and her appointed audience were now on Broad Street, the former still trailing the latter by just over an arm's length. (Leon had stutter-stepped several times to let the poetess catch up, but Poppy, each time, had subconsciously mimicked the action and so maintained their relative positions; to Leon it appeared the very notebook itself, held out, open between them, was somehow demanding its reader sustain the gap.)

And so it was, slowly approaching the top of Leon's road, lagging marginally behind Leon's right shoulder and looking every inch the deferential PA that Poppy started a new poem; or continued the last one – Leon wasn't sure which.

'Okay,' said Leon, coming to an abrupt stop. 'This is me.'

Poppy all but bumped into him. 'Ooh, Norris Avenue – *very* nice.'

'It's okay, I guess.'

'I wish the road I live on had trees. Or houses.'

'Houses?'

'Yeah, I live on the high street – it's all shops and flats.'

'Oh right.'

'Above the Subway sandwich shop. Honestly, I would kill for a little semi-detached.'

Entirely removed to an unseeing, protracted moment – Leon lingering quietly – Poppy eventually returned with: 'Come on, I'll walk you to your house. It is a house, right?'

Leon wasn't sure he wanted Poppy knowing *precisely* where he lived; he didn't know her well enough. *What if she turns out to be a nutter!* Time, he thought, for a polite goodbye. 'Actually, I've just remembered: I need to pick up something from the precinct.'

'Really?'

'Yep.'

'*Leon* . . .' Poppy gave him the eyes again. 'You're not worried about little old *me*, are you?'

She dished out a playful punch.

'*Ouch.*'

'*Oops*, sorry.'

Leon rubbed his shoulder. The girl was tougher than she looked.

'Because if you're worried about me seeing exactly where you live . . .'

'What? No. Why would I?'

'So, you really do have to go the precinct?'

'Definitely. I've got to get this thing I've got to get.'

'Cool. I'll come with. Give me a chance to read you some more of my poems – if you're still up for listening?'

No, no, no; not more poems!

'God, yeah – you try and stop me.'

'Excellent. Let's walk the canal again. I know it's the long way round but there's just something about water, don't you think?'

Leon found himself nodding. *Think of something – anything – just say no.*

'Canal it is,' he said.

AND BACK THEY WENT

Once again, at the pace required for mobile poetry recitals (i.e. unhurried) they set off, retracing their steps.

'See what you think of this one,' said Poppy.

Leon put out a smile he hoped would suggest a complete lack of mushrooming weariness, but by the time they had gone back along Broad Street, descended the steps leading down from Stickleback Road, and walked the towpath alongside the long narrow strip of scrubland before the concrete skateboard-park – finally nearing the bridge where they had reacquainted only a little earlier (though it was starting to feel like a *lot* earlier to Leon) – he was beginning to regret not taking the opportunity to fall in the canal and drown when he'd had the chance.

Poppy was lovely – if a little weird – *but all these bloody poems!*

'Should we take a short cut?' Leon pointed ahead, to the steps by the bridge.

'No, it's fine,' said Poppy, briefly interrupting her poetry reading. 'We can take the steps at the station.'

And so, one behind the other, they headed underneath the bridge . . .

As evening was underway the one remaining working arc-light in the skateboard-park was now on. Although its glow only marginally improved the odds of safer skateboarding, it did manage to spread a pool of gloomy shadows around the bridge's concrete support pillars.

In the cold, echoey air, as Sale Road passed noisily over their heads, the poetry took a turn for the melodramatic:

'*Ah, the violin strains,*
'*For the aches and pains;*
'*She reaches for the gun.*
'*If he can't find the courage,*
'*Her love will be undone . . .*'

Beyond the bridge but before half the allotments – stretched plots of root vegetables and winter cabbages interspersed with rickety sheds and compost bins, and not a gardener amongst them – had gone by, Leon realised he was walking a little more briskly; accelerating.

Yes, definitely quicker now. He could feel it in his legs, upon his face and about his hair. Sorry but he couldn't help it; endless poetry, it seemed, put him (eventually) into Flight mode.

Poppy did her best to keep up, but by the time they'd rounded the bend in the canal, Leon was several metres ahead. Poppy stopped and quipped:

'Hey, how about not walking so bloody fast?'

Leon slowed to a stop, apologised and waited.

Poppy arrived with a new poem but wanted to check something: 'Would you say you are open-minded?'

Leon stated that he believed so.

'Good,' said Poppy with a cheeky smile.

THIS ONE'S CALLED 'PASSION'

'I'd hate a passionless marriage;
'It's so not the thing for me.
'I've seen it with my sisters:
'Lily, Violet, Daisy; all three.
'One's square and dull, one timid and weak,
'The other's an overbearing nag.
'I say their husbands deserve them:
'The bag, the shrew, the hag.

'Happily Married my backside,
'I don't believe a word.
'Bet their sex lives are dreary, defunct,
'Or constantly deferred.
'And only ever in the bedroom, too.
'Why don't they go outside? –
'During the day, to woodlands,
'For a picnic . . . and a ride.

'If I had an adventurous man,
'We'd do it both inside and out.
'Under stars, in cars, flying to Japan,
'Library, tree-house, lake – a row boat, no doubt.
'Waterfall, stairs, cinema, nightclub,
'A haystack in the rain.
'Meadow, swimming pool, forest, tub,
'And up above the city, atop a tower crane.'

What had been feeling like a week to Leon – but was nearer an hour and twenty – now seemed to have flown by as he arrived at the door of Nobby's shop. Poppy hadn't even noticed they'd entered the precinct until Leon stopped suddenly. Her feet faltered for a moment but the recital, into its umpteenth stanza (each stanza revealing increasingly graphic details as they related to individual locations; she was currently in the woods) continued:

> *'Slipping off my coat reveals*
> *'Black lace hold-ups and high heels.*
> *'He undoes my Basque slow-handed;*
> *'Teases me till I squeal.*
> *'Then Romantic, but oh so raunchy,*
> *'I back against a tree.*
> *'He takes out his manhood,*
> *'And I guide him into—'*

'I have to go in here,' interjected Leon, the idiot. Getting *really* interesting and he had to butt in! Maybe he *was* a fuckwit, after all. *Stupid, stupid—*

'Okay,' said Poppy. 'No problem.'

She had thought to accompany him or at least wait at the door but quickly revised when she saw how he was just standing there like a lemon pointing silently into the Spar.

'I suppose I really should go and sit down somewhere; my feet are killing me.'

'What was that about hold-ups and high—?'

'Can you see my feet throbbing?' interrupted Poppy, waggling her shoes, one at a time (obviously) in the general direction of Leon's shins.

'Court shoes, leopard-print, round-toe, five-inch-stiletto-heel, patent leather uppers, size 6.'

'Wow, that's right,' said Poppy, sounding pleasantly surprised. 'Has someone got a shoe fetish?' she teased.

Richard's voice: *He wouldn't have the gumption to have something as raunchy as a shoe fetish.*

'I would,' said Leon.

'*You would?*' echoed Poppy.

'I mean . . . I haven't.' Denial.

125

'I wouldn't mind if you had,' said Poppy. 'I *love* shoes.'

Again, she flourished a shoe; knee high this time.

Check out those sexy mommas.

No, thought Leon, refusing to let his libido get the better of him. I mustn't be swayed by all this sexy talk. Steamy poetry doesn't necessarily rule out Bunny-Boiler.

In fact, it might make it *more* likely.

When Leon didn't come up with any kind of reply – like, *Actually I do have a bit of a thing for shoes; especially high-heeled ones* – the foot gradually re-found the ground.

Yeah, waggling your feet, Poppy, that was really going to work! And interrogating the poor guy about his personal fetishes after, what? – out came Betty Boop – *not even two hours! I suggest we give him some breathing space, withdraw for a moment and come up with a new spontaneous plan.* 'Okay, maybe I'll see you later, then.'

As Poppy walked away, only a little awkwardly, she glanced back, over her shoulder.

PIGGY IN THE MIDDLE

Fingers resting on DVDs, Leon's eyes cased the window, or rather, the bench beyond. He watched as Poppy, now seated, kicked off her shoes and jiggled her raised feet.

That's kind of cute, he thought. *But that doesn't mean she's* not *a bunny boiler.*

After a spell of adorable toe-wiggling and not-so-dainty foot-rubbing, Leon caught a sense of Nobby's beady eyes: watching him watching Poppy. As Leon made a show of focusing on the DVDs, it occurred to him that the newsagent was acting a bit like Seema did when she was orb-busting. Did that mean *he*, Leon, in a way, had become Reg – the piggy in the middle? *What a horrible thought.* But *this*, he told himself, *was* different. And, actually, none of nosey Nobby's goddamn business!

With a degree of defiance (*Yeah, that's right, Nobby, I am looking out the window, and yes, at a girl; what's it to you, ya toad?*) he returned his gaze to the precinct bench. Unlike Reg, he wasn't trying to catch Poppy out; just wasn't sure about her. Nothing he could put his finger on. He did like her. So what was the problem? An overdose of earnest, expressive poetry can be unnerving. Maybe that was it. Appealing as she was, a barrage of rhyming quickly becomes exhausting, mind-boggling, and downright—

Hang on, what was I thinking about?

Oh yes, orb-busting. And if Nobby was Seema, and he was Reg, did that, he wondered, make Poppy, *him*?

In a way, he wished she was, because Poppy had started writing – effortlessly, it seemed; fluently and with hardly a discernible pause: scribbling away, he imagined, like Keats, Byron, Shelley; Tennyson or Owen or . . .

Leon wished he could think of a famous *female* poet, past or present, but he couldn't. The only one that came to mind was Poppy: a poet in progress.

Leon was no great lover of poetry (had never really been able to get into it; to him it always felt too artificial – *too* made-up) but he respected the endeavour, appreciated the work that goes into any form of writing.

Not that it looked like hard work for Poppy.

Look at her banging it out. Impressive; doubtless with her delicate finger firmly on the emotional pulse – such a *busy* poet; line after line after line . . .

He thought she might be there for some time.

Leon now noticed Svetlana had joined Nobby. Restarted hands riffling blindly through DVDs, he smiled; acknowledged he'd registered their presence – their unwavering attention. Svetlana and her semi-see-through top smiled back. Nobby did not.

Miserable bastard. The Brontés! Of course, the Brontés. Oh, and Elizabeth Barrett Browning. I don't know why I didn't . . . never mind, better late than— and Shelley! (Mary *Shelley*, not Percy *Shelley*.) *Honestly, what am I like? Head like a sieve sometimes . . .*

Leon became aware that he was making some kind of face which Nobby and Svetlana couldn't have failed to spot.

Feeling outnumbered and increasingly self-conscious, he gave them a stiff grin before focusing his concentration exclusively on the DVDs. *For God's sake choose something!* On the next riffle, a film came up; a completely random choice but no matter; those behind the counter wouldn't know. He studied the back of the case, nodded a little, as if this were definitely the one he'd been looking for.

The chance selection was *Summer Holiday*.

Leon was sure he didn't want to see a film starring Sir Cliff (Lord, no) but for some reason it set his mind adrift – and though he didn't realise, he was smiling again.

CABBAGE CRATES OVER THE BRINEY

Welsh countryside: wide landscape with tall, rugged hills and summer sunshine; and Leon, eight, running around a smallish four-berth tent, arms outstretched, making Spitfire noises.

Lester, forties and handsome – hands full of suntan lotion and Veronica's shoulders – laughs at the boy's antics.

'Hey, Squadron-Commander Leon! How about when your dad finishes this, we head into Llani[3] for some of that meringue you like?'

Swinging around for another pass, young Leon shouts 'Tally-ho!' and guns the tent with arm-mounted machine-guns, his pursed lips flapping with the noise.

His parents' amusement has not ceased half an hour later. They are in the Red Dragon Café watching their offspring, still on theme, make a reconnaissance flight.

Having successfully reconnoitred a lemon meringue from 60,000 feet, he bails out, pulls the rip-cord, makes a perfect parachute-landing – right onto his chair – and tucks in. Everyone in the café is laughing. All find it funny and cute. Kids, eh? You've got to laugh. Like all children, little Leon knows that adults like nothing more than to be amused by a child.

A precocious brat, you mean. Showing off and being a twat.

Richard's voice again, the perpetual party-pooper calling out from the ether. Leon had heard the negativity so often Richard no longer had to be there for him to hear it. And despite knowing Richard would *never* make it as far as

---

[3] Llani: shortened, affectionate form of Llanidloes: a picturesque little market town in Mid Wales. Look it up. Go visit. You might enjoy.

Nobby's (not without blowing his cover; he was no doubt back at the house and almost certainly up to no good), Leon couldn't help himself – he fought back: I wasn't precocious, I just had a vivid imagination.

Yeah, right; really 'vivid'. Pretending to be a spitfire – how fucking obvious. You'll be doing your lame impression of King Kong in a minute.

I hadn't seen *King Kong* then!

Richard's 'presence' evaporated as Leon wondered how long it had been since he'd last watched *King Kong* (the original *King Kong*, not the remakes; he didn't like those – except maybe the Peter Jackson one). As he couldn't remember, not exactly, not even roughly, he decided instead to pit the pros and cons of the 1933 classic against the various remakes (the Peter Jackson one included), but as he made a start, a clumsy shopper bumped into him with her half-size trolley. Hard, too; an accident, no doubt, but she didn't apologise. Clumsy mare just carried on to Cheeses as if nothing had happened. Leon might have said *sorry* without realising. He hoped he hadn't.

Shit, what was I doing? . . . Oh, yes – pop the so-called Peter Pan of Pop back and choose a bloody film, already! A decent one!

Nobby and Svetlana had yet to find anything to do, other than man the counter, scan the shop, and wait for a customer to actually buy something. (The unapologetic lummox, now edging towards Ice Cream and Yogurts, still hadn't put anything in her trolley.) But Leon wasn't going to buy a DVD just to give Nobby and Svetlana something to do; he'd spent plenty here in the past and would not be intimidated. No way, José! He'd walk out of here without buying a thing and think nothing of it – definitely.

And with that, he slipped *Summer Holiday* back in at roughly the same place he'd found it. Not that it mattered; there didn't seem to be any semblance of order to the DVDs. Not that Leon could detect. Although Nobby had enough stock to rival a small Blockbuster store, the films weren't grouped in *any* way: not in genres; by Director; chronologically – not even alphabetised!

No, scrupulous riffling was the only—

Leon clocked Poppy's bench.

The seat was empty.

And something else: Pogo, over by Midas Well, on a mobile, waving somebody in. That somebody was a mean-looking street-fighter. Leon spontaneously ducked behind the DVD rack then re-emerged piecemeal, peering over.

Leon was stunned by the sheer size; the guy was *huge*: shoulders, arms, chest, head, neck, legs – everything. This was one big fucker; one big *ugly* fucker.

Stupid looking, too: ogre-like features beset by a permanently stupefied expression; cabbaged ears; flat, lopsided nose; and uneven, bee-stung lips that leaked drool over a jutting jaw. He had a face not even a mother could love, a face that had clearly taken many, many blows – although Leon suspected it had witnessed the giving of as many as it had received.

He imagined the man-mountain would have a ludicrous street-name like The Daddy or The Guv'nor or Mad Thing. Yes, Mad Thing; probably an ex-pro who lost his professional boxing licence after he'd assaulted a referee and bitten off an opponent's ear. That sounded right.

After Pogo and Mad Thing had become acquainted (clearly this was the first time they'd met) Pogo seemed to explain what he wanted; what he expected of this grotesque goliath – he did this by demonstrating on a passer-by: a middle-aged man with a paunch, hauling several carrier bags of shopping.

The clown punched the man in the stomach and after he'd doubled over, kneed him in the face. He then took his victim by the scruff of the neck and punched him in the face repeatedly. The beating went on for several minutes and culminated in a savage head-butt followed by a severe kick to the bollocks.

As the man twitched around on the concrete, surrounded by his shopping (and several upright members of the public who continued to mind their own business) Pogo put in a final flurry of hefty kicks and stamps before turning to Mad Thing.

The street-fighter nodded, somewhat vacantly, that he understood.

CHAPTER NINE

What happened is this:

LESTER SITS ALONE

Leon, dog-tired but unable to drop off, shuffled across the landing, in the dark, accompanied by the eerily low sounds of Veronica's snoring.

'Bit late for prowling around, isn't it?' asked Richard.

'Couldn't sleep,' answered Leon. 'What you up to?'

Richard, who was standing at the landing window, turned his head, revealing night-vision goggles like those sported by Jame Gumb in *Silence of the Lambs*.

'Mind your own business,' he said, quickly returning his assisted vision to the exterior.

'I saw the clown again today. I mean yesterday.' He gurned his face in the way exhausted people do. Richard sighed, muttered something. Leon fancied he'd rolled his eyes, too. 'In the precinct. With a mean-looking—'

'I told you, they're all in your head. Now piss off.'

Leon yawned, said nothing for a moment then asked:

'Kelly on night shifts?'

Leon found his dad in the kitchen, sitting alone in the dark, watching yet another home movie. After pouring a glass of milk Leon joined him at the table.

'This is when we first moved in,' Lester said. 'Do you remember?'

Leon did remember. Not the actual moving in; he was years away from being even a twinkle in his dad's eye. But the film of his parents moving in, he knew well.

Through sleepy eyes he observed a street of early-Seventies semi-detached houses: a newly-built council estate. Few cars: Ford Capri, Hillman Imp, Triumph Herald. The camera settles on one of the uncultivated front gardens and an open front door where Veronica, mid-twenties, waves us in; to the kitchen – *this* kitchen.

Veronica showcases the units, applauds excitedly and then beckons us to follow. A succession of cuts connects a tour: living room, bedrooms, bathroom, back garden. Veronica presents soil and a rickety wire fence; she laughs and shrugs as if to say: *What on earth do we do with* this?

As Leon watched the movie, he subconsciously anticipated every tiny film scratch, each random blemish. He knew all the flaws by heart: a brief focal blurring in the hall; an over-exposure in the box-room; a flash of green and a rogue hair trapped under the lens in the sitting-room; mysterious white dots that made holes in the driveway; a sudden sweep of light in the back garden . . .

For Leon, the film's imperfections did not detract. If anything, the small defects added to the whole experience. Spots, snags, speckles, smudges, and splotches. And the colours! He'd always loved the colours. They appeared rich, luxurious; reminded him of the saturated Technicolor of old movies like *Singin' in the Rain* and *The Wizard of Oz* – not *favourite* films but something in the lush pigmentation and lavish hues never failed to stir him. (Lester once told Leon that the vibrant chromaticity was the result of the Ilford Colourciné film he used.)

Another splice: ten or eleven years later. The house now has a neat green lawn lounging out front bordered by a multitude of flowers: mostly Hydrangeas, Marigolds and Zinnias; their blues, reds, yellows and purples, radiant and plush. The view tracks right, along a low brick wall, to open sunrise-design gates. The camera then walks the tarmac drive, the movement catching glimpses of cerulean sky spotted with fluffs of ivory cloud. We pass the recently acquired Volkswagen and find Lester sitting on a camping chair in front of another new addition: a garage, the first of its double-doors painted blue, like the heavens.

(Betty, a 1940s *Type 1* Beetle, was willed to Lester by Leon's great-grandfather, Percy Blank, after his unexpected death in 1977. Given to a lifetime of odd behaviour, Percy's last day on earth found him climbing down into the walled Gorilla enclosure at Chester Zoo – despite the numerous DO NOT FEED, AND DEFINITELY DON'T CLIMB IN! signs – to remonstrate with a Silverback who steadfastly refused to share any of the bananas Percy had just thrown in with his female companions. Percy's last words were reported by helpless onlookers to be: *'They're not all for you. Give some back, you selfish—!'*)

The painter, open paint pot at his feet, brush in hand, gestures to the filmmaker. The gesture asks: *Where were you when I was busy?*

'Isn't it typical, lad? You spend all day labouring and nothing, but sit down for two minutes and you're in the bloody spotlight.'

'I have the same problem with Reg. I could have been working all morning, but drift off at the stitching machine for a couple of hours and he's on me like a rash.'

Lester laughed. '*Couple of hours*; what are you like?'

'Health and Safety, he says. *Health and Safety!* The world's gone mad. So my mind wanders sometimes. It's not like I've ever stitched my thumb to a shoe.'

'Well, there was that time . . .'

'Okay, once. It happened once. Let it go already.'

They both smiled and Leon suddenly wanted to unburden himself; to say, 'Dad, I've somehow upset an evil clown. And now he's drafted in a half-witted brawler to beat me senseless. What should I do?'

He didn't of course. Now he thought about it in words, it just sounded comical and silly, not dangerous. Besides, his dad was enjoying the film. He didn't want to spoil that.

Look at him, thought Leon, lost in time, reliving all those moments.

Lester tweaked the focus from sharp to fuzzy and back to sharp. 'I was on a break, y' know,' he said, indicating his movie-counterpart, 'just resting my leg.'

'I know,' said Leon.

Lester gazed at the projection, massaged his troublesome knee. 'Bloody knee,' he mumbled.

Leon rubbed his eyes, studied his dad with tenderness and affection – the dad at the table; he knew what celluloid-dad was doing:

Movie-Lester jokingly jabs an azure thumb over his shoulder at the *unpainted* door, the tongue-in-cheek implication clear. The camera's outlook moves to and fro, the answer just as obvious. Whoever had been filming did not fancy getting their hands dirty. As Leon knew his mother would be appearing imminently and *he* was fast asleep (in that boxy, small-wheeled pram parked off to one side), he'd always assumed it must have been that lazy little bastard, Richard, behind the camera.

Leon's recollections of *It* growing up were vague. The really memorable 'good times' were mostly Richard-free, yet the little shit seemed to feature in so many *bad* childhood memories.

Like when Leon's pet mouse, Humphrey, mysteriously disappeared from his cage: there was Richard, ridiculing the tears. Broken toys; scratched records; pages missing from *Robinson Crusoe* and *The Count of Monte Cristo*; that time he awoke to discover Richard by his bed with a pan of water – funny how Leon didn't wet the bed *that* night! Coincidence? Leon didn't think so.

Or the time Veronica discovered someone had used Lester's new video camera to film that old slapper, Tina Dixon, sunbathing topless next door: Veronica accused Lester; Lester cross-examined Leon; and Leon blamed Richard – even though he hadn't seen him for weeks. (Richard often went missing.)

Leon said Richard must have sneaked in, done the dirty deed and left the 'evidence' to deliberately incriminate *him* – in fact, yes, now he thought about it, he'd seen Richard do it. (Why else would a video be found in Leon's dirty-laundry basket? On washing day of all days! *Another coincidence?*) Leon was urged to stop lying.

It's perfectly normal, he was told, to develop an interest in the female form, but filming someone without their knowledge and consent was just plain wrong.

Leon agreed, so why wouldn't they believe him? If only they knew what Richard was *really* like . . . the dirty, seedy, perverted—

Oh, get over yourself, Leon. Even though Richard wasn't present, Leon heard his scolding voice as if he were: *There's nothing wrong with a healthy dollop of carnal female pulchritude – revel in the joy of its voluptuousness, you big stiff!* This was followed by his grating laugh.

'Oh, fuck off,' blurted Leon.

Lester touched his hearing-aid. 'Sorry?'

'Nothing, I was just . . .' Leon feigned a yawn which turned into a real one.

'Hadn't you better get some sleep, lad? Work in the morning.' Lester nodded towards the clock.

'Sunday tomorrow, Dad. Even Reg doesn't ask us to—'

'*Monday* tomorrow, lad.'

'Shit, really?' sighed Leon.

' 'Fraid so.'

Leon wondered how he could have so easily lost a day. Had he slept away a whole twenty-four hours? Surely he wouldn't be feeling so tired if he had. Not only tired but now facing the unpleasant bombshell of a premature return to work . . . *In just a few hours!*

'Never mind, lad,' Lester patted his son's back, 'onwards and upwards, onwards and upwards.'

Leon slid down the chair, sinking under the weight of his unreadiness.

'Dad, I don't want to work at the shop anymore.'

'Everyone has to work, son.'

'They don't all have to do what I do – sticking on soles, fixing broken heels . . .'

'I'm not being funny, lad, but you were happy to take the job at the time.'

'Yes, but I didn't—'

'You've done that since leaving school; why the change of heart now?'

Leon didn't have an answer.

'What else could you do? What else *can* you do?'

Leon raised eyebrows as if Lester should know.

'Is this about the writing again?' asked Lester.

Leon made the noise a semi-blown inflatable doll might make if she had been gently stabbed in the heart.

'Cobbling is a good, honest job, lad. A *proper* job.'

'Oh, thanks.'

Leon tutted unintentionally and slipped a little lower.

'You know what I mean. People will always need their shoes repairing. Work hard and you could be there right up to your pension.'

'What a wonderful thought,' sighed Leon.

'Exactly. See, it's not all bad.' Lester squeezed Leon's shoulder.

The movie cut away now; spliced to Lester lying on a hospital bed, right leg held high in traction: the camera closes in then a hand, Veronica's, reaches out to tidy Lester's thick, lustrous hair.

After a moment, Leon heard his father say, 'So, what have we learned?'

Leon offered, 'You can't always get what you want?'

'No. That it's good to have a dream,' replied Lester. 'But don't be too disappointed if it doesn't work out.'

A few seconds later, the movie cut back to Norris Avenue and the half-painted garage doors, where Lester was still 'resting his leg'.

'Now go on, get yourself off to bed.'

'In a minute,' Leon said, letting out a long yawn. 'I need to wake up a bit first. I can't sleep if I'm too tired.'

Lester smiled and gave Leon's shoulder another squeeze before swivelling his head back to the movie.

Eventually, Leon sat up and stretched, then looked to his dad; no longer able to ignore something that had been troubling him for years. 'Dad?' he ventured, knowing the subject wasn't entirely relevant.

Lester's gaze remained on his movie-counterpart but he did manage a 'Hmm?'

'Do you remember Tina Dixon?'

'Tina Dixon, Night Nurse?'

'No, this wasn't a film. And that was *Rosie* Dixon. This was a video. Do you remember? . . . the video . . . you found it in the bottom of my—'

'Oh, here we go.' Lester pointed at the wall. 'This is the bit where your mother almost catches me sitting down on the job.'

Leon eyed the projection, let Tina Dixon go.

'I know,' he said warmly.

Movie-Lester's ears prick up and in one swift movement he's off the chair and painting. Two seconds later, Veronica appears with a biscuit tin and mug. Lester stops pretending to paint, acts like he's exhausted.

Lester smiled at the image.

'Have to be quicker than that, Vee.'

Having limped back, Movie-Lester sits, hands gratefully accepting the brew and biscuits. As Veronica checks inside the pram her attention is called to the camera. She turns, dispenses a rapid smile and performs an express curtsy (no doubt all slightly accelerated by the technologies involved).

Next cut: BLACKPOOL '82 scratched in wet sand. The camera rises, finds Lester and Veronica posing, the tower in the background; Veronica is expecting. Lester proudly pats her tummy. Then, despite their gesticulated protestations, the camera veers off, following two bikini-clad women who happen to walk by.

Another splice: another sunny day – the back garden. Centre screen, Veronica reclining on a sun-lounger in a floral swimsuit catching rays. She is fortyish but looks much younger. Sunlight inflames her long auburn hair. To her left, and only just in shot, is Lester, sitting on a plastic garden-chair. Looking to camera, he points a finger off to one side; a command. But the view moves the other way, to *our* left, edging Lester out – then creeps towards Veronica's breasts. Lester leans into frame and reinforces the instruction. Stubbornly, you feel, the camera operator takes heed, and the point of vision, pulling back out, shifts right, ahead of Lester, to Leon, age six, riding a small two-wheel bike (four, if you count training wheels).

When little-Leon eventually reaches his parents, after a protracted bout of laboured pedalling, he is snatched up, travels as if on a wire, and comes to rest on Lester's knee – the good one. Veronica applauds but the wheezing six-year-old is clearly in no mood for celebration, and with good reason: he looks like he's escaped a miniature building site, secured as he is within a high-visibility, orange-and-yellow safety-jacket ringed with reflective strips, and a bright-purple brain-bucket fastened tightly under a severely-pinched chin. As Lester waves at the camera, encourages Leon to do the same, Veronica gives her son's helmet strap an extra tightening, just to be sure.

Little-Leon is still attempting to poke out trapped neck-skin when his best friend whizzes into shot on a BMX and performs a sliding stop: the rear wheel orbiting around the suddenly stationary front. Little-Moss is a year younger than Leon but clearly has no need of embarrassing stabilising wheels, garish safety outfits or vice-like headgear – or inhalers (like the one little-Leon is now sucking on). Little-Moss is dressed in flares, tie-died T-shirt, and has shoulder-length blond hair: a mini-hippie. Veronica ruffles his mane as he gives us the Peace sign. Leon, still struggling to loosen his chin-strap, looks to his friend, no doubt wondering why he has to wear all this crap and Bob Dylan over there doesn't. Perhaps sensing young Leon's irritation, Lester pats his tyke on the Noggin Box.

Back in the kitchen, Lester simultaneously patted Leon's grown-up head. (Leon had known it was coming as surely as he knew the upcoming splice would bring another of Lester's football games: a winter match played in a virtual blizzard). Kitchen-pat, movie-pat; comforting gestures almost two decades apart – and Leon felt them both.

Meanwhile, on a frozen pitch on the kitchen wall:

Teenage goalkeeper Lester looks out through heavy, falling snow; watches a player in green-and-white stripes place a football where the referee indicates the penalty spot should be. The actual spot, indeed all pitch markings, are invisible under a thick blanket of white.

These were the days, Leon learned from Lester, when games were never abandoned for something as trivial as *a bit of bad weather*. Oh no. Not a chance. They would ignore hail the size of house-bricks; laugh at fork-lightning, the type that splits trees in two and incinerates people into ash-piles; slosh their way through the hardest of Manchester monsoons, wetter than any in southern Asia; play on during hurricane-force winds, even when they played havoc with free-kicks, corners, throw-ins, goal kicks, shooting, heading, and passing; they would yell themselves hoarse through heavy fogs and choking smogs, and we're talking real pea-soupers with visibility of four feet or less; they would press on despite being broiled by record-breaking freaky-hot face-melting summers. And when arctic-cold Christmases threatened to snap off frost-bitten fingers, they would— yes, well, you get the idea.

138

Oh, and gloves for outfield players – or orange footballs in winter?

For sissies.

Anyway, in the time it takes for the penalty taker to line up his run – goalkeeper Lester bouncing on the goal line, arms outstretched, ready to spring left or right – the non-fluorescent rock-hard football acquires a conical snow-hat.

The referee raises an icy whistle to frosty lips . . .

Leon didn't need to look, he knew the outcome. Instead, his eyes drifted to the side where he studied Lester, who had resumed the kneading of his dodgy joint.

Why couldn't things have worked out for you, Dad? It's so unfair. Why *didn't they?* This was clearly the question that needed answering; though Leon knew it was a question that, even if asked, could never be answered. (Not unless the answer was: Sometimes things just don't work out as they should.) This, however, didn't stop Leon's imagination slipping loose and playing out one possibility:

'Can you believe this, Gary? Deep into extra time and Manchester United have had to change their goalkeeper – and his first, perhaps *only* task in this game, will be to face a penalty. There surely can't be time for anything else. This should be the very last kick of the ball.'

'I know. It's incredible. The young lad; what's his name?'

'Blank. *Lester* Blank.'

'What is he, eighteen – nineteen? And he's being asked to keep United in the Cup. You couldn't make this stuff up.'

'And if all that wasn't daunting enough, he's facing the veteran, Rory *I've never missed a penalty in my life* McArdle. Over a hundred penalties taken in his career so far and not a single one missed. Hey, Gary, I wonder if that's how he got his nickname.'

'*Seriously?*'

'I seem to recall one *did* clip a post.'

'Yes, but it still went in. He's not called Rory *I've only ever missed one penalty in my life* McArdle, is he?'

'Good point.'

'And you can bet your life that's he's not planning on changing his nickname today. This young goalkeeper must be fair crapping himself.'

'Well, he's getting plenty of support from the Stretford End faithful, that's for sure. Just listen to that noise.'

From somewhere deep within the capacity crowd, Leon leads a chant of '*Lester! Lester! Lester!*' as out on the pitch, a few paces behind the penalty spot, Rory McArdle, spot-kick maestro extraordinaire, eyes the football intently – and then looks to the referee.

Goalkeeper Lester, gloves spread wide, bends his knees in readiness, set for action, primed to go.

The referee's icy lips encircle the frosty whistle . . .

TROUBLED SLEEP

Leon would have to be up for work in less than two hours, but for now, he lay twitching in a deep yet troubled sleep.

Three weeks short of twelve months ago (on 28th October 2006 to be exact), in climbing blackness, he had foraged for the reason the world had ambushed him, hung him upside-down in a burning car, and left his parents on broken glass, at odds with mangled, unmovable doors. Confounded and overwhelmed, Leon's conscious mind had disengaged, fragmented, and blown away like so many airborne dandelion seeds. Separate and lost, he'd floated into a darkening abyss . . . remnant light faded and the event slipped, as if through a crack in the past.

In the weeks and months that followed his time spent in a coma, he found recalling what had happened, an impossible task. He *attempted* to face the experience, *tried* to remember, and sometimes his exertions prospered a glimpse, but then the picture would invariably rush to shadow, don a murky cloak, and hide. Occasionally, unexpected threads breezed in, trailing like shimmering filaments, but they always remained stubbornly vague and intangible, and the very act of reaching for them blew them apart like delicate gossamer. Little wonder then that he soon came to accept the futility of trying to extract how this particular misfortune, like so many other misadventures he'd suffered in his relatively short life, had come about.

He simply couldn't remember; *would not be able to remember* – not yet.

What *had* happened is this:

Leon had been driving the Volkswagen back from the cinema. Despite a lousy night outside and the accompanying *squeak-squeak-squeak* of Betty's wipers working overtime against incessant rain lashing at the windscreen, the atmosphere inside the Beetle was happy and carefree. Lester and Veronica were singing along to 'My Generation' by The Who, part of a Sixties 'Mods' cassette Leon had put together for their 40th wedding anniversary.

The car travelled alongside the Manchester Ship Canal, took the usual detour to eulogise Old Trafford football ground, then slipped by White City Retail Park and to the sounds of 'Green Onions' by Booker T. & the MG's headed for home.

Leon didn't like driving; particularly in bad weather; especially at night; even more so if there was any degree of traffic; but the outing to the Trafford Centre for a fancy meal followed by the special screening of *Quadrophenia* had been *his* idea – a red-letter treat for Lester and Veronica's ruby anniversary – and he knew that if *he* hadn't driven, they probably wouldn't have gone. In stark contrast to their youth, when they were always out and about, his parents tended not to go out much anymore. (The designated chauffeur had intended to wait in the car park, get a spot of reading done, listen to music – Puccini's Madame Butterfly or Mozart's Don Giovanni, perhaps – told them this was *their* night. But on arrival they said they wouldn't go in unless he joined them – and so he had.)

'This is a wonderful tape,' Veronica said as The Kinks really got into 'You Really Got Me'. Lester gave her the glad-eye. Not driving was fine with him. He hardly ever drove Betty these days. The accelerator pedal had started to make his knee ache even more than it usually did. He commuted on foot, too. Said he preferred it. *His* car park was, he joked, just a ten minute limp from the house. In contrast, Veronica, as she'd tottered back to the car, said she *wanted* to do the drive back – insisted on it for a short while – but as she, like Lester, had knocked back several glasses of wine with the meal, Leon thought it best to refuse. Besides, Veronica couldn't drive. (According to her, she grew up in a time when young ladies preferred to be driven, and so, had never learned.)

As Betty sliced through an enormous pool of sitting water that had amassed outside what used to be the Odeon Cinema (currently a fitness centre; before that, a nightclub) the long whoosh of spray put Leon in mind of the Water Chute ride he'd seen in one of Lester's home movies: *A trip to Belle Vue, 1968.*

'Be My Baby' came on the stereo. 'Steak, drinks, cinema and now The Ronettes,' enthused Lester. 'Excellent!'

'Yes, it's been a lovely evening, thank you,' added Veronica.

Lester patted Leon's shoulder. 'A great day all round. Good job, son.'

Leon squinted through the windscreen; thankful traffic had eased even if the downpour hadn't. 'Glad you enjoyed it,' he said, smiling. (By the way: squinting and smiling at the same time? Not a great look.)

With only a few miles to go, a car that had been close behind for over ten minutes finally turned off, onto Maudlin Street. Leon was happy to be rid of its wonky bright headlight in his rear-view mirror.

'Ooh, it's our song,' lauded Veronica, shaking happy fists. The song was an old Motown classic by Eddie Holland: 'Leaving Here.' Lester cheered, squeezed Leon's shoulder and asked for more volume. Although the music, already loud to compensate for Lester's hearing loss, made the car vibrate, Leon obliged.

During the second play of the same track (Veronica had requested a rewind) a sudden gust of wind engulfed Betty in an extra-heavy barrage of buffeting rain. For a moment, Leon's visibility dropped to drive-through car-wash proportions.

By the third play (Lester's request this time), Betty was almost home. Now travelling along the top of Upper Church Street, headed for the dip, she ploughed through slicks of wet leaves that had recently abandoned tall oaks and ashes lining both sides of the road. As Lester, Veronica, and the band hit the chorus with gusto, the car passed the bus stop outside St. Mary's, the church where Lester and Veronica were married (or to give the impressive old place its full name: *St. Mary's, Blessed Virgin and All Hallows Trinity Parish Church*. A fading sign: silver letters on a mauve background, confirmed as much – then quietly warned, or boasted, depending on your point of view, that GOD SEES EVERYTHING). As usual, at night, the stone-arched entrance was barred by a rusty iron gate sealed with a hefty chain and padlock. Unlike God, Leon did *not* see this: his eyes were now aimed downhill, focused on Lower Church Street, which, he noted happily, was, like its lofty namesake, also free of traffic: not a single vehicle; not parking, not parked, and not in transit – so no dazzling headlights coming the other way. Leon hated that even more than dazzling headlights in the mirror.

Lester, who had upped his own volume considerably, was now singing flamboyantly about how the love of a woman is a wonderful thing. Leon chuckled inside; he knew his father would be addressing Veronica's eyes – the big crooning softy.

Leon felt all warm and fuzzy as Veronica giggled like a teen and rain battered Betty uproariously (was big-softyitis hereditary? he wondered). He joined in the singing and peered through the arching wipers to the upcoming bend, beyond the bottom of the hill.

Here, in defiance of the weather, a young woman – not much more than a girl, really; with a child in a buggy and another on the way – was feeding a letter into the mouth of the recently-painted Royal Mail letterbox.

Caught in the extremity of Betty's advancing headlights, the letterbox grew as bright as red can be.

ASHLEIGH

The letter in Ashleigh Fairclough's hand was addressed to Private Eckersley via a series of numbers: Private Eckersley's service number, the number of his Regiment, and a British Forces Post Office number. The latter digits would direct the missive to Afghanistan, where the private was currently serving.

Andy 'Snapper' Eckersley, stocky ginger-haired lad from Salford, was the father of Tyler, the ginger-haired sprog in the buggy. Private Eckersley might also be the father of Ashleigh's unborn; she just wasn't sure. The dates matched Andy's last leave, more or less, but there had been a rather eventful party a day after he'd returned to duty. Ashleigh had got extremely drunk that afternoon and a couple of random lads quickly took advantage, in turns, from behind, as she was being copiously sick out of a twelfth-storey window. She never did catch the cheeky opportunists' names. By the time she had cleared out the last of several Vodka Red Bulls, they had come and gone – so to speak.

Ashleigh had chosen to ignore the episode, hoped by burying her head in the sand it would go away. She would only ever discuss the matter with Snapper if he found out. And he wouldn't be doing that any time soon. Not unless some evil bastard sent him a copy of the video currently doing the rounds amongst her so-called friends.

She'd seen the footage only once. Watched it through laced fingers . . .

Taken on a smartphone, in eye-popping high-definition, the action had been captured in a towering flat (possibly in Salford) and showed two chancers, one black, one white, pants around their ankles, tag-team-humping the back end of a young woman whose head hung, unseen, beyond an open high-rise window; her attire down to clumpy trainers and a teeny-weeny skirt pushed up towards an unhooked bra. So vigorous and unrelenting was the pummelling and pounding, that the star of the show was compelled to cling to the windowsill, lest she be launched in the direction of her latest, still-falling upchuck.

Crystal clear sound had successfully caught the wild party atmosphere: the whoops, yells and cheers of an unseen crowd; machismo encouragements such as 'Smash that ass!' and 'Yeah! Do it! Do it!' The vociferous and bountiful heaving and hurling from the half-in/half-out female and pumping music that dovetailed perfectly with the orgiastic mood: The Prodigy's 'Smack My Bitch Up'.

Although the recorded events jerked around and no faces were shown, one distinct image repeatedly hogged the limelight: a tattoo of a pink butterfly, resting, wings-akimbo, on the lower back of the leading lady.

Ashleigh had one just like it.

Identical, in fact.

Should Snapper ever see the video, Ashleigh would, she'd decided, brazen it out: *Lots of girls have Tramp Stamps, Andy!* Doesn't mean they *are* tramps! Okay, *that* one's whoring it up a bit but that is *not*, repeat *not*, me. *What!* Yes they do; lots of girls have butterflies. *Jesus, Andy, there is such a thing as a fucking coincidence, y' know!*

With unbelievable luck and a conspiracy of silence bought by favours or threats (Ashleigh had a temper that matched even Snapper's), she might just get away with it.

What might prove harder to explain would be the chanting voices: unseen party-goers, male and female, joined together in an enthusiastic chorus of '*Ashleigh! Ashleigh! Ashleigh!*'

Yeah, that could be a tricky one.

Oh well, she'd cross that minefield when she came to it. For now, she just wanted to post her letter, get out of this horrible wind and rain, wheel the buggy home, get Tyler in bed, kick off her waterlogged trainers, put her feet up, grab a WKD Blue, light a spliff, and finish off her box of Celebrations whilst watching the TV series: Angel. *Mmm*, that David Boreanaz; he could flick her bean any night of the week— Christ, what was that terrible *squeak-squeak-squeak* noise? The sound was akin to a sick gerbil being repeatedly hammered with a large wooden mallet.

Leon, who knew nothing of Ashleigh's Tramp Stamp, was, unlike the brazen opportunists at the party, about to have a *face-to-face* encounter with its owner.

ALWAYS CRASHING IN THE SAME CAR

Before Betty reached the bend – occupants still warbling to 'Leaving Here' – a second vehicle drifted around the corner at high speed.

The blazing headlights spiked Leon's eyes, crossed the dividing lines and advanced head-on.

Shielding his eyes, and with no other option presenting itself, Leon swerved to avoid a collision. Initial phase of manoeuvres: avoidance of Object A (rogue vehicle) by Object B (Betty) was successful. The remainder of the impromptu venture did not fare so well.

Immediately following the swerve, something hit, Leon lost control, and Betty flipped onto her side. The encounter happened so fast, but in super-slow motion, too – with Leon's cognitive process experiencing every racing moment in minute detail.

As Betty skidded through a salvo of amber sparks, he smelled wet pavement rolling by, just inches from his face. Heard the grating sounds of crunching glass – gravelly and unhurried. He felt buffeted levity despite a creeping, oppressive weight. The moulded Mary Magdalene, liberated from her place on the dashboard, floated by spinning slowly, narrowly avoiding a collision with the little plastic football boots that until seconds ago had been hanging from the rear-view mirror.

Leon also distinguished an empty cassette case, insert missing, spiralling gently in mid-air; the path of its heartbreaking ballet imperceptible as it kept pace with the car's snail-like trajectory. Eddie Holland was singing about a train but this, too, was taking an eternity.

'Traaaaaaaaaaaaaaaaaaaaaaaai . . .' he droned – the vocal equivalent of wading through molasses.

Leon's eyes, now fully rebooted after the high dosage of full beam, alighted upon Ashleigh and Tyler framed within the vertical windscreen, their expressions frozen, illuminated, horrified, as Betty scudded towards them. The letter intended for Private Eckersley in the Middle East, having slipped from Ashleigh's withdrawn fingers, was, at present, floating past the stretched and rain-dappled skin of her bare midriff; heading south, towards her soggy white Reebok Classics. Tyler pulled in a soft toy clown, clutched it tight against his coat buttons.

Within whatever fractions of a second remained, Leon decided it was impossible for the pair to escape in time. Unable to watch he screwed his eyes and left it to God – although a facsimile of mother and child did persist on his retinas: witnessed as ghostly replicas on the back of his eyelids. The image persevered throughout a long metallic scrape: a shrill, rasping, painful noise which had already sustained far longer than seemed right.

There was another sharp blinding flash of light, this one internal, his head colliding with something *extremely* solid.

A thought, in milliseconds: *What the fuck was that? The kerb! Is that possible?* The idea horrified him.

(He instantly flashed on a time when he'd seen someone knocked senseless by a washing-machine slung from a passing flatbed truck. *Who* and *where* escaped him but he retained it wasn't pretty.)

And then air, rushing out; precursor to what would be a long-drawn-out, percussive explosion: chrome and steel impacting against stone and iron in a ponderous coming-together of metals and minerals: long, reluctant *cracks* and *crunches*; sandwiched bones, buckled joints, and the tearing of tissue; shattered pieces of debris falling all around; the short, sharp dance of metal parts; a clattering object that rolled and rolled before finally coming to rest. Betty's upended near-side wheels, almost in sync, repeated ratchet-like *click-click-clicks* as if by crippled, hindered clockwork as they set about exhausting the remnants of their gathered momentum.

Leon didn't hear any of that; or the nearby, high-pitched squeal: a screech of tyres braking to a sudden stop. As though sucked into a vacuum, he sensed nothing for a moment; nothing beyond falling through a great black abyss – tumbling and twirling . . .

Well, this is just great, Leon thought.

But even as he thought it, the falling slowed . . . then stopped, leaving nothing; only darkness – darkness and a deafening quietude. That and nothing more.

Eventually, in this space without time, Leon assumed he had to be dead. *Had* to be.

'What bollocks. Of course you're not dead.'

'Not dead?'

'No, you pitiful ponce. How can you be dead?'

'How?'

'Is there an echo in here? Yes; *how*?'

147

'Er . . .'

'Oh, for fuck's sake: René Descartes! . . . "I think—" '

' "Therefore I am." '

'Exactly – *because* . . .'

'Because . . . the very act of thinking we must be dead . . . means we have to be alive.'

'Bravo. Give the Neanderthal a banana.'

'Okay, but this is all really weird. I mean, where am I? What do I do now?'

'Fucked if I know – Right, balls to this, I'm off; things to do.'

'*Hello?*'

Leon wasn't sure he was speaking aloud.

'*Hello!*'

A few seconds after the tyres of the other vehicle had screeched to a stop, somewhere out in the pelting rain, a muffled voice yelled:

'Get back in the car! Come on, let's go! Let's get the fuck out of here!'

As with the tyre squeal, Leon failed to catch the yell; for him, time was trudging ahead, solemn-paced and grim, his *semi*conscious mind at the helm. And yet, despite being severely head-clonked during Betty's slide (and whiplashed on impact) he did regain, here and there, brief fragments of what felt like intense consciousness – only for split seconds, but enough to take a series of stirring snapshots.

The first thing he perceived was a trickle of moisture track across his face; it arrived with a hint of breeze that played upon his skin. He had a feeling of being light-headed yet top-heavy, isolated yet attached, punch-drunk but somehow wide-awake, all at the same time.

He heard Holland, arse back in gear and free of molasses, belting out something about how it wouldn't be long until they were leavin' here.

Leon liked how the singer sounded against the backdrop of heavy rain. The voice was forceful and uplifting, optimistic and hopeful.

Then his eyes blinked open, adjusted to the light, and took it all in; absorbed everything at once: Betty, on her side, crumpled and shattered; hard, wet, shiny road; a spiky throw of glass splinters under his shoulder; blood on his hands; a taste, like damp copper, in his mouth; the circling downpour – and the creepy dummy in the passenger seat . . .

'Hello, Leon.'

The ventriloquist doll hung over him, disabled by a web of contorted seatbelt, swinging gently under a broken side-window canopied by night sky and gloomy clouds, useless pyjama-trousered-legs dangling either side of the gear-stick. Big, ventriloquist doll eyes gazed down. Raindrops dripped from its pug-nose.

'I said . . . *Hello, Leon.*' The dummy's brightly-painted wooden teeth beamed.

'Who the fuck are you?' Leon barked through the pain that arrived like a rocket and burst like a shell, instantly radiating a brilliant incandescence that lit up his whole being. The reverberations flashed around his nervous system as if his spinal cord had been stroked with an electrified cattle-prod.

'Lord Archibald. Pleased to meet you. But please, call me Archie.' The dummy's words were punctuated with harsh wooden clacks. 'So, is this how you want it to end?'

In spite of the agony thundering around his skull – his head had abruptly taken on the sensibility of a shattered cannonball – Leon mustered a shaky 'What?'

'Is this how you want it to end – like this – to die in a car crash with your parents?'

'No,' was the instant reply.

'Well, someone has to die, Leon.' Lord Archibald's creaky, posh voice gave the statement an air of truthful authority. 'And it seems to me, that *you*, old bean, are just wasting *your* life.'

Leon didn't think he was wasting his life and said so.

'Aren't you?' the dummy asked pointedly.

'I'm only twenty-three,' asserted Leon, though the way he said it sounded kind of sad.

Archie, a deadpan look on his face, let out a slow 'Hmm.'

Not wasting and lots more to do, Leon decreed – *lots* more. He wasn't sure exactly *what* right now, but *lots*, nonetheless – probably. He would have to think about it later, when he didn't feel so wrecked and tormented. He had become heavy and exhausted.

Leon decided it was time to sleep; it felt like the right thing to do.

As if on cue, a strange coldness formed under his right shoulder; it opened up and he slipped, sideways into dead air; sideways and down, into an unnamed place where everything, it seemed, had gone – stopped. He'd almost *completely* blacked out now. The suffering and music and rain and everything else had ceased; once again, there was only inky nothingness and deathly silence – which Leon's *subconscious* mind, as it so often did, raced to fill . . .

'What?' he said, reopening his eyes, confident he'd felt something prod his shoulder.

'I said: *Someone has to die.*' The dummy's jaw clattered out the words. 'Someone *always* has to die.'

Leon wondered wearily why *anybody* had to die.

'They just do,' said Lord Archibald.

'Who?' Leon asked. '*Who* has to die?'

'Who indeed . . .'

'Not me?'

The dummy widened his eyes.

'Please, don't let it be me,' Leon pleaded.

'Hmm,' Archie said, looking Leon up and down.

Leon acknowledged (to himself) how drained he'd sounded; how even his internal voice was now nothing more than a whisper . . .

He accepted that he was almost entirely spent.

The dummy clacked his jaw, as if deliberating.

'Okay,' he agreed.

Leon felt a small wooden hand slide against his palm; it gripped and dealt a surprisingly firm handshake.

If Leon had been fully conscious, he might have witnessed the crunching of glass and folding of metal as Betty rolled onto her back.

CHAPTER TEN

Women ARE from Venus

KAYLEIGH

Now, nearly a year after the accident, Leon was again on Lower Church Street. Despite securing only two hours sleep and suffering a bad dream he couldn't remember (it had buzzed off with the alarm clock), he'd awakened feeling curiously refreshed and in high spirits. He'd cooked eggs for breakfast and washed it down with not one but two large mugs of Joe. His good mood and perkiness was not lessened by a damp early-morning walk to the Metro station to start another long week of key-cuts and cobbling; it was, after all, as his dad had told him: a *proper* job.

Leon took a short, presumably caffeine-fuelled run and kicked an imaginary ball. 'He shoots, he scores; the crowd goes wild!' Triumphant, he leaned back, fist pumping the air, imitating the sound of a crowd going wild; roaring their perceived appreciation into the quiet, dimly-lit sky . . . and that's when he realised he was not alone.

Across the street, a female, squatting by the letterbox, stared at him. For a second Leon thought he'd caught her at an inopportune moment; a young woman with lady-bladder problems, perhaps, seizing the opportunity for a discreet whiz on what had been an empty street till he'd showed up with all his bellowing and gesticulating.

But no, nothing lurid or embarrassing, she had simply been in the midst of placing flowers. (The anniversary of the crash wouldn't be for another two or three weeks yet – with all the medication Kayleigh was on, she wasn't sure what *year* it was, never mind which *week* – but she'd felt compelled after spotting others had already left flowers.)

After gently propping her bouquet against the letterbox, Kayleigh rose slowly, her bloodshot eyes fixed on Leon.

Leon thought it might be best to dial down the roaring at this point, so he did.

The twenty-something-year-old was dressed in vest top, grey sweat pants and fake, tan-coloured Ugg Boots, had love bites on her neck and bruises on her arms (both the result of an overbearing steroid-taking boyfriend), frizzy hair tightly-scraped into a side pony-tail, tangerine skin, and earring hoops large enough to attract dolphins.

Leon ceased pumping the celebratory fists and hid them in his pockets – an action he felt in retrospect could have been done sooner, perhaps even synchronised with the discontinuation of roaring. Oh well, better late than never.

As he needlessly cleared his throat, no doubt hoping to distract from his silly antics, the woman looked down; her bouquet had somehow slid from its upright position onto its side. Top heavy, Leon thought; the bouquet, not the woman. With the supine speed of a sorrowful sloth on sedatives, she gently lowered back onto her haunches and tenderly repositioned the flowers (nicked from the petrol station where she'd just worked a late shift.)

Leon studied her . . . He liked to believe he was totally non-judgemental, purposefully avoided unkind terms like *Chav* or *Chavette* (especially in their presence, and God knows there were a lot of them around here), and as a would-be writer abhorred the idea of creating any character that might ever be considered stereotypical (or situation which could be construed as clichéd) but sometimes there they were, right in front of you, large as life.

After an extended moment of contemplation Kayleigh shifted her troubled gaze back to the young man across the road. OMG, she thought (Kayleigh did a lot of texting), he's still here. I don't know how he's got the nerve.

Who does Ugg Boots remind me of? Leon wondered. And then, noticing what he suspected could be an irritated glare: *And what* is *her problem?*

He'd once called an ambulance after receiving a call from his grandparents' number. No one spoke but he could hear Bill in the background, shrieking and moaning.

Arriving at the same time as the medics, and gaining no answer to knocks and rings, Leon told them to smash the door in. They discovered the pair engaged in what can only be described as geriatric sex-games. Nana Norma was dressed as a PVC-clad dominatrix Nigerian prostitute (she'd actually *blacked up!*) and Granddad Bill was a naked, submissive Toulouse-Lautrec delivery boy (pince-nez eyeglasses, bowler hat, false beard, pizza box, and on his knees). Seems Nana's whip hand had accidentally knocked over the bedside phone which inadvertently redialled the last number called: Leon's mobile.

As Leon had escorted the medics out, clambering past the unhinged front door, everyone politely ignored the whoops and whip-cracks from upstairs as the interrupted pensioners got back to it.

The somewhat clumsy point is: our protagonist was never very good at judging the moods or intentions of others. Where most people would no doubt say Ugg Boots looked sad (well, duh, she *was* laying sympathy flowers) to Leon she appeared uptight, resentful – angry, even.

Has she got a problem with *me*? he wondered pointedly.

Kayleigh was wondering, too. Wondering: Is he just going to stand there, or actually say something?

Kayleigh was Ashleigh's sister.

Yep, she's definitely staring at me, Leon told himself. Okay, I guess I'm staring a bit now as well, but *she* started it. And that redness in her eyes – that's murderous intent if I ever saw it. *Jeez, if looks could kill.*

A fresh wave of paranoia washed over him. He'd been feeling overly suspicious for a few days. Why though? Was it the recent strange sightings? Maybe they'd freaked him out more than he'd acknowledged. Was Ugg Boots even really there? He closed his eyes, counted to ten then opened them tentatively. She hadn't disappeared or made an infantile dash for the station like that rickety old fossil. What had Leon called him . . . Dusty something . . . Dusty Dust? . . . Dusty dust, ashes to ashes . . .

No, he's definitely not going to say anything, Kayleigh decided. But what *could* he say? What could *she* say? As she watched him take out a notebook, find a pen, open the notebook, then bounce his eyes between her and the page, she had but one thought: How about saying you're *sorry* – one of the words she'd written on a little card now inserted amongst her flowers.

Tapping his pen against the notebook, Leon slowly concluded that, although Ugg Boots *was* freaking him out a bit, she was *unsuitable* for entry into the *Odd Log*. She wasn't an *especially* strange sighting as he'd come to understand them. Not like Chicken-Man or the freaky clown, for example.

Kayleigh fixed to address Leon but found she didn't know where to start. Maybe it was the weird notebook/assessing thing; or the way he was just standing there – or maybe it was the new tranquillisers she'd been prescribed.

Leon was sure Ugg Boots had something she wanted to say. But whatever it was, she wasn't letting it out, and he wasn't going to speak first. He never spoke to females he didn't know. Not unless they spoke to him first. Not since the whole high-school prom incident:

UK proms in those days, at least at the school Leon attended, consisted of an assembly hall decked with a line of twitchy lights and a string of bunting, a non-alcoholic bar, and the odiously cloying but striving to be effervescent DJ wannabe, Mr Crawley (aka 'Creepy' – boys' PE and Swimming), spinning up his meagre collection of original Rock and Roll vinyls. (And they weren't called *Proms*, but *End of School Discos*.) It was during Creepy's umpteenth play of Chuck Berry's 'My Ding-a-Ling' – as Leon had been busting out some awkward moves – that his so-called classmates (they might have been in the same class but they certainly weren't *mates*) assured him that girls love nothing more than a *really dirty* chat-up line; the filthier the better, in fact. They even gave him one to use on the girl he'd admired from afar since first year: Michelle Moore.

The wooing had not gone well. Unless your idea of a good time is having your face bitch-slapped by your true-love: little Miss *'No, I would not fucking like to sit on your face so you can guess my weight!'* in front of all your teachers and teenage peers and being depantsed by person or persons unknown in the middle of the dance floor.

A quick lesson about school:

Although everyone knew Leon would have breezed the entrance exam for the nearest grammar, he was instead sent to Thorny-Common High, the local comprehensive.

Unlike the grammar, Thorny was *co-ed*. Veronica disapproved of single-sex schools. With a naive sense of romanticism and blatant disregard for educational prosperity, Mother had sent Leon to the comprehensive openly hoping he, too, would meet someone special there, as she and Lester, inseparable from Year 7, had done.

She envisioned her boy encountering the love of *his* life, courting her, enjoying adventures together, producing offspring of their own one day.

Lester was swayed by Veronica's reasoned argument: *They're all taught the same stuff anyway* and definitely not because he was relieved to be saving on travel fares (the common lay within reasonable walking distance; the grammar was two buses there, two buses back) although he would later feel guilty when Leon, upon leaving school, confessed to having hated every minute; apart from English Language with Mr Greene and English Literature with Mrs Bernstein – he soaked up those classes. Leon suspected everything else about the school must have declined horribly since his parents were taught there in the late Fifties/early Sixties, the 'good old days' they had so often reminisced about.

Anyway, Kayleigh, who still hadn't said anything, now reached into her bag, produced a small teddy-bear (another Petropolis 'freebie'), patted its head, hunkered back down, and placed it beside her flowers. A tissue went to her nose.

As Leon watched, his usual feeling of unusualness met with a change: *Sadness*. He put this down to Ugg Boots' sorrowful demeanour and the presence of all the flowers and tributes. He didn't resist this locationally-new sentiment; why shouldn't he be sad, faced with this scene? Being sad was okay. He hadn't, he thought, had much heartbreak in *his* life – not *real* misery; not compared to others; he would let the reaction sit. He believed writers *needed* to experience different emotions. And it made a change from feeling *unusual*. Uncomfortable as the sense of mournfulness was, he would soak it up. Why not, he had a few minutes. Would Ugg Boots mind if he stayed a bit longer? He decided she probably wouldn't give it a second thought; what, with the woe and everything.

But Kayleigh was already on her feet, tip-toeing over flowers. Stepping onto the street, aimed Leon's way, she had barely left the kerb before he was on the move.

Stopping, watching him quick-walk away, she squeezed a handful of burns on her right thigh; results of much self-harming with a hair-curling iron. She grimaced and let out a low frustrated growl. 'A simple *sorry* would've been nice,' she muttered – then slapped herself across the face.

Leon didn't have time for an encounter or confrontation or whatever that was about to be. Even brave soldiers have places to be. He needed to get to work, had a tram to catch.

Fifty nifty paces later he entered the Metro station. After reversing two paces, he peeked around the entrance to make sure Ugg Boots wasn't following. He didn't like the idea of being followed; although in this case he was satisfied that, if needs be, he could easily outrun Ugg Boots – with or without his free-running abilities. (Okay, he'd never actually acquired these skills but he had watched *District 13*, seen kids performing gymnastically around the underpass and precinct, *and* viewed several Parkour clips on YouTube. How hard could it be?)

Outmanoeuvring and outrunning a clearly less-than-athletic Ugg Boots, Leon pictured himself free-running at great speed, performing astounding leaps and acrobatic bounds: a precision jump onto railings, monkey-vaulting a wall, a back-flip to the ground, scrambling up the face of a building, a cat-leap between roofs – wait, is it *roofs* or *rooves*? he wondered; doesn't matter – cat-leap between them, run along a ledge, drop from height onto a moving train, okay maybe not the train, a bit too James Bond, but a tuck-and-spin cannonball barrel-roll or whatever over the canal at the point where it narrows for the lock but is still pretty damn wide, now that would be— oh hang on, she's not following. Don't need to do any of that. Well, good; lucky for her. She would have definitely embarrassed herself there – and such a poor choice of footwear for urban Parkour. *Ugg Boots?* Do me a favour.

Leon was right, of course, about Kayleigh not following him; she was back squatting amongst the flowers, reading the attached cards – cards containing kind words from well-wishers: friends of the deceased or strangers moved by tragic loss and its anniversary.

Metro trams run every six minutes from here to Manchester. As he bought his ticket Leon hoped he wouldn't have to wait *that* long; for some reason he felt a sudden need to take a whiz.

Perhaps he shouldn't have had that second cup of Joe.

GIRLS

A forty-something woman with an ass like a mule and a horsey, masculine face (all lips and teeth and an abundance of saliva) waited at the counter watching Leon as he cut new front- and back door keys for her. Seema had overheard Desert Orchid say something about changing the locks after finally kicking out her useless boyfriend.

In the years that Leon had been working at Keys-n-Stuff, Seema had seen several women (of various grades and ages) come into the shop to establish contact. Some were upfront, some less so. The shyer ones would 'browse'; hang around the trophies or house-signs, stealing glances. A polite 'Can I help you?' from Leon could send the really bashful scurrying for the exit, usually mumbling, occasionally tripping over their own feet. Timid types braving it out might lurch into a panic buy – usually a cheap item like liquid shoe-shiner. One in particular, a skinny girl with a hawkish nose, unfashionable glasses and a smattering of chin-acne, came in every Friday afternoon; she never got the result she clearly hoped for, but she did now sport the shiniest shoes in Manchester.

Those with more confidence would sometimes employ body-part presentation techniques. Good Legs (or *Thinks She Has Good Legs*) might ask: *Hello, me again. I was wondering how much it would cost to repair these boots. They're a bit taller than the last ones.* She'd hitch skirt far higher than necessary, well above the knee, then hold. Once Leon had worked out the charge (thighs are an enemy of mental arithmetic), she'd readily agree and ask for help in getting them off – the boots, that is. A typical approach for Nice Tits (like there's any other kind) could be: *I think I*

157

might have a dodgy link in my necklace. Would you mind having a look for me? Aw thanks, Hun. And she'd lean in to present cleavage in unmissable widescreen 3D. Once Leon had recovered and come up with the repair cost (how easily these things can be forgotten) and agreed to fix it while she waited, she'd probably add: *Actually, the catch is a bit tricky, too. Could you do the honours?* Then she'd sweep the hair from her neck and wait. (Waiting, holding; are important moments in female mating-rituals – it puts the ball in the guy's court, compels him to join the dance.)

Yes, Seema had seen every approach in the book.

Some: the bold, the self-assured, the vain, the deluded, the desperate, or ones on a dare; the horny, the aggressive, the assertive, or those seeking an affair, would sidle/breeze/march over to the counter, and often with minimal or zero preamble – and no hint of a purchase – just ask him out, blatant and outright. Before Leon could recover from the shock, Reg would step in and escort the would-be suitors outside. He entertained no shenanigans during work hours, did Reg. Not unless they were putting money in the till. Big spenders would be given plenty of leeway but 'time-wasters' (those who Reg believed had no intention of spending anything) would get the bum's rush.

'Takes his lunch at one,' he would advise, and they'd be politely evicted with a 'Now, if you'll excuse us we need to close for a while to run some machine checks.' Their arse would get the door and the door the CLOSED sign until they'd cleared off. They might not appreciate the abrupt expulsion but if they weren't splashing the cash then Reg didn't care. He felt no remorse. Not even that time when Seema had rushed over to comfort one girl who'd burst into tears whilst being ushered by the elbow to the door:

She'd acknowledged, rather hysterically, that she hadn't intended to buy anything, only had a couple of pounds to her name, just wanted to give Leon a sketch she'd done, but that didn't wash with Reg; he'd showed no compassion.

Mind you, he beat a hasty retreat when her mother burst in to see what had so upset her eight-year-old. Calming the waters was left to Seema: she ignored whispered suggestions of '*Suspected shoplifter*' from Reg, hiding in the stock room, and after apologising profusely went with 'It's out of our hands, you see. We're part of a chain and the company's policy is for every branch to employ, wherever possible' – she'd leaned in as if sharing a confidence – 'a *Care-in-the-Community*.' Glancing back she added, 'We'll talk to his carer; see if extra medication might be in order.'

'Ah,' the woman said raising her head. 'I thought last time I was in he looked a bit *simple*, like. He did a lovely job of resoling our Terry's boots, though.'

She smiled benevolently, empathy for the shit-out-of-luck staff, conscious of the simpleton ensconced within the shadows of the stock room then turned to her daughter's no longer snivelling but plainly still-jittery face. 'Okay, Jaz, that's enough. How about we get you an ice cream?'

Little Jasmine clapped her hands and headed for the exit alongside mother. 'Did your dad give you your pocket money this morning?' mother asked. The child nodded happily. 'Good, you can buy me one as well, then.' But Jasmine had hardly stepped outside before she was running back through the shop and over to the counter.

Here, she offered up her art to Leon: a felt-tip drawing featuring some kind of weird multi-coloured long-necked thick-tailed creature with two stick figures on its back.

Leon exchanged a child-friendly grin for the drawing.

'Is that you?' he enquired.

Jasmine nodded. 'The pony's called Lucky.'

A pony! Mystery solved. 'Very nice.' Leon pointed to the taller stick figure. 'And is that me?'

Jasmine pulled a face, something between a frown and a scowl. '*No* – my dad,' she said. 'Get over yourself.'

Little girls can be puzzling. Little wonder, Leon thought, that so many become *impossible*-to-understand as adults.

'Come on, Jaz, we haven't got all bleedin' day,' barked Mother through the doorway.

Jasmine skipped outside and the pair disappeared into the afternoon.

Only then did Reg emerge from the stock room. He went back to his cobbling without a word. As if nothing had happened.

That must have been five years ago.

As Seema unpacked a bag of recently-delivered dry cleaning, she looked over; saw Reg had one eye on gluing a new sole onto an old shoe he was repairing, *and one on Leon* – as if he expected 'his junior' (a reference Reg used often) to make a mistake at any moment and spoil several pence worth of key blank. Like Leon hadn't successfully cut tens of thousands of keys in the past.

Despite feeling it morally within her rights to do so; as Reg hadn't yet furrowed brow, set jaw or tightened eyes (as per the checklist), Seema prudently resisted the urge to 'accidentally' sock-ball her boss's noggin with the not-yet-cleaned 'ammunition' before her. (Today was Friday, the day Mr Hawthorne's annoyingly-perky PA always dropped off her boss's shirts, ties, and a week's worth of oh-so-tempting highly-throwable-when-balled Cashmere socks.)

By the way, it wasn't just females who approached Leon in the shop with motives unrelated to shopping for goods or services as advertised. There were occasional guys, too.

Seema remembered one in particular: a German called Klaus; bold as brass, six-foot, a plethora of piercings and face tattoos; moved from Berlin, he said; recently started working at the tattoo parlour over the road; made numerous cool yet pushy offers of free piercings and complimentary tattoos. *Be nice, say Ja. Is it every day you are offered something for free?* (His accent made it sound like *some-zing.*) *It vill make you look super modern and exciting. Kommen sie bitte, you vill sank me later, I sink.*

Leon had courteously turned them all down and for once didn't mind when Reg finally stepped in (his boss had taken his time with this one; perhaps secretly enjoying Leon's slightly awkward predicament) but Leon certainly *had* minded when he heard, from the door: *Ja, ja, I vill* after Reg had shared: *He finishes at five thirty, why don't you come back, then.* (*Bloody Germans*, Reg had muttered as he closed the door.)

But back to females, for the significant majority of suitors over the years *were* females:

(And please remember we're not talking monumental numbers or swarming hordes here, we wouldn't want you thinking Leon was Johnny Depp or that bloke from

Twilight. Approaches didn't happen every day, not even every month. Maybe once every six to eight weeks on average. Still, pretty good though, right? Even if Leon, bless him, couldn't comprehend why.)

Seema totally understood why, and could never fathom Leon's eternal surprise at being asked out. Yes, he was a bit kooky and kookier now than he used to be, but what was wrong with *kooky*? Wasn't *she* a bit kooky, too? And who wouldn't be a bit kooky after an accident like the one Leon had suffered. Bottom line: he was a nice guy and he deserved some happiness. Like she'd found with Ravi. It would, she thought, be so nice. She doubted that anyone wanted it more: for Leon to find *his* soul-mate.

But where *she* saw a kind-hearted young guy with features aligned in delightful symmetry, chiselled cheekbones, great skin, nice eyes, gentle-natured and wacky sense of humour; *he* saw an awkward, troubled, unexceptional-looking misplaced nerd – someone unsure of his rightful place in the world, who used comedy as a way to get through a succession of sometimes dark, occasionally wonderful, often puzzling days. Still a boy in many ways, adrift and regularly disoriented, unable to put a handle on *what exactly* was troubling him.

Leon was happy being Leon most of the time, but he felt frustrated and wished he could see a more certain future. *What was* he doing? Other people seemed to have plans. *They* didn't get confused and distracted on a regular basis. Or did they? Maybe they did. That, too, was confusing. And he *hated* his scars; both of them. The one on the side of his head that appeared as a bald line, 8cm in length (visible if he wore his hair short; which he no longer did), and the one on his forehead, shaped like a crescent moon. Half the length of the other, it stood out, Leon believed, like The Joker's smile, in miniature, taunting him. Sometimes he would stare at it in the mirror, willing it to disappear. He'd stare so hard his facial features would morph, his phizog taking on the trippy appearance of a ghostly evil murderer floating before him, like a shady Dickensian villain.

Seema no longer saw the smiling scar, not unless she got close and really looked for it. She saw him touch it sometimes, though – subconsciously. He was doing it now, in fact, as he blew metallic dust from Red Rum's final key.

No, Seema didn't miss much at all.

She saw the indirect probing: *Oh they feel much better. Thanks for doing them so quickly. I was hoping I'd be able to wear them on the girls' night out tomorrow and now I can. How do they look? I have a thing for glittery stilettos. Does your girlfriend wear heels as tall as these?*

The hopeful long-shot fishing expedition: *Yeah, I'm looking for a new flat-mate; that's why the extra key. Castlefield, very nice, all mod cons, balcony overlooking the wharf café . . . know anyone who might be interested?*

The dragged out departure: *Okay, then, don't forget, our special offer on Frappaccinos runs out on Friday, the Starbucks round the corner, not the other one, well they have it, too, but we are, you know, nearer, so, right, maybe see you in there, then, if you'd like, okay, bye.*

And the dubious return visit: *You're right. That is the second key I've lost this week. Poor me, right? Never mind, maybe my luck will change with this one?*

To Seema, like every other woman, it was all so blatant. If only Leon could see the things *she* saw, the big lovable dope. And a thought occurred to her as she sprayed the armpits of Mr Hawthorne's fancy shirts with stain-remover and Leon handed over a batch of successfully cut keys to the grinning Shergar. The thought was this: *I wonder if I should ask Mowgli if anything ever happened between him and that quirky white girl; the one with the tiny tits.*

SVETLANA

Leon produced his wallet, and thinking this would be a good opportunity to be rid of some small change, unzipped the heavy, swollen coin section.

Svetlana arose from behind the counter, black plunge-neck top brimming with bosomy flesh. Standing over a foot taller than Nobby, she lingered for a moment – one finger needlessly poking up through the located DVD – all pouty, as if posing for a glamour shot. The newsagent's stare stood sentry, a warning to wandering eyes. Not that the Guardian of the Globes would actually do anything, other than be vexed, should he spot someone sneaking a look.

Svetlana slowly extracted her long-nailed finger from the disc, placed the disc on top of its case. 'I think you make good choice,' she glanced at Leon's rental card, '*Leon.*'

'Thanks,' replied Leon, already clacking silver onto the counter.

Leaning over, Svetlana placed elbows around Leon's initial outlay and propped her beauteous face on her palms.

'I like good Thriller,' she said. The Ruskie was husky.

'It's not really a Thriller,' said Leon, trying to stay focused on the count as Svetlana's voluptuous valley hovered forward, pulling his coins into shade.

'You like I should put in for you?' she asked.

Leon copped her large wolf-grey eyes.

'Sorry, what?' he spluttered.

Svetlana pointed a fingernail at the DVD.

Abandoning words, Leon nodded.

But Svetlana didn't move; she held position, waited, breasts imposing. By the way, Nobby's face was warming nicely now. Bubble gum pink.

Obliged to complete payment (tis the law) Leon carefully pushed a collection of copper pieces under the hypnotic overhang. *Easy,* he told himself as the back of his hand came within a whisper of the Russian's swollen symmetry.

If Nobby had been a *cartoon* newsagent, steam would presently be rising from his collar. He twitched and angled, umpiring for contact as Svetlana held firm.

Finally, coin gently kissed coin. Leon let out a small sigh then almost fell over the counter as Svetlana reversed her mesmerising mammaries. (You'd swear those things have the gravitational pull of large twin moons!)

Leon made a show of checking around his feet as if something there had disturbed his balance.

The Russian, her form back in the upright position, now popped open the DVD case. 'I like when it pops,' she said, firmly splaying the covers. 'Do you like when it pops?'

Nobby's toad-like head wobbled for a moment, stewing, reddening, but he said nothing to his Siberian spouse: a ridiculously attractive female, two or more decades his junior and innumerable leagues above amphibious-newsagent level.

The amphibious-newsagent wanted to say what his body-language was already squealing: *Put some clothes on, you Russian hussy. I know* exactly *what you're doing!* but he was lucky to have Svetlana around, blessed to be allowed to even gaze upon her east-European beauty – and he knew it. Knew it and didn't want to blow it. He couldn't camouflage the disapproval on his face, no more than he could hide his stiffening exasperation, but he could – *would* – bite his tongue.

'I said: *You like when it pops?*' repeated Svetlana.

'Popping, sure,' mumbled Leon, knuckling down to the job in hand; shipping cash requires concentration – so many coins and still a way to go. 'Hope I've got enough.'

Svetlana pressed the DVD home. The retaining stud issued a gratifying click. 'Oh, I'm sure you have *more* than enough,' she purred, ignoring the frog-like eyes now blow-torching her profile. (Nobby's skin tone, scorched by subtext, had elevated to chafed cerise.) The Russian beauty had learned that no matter how much she flirted with male customers (only the younger, taller, better-looking ones, you understand – so, most), Hubby would huff and puff but he'd say nothing. Not to her. Instead, he would aim his pique across the counter. And he did so now:

'Not often you see a boy with a purse,' hissed Nobby. 'Not unless he's . . . you know.'

'It's not a purse, it's a wallet. It just happens to have a coin section.' Leon had heard the 'purse' jibe before.

'*Looks* like a purse,' said the one that looked like a toad.

'Well, it's not,' Leon asserted, underscoring the now considerable brass mélange with a line of pennies.

Nobby scrutinised the item in question.

'Bit *girly*, though, isn't it?' The newsagent's tone was smug and superior; he sensed he'd gained the upper hand.

'I think is cute,' said the Siberian stunner, simultaneously unwrapping a Chupa-Chups lolly and undermining Nobby's advantage.

The balked newsagent visited his displeasure on two ten-year-olds by the magazine racks:

'Remember, it's not a library,' he barked.

As the kids ambled off, behind an aisle, muttering to each other, the Chupa-Chups wrapper, screwed and tossed, bounced off the till.

'Svetlana, *please*,' Nobby grumbled, 'there is a bin under there.'

Svetlana wrenched the lolly from her mouth. 'So put in bin if you know where bin is. Why bother me with this?'

A stream of Russian issued forth and it didn't sound like flattery.

The newsagent's head took on the appearance of a bubbling, boiling vegetable; something hot and purple.

'So how's that *friend* of yours?' he asked, cramming so much tone and implication into 'friend' that he was able to forgo air quotes.

Leon put coin counting on pause.

'If you mean, *Moss*—he's . . .'

Nobby licked his chops, tasting victory. '*He's?* . . .'

'He's . . .' Lacking a witty reply and losing a war of words with a watery newsvendor? What was going on! Leon *always* had a retort. Okay, not always, but most of the time; usually – quite often, anyway. And why was he even bothered? Perhaps indignation was contagious. Undeniably irked, Leon stared into the still crammed coin section of his wallet. This was taking forever.

'Actually, I don't think I *have* got enough change.'

Nobby sneered. 'Maybe you need a bigger purse.'

Elbowing Svetlana, he laughed like a peacock. A fucking peacock! '*Skwaahahahahahaha* . . .' He squawked on and on and on; relentless and infuriating.

Leon had heard this laugh before. Thought it the most annoying he'd ever heard. Found it grating. Especially now it was aimed at him. Svetlana smiled sympathetically. Leon had taken on the look of a gored matador.

'Don't listen to him. He is just jealous because I take charge of all our monies; shop, savings – everything.'

'Yes, well, at least *I* don't have *a purse. Skwaaahahahaha!*'

But it wasn't a fucking *purse*, it was a fucking *wallet* – and Leon could *fucking* prove it. He picked up all the fucking shrapnel, shoved it back in (this took a great deal of effort and a frustrating amount of time) then – under the relentless scrutiny of Nobby and Svetlana – made a start on what would clearly be an extremely tricky re-zip (this was obviously going to take even more effort and an embarrassingly ridiculous amount of time).

Svetlana returned her flawless tits to the counter.

'Don't worry,' she said. 'Take your time.'

She's right. Take your time. Do not get flustered. Jesus, this bastard zip! I should have just carried on paying with change; probably did *have enough. Why did I stop? Too late now. Keep going. Look at that smug bastard . . . he's* loving *this. Wonder if he's related to Reg? Not often I really despise somebody, but this guy. Have a long obvious stare at Svetlana's cleavage, that'll really piss him off. Piss him right off and he won't even say anything. Now that would be a result. Okay, I'm going to do it. Oh wow! They really are amazing . . . beautiful . . . such heavenly curves . . .*

Nobby's breathing grew louder, faster.

Bit longer. Stick it to the pompous newsagent bastard. Hold, hold. Really piss him off. Christ, it's hot in here.

'Warm in here today, yes?' tittered Svetlana. 'Here, I cool you down,' she said, blowing gently into Leon's face. Her sumptuous breasts rose and fell with each cooling breeze, her breath smelled of strawberries and cream.

'Aha!' blurted Leon. The zip had finally been forced across, back into the closed position. He now pulled apart the noisy Velcro-fastening, unfolded the obviously-a-wallet wallet then exposed the lightly-stocked but definitely 'manly' banknote section. *Do you see, you ugly-fucker tobacconist?* A macho note was whipped out and with a heroic grin offered to the pot-bellied toad.

'A twenty,' Leon announced.

Ka-ching! The bull was dead. The toad squashed. The peacock—

'Actually, it's a tenner,' said Nobby, snatching the note, 'but it'll do.'

Bollocks, the bull had scored another hit – both horns.

'Sorry, thought it was a twenty.' *Shit; had to apologise, I guess.* Oh well, the peacock might not be dead but at least it

166

had stopped cackling. Leon saw that, at least, as a triumph. He eyeballed Svetlana. 'I wasn't trying to, y' know.'

Svetlana patted the back of Leon's hand, sucked noisily on the Chupa-Chups. 'Don't worry, Leon,' she trailed the pink lolly over a glistening tongue, 'everybody make mistake.' Her lustrous grey eyes flicked out towards Nobby.

Jabbing till buttons, the nettled newsagent admonished the frisky Russian: 'Those do need to be paid for, by the way.' The drawer pinged open.

Svetlana jerked upright, stared down at Nobby.

'So put in till,' she said between slurps.

The tenner was tilled with a twang and a fistful of coins noisily scraped out and crashed firmly onto the counter.

Leon, admiring a wonderful display of side-boob, jumped slightly. Svetlana didn't flinch.

'Hey, what are you pair up to?' bleated Nobby, squinting (vanity precluded the wearing of glasses in front of Svetlana). He'd been distracted by suspicious activity near the sandwich cooler. One kid almost choked as the other grunted something akin to 'Piss off' through what might well have been a mouthful of bread-based comestibles.

Nobby danced with irritation but hesitated to leave the counter, torn between possible pilfering and potential hanky-panky.

'What are you waiting for?' asked Svetlana.

But still, Nobby dithered. 'Go, check!' she told him.

When Nobby finally left his post, aimed to tackle the Artful Dodgers, Svetlana returned to leaning over the counter, and Leon scooped his additional coins from under her rack (you can't just abandon your change). The seductive Siberian was all sucks and smiles.

Upon exiting, Leon glanced back.

The newsagent had cornered a pair of what appeared to be gibbering hamster-cheeked monkey-gargoyles. Waving an empty sandwich carton (Salmon and Cucumber) under the noses of the obstinate detainees, he spoke of devious little bastards and calling the police.

Leon's eye was drawn to the counter.

Svetlana made a phone of her hand and mouthed the adventure labelled: 'Call me'.

CHAPTER ELEVEN

Sense of Doubt

BANJO LESSONS

After only thirty minutes of jiggery-pokery nestled between a securely-chained bubblegum machine and a Cat In The Hat kiddy-ride, Leon had finally managed to cram his latest coin burden into the already bulging purse section (sorry, change compartment) of his wallet. Then, he'd tugged and jerked the zipper, wrenched and twisted for closure, yanked and strained until his thumb went numb. He'd made good progress, though; the zip was now almost halfway across.

Pressing on, questions were deliberated: Was it possible the toad-like newsagent secretly enjoyed his hot wife's flirty behaviour; found her waywardness disturbingly sexy – covertly arousing – a kinky, perverse thrill? Leon thought it a definite maybe; knew all too well the idiosyncrasies of the perverted – had witnessed them at close quarters. Yes, he'd just been admiring Svetlana's shapely attributes, but his interest was less *carnal*, more *aesthetic* appreciation. There was a difference. That's what he told himself, anyway.

Richard on the other hand; well, his sleazy depravities and furtive routines were notorious. At least, they *were* to Leon. He doubted neighbours realised the true extent of—

'Halle-bleedin-lujah!' exclaimed Leon. The zip was shut – *finally*; his wallet packed tighter than the back of a certain Siberian's stretchy, hot-pink spandex shorts (yes, there's no point denying it; he'd snatched an 'appreciative' glance there, too – when she'd bent for a Chupa-Chups).

After flexing some life back into his stiff fingers, he patted the coin section, hoping to bestow the gift of continued non-rupture. But why shouldn't it hold? The zip was good; *manly* – as manly, as Svetlana was womanly.

Just then: a ping and clatter of newsagent door. The tykes burst forth, snapped a sharp left and legged it, Nobby trailing in lukewarm pursuit.

Look at the state, Leon thought. Poor sap hasn't a chance. But wait, what's this? The newsagent ripped off his shirt, leapfrogged high into the air, eyes blinking, and landed and jumped, landed and jumped, flicking and re-flicking sticky tongue, long as a car, towards the runaways.

All to no avail, though; middle-aged frog-leaps are no match for spring-chicken limbs. Nobby was losing ground, wheezing on each bounce like a broken accordion and leaving a trail of gooey puddles in his wake. The only thing keeping pace was a nebulous ball of midges over his sweaty head. But there was hope: having sprinted 100 metres in less time than it takes to win gold, the tykes now stopped.

Tyke #1 flashed inside jacket pockets bristling with cider cans. Tyke #2 waved handfuls of chocolate bars and adult magazines. Both ridiculed and taunted the toady newsvendor as he laboured closer on shortening, exhausted hops. Sarcastic tyke applause rang out. One big vault, though, would be enough. Nobby hunkered down for a last-ditch all-effort bound. The tykes nodded to each other. 'Got you now,' croaked Nobby, leaping. Pump-action shotguns ratcheted; level–aim–*Bang!* The tykes cheered as the newsagent exploded in a green-and-yellow splat of slimy—

'So, you are still here,' said Svetlana from the doorway, smoking a cigarette.

'Yes, still here. I was just . . . uh . . .' Leon indicated the window, 'reading the cards.'

Svetlana craned her neck, scanned the handful of For Sale- and Wanted Ads. 'And this take you thirty minute?'

'Half an hour? *Really?*' Leon forced the turgid wallet into a front pocket; a pocket not really designed for accommodating something that combined the size of a fat orange with the weight of an iron bowling ball. He steadied his frame on the sweet-dispenser as the Earth and wallet pulled on their respective masses. 'Well, you know how it is. By the time you've packed away your change, bought–' Leon visually confirmed the sweet machine's true nature '–bubblegum, and had a ride on the Cat In The Hat.'

The Russian sized up the kiddy-ride. 'You fit in there?'

'It's not as difficult as it looks. The Postman Pat van that used to be here – now *that* was tricky.'

Svetlana laughed. 'You make joke, I think.' The cigarette revisited her mouth, the end burned brightly for a moment.

'Know what else I am thinking?' Smoke jetted from her puckered lips. 'I am thinking you don't want to leave.'

'Actually, I was thinking the opposite.'

'Explain, please – this "opposite".'

Leon thought for a moment then said: 'Okay, I don't really know why I'm telling you this but here goes . . . I was wondering if it might be time to fly the nest. Go. Maybe leave Manchester. Find a flat somewhere nice. What do you think? Is twenty-four too old to be living at home?'

'If you want to go, just go.'

'But then I think: Can I really just leave? Mum's not well. Dad's not getting any younger. And then there are my friends. Well, *friend*. We've always lived on the same street. How would he manage without me to keep an eye on him?'

'I had flat. In Norilsk. Is northernmost city in Siberia. Do you know? Is so cold. Like freezer. Arctic wind, *very* strong. Ice. And always snow. Snow *on top* of snow. Snow blizzards. Snow storms. Snow drifts. And in winter is worse. Some years, people must eat each other to survive.'

'But apart from that it's okay, is it?'

'No, we have *big* pollution. From ore-smelting factories and open mines. Everywhere factories. No trees. Only *dead* trees. Smog. Acid rain.' Discharging a grey plume she added: 'Still, is nicer than here. Manchester is shit-hole. I should not have left Norilsk. There are easier ways to make money, I think, than marry wealthy newsagent.'

'*Wealthy?* Are you sure?'

'In Norilsk, believe me, I could make good living by—'

The Russian's trip down memory lane stalled as Nobby returned, huffing and puffing. He addressed Leon: 'I can't believe . . . they got away . . . I was holding them . . . until the police . . . arrived.' He turned to the Russian: 'How long,' he wheezed, 'did they say . . . they'd be?'

Pink lips and grey eyes narrowed in tandem as Svetlana took another long, slow drag.

Nobby grew impatient. 'Svet—'

'I forget to phone, okay!' Svetlana blew a resentful cloud. 'But you went . . . into the back.'

'I know, but then I forget!'

'Dearest,' Nobby leaned on Svetlana, 'we have . . . to report these things.'

Her face went off like a princess opening a Glastonbury Portaloo door. 'So stop breathing on me and go call.'

Nobby eyed Svetlana. Leon eyed Nobby.

Nobby eyed Leon. Leon eyed the cards.

Svetlana eyed Nobby eyeing Leon eyeing the cards. 'You want they should leave area?' She widened her wolfish eyes. 'You want all kids should know everything in shop is free? Don't pay; he won't phone police.' To Leon she said: 'He wants to make poor helpless woman do man's job.'

Leon didn't feel the Russian was the type to pretend to cry, though he suspected females did that sometimes.

'Maybe Nana Varushka was right. I *should* go back.'

'No, no, *I'll* do it,' said Nobby, caving. 'I'll do it now.'

Svetlana backed against the door frame, tightening lest there be contact as Nobby squeezed by muttering about Nana Varushka and the price of salmon sandwiches.

The Russian, all smiles again, stepped over to Leon, nodded to the Ads. 'So, you don't find what you look for?'

'Oh, I wasn't really looking for anything. I just like to read them. I think they're funny.'

'Funny? What do you mean, *funny*?'

'Well, this one for starters. "Banjo lessons." I mean, come on . . . *Really? Banjo lessons?* Round here?'

'Banjo very popular at home. Banjo and throat-singing.'

'You don't think it might be like the old "*Large chest* for sale" or "*French polishing* available"?

'So "large chest" is not "large chest" – is . . .' Svetlana stuck out her chest. Not that she needed to.

Leon's raised eyebrows said: *I think you've got the idea.*

'And "French polishing" – that is . . .' A mime ensued.

'Could be.'

'I had no idea.'

'They're easily overlooked. The secret is to know what you're looking for.'

Svetlana settled in beside Leon. 'Show me, please.'

'Well, you don't have a large chest – I mean, on your cards. Or French polishing. They were just examples.'

'What about this one? *Shed for sale?*'

'Might just be a shed for sale.'

'Okay . . . *Large bike – hardly ridden?*'

'Possible, but unlikely.'

'*Hedge trimmer?*'

Leon shook his head. 'Look for subtle hints. *Retired Head Mistress offers private tuition; Water Sports DVDs For Sale; Ex Female jockey seeks new position* – that kind of thing. *Busty blonde will do anything for a tenner.*'

'Here!' Svetlana whooped with tickled-pink realisation. 'See? *Extensions R Us. Let us handle all your erection needs. Satisfaction guaranteed. And we clean up mess afterwards!*' There came such a burst of musical hilarity she had to steady herself on Leon's arm. 'Sound like *good* builder. But is *not* builder. *Is prostitute!*' Svetlana let out a volley of raucous laughter. She was getting loud. (Leon looked around. Not many people about but the nearest were now tuning in.) 'Nobby is their pimp-daddy, I think!'

'Like I said, they can be hard to spot. And it's not really a newsagent's job to—'

'Is very funny. But don't tell Nobby. We keep *our* secret.'

'Not a problem.'

Svetlana lit a fresh cigarette. 'So, what would you say to whore? If she came to you – offer blow-job and sexy time?'

'What would I say?'

'Yes. If I was prostitute . . . which I do not say I was . . . and I offered to . . .'

The sight of Svetlana expertly fellating her cigarette as if it were a small trombone silenced Leon for a moment.

'And I ask forty pounds for this. What would you say?'

Leon slipped into his Alan Partridge impression, a coping mechanism for answering awkward questions: 'Ooh, I'd probably say: Thank you for your generous offer, street-walking lady of the night—'

'No, you wouldn't. What you really say?'

Partridge again: 'I'd say, now listen to me you dirty whore—Hello.'

A big Turk had appeared: Hakan Memhet, owner of Big Chicken Fast Food; handsome, despite an overly-bushy tash; swarthy tan, slicked hair, vest, tight jeans – dull as

172

goat shit. The smell of burger, kebab and fried chicken had accompanied him across the precinct. 'Who is dirty whore?'

'Nobody.' Leon took an involuntary half-step back. 'We were just—'

'We were talking about when Leon visit whore.'

'*Hypothetically*,' Leon wanted to clarify. 'I haven't—'

'No, no, no, my Siberian Tiger, what have I told you about smoking?' The Turk took possession of Svetlana's cigarette, trod it out (army boots, black, laced, size 14).

What happened next was a blur. Leon recalled the Turk leaning on the Kiddy-ride, shoving his body in front of Svetlana, stealing her attention; clumsy innuendo about Oil-Wrestling (Turkey's national sport, apparently); her giggling like an enthusiastic groupie, him preening tash or running a hand over unctuous hair. And then they were gone; Hakan somehow mystically spiriting Svetlana away.

Leon watched the big Turk chaperon the Russian doll across the concrete plain, her laughter echoing around the inner faces of the precinct.

CONNIE

'Don't you hate it when men gate-crash your conversations with females?' asked a voice from behind.

'Yes,' said Leon, without looking back.

'You're allowed to enjoy their company, right?'

'Right.'

'The harmless flirting laced with humorous exchanges.'

'Exactly.'

'It's not like you want to smash her back doors in.'

'Of course not; she's a married woman.'

'I don't think she's bothered about that. But still, you could never do what that oily Turk is doing.'

Inside Big Chicken Fast Food, Hakan stood tightly behind Svetlana, guiding her hands, as together they sliced doner meat from a rotating spit.

'Half-witted men are not affected by beauty.'

'Not in the same way,' agreed Leon.

'*They* continue to function,' said the voice. '*They* can actually chat up an attractive female.'

173

Leon nodded, forlornly. 'I know.'

'Whisk her off.'

'Is that a euphemism?'

'Certainly not.'

'Okay.'

'I tell it like it is. I have no need of euphemisms.'

Leon turned now; saw an old woman wearing a Salvation Army uniform. She had a whiskery chin, deep-set eyes, face like a trodden-upon snail, and smelled of soup and ammonia. 'Sorry, didn't catch the—'

'Connie.'

'Leon.'

'No, it's definitely Connie.'

'No, I mean, my name, is Leon.'

'Yes, it's easy for you *now*, isn't it?'

'Sorry?'

'Because you're not interested in old women.'

'My Grandma's an old woman.'

'Yes, but you're not interested in her sexually.' Connie raised an eyebrow. 'Or are you?'

'Not really, no.'

'Not so easy on the eye, are we? Not full of delicious curves and youthful giggles. We don't make you feel all electric. But if I was younger, and not a fugly-munger[4] . . .'

'You're not—' Leon was going to say 'that old' or 'a fugly-munger' but she really was so he left it at 'You're not'.

'Don't patronise me, limp-dick. The point is, if I was outrageously beautiful, and your age, you probably wouldn't tell me your name because you'd have probably forgotten it. That's if you'd even talked to me in the first place. How long does it normally take you: about four weeks; five or six separate meetings?'

'You're very astute, Connie.'

'And you're a fuckwit.'

'I was just thinking about how—wait—what?'

---

[4] Fugly-Munger: Noun. British informal, well fucking uncomplimentary. A seriously unattractive person, especially a woman. An abbreviation of 'fucking ugly' followed by a combination of Minger and Munter. Jesus.

'You were wondering about Beauty; how it can stupefy intelligent, sensitive males – make them appear, ironically, stupid and pathetic.'

'Thanks, but yes.'

'Yet allow ignorant meat-heads to wade in, unaffected, with their hollow low-brow compliments, simple breezy jocularity, well-greased attentiveness, self-serving phoney kindnesses; and, despite this counterfeit conniving, get the girl.'

'Exactly!'

'Fucked if I know.' Connie discharged a long, slow, involuntary fart (at least, Leon assumed it wasn't planned).

'Ohhh-kay.' Leon wondered if Connie and Richard could be related. Maybe Richard wasn't a Blank at all. Perhaps he'd been adopted. That would explain a lot.

'But I do have a theory.'

'Go on.'

'*All* men are fuckwits. They either *are* fuckwits. Or they *act* like fuckwits. And we are what we do.'

'I thought it was *we are what we eat*,' joked Leon.

'See; acting like a fuckwit.'

'Sorry.'

'No, it's not *your* fault; it's *God's* fault – because He's a fuckwit, too.'

Leon frowned, eyed the uniform.

'Don't let this fool you. Charity shops sell all kinds of stuff.'

'Right . . . so Men are fuckwits. I'm a fuckwit. And God's a fuckwit.'

'That's what I was saying. Want to hear the rest?'

'Yes, please.' *You mad old bat.*

'I am convinced there are *many* gods. Not just ours.' Connie hitched up her drawers as if they might be falling down. 'Some have been around longer than others – are brighter, and, how shall I say – more *able*. I fear our God is callow and thick – the thickest. Yes, He created our universe. But it pales into insignificance when compared to the boundless multitude of universes beyond ours. Those created by the other gods. *His* was rather a puny affair as these things go. And the other gods were quick to ridicule

175

Him for being so stupid and inept. They laughed at such a pathetic attempt at creation; sneered at His weak, scrawny suns; pissed themselves at His rubbishy planets. So, God – *our* god – stamped His omnipresent feet, threw His divine dummy out the celestial pram, and decided *He'd show them*. Want to know how He got His own back?'

'Shouldn't you be on a couch somewhere?' asked Leon as Hakan lead Svetlana into Big Chicken's back room.

'He gave one of His planets, this one, a breathable atmosphere and weather and shit. And then He created Man, in His own likeness. The Earth would be a paradise he decided, but only for men like Him – the so-called "stupid" ones. Here, they would prosper and get the girls – who He now made. Here, they would receive the praise they deserved. Here, they would run lucrative fast-food joints and be blessed with big willies. Here, *smarty-pants creatures*, men like you, would be scorned and made a mockery of, as He Himself had been by the, uh, other gods I mentioned earlier. Are you following?'

'That would sort of make sense.'

'Praise the Lord!' rejoiced Connie, rattling a tambourine Leon hadn't noticed earlier.

'–If I wasn't an atheist.'

'It makes total sense, you Heathen. Remember when thicko Danny muscled in on Amy?' (Amy a soft-hearted girl Leon had once taken a major shine to. By the time he'd become accustomed to her strikingly-pretty face – enough to move beyond the odd witty comment and engage in meaningful conversation – Danny had indeed muscled in.)

'Ah yes,' Leon sighed, 'Amy.'

'Danny's got a *massive* cock, I hear.'

'I'm sure Amy isn't that shallow.'

'Which brings me neatly to my second theory: All women are sluts.'

'Whoa, Amy's not a slut.'

'Who's a slut?' enquired Nobby, appearing at the door.

'Nobody you'd know,' said Leon.

'I've got a nun's habit and a wimple back at the bungalow,' Connie whispered into Leon's ear. 'If you don't mind a few cat hairs . . .'

'Where's Svetlana? I thought she was with you.'

Following Leon's indication, the newsagent squinted across the concrete flatland.

'What's she doing in there?' Nobby wanted to know.

'Getting some mayonnaise in her kebab,' said Connie.

FROM ONE WINDOW TO ANOTHER:

After briefly scoping the busy interior of Kath's Kaff, DVD case held against his forehead to negate the reflection of the low autumn sun, Leon hurriedly navigated a way through a departing family, to their uncleared table not far from the window and took a seat overlooking the remains of four meals and accompanying drinks.

Jenny, the waitress, stood next to a table by the wall, her back towards Leon. From her demeanour, he assumed she was taking an order; he was focused on the tattoo, a red sunflower imprinted on the soft skin of her lower back (just above a marvellous bottom wrapped-securely in low-cut jeans). He only had time to admire the flower momentarily before it vanished as she turned.

Jenny spotted Leon straight away and headed over – in slow motion it seemed to him – the smile never wavering.

The name badge, clinging to the modest slope of her left breast, bobbled slightly as she walked; sending a warm, mechanical shudder straight to her admirer's nether-regions; instant semi – *shit, this boy needed to get laid!*

He tried to be respectful, focus on Jenny's face; not let his gaze be drawn by the undeniably eye-catching sight, knowing automatically that Richard, had he been here, would, without any doubt whatsoever, be making an uncomplimentary comparison between Jenny's gentle bobble and Kelly Buxton's full-on bounce.

Probably something like: *Bobbles are okay, but they really need to be bra-less if you want a full-on—*

'Well, hello there, Leon. Let me guess. Cup of tea, is it?'

Thankfully, Jenny's lyrical Irish tone easily drowned out Richard's lecherous telepathic transmission. Leon made a smiley-nod or noddy-smile, he wasn't sure which, but whichever it was, it got the message across.

'Now, how did I know that,' she said, scribbling onto her notepad. As thick and dark and rich and smooth as the body of a Guinness, her hair, tied into the usual pony-tail, was brushed from her shoulder as she tilted her head to check Leon's DVD, which he'd placed on the table.

'So what have you got this time? Not another one of those awful *Dirty Harry* type films, I hope.' ('Films' beautifully pronounced as 'Fillems'.)

'*King Kong*,' Leon said.

'Is that the one about the big hairy gorilla? No, I don't like the sound of that, at all.'

'Not at all, at all?' asked Leon in his best Irish brogue.

Jenny playfully slapped Leon upside his head.

'Now, what have I told you about that?'

Leon smiled back affectionately.

'*King Kong* indeed. Why can't you get something nice for a change?' she asked. '*Ghost*, or *Titanic* – or *Brief Encounter*. Or that lovely musical with Cliff whatshisface.'

'*Summer Holiday?*' spouted Leon, immediately wishing he hadn't sounded so repulsed.

'That's the one. Wow – I haven't seen that in ages. I remember it clear as day, though. They took a big old coach–'

'Double-decker bus.'

'–To America, I think it was.'

'Europe.'

'And they did all these really cheerful songs. Oh they were grand so.'

Grand wasn't the word Leon would have used.

'If it hadn't been for that daft Cliff Richard fella getting in the way all the time it would have been feckin' marvellous,' she added dryly.

Leon laughed; a woman after his own heart – a kindred spirit.

Then, with a degree of playful mockery, Jenny added: 'But *King Kong*, Leon? Dear oh dear. What on earth were you thinking?'

Leon beat his chest, growled low.

'Careful there, Leon, you might scare the other customers.'

He growled louder now, beat his chest a second time. Proper thumped it, as if he really *were* the giant ape from Skull Island.

'Leon, the customers . . .'

Some *were* looking. But Leon didn't bother; he chased his waitress, roaring like Kong, around the café. Joining in the game, Jenny made a pretending-to-be-scared face and play-screamed as she weaved between tables – waving her arms about in the air like a black-and-white-times B-Movie actress failing to outrun giant ants, or swampy lagoon monster – or, in this case, Kong.

Leon's performance wasn't just directed toward Jenny: he roared at fuddy-duddies eating chips; grunted at stiffs and squares drinking tea; thundered at party-poopers who were probably only pretending to choke; and, as he playfully chased the wailing waitress through their number, bellowed at well-behaved killjoys waiting at the counter. Customers of all ages eyeballed him as they would a crazy person, but he didn't care. *A bit of fun might liven some of these grouches up a bit.*

After Jenny had escaped to the safety of the kitchen, he returned – ignoring the gloomy faces – to his table and reminisced about the first time he had seen Jenny: the '*Jennysis*' as he now thought of it (the *Jenny Genesis* had instantly proved unwieldy).

JENNYSIS

The special moment happened less than a year ago; a couple of weeks after the accident. The perfect contrast, some might say . . .

A few details were *reasonably* distinct, despite much of the day being exceedingly hazy, but the Jenny part – that initial sighting – resonated clearer than a church bell; which was apt because the encounter happened on Church Street. Yes, that street again; it had headlined more than once in Blank family history and on this day it staged yet another significant event – this one up near the bus stop.

The reasonably distinct:

He, Leon, is extra smart today; wearing a jacket and tie for some reason, and looking out from behind a rain spattered car window. Stereo's off; no Mary on the dash; no football boots: the car isn't Betty – she's been scrapped, poor thing.

The hazy:

Is he in a taxi? Had he been for physiotherapy? Why would you dress smart for that? Could it be a hire car? Was he going for a job interview? And what's that: unseen hands? Yes – and heartfelt voices, quietly advocating fortitude.

The incontrovertible:

The weather is bad – that's easily brought to mind – grey and sombre, overcast and sunless, fraught with intermittent heavy showers. *Miserable* would be a suitable description. And he's not at the wheel – he's in the back, face 'resting' against the inside of the car window, nose squished, eyes droopy and tired – and no, he won't get out of the car; he just wants to go home.

The truly vivid:

Some women have a way of walking; like they really do move in slow motion; controlled and elegant. A refined deer spotted gliding past forest trees. Almost floating – proud, but not affected: beautiful; youthful; buoyant; nature in all its glory; organic; alluring; balletic; radiant and full of life. That's how Leon first sees Jenny: eyes widening to take her in; eyeballs fixing so as not to blink – so as not to miss a single second:

On the far side of the street, poised and graceful, Jenny carries herself like a catwalk supermodel. She sails down the hill, plain black coat and simple red bag (crooked over one arm) somehow made to look sophisticated and chic.

Leon is still taking in this amazing walk, when, without breaking step, her head turns, a penetratingly enlightened yet-slightly-coquettish smile upon her lips – *for him.*

Leon could recall the moment as if he were there; as if he had fallen through a rabbit-hole . . .

And, in remembering, in revisiting the scene, he sees her again – this woman whose name he does not yet know; whose life is, at this time, a complete mystery – in extremely sharp detail: the dark hair, the frock coat, the shoes, the walk, the smile. Transfixed, unable to move, *unable to think*, able only to witness, he watches her glide away, one slow, exquisite stride after another . . .

'Look at you,' Jenny interrupted, 'away with the fairies.'

The café looked just the same; still dreary, still full of losers, half-wits and untrustworthy philistines. Thank goodness for Jenny – a shining light amid the darkness – illuminating the place. The one face in here – of those still pointed his way – which he felt he could trust.

'Jenny,' he said, 'do you mind if I ask you something?'

'No, I'd like that, Leon. I'm waiting on your tea, anyway. What is it?'

Leon went for it quickly, before he could change his mind: 'I've been threatened by an evil clown. And now he's drafted in a half-witted brawler to beat me senseless.'

'Ah, you're not serious.'

'No, I am. Honestly. What should I do?'

'Well,' said Jenny. 'Not the question I was expecting.'

Reading her as a little uneasy rather than slightly disappointed, Leon added: 'I don't think they're real, though.' As if that somehow made it more agreeable.

'Well, why do you think they're not real? *Maybe they are.* Have you thought of that?'

'Jesus,' said Leon, giving the idea some serious thought. *What if they really are?*

'Hello,' said Poppy gently, trying hard not to startle this time. But her sudden appearance *did* startle and Leon jumped. And *his* sudden reaction surprised Poppy, and she, too, reacted with a jump.

'I'll give you two a minute,' said Jenny, slipping smoothly into reverse gear.

Once Poppy had calmed, she indicated the empty chair at Leon's table, asked if it would be okay.

Leon, not yet adjusted to Poppy's intrusion, hesitated, reluctant; this was meant to be his 'Jenny Time'.

Bollocks, think of something . . . something polite but discouraging, and think of something quick . . . come on, come on, think of something . . . anything . . . oh bollocks!

'Go ahead, make my day,' he said at last.

'Thanks, Clint.'

The unfortunate timing to one side, Leon was secretly pleased Poppy had got the film reference.

'Sorry, I thought you must have gone home,' he said.

'*Gone home?*' she echoed.

'When you weren't on the bench.'

'What bench?'

'You know: your aching feet . . . the Court shoes . . .'

Puzzlement tilted Poppy's face. 'Leon, that was Friday.'

'Yeah. *Today's—*'

'*Last* Friday.'

A lost, glazed smile took up residence on Leon's mug and showed no urge to move on.

Poppy discharged one of her snort-laughs.

'Oh, you big kidder; had me going there for a minute.'

As she pulled her chair in closer to the table, a bulldog-faced waitress with a large hairy wart, facial piercings, and bicep tattoos loomed large; imposed herself. The badge introduced Olive; the face declared, 'I hate my job so do not fuck with me.' The wart seemed to be saying: *If you think I look bad you should see the state of the growth on her—*

'Yeah?' Olive's manner was abrupt.

'Oh, uh, Skinny Cappuccino, please,' said Poppy, using a single finger to push back the previous occupant's still uncleared dirty plates. (Leon took the opportunity to covertly examine Poppy's shoes: high-platform/six-inch-heel, pointed-toe, purple faux-suede shoe boots – definitely *not* leopard-print Court shoes!)

'A what?' enquired the bulldog with a sniff.

'*Skinny Cappuccino.* It's a coffee.'

Olive switched eyes to Leon – who was now wondering if it was even possible: to detach for *seven days. A whole week!* Or was it that he just couldn't remember? Fuck, could *this* be a sign of early onset? Confirmation that he *was* now set on the same road his mother had taken: to the Dementia drive-through on Alzheimer's Avenue?

No, it wasn't possible, he told himself; he was *far too young* for that. He put it down to the working days being so similar; one often blurred into another. Yes, that was it; it's the repetition that fools you – catches you out. And so many other weird things had happened recently, why not that? He did vaguely recollect once thinking it was a Saturday only for it to turn out to be a Sunday. *But a whole week! Wouldn't that be a completely different ball game?*

Nah, not if it's a one-off, he decided. He resolved to make a note later in the log, only worry if it happened again, and with that the matter was put aside.

At arm's length, Poppy removed a long dark hair from the table but Olive's focus remained steadfast, and eventually, Leon realised she was waiting on him.

'Oh, I'm having tea,' he said, pointing in the general direction of the kitchen.

'One tea, one regular coffee,' Olive summarised curtly.

Poppy pointed to the plates and drying-out leftovers, but their waitress was already walking away.

'Friendly place,' said Poppy.

Leon made an *I concur* noise, his eyes shifting from Poppy to the kitchen, where he thought he'd caught a glimpse of Jenny through the serving hatch. But no, there was only Olive – Offhand Olive.

(He had heard, on more than one occasion, that Olive was a nymphomaniac but he wasn't one for listening to rumour and idle gossip – and looking at her now, index finger knuckle-deep in nostril, he couldn't believe it could be true; an uncouth shot putter, yes, a bed-hopping nymphet, surely not.)

'*Leon?*' said Poppy.

Leon caught the tone, knew it well: it was the tone of someone who hadn't received an answer the first time.

He gave her widened eyes: *What?*

'I said,' Poppy lowered her voice, 'wouldn't you prefer to go somewhere else?'

Leon shook his head. 'I like it here.'

Don't mention Jenny.

'Really?'

Leon nodded.

'Hmm, I suppose it does have a certain *Je ne sais quoi*,' said Poppy, unconvincingly, as she pulled out her notebook. 'So would you like to hear another poem, while we wait? I've written loads more since—'

'No,' Leon blurted.

'I mean . . . let's save some for next time.'

Damn, hadn't he said *next time* last time? And what did that get him? A two hour poemathon, that's what.

Mind you, some of them had been quite sexy . . .

Not as sexy as Jenny though.

'Again with the *next time*,' said Poppy, smiling. 'Still, I suppose it worked out okay last time, didn't it?'

As she waited in vain for a reply, she closed her notebook and set it on the table. Leon's focus, she noted, had again wandered to the kitchen.

How could he possibly like it here? He doesn't. But he won't admit to being in a place he doesn't really like. Right now, he's realising: this is embarrassing; the service here is humiliatingly slow and they don't clear the tables. But he can't go back on it now. And he's thinking, if only he'd suggested we go someplace else.

Or maybe, Poppy, he's planning where that other place might be for the 'next time'. Where he; might take me. Making manly decisions. Yes, that's it. And he's wondering how to phrase the big How To Ask Her Out question and still look cool; guys hate to appear too keen.

Perhaps he's a bit shy. Asking a girl out can be tricky. Shit, what if he's not shy; what if he's bored! Come on, Poppy, we're not losing this one. Sit up straight, suck that tummy in, undo another button (I will not, two's plenty) and think of something interesting to say . . .

'Have you ever written anything?' Poppy asked at last.

The inquiry got Leon's attention.

MEANWHILE, AT THE BUS STOP:

Moss seemed to spend half his life waiting for the Number 93. Maybe Janis was right – he *would* be better off getting a bike. He was working on the assumption that a second-hand one might not be too expensive when he heard the approach of aggressive Gangsta Rap.

A minute later, a black BMW sped past. As Moss's head turned, the air filled with the sound of screeching brakes and a smell of burning rubber.

Engine thrown into reverse, Danny and Carl backed up, heads banging to the oppressively loud beat.

'Alright?' enquired Moss with no hope of being heard.

Carl, passenger, nearest to Moss, raised a hand. Not a greeting, an indication to wait; they were hearing out the track.

Raised by a hippie mother, Moss was more used to the mellow sounds of Joplin or The Zombies. Gangsta Rap was very different: pounding and incessant – the reverberating bass made his teeth buzz. As the song went on (something about '*Brothas and suckers and crazy motherfuckers*'), Carl and Danny turned attention to Moss: to check he was fully appreciating the rap.

Moss nodded, hoped it would suffice ('*Sluts with butts and Niggaz with triggers—*'), thankful when the song suffered a sudden death. Having killed the volume, Danny looked past Carl, to Moss: 'Sweet, eh?'

Moss found himself nodding again, eyebrows up this time for emphasis.

'Got that stuff for you,' Danny said.

On cue, Carl raised a small bag of loose LSD tabs, gave it a little swing; it looked like he was bell-tinkling for Jeeves.

'Right,' said Moss, pausing to point up a potential problem: 'Sorry, man, I've only got my bus fare.'

Carl spat onto the pavement. 'Too bad.'

'It's okay, you can pay me later,' Danny adjudicated.

'*For real?*' griped Carl. He looked like someone had shat in his baseball cap.

'Yeah, why not? I know he's good for it. You're good for it, aren't you, Mossy?'

Moss considered the offer, hesitantly. Carl jiggled the baggie. Danny smiled and shrugged. 'No biggie,' he added.

'I dunno, Danny.' Moss rubbed his beard. 'You sure?'

'Yeah, yeah, it's cool, man. No sweat.'

Moss had decided; the walk to the car announced his decision. With each step, Carl's grubby claw drew back until the bag hung, swinging teasingly, above the gear-stick – if Moss wanted the tabs, he would have to reach in.

Moss – trusting, loving, hippie-hearted Moss – slid his arm inside. As an inevitable consequence of this action, his face came extremely close to Carl's — nose to snout, as it were. The car reeked of weed. Not that Moss could detect it above the whiff coming from his own dope-scented clothes.

As Moss's fingers gently gripped the plastic, what looked suspiciously like an illegal pit bull lurched for his arm, all teeth and snarls (the vicious brute had been sitting silently on the back seat the whole time).

Moss's panicked head retreated pronto taking the arm with it, but with no time to put legs in gear he ended up on his backside; the baggie, still pinched between thumb and forefinger, split, and several tabs fluttered to the ground.

Carl's rodent features contorted into an expression of cruel hilarity. 'Good boy, Butch, good boy,' he commended, slapping the devil dog's hefty, dense shoulder.

Butch's head hung out the window, slavering through fangs. The body of the dog, from Moss's point of vision, was missing. Tinted windows *are* dangerous. This proved it.

'And don't worry,' said Danny. 'I don't start adding interest on for a full seven days.'

Carl squeaked with ratty laughter, coughed then spat a huge green gob onto the pavement between Moss's feet.

'See you soon then, Bender,' Carl sneered.

Danny turned up the music, Carl blazed up a spliff, and the entourage sped away; all of them laughing — even Butch, it seemed. As the car squealed down the hill, a thick thread of drool trailed out from the dog's jabbering, windblown grin.

Moss, still on his backside, picked up tabs: little squares imprinted with Mad Hatters.

DID YOU EVER HAVE A DREAM?

Leon's notebook rested in Poppy's palm. 'Fancy us having the same notebook,' she said stroking the cover.

'Well, similar,' Leon replied.

As Poppy flicked through the pages, he wondered if she *really* had the same notebook; with hers covered by a hodgepodge of stickers it was hard to tell.

'What's this?' asked Poppy. '*Oddities Log.*'

'Not that—'

'*Pogo . . . Chicken-Man?*'

'No,' Leon described an arc with his index finger, 'further back.'

Poppy moved a few pages. 'This it?' she asked, looking up – *The Geisha and the Samurai?*'

'It doesn't matter, none of them are finished.

'*The canal was misty and quiet. A single barge drifted gently—*'

'Not out loud,' Leon prompted.

'Okay, no problem.' Poppy snorted gently.

Then she read on, silently.

Moss was also reading; he was rechecking the timetable – and there it was in black and white: every ten minutes at peak times, every twenty, non-peak (fuck all on a Sunday; well, a few, but that didn't matter right now). He had been waiting at least forty-five minutes. There should have been, at worst, *one* – no, *two!* – in that time.

Again the timetable was checked. It hadn't changed.

He looked up the road. No sign of a bus. After a lengthy internal debate he finally reached a conclusion: he would give up and do the unthinkable – *walk*. And so he did.

A bus turned up less than forty seconds later.

Moss scuttled back; the bus had stopped.

A passenger – an ageing punk with a green Mohawk, bondage trousers and ripped Nancy Spungen T-shirt – stepped off, the doors quickly hissing shut behind him.

Moss had less than ten metres to go. Arms outstretched he pleaded in vain to the smirking driver as the bus, windows full of faces, passed and escaped down the hill.

The punk, utilising the bus stop seat as a ledge upon which to tighten the criss-cross straps of his worn-leather boots, postured an expression that showed empathy, sympathy, and contempt for all things, in equal measure.

'Fuckin' shitters, the lot of 'em,' he slurred through the rash of spots and sores surrounding his thin-lipped sneer.

Before the bus had turned the corner at the bottom of the hill, the veteran punk crossed the road to a parked car, keyed the full offside length of its shiny black paintwork with one of the many spikes affixed to his studded PVC jacket, and nonchalantly ambled away as the car's futile alarm wailed and ululated in angry despair.

'That one's for you, mate!' he hollered over a buckled epaulette.

Incredulous, Moss watched as Sid Vicious senior shuffled up the road; back the way the bus had come. After half a minute he stopped, looked around, then squeezed through a ragged hole in the barbed-wire-topped fence that borders the rear of the abandoned Mayfield Station Arms public house (boarded-up since it was fire-bombed a couple of years ago) and disappeared.

Moss decided he needed a rest (well, he had just run a full twenty metres or so, uphill, without the aid of a relaxing spliff). He inspected his canvas-strapped analogue watch, went and triple checked the bus timetable, and then sat down with a sigh.

He pulled out the tabs and mulled them over.

Poppy turned a page, found it blank and flipped it back.

'It's not finished?'

'No.'

'Well, it's a fantastic opening,' she beamed. 'What happens next? I'm dying to know.'

'That makes two of us,' said Leon.

Poppy checked later pages for possible clues. Finding none, she put eyes back on Leon.

'Is it going to be a Romance novel?'

Leon noted how large and beautifully doll-like her eyes became when she asked the question. He wondered if she ever wore glasses. Those eyes, he thought, would look *really* sexy framed.

'*Leon?*'

'What?' Leon caught on. 'Oh, a *novel?* No. A short story.'

'That's a shame,' she said, closing the notebook. 'I love a big Romance. Long soppy sagas of girl meets boy . . .'

'It's not a shame,' replied Leon, perhaps a little too defensively. 'I *like* small books – big ones, too, but there's nothing wrong with a small one.'

Poppy grinned and Leon knew why.

'Well size isn't everything, Leon, but if you *can* manage a bigger one, I certainly would.'

'And it's not the dimensions of the pen; it's the quality of the writing.'

'We are still talking about books here, right?'

'Yep.'

'Good.'

The pair laughed then Leon said, 'Actually, I suppose I could extend it into a novella.'

'Hmm . . . I think you'd be better off either sticking with short stories or going for a full-length novel. Do people even read novellas anymore?'

'Course they do: "The Postman always Rings Twice"; "Breakfast at Tiffany's"; "Rita Hayworth and Shawshank Redemption" . . .'

'When were they written – the Thirties – the Fifties?'

'Not Shawshank; that was Eighties.'

'*Early* Eighties.'

'Yes, but—'

'Twenty-five years ago, Leon. That's what I mean. Today it's all Micro-Fiction and Flash Fiction. Yes, people still love novels – I'm sure they always will – but aren't *novellas* a thing of the past?'

'Definitely not.'

'Mind you, I do love "Breakfast at Tiffany's". Good film, too.'

'Well, at least there we agree.'

'So what?' said Poppy looking away dramatically.

'*So what?*' Leon parroted.

Poppy glanced back, giving her best Audrey Hepburn.

'Oh right,' said Leon, switching to as close to George Peppard as he could manage:

'So what? So plenty. I love you. You belong to me.'

'No. People don't belong to people.'

'Course they do.'

'I'm not going to let anyone put me in a cage.'

'I don't want to put you in a cage. I want to love you.'

Poppy didn't deliver the next line, just grinned, enjoying the moment. Leon smiled the stumped smile a simpleton might smile, laughed a slightly jittery laugh then set to stacking the dirty plates. He gathered drip-stained cups, glasses daubed with pudgy fingerprints, and herded the lot to one side, chastising himself for not doing it sooner.

A place for everything and everything in its right—

'So, is that what you'd like?' asked Poppy, raising a finely arched eyebrow.

'Sorry?'

As fun as coquettishness was, Poppy decided to let Leon off the hook – she indicated his DVD with her eyes:

'Someone to turn your story into a film?'

'Oh God, yes, that would be fantastic. I know I'm just dreaming, though.'

'It's good to have a dream,' asserted Poppy, reaching out to touch Leon's arm. 'It keeps hope alive.'

Okay, that was very cheesy, she told herself, smiling.

Perhaps it is cheesy, she thought, still smiling, but it's also *definitely* true. Fine, fine, but you might want to stop grinning now – unless, of course, you're hoping he's one of those rare guys who's actually *attracted* to bunny-boilers.

Oh shut up, I know what I'm doing.

Leon slipped the notebook into his backpack.

'So who's the guy hiding in the woods?' asked Poppy. 'Do Nathan and Ramona get together? How does it end?'

'I don't know yet. I can't seem to finish it – can't seem to finish any of them.'

'Really? Why not?'

'I don't know. There always seems to be something – a disturbance, an alarm, an interruption—'

As if Satan himself had decided to manifestly demonstrate how such mockery worked, an ambulance raced past on the main road, siren and lights, blaring and flashing – the cacophony bouncing around the precinct's inner walls.

'*A siren!*' exclaimed Leon, enjoying the comic timing.

They both laughed, Poppy snorting louder than ever.

Once her gleeful grunting had subsided she wondered aloud what was keeping their drinks. Leon didn't know and said so. She raised her palms and twisted her mouth to one side, and she was right: it *was* a mystery.

Leon wasn't so much interested in *what* was keeping the drinks, or even *when* they would arrive, he was more concerned about *who* would bring them.

If it was Olive, he would miss out on having the lovely Jenny bring him his tea. But if it *was* Jenny, she might assume that he and Poppy were 'together' – as in *an item*.

He couldn't allow that; he would have to explain – *have* to . . . *somehow*.

He set to thinking of the various ways Poppy could be 'explained' without it being too obvious what he was doing. And without making *him*, look like an idiot (or, as Jenny might say: 'Eejit'). He'd have to be clever – *very* clever – which was tricky because, as we know, only girls are good at that kind of thing.

He looked at Poppy. Boop was out.

Jenny, this is my friend, *Poppy . . . Jenny, this is my* old friend, *Poppy. No, no; Poppy might object to the word 'old' or get suspicious, raise awkward questions: Why are you telling the waitress we're 'old' friends when we've only recently met? In fact, why are you telling the waitress anything? . . . Jenny, this is my* new friend *Poppy.*

No, not 'new', that might open up a whole different can of worms. Just 'friends' having tea, or coffee, or whatever, in a café, that's fine, but 'new friends' having tea, or coffee, or whatever, in a café – that's a date!

Jeez, is that what we're having: a date?

No; arrangements have to be agreed for it to be a date. This wasn't planned. This was more like an ambush.

So what do I do? I like Poppy. But I think I like Jenny, more. Oh, God, this is a nightmare.

'I go to the park when I want to write,' said Poppy, slipping her Betty Boop watch back up her sleeve. 'Or relax in the bath. Where's your favourite place?'

'I had some nice holidays in Wales when I was a kid,' blurted Leon without really thinking.

'Go back then,' she told him. 'You could finish the story – great title by the way – and have a nice holiday at the same time. People need breaks, Leon.'

Leon discovered he was nodding – perhaps she was on to something.

191

'I'll come with you if you like,' Poppy petitioned, only *half*-joking.

She poked him, playfully. 'Don't look so scared, I was only teasing – kind of.'

Frickin' heck, Poppy, why don't you just offer yourself to him on one of these filthy plates?

But it wasn't the light-hearted solicitation that had concerned Leon: on the other side of Poppy's shoulder, a trio of dwarfs in carnival clobber were gawking in at the window. Leon's eyes scrutinised them in rapid succession; each face intent, scowling and meddlesome.

Leon had been feeling *fairly* neutral about his visions, as he was about most things, but the hateful clown confrontation had gnawed at his perception.

Before Pogo, visions had always seemed comical, entertaining, and in all probability, benign. *Now*, they had, he'd grown to realise, the potential to be threatening, hostile – become downright dangerous.

Pogo *definitely* had.

And so he wondered: What might these little bastards do? Their circus make-up and excited dancing around did nothing to detract from his sense of foreboding. If anything, their farcical appearance made it worse.

As they gawked in at the window, the tallest dwarf put stubby hands on the glass to improve his view. The shorter ones jumped up and down, attempting to see over table tops. Slowly – sudden movement might draw attention – Leon raised a menu to his face and peeped over the top.

'Yeah, I'm getting hungry too,' said Poppy to the eyes now frozen above the dessert section. 'Do you think that's why they make us wait for our drinks?'

She slipped a laminated menu from the plastic holder and scanned for the café's least disgusting snacks.

On the other side of the window, just feet from Poppy's back, more of the little horrors had gathered; a whirling, seething mass of them. A few climbed onto the shoulders of others; their curious, diminutive bodies consolidating to eclipse huge chunks of light and cast a gloomy, voluminous shadow over the café interior. One of the female dwarfs – pretty – raised her top, flashed her bantam boobs then

192

pressed them hard against the glass; not so much *flirtation*, more an act of *aggression*, Leon believed.

'Hmm,' said Poppy, 'I don't like the look of any of this lot. See anything *you* fancy, Leon?' She returned attention to the visible part of Leon's head to discover eyes bulging with what appeared to be apprehension and dread.

There was a lot of window thumping and pulling of faces then one dwarf, encouraged by those nearest to him, pulled out a mobile phone, keyed a number, and passed around confirmation that it was ringing. Who was he phoning? Jesus, were these little shits friends of Pogo? Some – the ones now pulling out dinky knuckledusters and short-bladed knives – protested to the caller; their body language spoke of sorting this themselves.

'Are you sure you wouldn't rather go and eat somewhere else?' asked Poppy.

Look how they're dressed. They could easily be friends of Pogo.

'. . . Leon?'

Jenny hadn't yet returned but Leon heard her lilting Irish voice as if she were whispering in his ear: *What makes you think they're not real, Leon? Maybe they are. Have you thought of that?*

PANIC IN MANCHESTER

Leon darted back and forth between bed and wardrobe, between drawers and bed, stuffing clothes into a rucksack.

Richard tracked him like a shadow around the room.

'You can't just leave. I refuse to be left on my own.'

Leon said he just needed a break. Some time to think. A couple of days away would be good for him. The words were panted. His run had been eventful: he'd had to change direction when he saw Mad Thing lumbering through the precinct's north entrance (the fighter bore all the hallmarks of an enormous, oft-repaired boiler, banging and thumping, its needle high in the red zone and in desperate need of pressure release, lest it explode at any moment) then scurry, skip and sidestep, around, over and through a bunch of erratic, shifting, unpredictable dwarfs.

Leon had caught them by surprise as he'd suddenly exited at speed from Kath's Kaff, but once he'd turned back they were ready for him. One dwarf tried a rugby tackle, though any slowing was negligible as he was immediately sent tumbling over his own, surprisingly-large arse.

Leon did stop briefly, moments later, to pick up his wallet (flown from his pocket as he'd turned sharply after bolting from the south passage) but hadn't lingered.

Not even when all his change was rolling around on the pavement (the zip had held; the coin compartment stitching had not). Not even when a pack of youths yelling 'Yeah!' and 'Mine!' appeared from nowhere to descend like greedy poltergeist-hyenas upon the free bounty.

Not even when the unruly mob abused him for failing to provide any kind of response to the straightforward question: 'Got any more on ya, ya don't want, mate?'

He had left them there with their shame and his plethora of coinage, confident in the knowledge that refusing to hand over your hard-earned banknotes to a riotous rabble of preadolescents does not make one a selfish cunt, as they claimed.

'And how am I supposed to eat?' Richard demanded to know.

'Have you tried looking in the fridge like a normal person?'

'Yes, I have, and for your information, it's empty; unless you count a mouldy tomato and a few drops of moisture.'

Leon muttered 'unbelievable' as he opened the final drawer, picked out three identical pairs of socks and three indistinguishable pairs of boxers from the neat rows of balled socks and rolled-up boxers.

'Wait, let's talk about this,' urged Richard, blocking.

Leon elbowed the obstruction aside and packed.

'But what about work? You can't just disappear.'

'It's Friday, you idiot. Perhaps if you had a job you might know that.'

'So are you talking about a whole fucking weekend? That's ridiculous! What about *me*?'

'Richard, you really have to stop relying on others.'

'You know I can't leave the house!'

Panicking and packing stopped abruptly. Leon gawked suspiciously at Richard. 'Is that so?' he asked.

A minute later, Leon was fleeing the house, tightening the straps of his rucksack. Richard was on his back, too, metaphorically speaking. 'And what's that's supposed to mean, exactly?' he inquired from the front door.

From the gate, Leon replied, 'I mean, I don't believe you're agoraphobic at all. That's what I mean!'

'Of course I am. Stop talking bollocks.'

Leon waved nonchalantly – the nonchalance surprised him a little but it felt *fantastic* – and then he strode away.

'Leon? *Leon! LEON, YOU SELFISH, SELFISH CUNT!*' Richard danced around like a witch doctor possessed by raging spirits. 'CUNT!—CUNT!—CUNT!' he spat, his whole being taking on the appearance of an angry boil – one about to burst.

Leon strutted along the pavement knowing Richard would have desperately loved to argue the validity of his invalidity. But he also knew Richard would have to follow him down the street to do so, and to do so would prove Leon right. Catch 22. Leon stopped, turned and blasted:

'Actually, do you know what? I'm not coming back. *Ever.* So fuck you!'

'*BASTARD!*' shouted Richard at the top of his lungs.

'Byeee!' yelled Leon, soon hustling through rustling maple leaves and donning a true Mancunian monkey-man swagger in full-on 'Ian-Brown-style': toes out, shoulders rolling, knees bending, elbows akimbo, head bobbing in sync with the gait; a sense of overblown pride, self-aggrandisement and pompous bluster . . . yes, he looked a right pretentious prick; a proper knob – but he felt *great.*

In spite of the expanding distance, Leon heard the front door slam. He wasn't concerned, though: he was a man on a mission; no time to think about Richard. That problem and all his other problems were behind him – and getting more behind him with every stride.

'Wales, here I come,' Leon said. And he said it loudly; confident he wouldn't be seeing Richard, Pogo, Mad Thing, or Circus Dwarfs, or whoever else, again.

'Goodbye, Manchester,' he yelled. 'And good riddance!'

195

CHAPTER TWELVE

Go West, young Man

PICCADILLY

Piccadilly train station, in the heart of Manchester, is a huge, bustling space endlessly stocked with people; so many people – all moving and waiting, boarding and disembarking, meeting and parting, eating snacks, drinking coffee, and staring at information boards; talking into mobile phones and to other people, riding escalators and taking stairs; people filling shops and surrounding stalls; people coming, people going; flowing away on trains and through exits only to be simultaneously replaced with more people arriving through entrances and on trains.

(This happens twenty-four hours a day, seven days a week. Over 28,500,000 people a year; an average in excess of 78,000 a day – more than 3,250 an hour. *Every* hour!)

Leon arrived at 19:25. Whatever the time he always thought the station seemed bloated and infected, as if swollen and contaminated by its colony of swarming passengers, commuters, travellers, non-travellers and workers of various kinds: security personnel, guards, law enforcement officers (Transport Police and regular Police), drivers, ticket inspectors, cleaners, and other unidentifiable species of staff. Leon didn't like crowds, especially in closed spaces. He wasn't claustrophobic exactly; it's just that he liked elbow-room, and the more the better.

As he rode the busy escalator down toward the large central atrium of the station, he scanned the familiar yet always slightly uncomfortable surroundings: this intense, bustling ape-house/ant-house/bee-hive, constantly shifting and changing; its transition so filled with bright light and oppressive hubbub, it seemed to vibrate. Leon wondered if anyone else sensed these things: how the station quivered under the rumble of locomotive engines, jarred to the painful squeal of air brakes, shivered with squeaky luggage wheels, resonated to unrelenting announcements and clicking heels, pulsated with a thousand footfalls and throbbed under a barrage of cacophonous voices: filtered, semi-robotic voices squawking through PA systems with their crackly communiqués and reminders of departures or arrivals amidst warnings for any would-be skateboarders; and the unfiltered, human voices: snatched conversations rushed with the pressing need to be on the move and elsewhere, and long unhurried standing/sitting idling-away-the-time chats, incessant and mundane – a filtered and unfiltered fizzle of utterances akin to background radio static, everything merged into a general drone – a murmuring hum that buzzed and echoed under the enormous roof space and yet was curiously muted and lost to it at the same time.

Hiding amongst the roof's innumerable cross-beams and stanchions, or braving it out on one of the twelve platforms (fourteen, if you count the two outside) the usual motley handful of urban pigeons, including the one with the deformed foot, scavenging for whatever they could find, indiscriminately pecked at anything in their path – food or filth – the question of spit or swallow somehow decided in a split-second, leaving time aplenty to hop away from marauding legs and troubling trolleys.

And then, as you would expect, there were the trains; lots of them: trains pulling out, trains pulling in, and trains awaiting their time to depart; snub-nosed local and medium-distance engines; sleek, stretched, high-speed long-distance engines; and carriages – so many carriages – long lines of them, most clean, some caked with the crud of whichever parts of the country they had crossed since their last visit to the train-wash depot at Ardwick.

Leon loved trains; so much better than travelling by car. Someone else does the driving (if it can be called 'driving' – they just keep hold of a handle, you know. Don't even have to steer. What a cushy number! They want to try restitching a thigh-length boot sometime). You don't have to watch out for other vehicles. And you can read at the same time!

Leon's train stood at platform 8. Several passengers waited alongside, unable to board, as the train's interior was cleaned. 'Cleaned' in the sense that a sole employee would walk from one end to the other transferring anything left behind to a rubbish sack (or Lost Property if the item was too heavy or bulky for the bin liner: laptops, luggage, guide-dogs; that kind of thing). Leon hoped the cleaning was nearly done; he liked to settle into a seat as soon as possible – and the train was due to depart *in five minutes!*

Upon arrival in Shrewsbury he would change for a second train, destined for the west coast of Wales. All being well, he should disembark at Caersws at 22:29. From there he would, hopefully, hitch a ride as far as Llanidloes, the small town he so often visited as a child with his parents.

The plan (*Operation Artistic Licence*) was to pitch his tent on the outskirts of Llani, study his notebook, regain the *feel* of 'The Geisha and the Samurai', get a good night's sleep, walk into town for lunch, then, once sated, return to the tent to indulge in some intensive writing.

Leon felt like he was going back, not just geographically, but also in Time – and he was *really* looking forward to it.

Almost at the bottom of the escalator he could still see his train: they had started letting people on. He felt a smile break out but it didn't last long: he'd clocked the bleeding Führer himself – *Adolf fucking Hitler* – standing near the foot of the moving stairwell.

And he was talking to Pogo!

(Being deep in conversation, *they* hadn't noticed *him* – – so far . . .)

Leon didn't have to make a decision – Flight mode had kicked in automatically and he was already heading back up the escalator, weaving like a determined (demented?) salmon through a stream of disgruntled bears. But it was taking an age. He did gain some ground only to lose it again as he was forced to squeeze by a group of holidaymakers with matching bulky suitcases.

Having scrambled inelegantly over their fat luggage, Leon finally began to generate some headway. He would cross the mezzanine, take the far stairs and sneak over from the adjacent platforms; it would be a push, but with luck and a mad final dash he should just make it. He was only six or seven moving steps from the peak (and starting to feel confident) when a large Chinese family, four generations of them, commenced their descent.

Two abreast!

Don't they know the mother-flippin' rules! Don't they Google these things before leaving home? Then they'd know: escalator code[5] demands you stand to one side and prevent your crap from obstructing the 'free lane' – in case someone in a hurry needs to pass. Like now!

Leon suffered the distance he had put between himself and his nemesis slipping away as he considered the descending oriental obstacle . . . and, at the last moment, seeing no other choice; he moved to dissect the group.

As he apologetically attempted to pierce their tight ranks, they dipped shoulders, pushed him left, right then left again, their many hands – hands of all ages – shoving fiercely at his rucksack. Mouths cursed in Chinese and broken English (again, the word *fuckwit* cropped up! When Chinese kids learn English, they *really* learn English) but in the end Leon broke through the great wall, popping out the other side like a relieved but rather worn-out party-popper. After that, he passed several stationary persons standing to the right and ducked in and out of various 'movers' flooding down on his left: people who wishing to hasten their brief escalator journey not only 'rode' but simultaneously walked down.

Eventually, after countless grumbles and endless apologies, Leon slowly recovered all the ground sacrificed and regained his previous height – half a dozen moving steps from the top – and here, at last, like a wonderful gift from above, Lady Luck took it upon herself to shine down and open up a relatively clear course, right to the summit.

As Leon passed the one remaining person (a boss-eyed construction worker with a head shaped like the top of a ten-pin bowling pin) between him and escalator emancipation, he checked below:

---

[5] Oddly, escalator etiquette in the UK requires 'non-moving' persons to stand to the *right*, even though on UK *motorways*, the *left* is considered to be the *slow* lane. Brits, eh? Dear, oh dear.

Pogo and Adolf were still engrossed in conversation. Excellent, Leon thought, stay like that. He put eyes on the pinnacle and pushed for the finish. He was virtually there, just two steps from the apex, when the access zone swiftly filled with a stream of oncoming suits. Lady Luck can be a right bitch when she wants to be. And she hadn't finished:

The business party was immediately followed by a wavy-haired teenager, gripped and flanked by two robust police officers; no doubt, escorting the black-hearted, highly dangerous criminal and his skateboard from the premises.

As Leon once again rolled backwards, he wondered if the skateboarder was deaf or just irresistibly anarchic. No matter, his own undertaking, to wit: catch a train, was fast turning into the most farcical of Norman Wisdom films.

A full three minutes after first sighting Pogo and Adolf, Leon *finally* completed his first objective: having vaulted onto the adjoining up-escalator (not as tricky as you might think, even with a loaded rucksack and two police officers in close attendance; but why the hell, he now wondered, hadn't he done that sooner!) he peeked over the top of the stairwells – making sure he wasn't swept back onto the down-escalator as he did so – in time to see Adolf tap his chest; the message clear: *Leave it to me.* From what Leon had seen, what he could make out from their body language: No, Pogo definitely wasn't satisfied with Mad Thing (had Adolf arranged that?) but not to worry, the Führer had something else – or some*one* else – in mind.

Leon didn't have time to wonder who or what that might be. He compared the time on his mobile phone to the departure board clock: 19:29 on both. He looked to his train. Apart from a couple of late arrivals, all passengers had boarded. At the head of the platform, someone ran; well, the train *was* due out any moment. Almost immediately, the only people left on platform 8 were a couple of middle-aged smartly-dressed would-be wavers awaiting their cue, and an inordinately-tall guard milling about by the engine.

Leon's face contorted with frustration; he no longer had time for the roundabout route via the stairs and far platforms. Still peering over the crest of the escalators, through the people getting on and off the stairwells, his eyes darted between his two sources of irritation: obstruction and salvation. Below, Pogo and Adolf nodded to each other, came to an agreement. Ahead, a no-time-to-spare Trolly-Dolly shoved his refreshment-laden cart up a small ramp, onto the train. The ramp followed, disappearing with a metallic scrape. Pogo shook hands with the big-shot Nazi then handed over a wad of cash. The guard on platform 8 scrutinised his watch against station time. The hang-fire wavers now commenced *actual* waving: furiously, to the young woman: a Goth with high-pigtails and purple fringe, sitting just feet away on the other side of the window. As *Raven Twilight, High Priestess of the Eventide* – or, until the age of fourteen, *Susan Barnes* – returned a fraction of the gesture (looking more than a little embarrassed), Leon moved his eyes back to the foot of the escalator . . . Adolf and Pogo had gone.

Quickly on his toes, Leon rushed down the escalator, pausing only to curse at some idiot coming up the wrong way. No time to buy a ticket (he would pay on the train), he ran across the central lobby, onto platform 8, alongside the engine, and entered, after stabbing away at the portal's button like a deranged knife-attacker, the first door he came to. No sooner had he jumped aboard than the guard raised his whistle to prepared lips.

Leon walked to the front of the train, shrewdly checking the occupants of each carriage as he passed through. In the last carriage, or first, depending on your standpoint, he made a final scan of the immediate vicinity and having seen nothing *too* unusual, dumped his rucksack on a platform-side window seat. As he slumped into the adjoining aisle seat, a jangly jingle played over the train's public address speakers. The jingle was followed by a female voice; not as sexy as *Gabrielle*, but still pleasant (Leon decided to christen her *Gloria*). She spoke thusly:

'Ladies and Gentlemen, welcome aboard and thank you for travelling with Arriva Trains Wales today. This is the – *nineteen thirty* – *Manchester Piccadilly* – service to – *Shrewsbury*. We will be calling at – *Stockport* – *Cheadle Hulme* – *Wilmslow* – *Crewe . . .*'

Gloria went on but she could have been saying anything. Leon wasn't really listening; he was more concerned with why the train wasn't moving – the platform clock said they should have set off.

'Please study the safety notices . . .'

Leon checked left and right: nothing but Virgin train at platform 7, its long sides extending off in both directions.

'And familiarise yourself with the location of emergency exits . . .'

Leon almost panicked when the train, *his* train, seemed to move deeper into the station. How was that possible? The engine was parked up against buffers!

'And if you should fancy a blow-job at any time during our journey please venture to the buffet car situated in the middle of the train where one of our friendly employees will be more than happy to provide service.'

Of course, *his* train wasn't moving at all; his mind was playing tricks – the *Virgin train* was on the move; pulling out from platform 7.

'And once again, thank you for travelling with Arriva Trains Wales today. Oh, and by the way,' she added at breakneck-speed, 'there'll be a short delay before we get underway.' There followed a rapid, sped-up replay of the jangly jingle and the announcement cut off sharply.

A short delay? That's just great, thought Leon, hastily but cautiously re-scanning the platform for signs of marauding clown, prowling dictator or God knows what . . .

Nothing – well, that was something.

He reached into a rucksack pocket and pulled out a book: *Strange Case of Dr Jekyll and Mr Hyde* by Robert Louis Stevenson. And sinking into his seat, head behind the rucksack as low to the window as possible, he settled down for a read. Even if it was written in the 19th century (as this was), a good novella, Leon reflected stubbornly, is the perfect way to make Time pass quickly.

'Right,' said Gloria, 'the idiot driver has found the key . . .'

Wow, that was either a very short delay or this is the most riveting story ever. I didn't realise trains had ignition keys, though.

202

'Of course they don't have ignition keys, you moron; I was joking. Right, here we go. Hold on to your hats. *Toot toot whoooo-whoooo chuffa-chuffa diddly-dom diddly-dee diddly-dah . . .*'

No, I can't read with that racket, decided Leon. He switched places with the rucksack, put his face to the window, and watched the station and all concerns of Pogo, Adolf, and Richard slip away.

'*Tickety-boo tickety-boo peweeeeeeeeeeeeeeeeee . . .*'

Oh shit! Leon tapped feverishly at the pockets of his cargo pants – of which there were many – then shot an anxious look to the rucksack.

Please tell me I packed my notebook!

CARRY ON CAMPING

Eighty-two minutes later found Leon in Shrewsbury and not a peep out of Gloria the whole way there – not since they'd left Manchester – other than to announce the train's imminent arrival at the handful of scheduled stops and repeat the safety instructions for new passengers to ignore (for some reason he couldn't put his finger on, Leon kept expecting her to say more). The slightly late arrival had shortened the interval between Network Rail's impressively coordinated trains by five minutes so Leon only had to wait a mere fifty minutes.

In less time than he'd had to wait (exactly forty-seven minutes for those of you taking notes) Leon's second train delivered him safely to Caersws, a small Welsh village midway between Shrewsbury and the west coast town of Aberystwyth. Caersws had a train station, an empty space where a Roman fort is said to have once stood, two shops (including the chip shop), a petrol station, and the population of a well-attended party.

Less than half an hour later, he was on the outskirts of Llanidloes, pitching his one-man tent in a field. (He'd managed to cadge a lift from a tractor driver heading in the right direction; it wasn't comfortable riding in the trailer with so many sheep but needs must; and he soon got used to the smell – if anything, the sheep seemed more concerned than he did but we won't go into that.)

Now, as he stepped back, admiring the finished canvas construction, he felt confident it was positioned on the exact spot; upon the selfsame patch of grass he'd once circled as a child-Spitfire; the identical location as had appeared in his dad's home movies; yes, he'd recognise that gentle slope anywhere – even by feeble torchlight.

As he reversed, though, he tripped over; a rock, perhaps. (Well, it *was* late by this time and very dark out there. Note to self, he thought, belatedly: tomorrow, buy new torch batteries!) His Surefire 'Gladius' Maglite hit the ground with only a dull thump but the faint light died instantly.

Finding nothing after a lengthy fingertip search through cold damp grass, Leon decided to put off the hunt until morning. Guided only by the muted lights of the town in the valley below and a countless array of conspicuous but far from illuminating stars, he made his way back to where he assumed the tent should be; lost his footing on the body of the fugitive torch and ended up sitting in something soft.

Oh, well, he'd found the main part of his only light source; might as well find the rest now.

So Leon spent a further ten frustrating minutes scrambling around on hands and knees: located one of the missing batteries, the head of the torch, and, finally, the other missing battery. He eased the batteries in, re-screwed the head, and with the click of a switch . . .

'Bollocks.'

He unscrewed the head, slid the batteries out – being extra cautious not to lose them again in the dark – carefully put them back in the *right way* round this time, re-screwed the head, and bingo, enjoyed weak light once again.

Tapping the torch made the unsteady beam strengthen from *exhausted* to *slightly-better-than-exhausted* but Leon wanted something more: he wanted to build a fire. Camping isn't really camping, he believed, without a small campfire. Yes, it was time for the boy from the city to collect sticks! That was a proper *country* thing to do.

As he set off for the nearest copse, ailing torch struggling to pick out distant trees, Leon suddenly questioned if it was still okay to camp here. Perhaps farmers were less keen to have city-types on their land these days. Were visitors and holiday-makers still welcome to put up tents? And if not, would the farmer recognise him and make an exception for old times' sake? Leon could recall seeing the farmer no more than three or four times but remembered him as a jovial soul who wore mud-splattered Wellington boots and drove a battered Land Rover *Defender*; his wise old dog riding shotgun, peering out though the mud-edged windscreen – perhaps on the lookout for escaped livestock.

Leon didn't foresee a problem; as far as he could recollect, the jolly farmer had *never* minded – not only that, he had always refused payment of any kind. *As long as you clean up after yourselves,* Leon heard him say.

But what if it wasn't the same farmer? It had been a while. Leon decided it was too late now, he wasn't moving. He knew the locals to be friendly – he would take the risk.

Any residue of concern Leon may have had, drifted away with the collection of wood and stayed behind when he exited the copse carrying an armful of sticks and twigs. How excellent to be amongst the hills and valleys. Ahh, the air was fresh and clean; none of that shitty city atmosphere here – none of the crud and grime that clogs up your nose and irritates the lungs. And the sounds were sharper, too – crisper; yet, at the same time, more harmonious and *natural* – so very different to the cacophony of annoying and alarming man-made sounds of the metropolis. He felt at one with the countryside, somehow more vital and at peace. And he'd enjoyed how the copse had seemed to stir with his arrival, as if it had known he was there:

Dried leaves had rustled beyond his presence – hidden nocturnal life, perhaps, getting into gear; a chorus of crickets (or grasshoppers; Leon was no expert) upped their game in the undergrowth, enticed him to dally with their hypnotising *reeeeee*; and a screech owl politely announced she was in the area. Leon couldn't pinpoint where, exactly; closer than the cow – which called out but once for reasons unknown from, Leon assumed, a distant farm somewhere up on the hill – but not as near as the series of low-pitched grunts and high-pitched yelps that he guessed had emanated from a fox or badger roving beyond the outer-circle of trees. The river at the bottom of the valley sang its quiet song of tranquillity and repletion throughout Leon's foraging, and, as he'd collected a final few 'starter' twigs, a jet-black Carrion-Crow indicated it was time *he, too,* should be going, with a loud cah-caw.

Gnarled and barren branches had raced through the chilly night air as Leon whipped around in a keen attempt to follow the sound of the fleeing bird's swishing wings with his ray of fading light. In this place, alone, in the ever-so-slightly illuminated dark, amongst trees and country wildlife, Leon had felt no fear – not a jot.

With Leon's parting, the copse again fell quiet – as if missing him already. Night was everywhere here, and all-consuming. The diurnal creatures of the land had long since taken to their slumbers – but not Leon; he was snapping sticks and watching the moon now rise silently over the peaks of the hills, notebook resting in his lap (he hadn't forgotten his notebook, after all; he'd found it lying snugly between layers of T-shirts – must have packed it without thinking whilst fending off you-know-who).

Oh, it was good to be away.

All around, the ancient Welsh landscape reposed under its canopy of stars, framed by hills, bathed in the light of an intense full moon (now the silvery sphere had climbed above the hilltops); and in the centre, warmed by the glow of a small campfire, a little tent blushed fitfully. In the mouth of the tent, sat Leon, content and thoughtful, scribbling away; writing at length in his notebook. Sentences flowed onto the page and only occasionally did they stop, as he broke from writing to gaze up at the constellations and moonlit peaks. *Operation Artistic Licence* was already ahead of schedule.

The next morning, after only a few hours sleep – he'd written well into the early hours – Leon unzipped the tent door to find lush countryside invigorated by morning sun.

Perhaps sharing the joy, a sheep let on with a whimsical *baa.*

'Yes, good morning to you, too,' Leon replied.

A GLIMPSE OF A BETTER FUTURE?

After an additional hour of pen to paper, a brisk walk, a surprise breakfast of eggs (bought from an honesty box spotted outside the entrance to the nearest farm and boiled in a pan on a tiny but trusty calor-gas camping stove), four more hours of all-out creativity, a lunch of boiled eggs (eating in Llani was put on hold so as not to break the flow) and a few extra hours of intensive writing, Leon finally decamped in search of his next meal (which definitely *would be* in Llanidloes and definitely *wouldn't* involve eggs). He knew what he was going to have and exactly where he was going to have it.

As Leon approached a rusty gate at the bottom of the field, his phone rang – he must have come into signal range (the hills play havoc with mobile communications). The ring surprised him; he thought he'd turned it off again after checking the time earlier (he regularly turned it off so as not to be pestered by Richard). The phone was fished from a pocket, the caller checked. Guess who. The call was cancelled and the phone quickly switched off; Leon didn't want to speak to *It*, thanks very much. He hopped over the gate, avoiding most of the rutted wet mud on both sides of the barrier, and set off across the adjoining pasture.

This truly was a beautiful place. As far as the eye could see: rolling green hills, big wide sky, trees, wildlife, and oh so quiet; ideal for writers – or *would-be* writers. *The soft peacefulness of the countryside has a way of setting the mind free.* Leon knew this to be true. He felt the notebook, brimful of recent ramblings, alive with the additions, heavier in his pocket.

Could he live here, though? *Could he really?* Would that be possible? Why not? Hadn't he told Richard he wasn't coming back – *ever!* Yes but he'd have to, of course. You can't just decide and move on the same day. Things need to be sorted. But could he *actually* do it? He'd lived his whole life in Manchester. Could he genuinely make the move to Wales? Or was he, in truth, just a 'barnacle' as Richard had often declared?

And what about mum and dad?

They might follow me once I'd made the move. They'd definitely be better off here. Safer, surely. *I'd never have to worry about them in a place like this.* Being in Wales would be like being on holiday, every day. And they *loved* their holidays.

A Red Kite soared majestically on high, gliding, scanning the ground.

But what about Moss? Could he cope on his own—Shit!

Leon had bumped into an easel. Somehow managing to save it and its resident painting from tipping over, he apologised profusely and reset the arrangement. He had happened upon an artist attempting to replicate, on canvas, Llanidloes, the small town nestled in the valley.

Leon admired the work and expressed this to the painter. Stella, for that was her name, appreciated the appreciation and said so.

Stella, Leon soon discovered, was from Newcastle, 'forty-*ish*' (Leon thought she looked more fifties or sixties but kept this private), recently widowed from Frank, and had taken early retirement to follow her love of art – painting, in particular – of that, she was specific. She liked to talk did Stella, a real motor-mouth, and Leon found out lots he didn't need to know. And much he hadn't *wanted* to know. He learned that Stella, a pushy, in-your-face type, with eyes that bulged relentlessly, was – and for as long as she could remember, had been – liberated, adventurous, open-minded, permissive–

'Excellent brushwork,' Leon managed to squeeze in. 'Do you prefer water colours to oils?'

–and had been known to dabble in groups, threesomes, swinging, and, on more than one occasion, women.

Leon asked if she'd ever had any of her work exhibited – perhaps in Llanidloes, which he knew to have two art galleries of its own.

Undeterred, Stella went on to say, unprompted and quite unashamedly, that she was now, 'to use the modern vernacular: *a Cougar.*' Leon indicated an approval of her flowered wellington boots ('very arty') but Stella would not be side-tracked by irrelevant talk of footwear, said she'd preferred younger men since she'd hit fifty.

'I mean *forty*,' she corrected quickly, laughing off her 'slip of the tongue' as she energetically waggled a brush in a jar of water.

'It must be nice,' Leon said, 'spending all your time doing something you enjoy.' By which he meant Painting. 'Being able to afford to—'

'In fact, the younger the better,' added Stella with a smile far less ambiguous than any da Vinci had to capture.

Leon asked how old Frank had been when he—

'Fifty-four,' she replied, indifferently fisting out a splurge of Burnt Umber.

Leon wondered how her husband might have died but didn't get time to postulate because Stella wanted to know if he'd ever posed for an artist. Leon was certain he hadn't and communicated as much. An armada of questions followed: Yes, he'd think about it; yes, he agreed, she did 'look good for her age' (whatever age that might be); no, he wasn't free now; and, what – *naked*? He was sure no art-lover would ever want to see *him* naked; yes, he really had to leave; no, he hadn't had lunch yet; yes, that's where he was going; no, he'd already made arrangements but thanks.

As he hit the trail, Stella winked at him. Leon was sure of it.

WE SHALL GO TO TOWN

Llanidloes, also known as 'The First Town on the Severn', sits quietly by this river surrounded by some of the most spectacular scenery in Mid Wales.

Fair to say Leon loved it here: this little town so full of happy holidays and happy memories. After an invigorating walk down the hill, he gravitated towards the centre.

Some history for you:

(To the philistines, we say: *Feel free to skip ahead a few paragraphs.*)

The origins of Llanidloes, as understood today, go back to the 7th century, when Idloes, the Celtic saint, laid the foundations of a church on a plateau overlooking the river. In place names, the Welsh word *Llan* originally referred to an enclosure but later came to mean 'church', especially a parish church. Not difficult then to see how the church of Saint Idloes would become Llan Idloes . . . Llanidloes.

Leon knew all this from regular visits to the town museum as a child. Lester would often tease his young son that he really just wanted to see the two-headed lamb exhibit again, but Leon – although he *was* fascinated by this strange creature – was also genuinely interested in the history of the town. In fact, the museum visit became a bit of an annual tradition for the family, and the Blanks probably learned as much as anyone about the place.

What did they know?

(*Thank you for asking* . . .)

They knew the medieval town had begun to expand after the Norman Conquest of Britain in 1066, when a motte-and-bailey castle was constructed at the then western end of town. They knew that in 1280 Llanidloes obtained its first charter, granted by Edward I, and this was followed in 1344 by a charter making the town a self-governing borough (a status that was retained until as recently as 1974). They also knew the original medieval town was designed in the shape of a cross and had retained this structure throughout the centuries, and that a market hall was built at the crossroads of the four original streets in the early 1600s. The hall still stands there today and is considered to be the *heart* of the town. The black and white timber-framed building, the size of a large barn, has two floors. Thick wooden posts corral the cobbled open-air ground-floor and support a walled upper-floor. In one corner, an enclosed section filled with twisty steps connects the two. At the top of the ancient stairs, a spacious single room sits regally within stone end-walls and a lofty apex roof. The room looks out through ten latticed windows – five along each of its long but diminutive side walls. The old, polished timber floorboards, with their marks and indentations, hold some small record of the countless heels and happenings they have so clearly witnessed.

Below this scarred timber floor, in the cobbled open-area bound by herculean stilts, sat Leon – on a wooden bench. How many weekly markets must this building have seen in the four hundred or so years it had been around?

Leon had often wondered but had never actually bothered to work it out. Today was no different. Instead, he watched the comings and goings of the good people of Llanidloes.

(For the record, the obligatory history lesson isn't quite over so the uncultured amongst you may want to stay in the cupboard a wee bit longer.)

Leon had always found the locals to be a friendly, welcoming bunch – more so than many places he'd visited. Manchester, too, was known as a friendly place, but Leon felt his 'home town' also had, unfortunately, more than its fair share of undesirables. *Nob-heads*, Richard called them.

Llanidloes appeared to have completely avoided the problem of 'nob-heads' as far as Leon could see. *Why* did Manchester have such a plethora of undesirables? Maybe it's just because Manchester is so much bigger, he thought. (Greater Manchester has a population fast approaching the 3 million mark.) *That many* people, there's bound to be *lots* of undesirables, nob-heads, call them what you will.

They are emboldened in the masses; hidden by crowds, they feel invisible, unaccountable – anonymous. Most people who live in big cities, it seemed to Leon, don't know who lives below, opposite, or next-door-but-two – even though they may have lived in the same house or flat for years. When someone loiters in their street, they frequently have no idea if that person should be there or not. Manchester is, after all, a huge, sprawling metropolis, home to the largest housing estate in Europe and harbours a populous over a thousand times that of little Llanidloes.

Here in Llani, every one of the 2,500 population appears to know everyone else. They went to school together (there's only one school). They buy from each other's businesses. They have a sense of community. Apart from visitors and holiday-makers, there are no strangers here. The locals are accountable and there's no hiding. They have their reputations to think of. Nob-heads are shamed, not avoided. Kids here would no sooner have guns or knives than they would, crack cocaine or heroin. Perhaps that's why this area – and indeed the whole county, Powys – has one of the lowest crime rates in the United Kingdom.

A reasonable thought, thought Leon.

Leon was a visitor, and had been a holiday-maker, but he didn't feel like a stranger here; he remembered enjoying all the smiles he had collected walking around the characterful town – around the friendly bookshops, the cafés, bric-a-brac stores, bistros, art galleries . . . and Lester and Veronica's favourite: the antique shops. And let's not forget the public houses: Leon had eaten many lunches in the town's various old inns – knew their histories by heart and could even recall certain meals: Ham and Eggs in The Crown and Anchor (built in the 17th century); Bangers and Mash in the Mount Inn (a beamed coaching house built in the 14th century on the site of the old motte-and-bailey castle); home-made Pizza in the Angel Inn (another beamed coaching house, this one 18th century); a so-called Stag Burger and being allowed his first taste of cider – *real* cider – in The Stag . . .

The past was lost, consumed in the fire of gastric memories, as Leon became aware of growing hunger. He turned his head towards Great Oak Street, the Red Dragon Café, and lunch.

(By the way, the lowdown on Llanidloes history is over for the time being so you can stop tutting and exit the cupboard.)

As Leon passed Llanidloes Museum (sited within the Town Hall) and The Great Oak Bookshop, he wondered which of them to visit first, after lunch. Walking the narrow pavement, and still deciding, he suddenly hesitated: two hulking teenage lads lumbered straight towards him: young men with weather-beaten faces and hands like shovels.

Leon's reaction was instinctive and involuntary: deep-seated; as if inbred – almost primal.

He froze.

The hefty youths were clearly farmers: sons of farmers: grandsons and great-grandsons of farmers. Farming was in their blood . . . 'Steeped in sheep,' Lester had once said.

(He'd gone on to add 'Packed with pigs,' – 'Immersed in milk,' – and 'Bursting with beef,' and might have continued further had it not been for the 'Filled with frustration' slap from Veronica.)

But Leon needn't have iced over, the teenage farmers, already separating to circumnavigate the momentarily stationary visitor, smiled as they passed; polite and friendly – and the visitor castigated himself for having flinched unnecessarily. Leon knew Llani lads weren't like Danny and Carl and the rest. He put the flinch down to being in Manchester too long.

As he watched the young farmers go, the word 'beef' reoccurred to him. The boys were built like oxen: wide shouldered and thick necked; arms like Minotaurs on steroids. Leon wondered if they played rugby at the weekends; assuming their farms could spare them – farmers don't get much more than Christmas day off, and even then, they'd probably work half a day.

Leon's stomach reminded Leon's mind that it had wandered (again) and needed to get back on track. He walked on, but a moment later stopped anew . . .

The Red Dragon Café.

Leon's face – his very soul, it seemed – basked, taking the place in. The café was just as he remembered – and exactly as it appeared in Home Movie World.

As he stood there soaking it up, reminiscing, his mind questioned if 'Immersed in milk' was an authentic and accordingly allowable alliteration. His stomach didn't care, didn't have time for this nonsense, and pleaded for his mind to shut up, to hurry up, and to get in there.

THE RED DRAGON CAFÉ

The cosy, quaint interior of The Red Dragon Café hadn't changed in the slightest; still contained the same sprinkling of old wood tables and matching chairs. Wood-panelled walls sported various paintings by local artists: the odd abstract and several scenic views featuring local landmarks, each priced and available to purchase.

Leon hadn't wanted a painting. He'd wanted lasagne. They'd always made great lasagne here. And today was no different. He'd enjoyed it immensely. And now he was tucking into their famous (locally, at least) home-made lemon meringue, as he had done so many times in the past:

the cool zingy lemon bit, the fluffy, soft meringue. Each melt-in-the-mouth spoonful almost made his eyes flutter with the pleasure of it all. He'd have to watch out for that.

Between heavenly mouthfuls, Leon read his notebook.

Last night, in the tent, he remembered how Poppy had said she wrote in the bath. As he'd thought about that (the process of writing in a bath – after he'd managed to get beyond the sensual image of Poppy lying naked in hot, soapy water with only a pair of steamy glasses and a layer of translucent bubbles to hide her modesty), he discovered, located on an upper floor somewhere towards the back of his head (at least, that's how it felt), a special room, illuminated by hundreds of candles of all shapes and sizes.

Warm, clean, and most importantly, quiet, the room smelled of nothing – except maybe a hint of vanilla. And, at its heart, sunk into a tiled floor, lay a large, circular hot tub; a deep, protective sauna pool – a steaming, all-enveloping spa, full and intensely inviting.

He stepped in, reclined slowly, stretched out, let out a protracted sigh then submerged fully.

The soothing water felt wonderfully hot; the temperature perfect – beyond relaxing.

Unfurled and unwinding, he weighed up the contents (the narrative work, not the Sightings log – definitely not the log) of his notebook: the story so far, the creative details of his annotations, the comments and footnotes . . . *weighed them up*, yet didn't really *think* about them. Not in a conscious way. In the physical world, the notebook was before him but he was no longer aware of it. Not in a material sense. He dialled down the conscious part of his mind and as it rested, his subconscious mind became liberated. And it wandered, easy and free, drifting, roaming. He became immersed in his psyche, his under-consciousness.

He'd found 'the Hole' – or perhaps, more appropriately, 'the Pool'.

Leon's disparate notebook ideas washed over him; mixed with story-so-far and swirled around, independently. Tenuous, nebulous, illusory and illusive at first, then, in the blend, connections were made. Resultant fusions formed shapes; apparent, but not yet meaningful. These unions then synthesised further, coagulated through some mysterious natural force; joined together to become a different thing entirely – a new total. Some parts were gently dropped. More bits added. The *different thing*, whatever it was, continued in the process until, at some point, it evolved, metamorphosed into something significant and beautiful: segments of Story; components of Character; pieces of Plot.

At times: notions, suggestions, instructions, proposals, setups, advancements, resolutions and the like, were conveyed to him via a genderless voice; an inner- or outer voice he wasn't sure, but he definitely heard it; sometimes faint – he had to listen intently – other times as sharp as a well-cut diamond. (He did wonder if the voice was his own or a newly discovered muse; he'd heard about writers having muses but couldn't recall ever having experienced one before – not first-hand – not like this – not so acutely. He found the idea of a muse exciting but chose not to examine it too closely in case he broke it.)

And all the time – as these segments, pieces and components had continued to ebb and flow, surge and swell, rush and churn, twist around as if in a whirlpool; and the ethereal, mystical voice (be it from outer- or inner space) had spoken – up on the surface, back in the *real* world, Leon's hands had been writing—writing—writing.

Presently, still in The Red Dragon Café, after re-reading his new, improved story and going over his notes, Leon was feeling extremely satisfied. He reckoned he'd now written over 12,000 words. He'd improved the beginning, had a fleshed-out middle, and now – hallelujah – an ending! Only first-draft quality but the words were there: *down on paper*. And if he could expand the story by another 8,000 words – and he now believed he could do exactly that – he would have enough, once everything had been polished and tweaked and perfected, for that novella!

He placed his notebook on the table, open to the title page of 'The Geisha and the Samurai', and slipped another spoonful of lemon meringue between his lips; made a conscious effort not to *Mmm* out loud and wondered if he should order a second helping. He decided not to; he wanted to dwell on his story: about the writing; about how much he'd produced last night and again today (with plenty of today still remaining); about how much extra he might conceive before he returned home tomorrow evening; about how, with further cogitation and musing, he might come up with additional memorable scenes, crank up the excitement, devise another twist – or two! – add more laughs, intensify the romance . . .

Leon drifted off for a time but then the mind-trip vanished in much the same way it had arrived – mysteriously, easily, and without fanfare – as he became aware of a young girl standing by his table. Her name was Molly, though Leon didn't know that yet. She was staring at him and he got the sense she'd been there a while – watching him. He looked at her, she stared back; she standing, he sitting – their heads at roughly the same height. Leon gave her a smile. That was okay, wasn't it? That was cool? It wasn't weird, he reminded himself, for an adult male to smile at a child here – even a child the man didn't know – they were in Llanidloes; people smiled all the time in this town. People *here* were innocent – they hadn't been hardened by city life – made insensitive to the feelings of others by the overwhelming proximity of the self-centred masses with all their 'fuck you!' behaviour and— Hang on a minute, *he'd* lived in Manchester all his life and *he* hadn't turned out that way, he wasn't *hard* or *cold*, not even—

Molly drained a milkshake, long and noisily, through a straw. Pretty as a princess, seven or so, curly hair, charming button nose and bright blue eyes. A toy angel, her long thin legs gripped in her owner's dainty fist, swayed back and forth near the hem-line of a cute lilac dress. Molly hadn't ventured far. Two tables away, her mother sipped a frothy coffee, attention focused on an open paperback, spine-cracked to lie flat on the table.

Leon was sure he'd smiled but to make doubly sure, he smiled again.

Continuing to stare, Molly sucked unashamedly – the bottom of her straw now dredging little more than milky dregs. Leon studied the little princess, who still hadn't moved an inch or uttered a word. Her eyes were intensely piercing; the unblinking gaze, borderline crazy. She could have been menacing, if she hadn't been so adorable. But Leon was all smiled out. He felt he should speak:

'Hi,' he said, in his most affable child-friendly voice.

'Hello.' And then, after a girl-sized pause, and in a lilting, almost musical, Welsh accent, Molly asked: 'What were you doing?'

'What was I doing?'

Molly gently tapped the pint-sized angel's head on the notebook then let her rest there.

'Oh,' said Leon, catching on. 'It's a story.'

'What kind of story?'

Good question. Leon needed to think for a moment. *What kind of story was it?*

'Is it a fairy story?' Molly asked, a sprinkle of excitement added to her rhythmic tone. Leon's answer, an apologetic thumbs-down, hadn't yet gained form when Molly's eyes widened in anticipation of her next question:

'Is it about an angel?'

The angel shifted: one second resting her wings on Leon's notebook (as if asleep), the next, flying. Assisted by Molly, she set down, spotting her landing perfectly, and stared Leon full in the face. Her lovable little pinched-features and proportionately huge eyes bore into Leon's correspondingly massive mug. He felt like a giant ugly ogre in comparison.

'This is *my* angel. She's called Jayne.'

Leon wasn't sure how to respond. He'd never had a sister. Didn't have any nieces . . .

'Jayne Angel.'

'Right. That's nice.'

'Jayne with a Y,' Molly added, as if it were an extremely important, perhaps vital, detail.

'Well, hello, Jayne with a Y,' he said, looking into the angel's big green eyes. 'My name's Leon.'

Molly pulled a face that simultaneously involved twisting her lips, pulling her eyebrows down, and dropping her head to one side.

Worried that his voice had taken on an ogre-like quality, Leon softened his next utterance: 'You look nice,' he whispered. A well-meant but decidedly weak observation; he felt it straight away. And was equally struck by a new concern: had he *over*-softened his voice? He thought it might have sounded anaemic and too – well, *girlish*.

'She's not *real*, Silly,' Molly reprimanded, her head now back to vertical.

As Leon reverted to his dealing-with-children fall-back position – an inane grin – Mother finally came to life.

'Molly, come over here,' she said. 'Stop disturbing people.' She moved motherly eyes to Leon, apologised by means of a smile or a shrug or a combination of the two (Leon wasn't sure which), then got back to her book, re-cracking the spine in the process. One page proved extremely unruly and had to be pinned under a salt cellar.

'I have to go now,' Molly said, at last.

'Okay,' Leon replied, feeling her unwillingness to leave. Not only felt it, he saw it: she hadn't moved a muscle.

'Molly!' Mother chimed. '*Now*, please.'

This time there was no shrug or smile; just a gentle but pointed stare at the back of her daughter's head.

Dragging her little pink shoes, Molly rejoined Mother. Jayne Angel spent the short return journey upside-down, swinging, suspended by her skinny ankles, her long shiny black hair brushing the ground.

As Jayne with a Y set down on the table (an ungainly, heavy landing on this occasion), Leon returned to the notebook and the last of his zesty dessert.

But Molly was a persistent little girl. Her eyes remained fixed on Leon, and the soft sap, feeling her attention, couldn't help but smile anew. He had caught the Llanidloes affliction.

A minute later, having finished his lemon meringue – he'd been careful not to flutter eyes or '*Mmm*' too loud – Leon decided he *would* order a second helping, after all.

He looked for the waitress but couldn't see her. Probably chatting to the chef, he thought. Around here, people didn't rush – *ever*. That's just how it was. She'd be back in her own good time.

Someone, though – or rather, some*thing* – had caught Leon's attention; it was Jayne Angel again: she was, with a little help from Molly, waving – waving, and crooning:

'*Yoo-hoo, Leon!*'

Leon chose not to croon *Yoo-hoo, Jayne!* Instead, he waved back. Only a small wave, mostly fingers, but the waving somehow mutated into bowing: the toy angel, full bows from her waspish waist; Leon, straightforward head bowing (he thought it best to keep it simple when dealing with a toy). He felt a bit silly, sure, but not as silly as he did when Molly's mother looked up and witnessed the curious event: Leon and a foot-tall plastic angel exchanging salutations. How do you explain that? He doubted *She started it* would help.

In the city, this kind of thing could get you arrested, or killed, or worse. Luckily, everyone was smiling. Mother was smiling (most importantly), Molly was smiling, Jayne Angel's face looked happier than ever, and Leon, too, was smiling – smiling like he didn't have a care in the world.

Late the next day, Leon was back on the train; leaving Llanidloes behind and heading home – although, for some reason he wasn't sure of, his destination was starting to feel less and less like 'home'. Other than this feeling (as the train sped north, exchanging the fields of Cheshire for the urban landscape of Manchester) Leon's mind was, on the surface at least, quite blank.

One day, he would look back; look back and agree that he really had no clue. Not then. Not consciously.

Of course, he *must* have known, somewhere deep in his subconscious; locked away in one of his many 'rooms'. Not the pool room. Not the library. Not the internal cinema. Nor the Records Room; a space stuffed with filing cabinets overflowing with lists and logs, both old and new. No, a different room entirely. A 'vault' or 'walk-in freezer', perhaps; its contents out of sight, packed away, stored, mothballed and iced over – a heavy door, closed, bolted, chained and padlocked.

But things can only stay hidden for so long.

As Leon would soon find out.

CHAPTER THIRTEEN

Dancing with the Big Boys

BEGGING YOU

By the time Leon stepped off the train, Manchester was getting dusky. By the time he stepped off the tram, the city was under rain. That it *always* rains in Manchester is a myth, but on this early evening, the legend *was*, once more, *true*. Only drizzle though so no big deal.

Despite the travelling, Leon returned feeling refreshed. He had panicked once on the train, when he thought he'd lost his notebook. All that work! He doubted he'd be able to replicate it easily; not *exactly* – and certainly not in its entirety. When he got home he would type the story – every single word – into his computer where it would be safe; he would make several copies, store it on a recordable disc, flash pen, external hard drive, and print out a hard copy – just to be sure. Not tonight though, it would take too long – he had to be up for work in the morning.

Leon was making tracks along the canal tow-path. As he was in such a good mood he'd again chosen the scenic route home; the drizzle would, he had forecast, blow over. Now, his body arched against the ferocious downpour, he wished he'd taken the more direct route. The harsh, pelting rain made a heavy patting noise as it bounced off his head and rucksack. Up ahead, the road bridge offered shelter.

Beyond this bridge lay the skateboard-park then the long, narrow strip of scrubland (within a high mesh-wire fence) which bent left as it followed the curve of the canal. As Leon broke through a wall of stair-rod rain and entered the murky cover of the low-slung bridge – the skateboard-park's dim floodlight vaguely contrasting the span's gloomy interior – Leon immediately had a bad feeling.

And sure enough, from the shadows behind the bridge's support columns, out stepped Danny, zipping up his fly.

Leon had intended to shelter for a few minutes, see if the monsoon-like rain eased. Now, given the choice of Danny's company or rejoining the deluge, Leon chose to press on. He didn't get far. Danny intercepted his course and blocked the way.

'Fuck me; look who it is. Hello, *Halfwit*. Out for a stroll?'

'Oh hello, Danny,' said Leon. 'About that halfwit thing—'

'You're wet.'

'Yes, it's raining.' *Jeez, what is this – the Rocky Horror Picture Show? We'll be singing Time Warp in a minute.*

Danny took his time installing a cigarette and for a moment, all Leon could hear was the sound of rain falling, behind, above, and ahead of him, pounding on the towpath, splashing the surface of the canal, pummelling the road. Danny popped a chrome lighter, deftly igniting a large flame. As the cigarette end sought heat, Leon noticed the lighter's illuminated motif: a naked, black woman posing provocatively within a playing-card design: the Queen of Spades. Not a range they sold in Keys-n-Stuff.

Leon wasn't sure if the lighter was offensive or celebratory but it certainly looked expensive; high-priced yet crude. As the flame lit Danny's indifferent-but-in-control face – a multitude of tiny fires appearing in his gold teeth, iced grillz and fancy bling – Leon noticed the blue-grey eyes staring back; they were icy and remote – and yet Leon thought he detected a hint of warmth he hadn't noticed before. Was Danny all show?

Danny took a long drag; tobacco cracked and sizzled. As he exhaled, he seemed – though they had known each other for years, attended the same schools – to be trying to figure Leon out (like a stand-off in *Fistful of Dollars* – except that Leon wasn't armed and Danny might well have been).

Leon wondered if he should speak or wait and see where this went. He had the option of running, of course; turning, and legging it as fast as he could . . . No, the rucksack would slow him down; and dumping all his stuff would be a high price to pay for improved velocity – and who knows, Danny might be faster than he looks. Besides, slipping off the rucksack can be tricky at the best of times, on the run might prove impossible. Maybe push him in the canal? Nope, that would only invite future problems – especially if the oaf could swim. Maybe *he* should jump in, swim for the far side . . . Nah, the high probability of drowning or being stoned – or shot! – put him off. He would sink under the weight of his water-logged rucksack and never be found. Lost forever! Nobody would ever know. No-one would ever read his stories. Perhaps it was due to the positivity of his trip to Wales that Leon now felt it might be better to stand his ground for once. In the city, any sign of weakness can—

'Been away?' asked Danny finally, peering over Leon's shoulder – his voice amplified by the low bridge but also muffled by the relentless rain.

'What do you want, Danny?' said Leon in as neutral a voice as he could muster.

'That's not very friendly,' said a disembodied voice from behind a bridge support column. Undoubtedly Carl's soprano whine but it wasn't Carl who came out. Two girls, young teenagers, thin and tired-looking, super-short skirts and skimpy tops, appeared: one wiped her face and mouth, flicked her hand towards the canal (there followed a small *ploop* sound); the other, an unnoticed pendulous blob of what Leon took to be fresh ejaculate swinging from her chin, smiled stiffly at the newcomer.

Each girl deposited something Leon couldn't make out into their handbags (Leon assumed this had been a drugs exchange of some kind; perhaps a baggie for a faceful of discharge type of thing; a take-one, get-the-other-free deal) then the girls linked arms, opened a weedy brolly, and tittering to each other, headed out into the rain, their uncovered arse-cheeks twitching in tandem.

Carl now put in an appearance, adjusting his clothing.

'I said: *That's not very friendly.*'

'Hello, Carl. Sorry, I didn't see you back there.' Leon shrugged the rucksack, starting to feel its weight.

Carl produced a mobile phone, held it up. He intended to film the encounter.

'No,' he said, coming up close. 'I'm the Shadow Man.'

'That's nice,' said Leon somewhat bravely given his situation. He thought it put a smile on Danny's face, though – momentarily.

•

Carl circled like a jackal, prodding at the rucksack with his free hand. Leon shifted his feet; spontaneous moves preserving equilibrium.

'Seen your boyfriend, lately?' Carl enquired.

'He's not—'

Carl spoke into Leon's ear: 'Coz we fucking haven't.'

'He owes me money,' Danny said. One eye squinted as he took a pull of his cigarette and Leon wondered, briefly, if he was trying to imitate Willis, or maybe Eastwood.

'What are you telling *me* for?' Leon asked, with a hint of weariness. He couldn't help it; he was tired and wanted to get to bed. *Some of us have work in the morning . . .*

'Well, it's like this,' Danny said, almost apologetically, 'if he doesn't pay soon, the debt increases.'

'Always a shame when that happens,' Carl added, his circling picking up speed.

'And you know what it's like,' Danny said, 'when a debt spirals . . .'

Carl leaned in: 'Someone ends up getting hurt.'

They were taking turns to speak. Leon wondered if they'd rehearsed. 'And when exactly did he borrow this money? It's the first I've heard—'

'Carl,' said Danny clicking his fingers.

Carl didn't appreciate the finger-clicking – like, what was he, some kind of fucking servant? And couldn't Danny see he was filming? Nonetheless, Carl dug out a battered notebook, flicked clumsily through crumpled pages.

Leon nearly laughed. The notebook was no bigger than a ticket-stub. He wondered if Carl had a tiny pencil to match.

'Friday,' announced Carl gravely, as if Friday was months ago rather than the day before yesterday.

Oh, this was ridiculous. Was it too late to run – to escape all this hideousness? Probably; they were too close. Besides, Leon knew he shouldn't; this was just a farce – a couple of dolts acting out a hard-man pantomime. They wouldn't actually do anything *too* murderous to him. Would they? And anyway, it wasn't *his* debt; it was Moss's – surely if anyone was going to get hurt . . .

'Maybe if something happened to his boyfriend, he'd be a bit quicker to pay up,' suggested Carl.

'*Quicker?*' Leon turned to Danny. 'I thought he said *Friday* – that's only two days.'

Danny remained silent but Leon believed he witnessed a brief, unspoken acknowledgement that recognised the fairness of this observation.

'Sometimes *two* days,' Carl advised with venom, 'is *too* fucking long.'

As Leon wondered if Carl thought *two* and *too* were spelt the same, the rat-faced one lit the tail end of a previously-smoked joint (from a plastic lighter), inhaled, exaggerating the pleasure drawn, exhaled slowly then said:

'What do you think, Pussy? Would it send a message to *your boyfriend* if something bad happened to *his?*'

'*Me?*' Leon said, letting the whole 'boyfriend' thing slip (it bored him now). 'Why would something happen to *me?* It's not my—'

The question went unanswered as Carl suddenly whipped out a hand gun and slammed the butt down hard into Leon's nose. The crack reverberated within the solid structure of the bridge. Leon took an unsteady stutter-step; one hand went out to the side, reaching for support that wasn't there, the other cupped a bleeding nose.

'Oh, that's *got* to hurt!' screamed Carl jigging excitedly.

Leon dropped to his knees and collapsed forward as if praying to Mecca. A truck thundered overhead and he felt the full weight of the rucksack judder against his back.

'When did you get a fucking gun?' Danny steamed.

Carl ripped away the rucksack (after much trying had produced nothing more than comically jerking around its tightly strapped-in owner) and tossed it into the canal; the pack bobbed for a while then sank under a trail of bubbles.

A swift kick was now dispensed into Leon's side.

'Think you can remember to give him the message, Pussy?' Carl leaned over, spat at Leon's face. 'Hey, Nutter, are you hearing me? Do – you – understand?'

Leon had barely enough faculties remaining to be thankful his precious notebook was safely secreted in a trouser pocket.

'I think he's got the message,' Danny said. 'Remember, he's not the one—'

'He's a cunt! They're *all* cunts!' hissed Carl with the contempt he thought cunts – *all* cunts – deserved.

He flicked the last of his joint at Leon's head to punctuate his assessment. A small spray of sparks bounced up and fell away; some dying mid-air, some on the ground.

'I know *he's* a cunt!' barked Carl, pointing. 'He's the biggest *cunt* of all! BIGGEST CUNT EVER!'

Contorting his face, Carl stamped down hard on Leon's leg in what Danny knew to be an overblown impersonation of Carl's hero: Bruce Lee.

'Come on, Carl,' Danny said. 'I've got fucking things to do, even if you fucking haven't.'

'Hello, what's this? . . .'

Carl patted Leon's thigh pocket.

Danny watched as Carl, still filming, rolled Leon onto his side, rifled a pocket and came up with a notebook.

'You know, I worry about you sometimes,' Danny said. 'I really do.'

'He'll be alright,' Carl insisted. 'It was just a fucking tap.'

Calmed now (Carl's anger quieted as quickly as it had flared) he turned random pages. 'And what have we here?'

He nudged Leon with his foot.

'Fuck me, it's Fuckwit's notebook!'

'We don't need his fucking notebook,' said Danny.

'You're right. We don't.' He gave Leon another toe-jab.

'What shall I do with this, Fuckwit? Chuck it in the canal? Or should I keep it and maybe read it later?'

'Please don't throw it away,' Leon whispered.

'What's that, Ichabod? *Throw it away?* . . . Oh, *don't* throw it away.' He addressed Danny: 'He's gone for option two.' Laughing uproariously – he sounded like a dog's squeaky toy – Carl stuffed the notebook into a back pocket.

'Right, fuck this for a game of soldiers, I'm off,' said Danny moving away, back the way Leon had come.

'Yeah, and I need to eat. I'm well fucking starving.'

Walking, Carl viewed the recording on his mobile, laughing in unnaturally high-pitched squeaks at the high-jinks . . . he offered to share the footage.

Danny declined.

Undeterred, Carl continued to review his handiwork: left-handed filming; right-handed pistol-whipping. Seconds later, dancing like a kid on Christmas morning, he put in a big 'OH!' at what Danny assumed was the key moment. He made a fist, satisfied he'd been able to capture the quick-fire gun-to-the-bridge-of-the-nose incident so well.

'It'll sting like a fucking bitch in the morning, though,' the ratty one said. Then he noticed Danny giving him the eyes. 'What?' he asked.

Danny shook his head. 'You're fucking crazy; you know that, don't you?'

Carl laughed and stowed the phone . . . they had stopped at the edge of the bridge – *before a waterfall* – the rain had become torrential; heavier and noisier than ever.

Pulling the hood of his top over his baseball cap, Carl shouted: 'Shit, man, we're gonna get fucking soaked!'

Danny extracted a beanie hat from inside his jacket, donned it, and adjusted its position.

As Carl launched into the deluge Danny looked back at Leon, lying stationary in the foetal position, head slightly off the ground, as if watching. But in truth, Danny was more concerned about the gun tucked in Carl's pants.

Might be time, Danny thought, for a bit of serious wing-clipping (and not just because Carl's Heckler was bigger than his own Glock). Then he zipped up his jacket and barged through the curtain of rain.

Nose purple and bleeding, rattled-eyes aimed towards the tow-path, Leon tried to focus on his assailants but the image was hazy and double. Carl and Danny – or rather, their imprecise shapes – left the dry shelter of the bridge then disappeared as they broke into splashy runs.

Their wet footfalls died instantly, swallowed by vicious downpour, and Leon's cheek settled on the cold, dusty concrete . . . he could smell the damp, musty air – and something else – something unexpected and out of place.

Oranges? . . .

Before he passed out, he may have uttered: 'I am not an animal. I am a human being.' If he did, it was quiet.

After that everything went black –

– *Very* black.

Later, when most of the black had leaked away and what was left lightened to fog-grey, Leon sensed he was lying on the ground. Heard slapping or ripples or lapping; something wet, anyway – his head, on cold rock (an edging stone?), had to be near water. He blinked open weary eyes and felt their sting as a clouded brain tried to make sense of the slanted, unfocused view now streaming in through out-of-whack lenses.

As his vision slowly focused, adjusted and readjusted, he made out the waterway and tow-path ahead; equally blurry, they meandered off side by side into the near distance past the skateboard-park and scrubland. A fox scaled the mesh-wire fence and padded down the tow-path, along the water's edge. The vixen stopped at Leon's side, brown eyes staring inquisitively over the cooked chicken carcass gripped in her thin jaws, then trotted off to where Leon couldn't see. He was alone again.

Although he felt overly heavy and unable to move, Leon thought he really should try . . .

His legs were stiff, and one, around his thigh or knee, or both, was extremely painful but after a lot of panting and pushing of arms, he finally managed to sit up.

Behind – in the direction Leon was vaguely starting to recall coming from – dimly lit from the left by the lights of Precinct Crescent (a service road that runs around the back of the shopping centre), the tow-path and allotments offered a subtle, low-key winsomeness.

In the same direction – on the other side of the canal – numerous security lights, perched loftily on the rear of a series of retail warehouses and commercial properties, reflected upon the canal surface. Most people would find nothing to appreciate when faced with the backside of Carpet World, Halfords, Pizza Hut, DFS, and Comet. But Leon saw beauty in how their myriad illuminations replicated as thousands of frivolous glossy ribbons upon the sluggishly-undulating mercury-like water. And he liked how the two scenes contrasted perfectly in terms of light and energy, the way they balanced one another, counterpointed and contradicted yet complemented each other's . . .

He lost his train of thought but eventually found another. Oblivious to the ridiculous reality of lazing, like some kind of hobo, next to a stinky canal full of dumped furniture, rotting mattresses and corroding domestic appliances, Leon found pieces of Presently and Previously – as with a considered jigsaw – gradually coming together, one at a time: it was night (the *same* night, he hoped); the rain had ceased; his face hurt; the rucksack had gone; and, apart from a dull ringing in one ear, it was quiet again.

Trying to remember more, searching between the clouds in his head, he turned to face the interior bridge wall. And there before him, on the concrete, as if watching a home ciné film, the images slowly began to play out in full: the train station; the tram station; the wooden steps; walking south of the precinct (away from the narrow bridge that carries the tramway over the canal); torrential rain; a severely puddled tow-path; this bridge (Sale Road Bridge); Danny lighting up; girls in short skirts and skimpy tops–

(a shame Leon couldn't remember other facts so easily, but more of that later)

–dribbling chins and hand-flicks; Carl, the ratty rat-faced rat; an object (a gun?); one flash of light . . .

There was nothing else – just concrete again.

Leon touched his nose and winced from a burst of pain, then jolted when a sudden noise startled him: an eighteen-wheeler rumbling noisily overhead, shuddering the bridge.

Once the shock had passed he felt woozy again, the need to lie back down. And so he did. Surprisingly, it proved only a little easier than sitting up had been.

Prone once more he looked back to the water. There was, Leon had always believed something invigorating, yet, at the same time, calming – both sobering *and* intoxicating – about a body of water (the sea, a lake, a river, a stream, even a not-particularly-pleasant canal).

Despite his situation, as he eased his limbs back into a foetal position, he felt unburdened and absolved. Although in pain and wronged, he became – as odd as it sounds – *comfortable* lying here, unseen and abandoned.

After a length of time (he wasn't sure how long but a goodly amount) he perceived even bigger clouds rolling in. Was it the old familiar blackness returning? For some reason, he didn't care; wasn't worried at all – a *new* emotion had enveloped him. But what was this feeling – *Bliss?* The sensation was definitely exhilarating. Could he be drunk? He *was* lying down. No, he hadn't had a drink for as long as he could remember. Something else . . . Felt like – *Euphoria.* Or at least what he imagined euphoria to feel like.

From his renewed slanted view of the canal, he grinned at the surface; he wasn't sure why – just sharing the joy. He started to hum a tune he recognised but couldn't remember the name of. He stopped humming when he detected the smell of fruit. Tangerines? Satsumas? What *was* that? Was it Christmas again? Like when he was a kid. Is that why he was feeling so happy?

He laughed. Laughed hard and loud and long, a noise such as a downed and demented crow might make. What a sight he must have looked, this broken young man lying beneath a cold bridge, isolated beside a stagnant canal, cackling like a loon (no one could have blamed you, had you been there, for walking by without stopping).

When Leon was all laughed out, he let out a long, tired sigh and stared vacantly at the canal – at a bright mist that floated graciously over the water. Had the mist been there before? And was it really there on the water, or just in his eyes? He blinked slowly (through swelling, stiffening eyes) but the mist didn't clear. He'd seen night mists before but never one that appeared to be lit from within.

He watched for a moment and became mesmerised; the mist seemed to be moving – or rather, reshaping – and at a speed that felt increasingly unnatural. The outer edges pulled in and the centre cleared as the individual wisps gathered to form a shallow ring. This ring, hovering inches above the canal surface, now began to spin excitedly, the millions of tiny water droplets whisking themselves into frenzy. They rushed together, coiling upwards, to form a tall, thin column – a spinning vortex that proceeded, over the immediate vicinity of the waterway, to move out in expanding spirals, orbit a few times, then return, in ever-decreasing circles, back to its starting point – then, as quickly as it had formed, the performing mist was gone.

So profound was Leon's sense of elation at this point that he wanted to stand, or at least sit back up, and applaud, but the pain in his leg was so intense, he settled for '*Wow.*' And there was more to come; he could sense it.

Perhaps he was dreaming or delirious (he vaguely recalled a recent blow to the head or face) but no matter, he would enjoy whatever came next; whatever it was, he decided, did not intend to harm him.

He stared at the water for what seemed like an age but nothing happened.

Then:

Tiny coloured-lights, glowing deep within the dark water, proliferated and rose like bubbles. Countless numbers broke the surface, spreading an effervescent film of sparkles that fizzled and danced as they radiated out across the water. These lights felt like a sign, a precursor; the herald of a coming event. The spectacle gave a sense that something momentous was approaching. A strange sound, high-pitched but pleasant, with an almost angelic quality, grew nearer, filling the air . . .

Paralysed with awe, Leon watched as a form rose in the inky water: female, shapely, but only part human; the water shimmered as it streamed off her lithe body. Waist deep, she drifted effortlessly in his direction.

The mystical creature suggested a divine fusion of mermaid, angel and water-nymph. Most immediately noticeable were coral red lips, spell-binding green eyes, and flowing auburn hair that cascaded from a crown of dew-covered water lilies. Motionless, but smiling, Leon could only stare as she glided towards him.

Suddenly near, the creature leaned in and whispered into his ear. She smelled of rainforest and cinnamon and oranges. Leon listened attentively but the whole experience quickly took its toll and his eyes closed, as if drifting to sleep.

✳ ✳ ✳

When Leon next opened his eyes, his eyelids flickered apart to find the rucksack, mysteriously returned, close to his face; so near as to briefly fill his field of vision.

After lying there for a moment, he slowly, gently, pushed himself up into a sitting position. Surveying the waterway in both directions, he saw nothing unusual – no mist, no mystical lights, no water-nymph. He did though rediscover the pain in his face. Having fished the torch from the rucksack, he leaned over the water and illuminated his pitiful mug; the light hurt his eyes but it was the sudden shock of the terribly swollen features gawping back that made him lose his grip. Dropped, the torch disappeared with a resounding *plop*. New batteries as well!

Never mind, he thought, it's just a torch – albeit a Surefire 'Gladius' Maglite – and easily replaced. *Shit!*

Leon instinctively tapped his pockets as he remembered the notebook. Damn that rodent-faced thug! Could he get his notebook back somehow? Maybe offer the rat a 'finder's' reward? Or might Carl already be using torn-out pages to blaze up spliffs? Jesus, all that work! He looked around as if the landscape might help evoke a workable plan. Nothing came. There was only night. And in the morning there would be work – *and Reg*. How depressing.

Christ, was this the same night? What, Leon wondered, if he'd already missed a day! Or more! He turned on his mobile and discovered he had only lost an hour, give or take. Though pleased with that, he decided to get a move on so as not to lose any more time.

'Not now, Richard,' he said turning off the phone as it rang; it was time to face standing:

With much effort and huffing and straining, Leon slowly climbed to his feet. The elevation brought an unwanted gift: unsteady legs, like a newborn giraffe. (Luckily, the pain in his face helped to distract from the pain in his legs.)

After steadying, he picked up the shockingly-heavy water-logged rucksack and gave it a shake. The sudden movement caught his still-rubbery legs by surprise and he almost ended up in the canal. He felt as if he'd just come ashore after a long boat trip and was still acquiring land-

231

legs (like that time he landed back at Aberystwyth after his dad had hired a boat for a four hour mackerel-fishing-trip).

Four hours? You only lasted *five minutes!*

'Shut up, it wasn't my fault I got sea-sick.' Leon discovered, a little surprisingly, that putting on the weighty rucksack actually *improved* his balance. 'I was only seven.'

You were sixteen!

'I was seven! – Nine, tops.'

Don't listen to the voice of doom, Leon. Just get yourself home – and sharpish.

Was that his dad's voice or his own? He wasn't sure. They sounded so alike.

Loaded with sodden rucksack, water soaking through his top and dripping onto his trousers, his puffy eyes checked out the route home – a puddle-laden tow-path – and he set off on as straight a line as the wobbles allowed, concentrating hard on not pitching left, into the canal, and not stumbling right, headfirst into concrete pillars.

As the baby giraffe gradually found his legs, noticing one of them had a limp–

(*When was the last time you saw a car park attendant without one?*)

–Leon put the bridge behind him and, already thinking ahead, set to weighing up various alternatives for tomorrow's certain hurdles: like when Reg's curious mug will immediately react to his own and say: *Oh yes, what happened to you, then?*

How could a haematoma, perhaps two, be explained? *Oh, just some joker with a gun – a mistake, really – it wasn't even* me *he was angry with.* No, he would have to think of something less honest and more convincing. *Oh nothing* or *Mind your own business* would not suffice. Such a reply would only encourage further interrogation.

No, he needed something which, even if it sounded extremely unlikely, would, as long as he stuck to it and didn't waver, eventually quell the inquisition (not wavering was key, because Reg can – for a while, at least – be like a dog with a bone).

By the time Leon left the tow-path he'd decided he would, when confronted, start with: *What? Oh, this. Man,*

it was the dumbest, most crazy thing . . . He had discarded
*I got hit by a stray cricket ball, fell off the train, walked
into an unseen low beam, was bushwhacked by a
runaway tractor*, and other, even more bizarre options –
including one about a frozen chicken – in favour of a
simple: *I walked into a door.*

And after disbelieving faces had been pulled and sounds
of doubt vented, he would add: *I know; I can't believe it
myself. What am I like?*

HEROES

A short while later, as Leon limped along Broad Street, past
the shops facing the park, he noticed a broad-shouldered
guy with long straggly hair and greasy blonde beard, sitting
– a few degrees above *slumped* – in Specsavers' doorway,
supping from a large, blue-plastic bottle.

Ronnie was ex-Army but his once buff physique, like any
looks he might have previously possessed, had long since
been ravaged by alcohol abuse. The face was so flushed it
was hard to gauge its age . . . forties . . . sixties? A nose like
a big bad raspberry eclipsed three teeth; none of which,
chance decreed, lined up. He wore a filthy trench coat,
shabby trousers, and exhausted brown shoes in dire need
of new soles and heels; one lace was broken and tied tight,
the other had been replaced with nylon twine.

'Fuck me, what happened to you?' said the wreck of a
man. The accent was as uncertain as the age. Leon had
always assumed it was because Moss's uncle moved around
a lot. At least he did when he was in the Army. Now, he just
ricocheted between Bargain Booze, the park, his scuzzy flat,
and, for the occasional meal, Moss's house.

'What? Oh, this. Man, it was the craziest thing. I was
coming out of the bathroom . . .'

Ronnie's ruddy face pulled to one side, a massive tic
Leon had never seen before. In a mild panic he assumed
the ex-Sapper would never swallow the hackneyed door
thing and switched: 'And walked into a lamp post.'

'*A lamp post?*' parroted Ronnie. He glugged more White
Lightning then stared blankly at Leon. Had he spotted the

233

glaring lie? If questioned, Leon decided, he would claim he'd meant to say: 'Coming out of the *house.*' Just a slip of the—

'Fucking hell – and I thought *I* looked bad.'

'I know, I know, I can't believe it myself. What am I like?'

Ronnie took another long swig then put his bloodshot eyes back on Leon. Silence – a *long* silence. Was Ronnie still in the room? Leon found it hard to read the alcohol-fuelled face, if indeed there was anything to read.

'So how are you, Ronnie?' Leon asked at last. 'Been to see Moss?'

'Don't get me started on Moss,' Ronnie blurted. (Leon would swear blind if you asked him that Ronnie's face went even redder.) 'That greenhorn's walked into a fucking minefield and doesn't even know it.'

Ronnie's sombre comment made Leon rethink: rather than go straight home, as he'd planned – and considering the face-ache, congealed blood, swelling, possible concussion and in-and-out vision, it might be advisable – he decided he would, instead, call in and see Moss.

INTERESTING DRUG

The bedroom was New Age Traveller meets old-school Hippie. An acoustic guitar lay on the unmade bed (by 'bed', we mean, mattress on the floor). A rug, dream-catcher, and poster of Bob Marley hung on the walls. A set of tom-toms leaned back in one corner. Figurines of Ganesha, Vishnu, and Buddha, sat, stood, and squatted around the room (Leon couldn't see Ganesha without thinking of John Hurt in *The Elephant Man*). A ripped and repaired zodiac chart had been Blu-Tacked to the back of the door.

Across the floor, under piles of discarded clothes and odd sandals, lay a long rug: a woolly shag pile in a bar design, each stripe a colour of the rainbow. As with all Moss's vintage clothes – time-warped here from the Sixties and Seventies – the room, as usual, stunk of cannabis.

Moss was dancing to Psy-Trance or Psybreaks or Psy-something; Leon was never sure of the distinctions. Moss had explained it to him many moons ago but they'd both drifted off somewhere between splicing breakbeat basslines and beats per minute. Anyway, Moss (dancing to whatever it was) spotted Leon at the door and waved him in.

'Wow. Great eyes, man,' Moss said.

Leon knew instantly that Moss was high on something, and not just the regular spliffs. After a fraternal handshake and a brotherly embrace, Leon set off for the small table that attended an old, cracked leather armchair by the window. As he crossed Indigo, he realised he had shaken off the last of his limp. Perhaps he'd just had a dead leg.

'Hey, man, look at you. You left a trail,' said Moss staring into Leon's wake. 'That's *so* cool.'

As Moss got back to dancing, all arms and head, Leon rummaged through a bunch of CDs covering the wooden table – but it wasn't the music he was interested in.

'Check out the walls, man,' Moss said. 'See the patterns, how they're moving?' Then, a little disturbed: 'Oh no, spider lines.' As Moss whirled his arms around, collecting invisible airborne 'cobwebs', Leon found LSD tabs between CD albums by God Is An Astronaut and Guided By Voices. Disappointment closed his eyes.

Moss had either stopped collecting cobwebs or had collected them all; he was pointing at Leon's back. 'What's that, man? That's so weird. Like a snail.' After a fit of maniacal laughing he dropped onto all fours.

As Leon looked over his shoulder at the rucksack, Moss proceeded to crawl around the room. 'Wish I was a snail,' he said passing behind the armchair. 'How cool would it be to have your home on your back? Wherever you went, it'd be there – like a shelly caravan.'

Still focused on his rucksack, Leon had an epiphany, brain wave and revelation all at once . . .

'Moss,' he asked, with the quiet seriousness he thought the question demanded, 'how would you feel about moving to Wales?'

Moss's crawling stalled. 'Wales?'

'That's right,' answered Leon. Then, in a voice as close to John Hurt's as he could muster, he added:

'The best thing to do is to get your ass out of here. Best way that you can . . . Catch the midnight express.'

'Huh?'

'Well, it's not a train,' said Leon in his best likeness of 'Max', the character portrayed by Mr Hurt in *Midnight Express*.

'Sounds great, let's go,' Moss said, getting back to his feet – barefoot feet.

'What, *now*?' Leon asked, taken aback.

Moss moved quickly to the door but then stopped. He suddenly looked queasy, leaned against the door frame.

'Are you okay?' Leon asked.

'Yeah,' replied Moss. 'I think I just need some air.' He bent to his bedside table, which stood far higher than the height of his mattress, and picked up a football-sized candle. He turned to Leon, the heavy, waxy sphere between his hands. 'Let's play some football.'

Before Leon could say *I wouldn't fancy heading that*, Moss got deeply anxious; his eyes rolled left and right, taking in the room – he backed into a corner, big pupils shifting continuously, and attempted to squeeze inside a clutter-filled wardrobe whilst simultaneously endeavouring to close the door. He was still failing when Leon stepped forward, peered into the gap, over the only visible part of Moss – an index finger, hooked around the door – and said, 'I think you need some rest, Moss.'

Leon was escorting his friend to bed when, somewhere around Yellow, Moss got into a new flap about something else only he perceived. He put both hands on the mattress and pressed.

'Aha! Look, see, all matter *is* energy – condensed to a slow vibration. It's true. I knew it was. *I knew it!*'

'Yeah, yeah, take it easy.' Leon pulled back the covers and helped Moss in. 'Get some sleep,' he advised.

'But hang on, man, what about Wales?' asked Moss, his head sinking into the African Tribal design on the pillow.

'We'll talk about it later,' said Leon, tucking him in like a sick child.

WHAT IN THE WORLD?

The hall had low-hanging Moroccan lights, beaded-curtain doors, and walls rich with hand-painted flowers and Age of Aquarius swirls. All was funky and psychedelic (lots of purple, like Leon's eyes). Jefferson Airplane's 'White Rabbit' played in a side room.

Leon stepped carefully over a fat, treacherous-looking cat sprawled across the whole of the fifth stair; Dylan kept his beady eyes on him as he descended.

'Bye then,' Dylan said scornfully.

Leon stopped in his tracks, sized up the cat. No way did he—

'*Yeah?* What do you want, a photo?' asked Dylan. 'Go on, fuck off, you crazy bastard. And don't think you're taking Moss anywhere. You mother fu—'

Dylan clammed up as Janis entered from the side room, swaying to the music. 'You off then, Leon?' she asked.

Moss's mother was nearly sixty, barefoot and dressed like the ageing hippie she was: circular, wire-rim pink-lens glasses; Grateful Dead T-shirt; long (greying) hair ringed by a beaded head-band; tasselled top and yellow bell-bottom pants tied with a brown suede belt.

'Yes, it's getting a bit late.'

'Are you sure you won't let me get some Arnica oil for those bruises? Might bring the swelling down.'

'No, I'm fine, really.'

'*Fine?* I'm surprised you can see anything through those bumps.' Still getting down with the Jefferson Airplane vibe, Janis stroked Dylan, now purring innocently.

'Honestly, it's—'

'Fancy walking into a tree; what are you like? Let's hope the council fix the light before anyone else walks into it.'

'Hope so. Right, I'll say goodnight, then.'

'Sure you don't want to get high first?'

A spliff appeared in Janis's skinny hand as if by magic.

'Get those eyes feeling mellow?'

'No, I'm good thanks.'

'You don't know what you're missing,' she said igniting.

'I do,' said Leon quietly.

237

Janis's eyes narrowed as she inhaled. After the smoke had done its work, she blew it out through a satisfied smile.

Leon had moved for the front door but Janis, remembering something, raised a hand.

'Just a tick,' she said, reaching into a little wooden cupboard near the bottom of the stairs . . .

'Here, take this with you.'

Janis handed over Veronica's biscuit tin. 'Thanks for letting me have a look. I could really dig it, you know.' A Peace and Love smile broke out across her wrinkled face.

As Leon slipped off the rucksack, packed the tin, and shrugged the rucksack back on, Jimi Hendrix broke into 'All Along the Watchtower' in the side room.

Janis grooved with another blast of Herb.

'And make sure you do something with that blood blister when you get home. I can hardly see your lip.'

As Janis, eyes closed, drifted with Hendrix, Dylan, on the periphery of Leon's vision, scowled. Perhaps compelled by the feline intensity, Leon accidentally eyeballed him directly . . . Dylan hissed.

'Quiet, Dylan,' said Janis softly. 'It's Jimi. You like Jimi.'

THESE THINGS TAKE TIME

Excluding a pyramid of junk-mail (had all that accumulated in just two days?) there had been no post over the weekend. The answering machine was definitely switched to *on* – Leon had checked – but nope; no telephone messages either. Not that he was expecting any.

Now he lay in bed, *Titanic* playing on his TV (Leon had bought the DVD, and another: *Ghost*, from a charity shop in Llanidloes). As Jack and Rose cavorted on the 'unsinkable' ship, Richard passed outside the unclosed door with an ear to the phone.

Stopping suddenly, surprised to catch sight of Leon; Richard swung the door wide and stood within the frame.

'How long have you been back?' he barked, lowering the phone. 'I've been calling your mobile for ages. Have you been turning it off again?'

'Not now, Richard.'

'Don't give me that old *not-now*-routine, you loafing oaf. This is an emergency. We need coffee. There's no coffee!'

Leon reached down, lifted his soggy rucksack and threw it against the door. The pack made a resonating, wet thwack as it struck the wood. The door swung shut removing Richard from sight. From behind the door, he bellowed, 'I can't function without coffee!'

'You'll have to get used to it when I move to Wales.'

'You haven't got the balls.'

'I have, and I will.'

'You wouldn't last more than a week out there.'

'I've spent enough time there already to know that I—'

'And don't think I haven't noticed that extra pin. I know you only have that stupid map to torment me; remind me of all the places *I* can't go!'

'Yes, that's why I have it, Richard. Not to remind me of happy times, memorable trips; just to annoy you. Now go away, quickly, please.' Leon was digging in, steadfastly refusing to be wound up; annoyed now that he'd thrown the rucksack: an admission he had let Richard get under his skin.

'And what's wrong with your face?' asked Richard's voice.

Leon increased the volume remotely to mask Richard's ongoing complaints and demands: basically, continued reminders of his total inability to operate on any reasonably human level without caffeine.

WHERE I END AND YOU BEGIN

In the morning, Leon rose and put on a dressing gown. The robe was the same colour and design as Richard's but unstained and not as tired or worn-looking. As he was tightening the tie-cord, a fluffy, bulbous robin alighted on the window sill and tweeted noisily.

'Good morning, Robin,' Leon said.

The bird chirruped persistently.

'Yes, yes, I know what you want.' Leon grabbed a few bird-seeds from a drawer and spread them on the desk. The chubby robin hopped in through the open window, looked at the seeds, twittered, took one, and flew out.

Minutes later, Leon entered the living room to find it full of smoke, and Richard, in dressing gown and Che T-shirt, sprawled on the sofa watching some banal, morning TV program.

'Jesus, it's like the black hole of Calcutta in here,' said Leon, carrying a cough across the room.

Failing to spot the peeping Tom spying from the sill outside, he opened the window.

Dylan sounded his annoyance as he was sent flying.

'What do you know about Calcutta?' asked Richard. 'Anyway, the window's open so stop complaining.'

Leon turned, squinted through the thick cloudy haze.

'And don't give me that look,' said Richard.' I'm only smoking because there's nothing in for breakfast. I've been sitting here for over an hour.'

In the brief silence that followed the accusatory claim regarding le petit déjeuner, an over-tanned Breakfast TV Presenter announced the arrival of 8:30.

'What? It can't be!' Leon moved closer to the TV for confirmation. At two feet from the screen, those all important numbers were affirmed: zero, eight, three, zero.

Leon rushed into the hall. 'Reg is going to kill me!'

Richard heard the front door slam. Up like a shot, he gained angle on the window and burst out laughing.

In the front garden, Leon, in dressing gown and slippers, was anchored to the spot, optics firmly fixed.

A wild-looking mongrel, drool slipping from its angry mouth, raised eyes from a jagged bone. Large paws planted, it set to growling.

Richard and Leon entered the hall at the same time.

'Better get dressed first,' said Leon.

Richard laughed psychotically as Leon ran upstairs.

'You're losing it, Leon,' Richard shouted. 'Losing it!'

When he'd finally stopped laughing, he shook his head, and returned to the living room.

Lighting a fresh cigarette he mumbled: 'Crazy kid.'

CHAPTER FOURTEEN

As The World Falls Down

YOU SHOULD GO, LEON

The working week had passed slowly but by Saturday, today, most of Leon's facial ballooning had subsided; just one eye remained stubbornly swollen – and both had entered the purple-to-blue stage. The questioning had blown over, though. The plan of sticking to 'Honestly, I'm not joking, I really did walk into a door,' seemed to have done its job. Reg claimed he wasn't surprised, said it was 'typical' of daydreamer Leon. Seema remained sceptical – she *knew* something had happened – but if Raccoon Eyes didn't want to talk about it, she wasn't going to press.

Currently busy in dry cleaning, Seema shifted eyes as Leon entered. *My goodness, I thought even Leon couldn't look groggier than he did yesterday but how wrong I was. And then there's the panting. That is so not a good look.* In unison they checked the wall clock (9:03) and Reg, on the phone, back to the door (the door pinged as Leon entered but a customer had been in the process of leaving at the same time so Reg's attention had not been drawn – so far).

Seema, hurrying quietly, helped Leon into his tabard and he quickly got to work. Seconds later, when Reg put the phone down, he turned, saw Leon, and suspiciously noted the time. For the next few minutes, he watched Leon apply glue to a resole. Leon knew the boss was watching but that didn't matter, he had made it. Just. He carefully rubbed his bleary eyes and tried not to yawn; another night without sleep – how many days was that now? He had lost count.

The rest of the morning and most of the afternoon passed without incident of note: more shoe repairs, key cuts, sales of laces or shoe deodorisers, blah blah blah – and oh yes, just minutes ago: a lecture on the importance of maintaining good personal hygiene. Like it was Leon's fault he'd worked all day in a hot, stuffy shop; it's a physical job for pity's sake! Who wouldn't get a bit clammy and sweaty? Just because Reg was a cold-blooded son of a—

'Hello again,' said Poppy, all smiles at the counter.

'Oh hello,' Leon replied, looking up from restitching the upper on a Moccasin shoe.

'Jeez, what happened to your face?' *Your beautiful face.* 'You look like you were in a car accident.'

Seema nearly said something but didn't.

'Oh, nothing exciting,' said Leon. 'Something wrong with your key?'

Reg's ears pricked up.

'What? Oh no, the key's fine, thanks.'

With a sense of some relief but mostly disappointment – he would love to have been able to give Leon a bollocking before they closed for the rest of the weekend – Reg got back to completing the end of week paperwork only for the phone to ring. He answered it and instantly fell into a deep conversation with Head Office about a promotion they wanted the shop to run.

'It's a *great* key; works every time. No, I was wondering if you fancied a coffee.' *One where you don't have to run off this time.* 'You know, later, if you're not too busy. I realise it's the weekend and you might have plans.'

Poppy sensed a bout of waffling coming on so she stopped talking and switched to her Waiting Smile.

Leon approached the verge of smiling back. 'Well . . .'

'You should go, Leon,' chipped in Seema, who had begun to empathise with this curious girl's persistence. 'You should definitely go.' *Grab a coffee; get something to eat; take her home, shag her brains out – she clearly wants you to. Then get some sleep!*

Poppy gave a quick thankful nod. Seema reciprocated.

'Well,' Leon continued,' I've got to see a friend . . .'

'A girlfriend?' asked Poppy before she could stop herself.

'A mate,' said Leon. 'I've got to see a mate.'

'So, will you have time for coffee? It doesn't have to be later, it could be tomorrow. Or next week.' Poppy reprised her smile. Leon checked the clock as if it might somehow shake off his tiredness and help him formulate his plans.

'It doesn't have to be that *Kaff*,' she added. 'We could—'

'No, no, the Kaff's good,' he said. 'I like the Kaff.'

'*Are you sure?*' Poppy immediately realised she'd sounded somewhat revolted; she pushed on trying to sound more upbeat: 'I know a lovely little Italian place.'

JENNY, MEET POPPY

Leon was in two minds, both fatigued. One mind was glad to be back in the Greasy Spoon café, though he was saddened he hadn't yet spotted Jenny (the waitress's days off were hard to judge and he was hoping this wasn't one of them); the other mind was, if he was honest, again finding Poppy's endless poems a bit of a grind.

They were sitting at the table nearest the door, the only one free when they'd arrived ten minutes ago. She was currently reciting some sad poem about her childhood or something (Leon hadn't really paid attention to the work's rather long introduction) and he was trying hard to look suitably interested. He knew it was rude and unsociable not to be attentive but couldn't help himself. He'd look at Poppy, hear the procession of words, the long, long succession of words, a sequence he could only tune in to for so long, and in his head, it inevitably turned into a drone, a tuneless hum, and his eyes would slowly drift back to the serving hatch window, his portal to the kitchen, and potentially – *hopefully* – Jenny.

Was that wrong? Probably, but he just couldn't stop. Although, to be fair, in an effort not to make his vigil *too* obvious, Leon did what he could: smiled, nodded, feigned high interest at certain points (head tilts, eyebrow shifts) and tried to remember to use mainly peripheral vision in his search for Jenny; reserving the bulk of direct surveillance for when Poppy was concentrating on her notebook and not him. This is a similar move to the one most guys use for snatching cheeky glances of cleavage or craftily checking for nippleage[6]. Here the move was used

---

[6] Nippleage: Nipples that can be seen poking through articles of clothing. Not to be confused with camel-toeage.

for a more honourable purpose. At least, that's how Leon felt about it. It's not like he and Poppy were a couple. He wasn't doing that thing where married men check out other women. He was single *dammit* and Poppy was just a friend and he liked Jenny, and Jenny, he suspected, liked him, so what's wrong with that?

At this point, serendipity stepped in: Leon spotted Jenny, in the kitchen, taking off her coat. Had she nipped out? Was she just starting? If she *was* part-time and worked shifts, as Leon now believed, it would be hard to keep track of when she was in and when she wasn't. *Hard* – it would be impossible. Should he implement a log of her hours? Could he do that *now* (in his new notebook)? Would Poppy notice, think it odd if he made notes during her poem recital? Maybe she'd be flattered. *Maybe she'd be offended; think I wasn't listening.* Then a familiar problem presented itself: Leon worried that Jenny, if she saw them together a second time, would assume Poppy to be more than just a friend. His mind churned, again rummaging for the best possible subtle-but-clarifying introduction:

Hi, Jenny, this is my friend *Poppy.*

No.

Jenny, hi. Can I introduce you to Poppy, an old acquaintance of mine?

No!

Hi, Jenny. This is . . .

Poppy, still going strong and showing no signs of fading, noticed a couple holding hands in a booth at the back of the café; they smiled to each other as Olive unceremoniously plonked a single banana sundae in the centre of the table between them.

Oh how sweet is that? thought Poppy, reading on:

'*Love is blind, Love is careless;*
'*Possessing and caressing us.*
'*Moving words pass back and forth,*
'*Like some kind of shuttle bus.*'

Leon yawned, long and hard.
'Sorry, am I boring you?'

'What? No, sorry. Just not been sleeping very well.'

'No, no, it's me that should be apologising. That last one was terrible.' *Damn! Why had she read that one? She didn't even like it. Shuttle bus? Pile of crap!* 'I've got some much better ones.' *And worse, hadn't she read it before, by the canal?* 'Back here somewhere.' *Or had she?* '*New* ones.'

Several pages were flicked through. *If I have read it before it's a bit rude not to make a joke about it; even if he is tired. Unless, of course, he's just too polite to say.* She glanced up. *Oh dear, he does look rough, bless him.*

'Has someone been staying up late writing when they should've been sleeping?' asked Poppy.

'Uh . . . let me think. Last night was a house alarm going off . . . *all night.* The night before that was . . . what was the night before? God, I've gone blank.'

Poor thing. Perhaps I should just take him home and get him into bed. 'Ooh, Poppy.'

'Excuse me?'

'What?—Nothing—I didn't say anything.'

'Could have sworn . . .'

'Okay, listen to this.' She'd found a new poem; one she liked; one she knew for sure Leon had not heard before . . .

'If this doesn't put you to sleep nothing will.'

Poppy laughed, inviting Leon to do the same.

'I'm joking, of course. You'll love it. And this is definitely one you've *not* heard before. I wrote it shortly after we first met. Do you remember? I was sitting on the bench . . .'

She searched for a reaction.

'Leon?'

Still nothing.

'What *are* you looking at? You seem distracted.'

'No. Nothing.' He shot the better eye back to her.

Poppy shifted in her seat, followed where his line of sight had been, through the kitchen serving hatch to where Jenny and Olive were milling about, each busy in their own way: Olive waiting for two Belly-Buster orders to be plated, Jenny preparing a couple of strawberry milk shakes.

'Oh my God, you fancy the waitress!' announced Poppy.

'Okay. Don't tell everybody.'

'Just my luck,' she said. And with her keeping-things-light voice she added: 'Oh well, I guess you never can know; where Cupid will aim his bow.' The notebook was returned to the snazzy beaded purse (1920s?) from whence it came.

'So have you asked her out?' asked Poppy trying to ignore the sickly-sweet, annoyingly over-affectionate lovey-dovey couple; the ones in the booth who insisted on feeding each other spoonfuls of their shared banana sundae. *Get a bloody room, why don't you?!*

Leon shook his head. 'We've just flirted a bit,' he said.

'Then ask her. Maybe she's waiting.' Poppy exhibited a fist that squeezed. 'Courage, Leon, courage. Faint heart never won fair lady, you know.'

'No, there's no point really. I won't be here that long.'

'Oh right. Are you moving?'

'That's the plan.' Leon yawned again.

Poppy tried to mask whatever degree of disappointment she was feeling with her elaborate Good-For-You smile.

FIRE UP YOUR MUSE!

Leon, approaching Moss's house, suddenly stopped dead in his tracks. Up ahead, standing near a fluorescent daisy-themed Citroen 2CV – Janis's long time pride and joy – he caught sight of Pogo and Adolf with what has to be described as an axe-man. Leon automatically ducked into a side path and peered back round.

The lumberjack was tall, almost seven feet; wore a clichéd short-sleeved red-and-white checked flannel shirt, heavy boots, and filthy pants held up by wide braces. A massive axe rested against a huge shoulder.

Leon knew the three had only just got there because Adolf was making introductions: Pogo, Axe Man; Axe Man, Pogo. Adolf pointed out the size of Axe Man's biceps in case Pogo had missed them (he'd have had to be blind not to have noticed). The clown tried to fit both gloved hands, thumb to thumb, fingers to fingers, around one bicep but couldn't get near to closing the circle. He nodded to Adolf.

Axe Man now demonstrated some aggressive axe wielding that culminated in a near-by sycamore losing three quarters of its height. Pogo gave a contented thumbs-up then shook hands with Adolf. As an extra wad of cash changed hands, Pogo and Adolf furtively checked the area.

Leon jerked his head back, deeply troubled. He felt sure he wasn't just being paranoid; this *had* to have something to do with him. A plot was afoot, no doubt about it.

The notebook came out.

As Moss, smoking the latter half of what had been a fat spliff, gently strummed guitar in his room; he cast an eye over the Sightings list in Leon's notebook, now laid out before him on the bed. Leon was wiping traces of soil and vegetation from his trousers. Moments ago he had dragged his body over the large fence at the bottom of Moss's back garden, got it horribly wrong and belly-flopped into Janis's extensive vegetable patch.

'Your notebook looks different, man.'

Leon's fatigue slurred his words: 'Yeah, it's a new one.' He declined Moss's spliff.

'Why the change?'

'*I told you.*' Leon recognised his tone had become, at best, impatient. He attempted to adjust: 'Sorry, look . . . I've *rewritten* the list. Just look at it, please.' The heady mix of agitation, sleep deprivation, falling into a wet potato patch, concern over the renewed conspiratorial meeting between Pogo and Adolf, and now the inauguration of this chopper-swinging lumberjack, was really getting to him.

After lengthy consideration Moss spoke: 'So the same clown, and Adolf again – but this,' he leaned in to confirm the entry, ' "*Axe Man.*" He's new?'

'Yes, exactly,' said Leon, trouser-scraping done.

'Yeah, it *is* pretty weird. What were the others again?'

Leon raised his eyebrows. This was getting to be hard work. He pointed to the notebook. 'They're all in there.'

Leon schlepped over to the window, looked left and right. 'There's getting to be more and more of them and the fuckers are looking for trouble, I can feel it. They're out to get me, Moss. *They* . . . are out to get *me*.'

'Alright, man, be cool. Relax a bit.'

'Sorry, Moss, it's just . . . you know.'

'Here,' said Moss offering the spliff. 'This, my man, will definitely help to calm you.'

Leon accepted (it's not like he'd never smoked a spliff with Moss before; he just didn't need it all the time like Moss seemed to), took a drag and immediately felt the weed kick in; and actually, yes, it did relax him – *big time.*

'Wow.' Leon sat on the bed and a second drag followed.

'Nice, huh?'

'Yep,' said Leon catching the buzz (suspicions that Moss's spliffs had been growing more heavily-loaded of late appeared to be confirmed).

Moss read from the notebook: *'Lifeguard with a massive head.'*

'That was this morning,' said Leon exhaling smoke. The weed made his voice sound different. 'Bastard just kept staring but I knew he was—'

'Zombie pensioners?'

'Chelsea zombie pensioners; yesterday; five or six of them – fuckers chased me out of the allotments.'

'What were you doing in the allotments?'

'That's the other thing; I don't even know.'

'But you do know these things are just in your head, right?'

'Are they, though, Moss, are they? Can I afford to risk finding out?' Leon handed the joint to Moss.

'I know what you mean,' Moss took a long toke, 'sometimes I feel like I've discovered hidden portals to other dimensions; whole other worlds full of weird and crazy shit. This one time, I saw an elephant in a blonde wig; said his name was Floyd or something . . . followed me around for weeks. I still get flashbacks.' Moss drifted off.

'Moss?'

'What?'

'The list.'

'Oh yeah, man, sorry.' Moss returned the spliff and got back to it: *'Astronaut in the Chinese.* I remember him.'

'Yeah, he was alright. It's the more recent ones doing my head in. Like that Beefeater bloke wielding a humongous spear. Or the garden gnome, who leaned out of the telly, called me a lightweight and told me to Fuck off.'

'Oh, man, that's Gnome Chompski. Everybody's seen him at one time or another. I saw him once. Think I was on shrooms. All red and green and—'

'But I *hadn't* taken shrooms. I hadn't taken *anything*.'

'Well, maybe you should.'

'What do you mean?'

'Something for the road . . .'

'What; like this?' Leon held up the spliff. 'This is extra-strong shit, even for you – I can tell.'

'Well, sure. I can give you a couple of joints of White Russian or Armageddon Skunk to take home. Might help you sleep. But I was thinking more like . . .' Moss hijacked the spliff, had a blast then returned it.

'Like what?'

'Like something trippy. *Really* trippy. An E or Acid, maybe. Or Salvia; it's legal but it's really good.'

'Yeah, right; my head's already like a mad hippie's playground. I can't afford to make it any worse.'

'No need to get uptight, man. I'm just saying.'

'What? What are you saying?'

'I'm suggesting, instead of *making it worse*, one might cancel out the other.'

'Neutralise?'

'Exactly.'

'I don't know, that sounds . . .' Leon took another draw. What was the word? He'd got *neutralise*, why couldn't he—

'Counter-intuitive?'

'Yep.' *That's what I was looking for.*

'Sometimes things are, man. Sometimes things are.'

'That's true. That's very true.' *Or is that just making sense because I'm getting incredibly high?*

Leon took a deep pull then handed back the joint . . .

'Jeez, how much did you put in this thing?'

Moss grinned, took a hit then chased the spliff around the ashtray. After blowing the end, he said:

'If you want to try a tab . . .'

'Thanks, but all I need,' Leon flopped back limply on the bed, 'is to know what's going on.'

'Fair enough. Shame though. With your imagination it might have been spectacular.'

'That's what worries me,' said Leon.

Moss chuckled.

'I envy you the nymph, though, man. She sounded cool.'

'Yeah, she was amazing – I mean *really* amazing. But some of the others . . .'

'Was she *completely* naked?'

'*Moss.*'

'Sorry, man. Just wondering.'

Leon sat back up slowly and after a brief gap asked what Moss thought it all meant.

But Moss didn't offer any real insight. Maybe he was too stoned. Leon had only ingested a few burns and already felt *extremely* light-headed. Leon tried to put things into words his friend might better understand but it just came out sounding kind of pathetic and whiny (and a little like a parody of Moss); he said: 'It's twisting my melon, man.'

'Yeah, yeah, I get that, man. I get that totally.'

Leon leaned forward, forearms on his thighs; feeling a shade queasy. 'So, any ideas at all?' he asked.

Moss did have a theory, a cast-iron incontrovertible and unequivocal theory as it happens, but whenever he'd broached the subject in the past, Leon had completely zoned out on him so he no longer liked to bring it up. He offered another puff; not much left now. Leon declined.

Moss gently plucked his guitar.

'And you definitely weren't tripping on something?'

'Again, no,' said Leon calmly, 'nothing.' Then, privately, he mumbled: 'Don't think it was Gnome Chompski, either.'

Moss strummed thoughtfully.

'What rhymes with Nymph?' he wondered aloud.

Moss hummed a sketchy melody, took a puckered drag.

'I tell you, Moss, the sooner we move to Wales, the better.'

Moss choked, coughed at the roach. 'Come again?'

Moss leaned against the open front door looking half-asleep as Leon, now wishing he hadn't shared quite so much spliff, stopped on the driveway and used Janis's 2CV for support.

'But you agreed,' said Leon.

Leon instantly recognised that he sounded pitiable but it was the least of his concerns.

'I was totally out of my gourd, man. I didn't know *what* I was saying.'

On a normal day Leon might have thought this a fair point but he hadn't had a *normal* day for as long as he could remember. That, and some deep-rooted persecutory sensibilities, perhaps reignited by the weed, had climbed back out of their box: 'But we had a deal,' he said.

'Anything can happen on a trip, man. *And that was some trip.*'

From Moss's expression, Leon assumed it must have been a *good* trip but he wasn't going to let him off the hook that easy.

'And what about the money?' he asked. 'The money you owe Danny.'

'Already paid him.'

'What?'

'Yeah, yesterday. It took me a week but he was really cool about it. Said his customers always get a week before he adds interest on. A *full month* before he rips their heads off.' Moss laughed, like he believed Danny had been joking.

'Really?' said Leon not laughing.

There was heavy silence for a moment and in the pause he realised night had fallen (how time flies when you're stoned and flush with anxieties and paranoia).

The hush was finally broken by Moss:

'Look, we both need some sleep. It's late. Why don't you let me think about it?'

Leon thought this fair, too, but for some reason didn't say so. He moved to the gate on what felt like puppet-legs, checked the coast was clear then plodded away, taking a last, almost pleading look back at Moss.

A pang of profound concern – no doubt instigated by all that he knew about his best friend and underlined by the hang-dog expression on Leon's blue and big-eyed face – pushed through Moss's cannabis-induced languor to make him shout:

'Hey, man, you caught the buzz; why not try a Hatter – it might fire up your muse!'

KING KONG AND MAD HATTERS

Two hours later, King Kong playing quietly on the TV, Leon lay on his bed, notebook open, trying to recreate 'The Geisha and the Samurai' from memory – the lingering weed had made him optimistic a full restart would be possible but in truth, he was getting nowhere. And then a solid *thump-thump-thump* took up residence in his head.

Disturbed, he opened the window and scouted for the source but as he did so the noise stopped. The thumping might have been coming from the garage, Leon couldn't be sure; all he could hear now was inharmonious Ragtime piano music (a heavy-handed version of Scott Joplin's 'Maple Leaf Rag') emanating from somewhere in the area.

Through the illuminated garage window he saw Richard drop a rubber mallet onto the workbench, swap it for what appeared to be an electric buffer, hold it aloft, spin it up, then seemingly satisfied, move back to whatever he was working on. Or *who*ever. The object of Richard's attention lay beyond Leon's vision.

'What is he doing in there?' Leon wondered aloud.

A shrill squeal ensued. Was that human or mechanical?

Leon didn't want to think about it; he had sentences to reconstruct. Closing the window made it quieter, but not enough. Still, he tried to recall at least some of the words that had come so easily in Wales.

At the exact same time, by complete coincidence and in total contrast, Poppy was relaxing in a deep bath filled with bubbles, surrounded by candles. As she scribbled away in her notebook, lines of poetry surged fluently onto the page.

A million miles away from this, metaphorically speaking – half a mile as the crow flies – Leon tossed his painfully barren notebook to the foot of the bed and growled with frustration. He picked up the remote and aimed; the TV volume rose bringing with it a dramatic score accompanied by a barrage of sounds: bi-planes flying; King Kong roaring; machine-guns rattling; and a woman, perhaps, Fay Wray, screaming.

As Kong swung a frustrated fist at a passing, out-of-reach bi-plane then caught one that flew too near, something occurred to Leon: *Hey, man, you caught the buzz; why not try a Hatter – it might fire up your muse!*

Leon picked up the notebook and shook it.

Three LSD tabs fell out.

One got held up for scrutiny.

The tab had an imprinted image of The Mad Hatter.

EMPIRE STATE OF MIND

Leon is above New York, in a skyscraper construction, leaning against a strong wind that waters his swollen eyes. He's standing within an open metal framework: the Empire State Building. Or, at least, it will be. He looks down. Far below his feet is the 1930s. The view is grainy black and white but he gets a sense of faint colour he can't see.

His feet – *bare* feet – are on a large horizontal girder. Shouldn't they be cold? If they are, he can't feel it. Under him, *far* below his muddy size 9s – over a thousand feet below – he sees the streets of mid-town Manhattan (West 34th Street and 5th Avenue), the Public Library, the Chrysler Building, and in the distance, Central Park. But how did he get here? And what is he doing so high up?

He becomes aware of being rooted, stuck to the girder – and feels rising dread as he remembers his fear of heights. A sudden feeling of nausea and vertigo makes him swoon. Invisible hands push at his back and chest. Laughter. He's not alone, then? His eyes move along the girder.

Construction Workers, eleven of them, all sitting, in vests, dungarees, gloves, caps, and lace-up boots; some have cardboard lunch boxes. No harnesses. No hard hats. No safety net. Can that be right? Then Leon realises *he* is one of the workers – the guy planted right in the middle. But he's dressed only in boxer shorts. Under his thinly-protected backside, the long steel I-beam feels cold and ominous. And everything seems even higher than before.

His feet, now in loose, unlaced hob-nail boots, dangle over the vast drop . . .

Just keep still, he tells himself.

And why is no-one talking? He knows the others aren't concerned about the height but why are they so silent?

All of a sudden, they speak (in New York accents):

'Whatcha got, Tom?'

'Cheese and pickle today, Al. What about you? As if I didn't know.'

'Yeah, salami again.'

The workers laugh. One slaps Leon, jovially, on his back.

The blow almost launches Leon off the girder; he wobbles but keeps his balance, looks at the drop and feels sick. A worker stands – it's Carl.

'Hey, Faggot, watch this.'

'Oh yeah, ya gotta see this, Leon,' says Al.

Carl does a full back-flip and lands unsteadily but then raises his arms in triumph. The others clap and cheer.

Again Leon's back is slapped, again he wobbles. *Who keeps doing that?*

'Come on, Leon, have a go,' urges Tom's cheese and pickle sandwich.

'No, thanks, I'm fine,' says Leon, pleased to have found a voice, at last.

Leon's fingers feel like they are about to burst; he becomes aware that he's gripping the girder, vice tight. And the workers, they're laughing; laughing at him – and the laughing is louder than it should be. Leon senses a change is coming. Something is about to happen. He knows Carl is going to speak. And he does:

'Hello, dollface, what's *your* name?'

All eyes turn . . .

Jenny, standing at the end of the girder, dressed in what Leon believes is a 1930s New York waitress outfit, unties a red ribbon in her hair; shakes it loose, lets it fall.

'Jenny . . .' Leon finds he is rising to his feet.

A cup is held out. 'Leon, I've got your tea for you.'

Leon sets off towards her but it's hard scrambling by; especially in . . . something doesn't feel right . . .

Pointed-toe, purple faux-suede, high-platform/six-inch-heel, shoe-boots!

The workers laugh, hoot and holler; one makes an 'Ooh, get you, sailor' comment.

Unsteady but undeterred Leon pushes on. *Why don't these guys fuck off? Can't they see I'm trying to get past?*

Carl feigns a push. Leon teeters . . . on the brink of falling. *Oh, shit . . .*

'Whoa, steady, mate,' Carl says.

Yeah, right, like you care.

'Leon, what happened? Have you got a black eye?' Jenny giggles then jokes: 'Have you been fighting over me again?'

Some time passes; hard to gauge. But Leon is close now.

He reaches out. Jenny leans in. Hand and cup inch closer . . . but shit, he's slipping . . . arms swing wildly.

'Come on, balance!' Leon yells. '*Please* balance!'

He sways side to side but swiftly realises it's a lost cause.

'Leon!'

'Jenny!'

Leon falls and screams like a girl, all the way down.

OILY ANNE

Leon lay in the long grass that had overwhelmed the back garden. He couldn't remember the last time it was mowed but that could be because he'd only just woken up. Anyway, that didn't matter right now; it was cold, night dark, and he wore nothing but boxers. He shivered, wiped his eyes, and discovered Richard, overexcited to the point of manic, kneeling over him, spying with the Big-Eye binoculars.

Leon sat up and followed the line of observation.

Richard was focused on an illuminated bathroom window, above and beyond the back fence, where a middle-aged woman applied moisturiser to her naked body. Despite lots of steam, she was clearly visible, and not unattractive in a Rubenesque kind of way.

Leon, strangely merry, placed a hand on Richard's shoulder. 'Alright, sonny, you're nicked.'

'Shush!' said Richard, flapping an arm in Leon's direction. 'Anne's putting on a show for us. She loves it. Look at her.'

'You big letch, give me those.'

'Balls. Get your own.'

Leon made a grab for the binoculars but Richard defended with his free arm. 'She's oiling her breasts, look!' he intoned, before tagging on a creepy, satisfied sigh.

255

Leon couldn't help it, he had to look – no, *ogle* – as Anne anointed her breasts with handfuls of glistening lotion. Quietly, and without averting his eyes, he said:

'This is so wrong.'

'Of course it's not. Anne's doing it on purpose. It's for us. She wants us to watch.' Richard had the flushed look of a horny teenager discovering his first glimpse of forbidden flesh. And *real* flesh. Not someone in a magazine or on a screen but actual, just over the back (so no fence-climbing sideways required to reduce oblique viewing angles), through the window, in the buff, neighbourhood flesh – and moving, doing things, not just your common-or-garden simply-lying-there sunbathing *semi*-nakedness.

But Leon was puzzled. Was he awake – *really* awake? The last thing he could remember was being in the Empire State Building. That *must* have been a dream. But had he woken after that? The damp grass under his backside and cold night air on his skin seemed to say he had. Still, something wasn't right. If only he could put his finger on it.

Shouldn't bathroom glass be frosted or something?

Richard pushed the binoculars at him.

'Here, hold these. I'm going to get the camcorder.'

Leon accepted the Big-Eye lenses as if by default and said, almost as an afterthought, 'And don't think I haven't noticed you're out of the house again.'

'I couldn't miss this. Look at her. Look at oily Anne.' His wild eyes shifted back to the slippery full-bodied Venus and her rigorous lubricating then returned to Leon, still sitting in the tall grass. 'I'll be back in a second. Shout me if she heads south of the equator.'

As Richard headed for the back door, Leon spotted Dylan near the wheelie bins – perhaps on the hunt for an unsuspecting mouse. Richard must have spotted him too because he ran a detour and kicked Dylan over the fence.

Leon vaguely registered the cat screaming on his unannounced flight but failed to witness the *whole* event as he'd succumbed to the power of the binoculars.

'Anne, you're so bad,' he said.

Just then, Anne stopped oiling and peered through the window.

256

'Oh shit,' said Leon thickly.

Anne wiped away a circle of condensation from the glass. As she leaned forward, squinting, her nipples made little holes in the steam.

Leon dove to the ground – the back fence now shielding him from Anne's watchfulness – but far from taking matters seriously, he delivered a line oddly reminiscent of *The Blue Lamp*: 'Here he is, Sarge; we caught him red-handed, in just his boxers, spying on his neighbour as she went about her personal ablutions.'

Leon laughed out loud. On top of a general feeling of ongoing merriment, and despite the arguably twisted situation he'd somehow ended up in, he had successfully amused himself – and that's a good thing. He stopped finding it funny when he spotted a vengeful Dylan bounding towards him at wildcat speed.

The condensation quickly returned and Anne was forced to re-wipe her makeshift porthole. She had definitely just heard *something*, though she wasn't sure what. The noise came from outside, a yell of some kind, quite high-pitched, possibly a young girl in sudden pain.

She found the radio amidst the thick, floating bank of steam, turned off Jazz FM, and now, her undependable portal already re-fogging, she finally opened the window.

As she looked out, her shoulders leaning into the chilly night, a cloud of steam billowed out behind her and up into the late evening sky.

Elsewhere, in a bedroom containing little more than a lacquered mahogany wardrobe and a small double bed, Bill peered out the window through a pair of tiny binoculars.

'Do you know, Norma,' Bill said, 'it never ceases to amaze me; the things people get up to.' He tapped a thin cane against his leg, then closed the window to cut out the shrieking and walked towards his wife.

Norma was on the bed, on all fours, dressed in a St. Trinian's Sixth-Form schoolgirl uniform, suspenders, stockings that showed off her varicose veined thighs, short skirt hitched over a saggy bare arse, and with her knickers around her knees.

'Ready when you are, Headmaster,' she purred.

257

CHAPTER FIFTEEN

Day of Reckoning

IN THE LIGHT OF THE MORNING

Leon replaced the ointment, closed the bathroom cabinet and stared at the fresh marks on the face of the other Leon, the one staring back from the mirror.

Standing in the harsh morning light, evaluating, examining, he tried but failed to call to mind how the scratches had got there. Like trying to revive a recent dream . . . the more he chased, the further away it moved.

Had he been sleep-walking . . . off his tits . . . or both?

Tits?

Had he *dreamt* of tits? Or was he just thinking of tits *now*? For some reason he flashed on a picture of a huge ball of oil falling from a skyscraper towards a figure on the 'sidewalk', a woman, naked apart from high heels and a red sou'wester—*Ouch!* – A razor-sharp pang stung his top lip.

Hang on . . . but no; the image had vanished as quickly as it had arrived and now he couldn't remember it at all.

Damn, he was sure it had been something nice, too!

He stooped to the sink, threw cold water at his face then reinvestigated his reflection.

The claw scrapes hadn't gone – they were real enough – and there were several of them; running in parallel lines, angry red grooves across his cheek, lip, and the lids of the non-protruding eye. Luckily, the stubbornly distended eye had escaped further damage. (Both eyes had now entered a green/yellow phase.) To say Mirror-Leon had a serious morning-after-look would be a grave under-statement.

Leon could hardly recognise the wretch looking back.

Although the cold water had helped a little, he continued to feel listless and lethargic, unsettled and bewildered . . . washed but somewhat slightly dazed.

Back in his bedroom, Leon opened the curtains. The 'good' eye blinked rapidly at the surprisingly bright morning sun. After an initial twitch, the other eye settled back to its enduring state of semi-immobility. And although he didn't actually see it, Leon felt that Batman also flinched, fractionally, as he was suddenly bathed in light.

As Leon's vision adjusted, he checked his mobile. Today was Monday . . . *Monday!*

I know what you're thinking, said The Dark Knight.

'You do?'

You're wondering what happened to Sunday. Well, I'll tell you: you slept it away – which is good because, boy, did you need it.

'So . . . it *was* . . . *Saturday* night?'

Yeah, and it was a doozy.

'A *doozy?*'

I'm an American, go with it.

'Okay.'

You took the tab—

'I took the tab?'

That's what I said. And you were tripping – *as I believe you kids call it – for several hours.*

'I saw . . . things.'

No, you only saw colours and shapes. Like a psychedelic light-show. Kind of fun, actually.

'Fun? It was bloody terrifying.'

Language, Leon.

'God, you sound like my mother.'

And no need to blaspheme either.

'Now you *really* sound like my mother.'

The Dark Knight can't condone blasphemy or bad lan—

'Hang on; it wasn't just colours and shapes.' A rush of images, like frames from a long-forgotten, badly-edited film, flooded his mind: New York—Carl—Jenny—Falling.

That was later, when you'd fallen asleep.

'And Anne? Oily Anne. Was that real?'

Who knows? – Hard to tell with you. But a word of warning: whatever you do, don't look over there.

Leon followed The Dark Knight's little masked eyes and spotted two brownish red feathers on the window sill. He picked them up and squeezed. 'No, not Robin,' he groaned.

Kind of ironic, isn't it?

'Come again?'

You know, with me being Batman. Hands on his hips, he bounced his eyebrows under his mask (at least, Leon imagined he did). *Robin, Batman. Batman, Robin.*

'Shut up, I need to think.'

The 'recall-film' dispensed another couple of frames: Richard, yes . . . but more importantly: *Dylan the cat!*

'The fucker!' spat Leon.

Holy shitting arseholes, where?! Batman's eyes darted from side to side.

To his surprise, Leon found he'd adopted one of his mother's poses: arms folded across the chest; he'd nailed her unyielding stare, too. 'So what happened to "The Dark Knight can't condone blasphemy or bad language"?'

Yeah, sorry about that; thought you said, The Joker. *Because he really is a fucker. You know that, right? He fucks with my mind, Leon. Fucks with my mind! You of all people should understand.*

Leon opened a desk drawer, dumped The Caped Crusader inside, and kneed the drawer shut.

Awfully dark in here, Leon – but that's okay – I am the Dark *Knight, after all. Good talking to you, though. We can always catch up later. You will let me out later, won't you, Leon? . . . Leon?*

By the way, you know it's the 28ᵗʰ next Sunday, right?

Are you there, Leon?

Hello?

✷ ✷ ✷

Later, on the tram, Leon was still wringing the feathers; held them locked inside a clenched fist. He had the persistent notion that Dylan had ambushed Robin. And that it was deliberate. Cats *are* evil, he thought (he'd suspected it for a while). Cats *know* things. And they definitely have the ability to plan; dispense retribution for a perceived slight. Dylan could easily have—

The thought trailed away as the tram pulled into a station and Leon – standing away from the opening – spotted Pogo on the opposite platform. He looked alert, like he was on patrol. Leon got the sense the clown was monitoring his movements. Despite the tram being full, Pogo noticed his quarry almost instantly. His painted mouth broke into a confident sneer. Leon understood Pogo's message to be: *It's just a question of time.*

Angry before, seething now, Leon glared back, his indignation making him firm; resolute. A steely resolve hardened within. Without forethought (and definitely not just because he knew Pogo could never make it over the footbridge before the tram pulled out; not in those stupid shoes) Leon reacted: 'Oh yeah?' he shouted, searching for more. 'Well fuck you! – you – you – Clown!'

But Leon's sudden aggressive incandescent boldness didn't seem to bother Pogo; a pernicious, self-assured smirk settled on his painted face and he dragged a white-gloved thumb, slow and menacing, across his throat.

'You don't scare me, you stupid bozo! *You big FUCKWIT!'*

As the tram pulled away Pogo's smirk hardened.

Leon jumped and turned (no mean feat at the same time) as Poppy gripped his shoulder.

'Sorry, you're right,' she said reacting to his startled face, 'I really must stop doing that.'

'No, no, it's fine,' said Leon catching his breath. 'Who doesn't like a good jump in the morning?'

I know I *do*, Poppy wanted to say. Almost did. Would it have been too forward? – Probably not. He'd have just laughed, she thought. And that would have been nice. *Damn, I should have said it.* Oh well, too late now. But actually, it didn't really matter; she'd been thinking it was probably too late for *them* now, anyway. That Leon wasn't the one for her; it just wasn't feeling right – like when you stir your coffee with the spoon the wrong way round, or put a shoe on the wrong foot, or pants on back-to-front.

She'd given him more than enough encouragement but thinking back, he'd never seemed keen to take the bait. *Oh well plenty more fish.* And speaking of fish, he could do with a shower. She'd thought he whiffed a bit the last time they'd met, at the café. Now, he smelled *worse*. Should she say something? No, it wasn't her place. Besides, she might embarrass him. She definitely did not want to do that.

Instead, she went for: 'So, who were you shouting at?'

'What? Oh, just some clown.'

'Oh well, at least you look like you've had some sleep.'

'Yeah, finally.'

'But what happened here? Had a run in with a cougar?'

Something like that, Leon thought.

'Or did you walk into another telegraph pole?' Poppy wanted to touch the scratches – gently – almost moved to, but something *had* changed, something held her back.

Telegraph pole – Is that what I told her?

Poppy had intended to come across as caring (if they weren't to be Turtle Doves they could still be good friends) and worried now that she may have sounded meddlesome. With no reply and not wishing to appear as one of those maternal, busybody Spanish-Inquisition-type girls, she quickly changed the subject. In as breezy and far from her own mother's interfering voice as she could manage, she asked: 'So, how's the story coming along?'

'Don't ask.'

'Oh dear, is it that bad?'

'Bad? No. Well, only in the sense that everything I'd written has been scrapped and I'm now back at square one wondering if I'll ever be able to put down in words again . . . the uh . . . you know, what's in my head.'

Leon cursed inwardly for not being able to put out a full and coherent sentence; if he couldn't *talk* properly how could he possibly hope to *write* well?

'Yeah, sometimes just starting afresh is the best way,' said Poppy. 'I do that all the time.'

Because Leon had grown to like Poppy, and because he now considered her to be a friend – a true and forthright friend – he felt he didn't have to let her comparison, between writing a relatively short *poem* and a *story* containing *tens of thousands* of words, slide.

'No offence,' he said, surprised at how terribly patronising his voice sounded – and though he mentally scolded himself for it, he couldn't stop now – 'but I think *poems* might be a slightly different kettle of—'

'I say *that*,' Poppy thrust two fingers into the air, 'to Writer's Block, turn over a fresh page, put my nib to the blank paper and wait. Just wait. It'll come, eventually.'

'Yep, me too, I do that,' lied Leon. Then he remembered Wales where it *had* been true. *Good, he wasn't a liar; he couldn't face being patronising and lying on the same tram journey.* Although he would tell a *white* lie if he thought someone might be upset by the truth, he always preferred not to lie if possible. He was, after all, an *honest* person.

'Speaking of poems, I've got a new one if you fancy it. No pressure.'

'Brilliant,' said Leon.

The rest of Leon's week was unremarkable: a few concerned questions from Seema regarding the latest addition to what *had been, decreasing* facial injuries; and Reg fawning over customers. The boss was leading by example after he'd cautioned Leon and Seema that the store, as decreed by Head Office, needed to increase sales: additional keys and shoe repairs, more engraving and dry-cleaning, shorter lunches and later finishes.

By the time the shutters came down on the following Saturday, Leon and Seema were worn out. (Reg boasted he could have worked all night and done Sunday too, but Leon reckoned it was all an act; he'd probably collapse as soon as he got home, the ungrateful little toe-rag.) Never mind, as Leon began the trudge up Church Street hill, he looked back over the week and decided the time had passed quickly. And he hadn't had a single vision. Not since Pogo's throat-cut mime – progress, right? Not really; somewhere deep in Leon's core, he sensed they would be coming back; soon – and in numbers. *Just a question of time.*

Across the road, a huge, solemn collection of floral tributes, messages and soft toys, had sprung up around the letterbox and against the wall.

Tomorrow would be the 28th of October 2007.

'Exactly one year after the terrible accident,' said Leon, mocking Kay Burley's affected touched-by-tragedy and oh-so-fucking-deeply-understanding Sky News Reporter voice.

He did not hear himself do this, did not even realise he had spoken.

THE 28th

Filling the bathroom sink with water, Leon checked his face in the mirror. The scratches had faded, his face bore only a few remnants of light-yellow/grey shading, all tumefaction was gone, and he could now see clearly from both eyes.

'This is quite a list,' said Richard.

Surprised, Leon half-turned to find Richard on the toilet, pyjama bottoms around his ankles, dressing gown pulled up to the waist, and a burning cigarette wedged in his trap. He was reading Leon's notebook.

'A court jester?' scoffed Richard. 'When was that?'

'I don't know, last week sometime; he threw his puppet-stick at me,' replied Leon, turning off the taps.

'Hilarious,' said Richard. Then, gripping the notebook firmly, he grimaced, pushed and strained until a single, mournful fart was born.

Charming, thought Leon. 'Couldn't you have waited?'

'I'm amazed I need to go at all,' barked Richard. 'The only sustenance I've had in the last twenty-four hours is a thin rasher and a single slice of Farmhouse.'

Leon snatched away the notebook and slipped it under a used towel on top of the stuffed laundry basket to his left.

Richard sighed as the thunderbox echoed with scatological success. 'By the way, you missed out the one-armed wrestler,' he said. 'And what was that other list? It looked like *Times:* times *on*, times *off*.'

Leon ignored the enquiries and the awful goings-on beside him, and dumped his face into the lukewarm water.

After a final pipsqueak fart, Richard reached for toilet paper. Alas, the roll was empty, bar half a sheet. And that wouldn't give up easily (maybe it knew where it was headed); it clung to the cardboard tube like a non-swimmer to a floating log; the wooden kind, not the lavatorial type. A hard tug was rewarded with a single-ply of the half-sheet.

'For fuck's sake!' blasted Richard. 'This is getting ridiculous. Doesn't anybody do any shopping around here?'

As Leon straightened, lifting his dripping face clear of the water, Richard stood, yanking his grubby pyjama bottoms up to the waist. He coughed fiercely and spat the resultant mucus into the sink; the glob hitting the water with an unpleasant *plunk*. The hack and hawk was followed by a casual dumping of fag end – also into the sink.

Richard exited the room without further word, without washing his hands, and without flushing the toilet.

Leaning on the sink, Leon regarded the floating lump of phlegm and buoyant yucky stub – the latter slowly coming apart and browning the water – and it occurred to him that bathrooms witness far more than their fair share of appalling noises and events. Then he returned his gaze, almost reluctantly, to the mirror. A misty, unshaven face stared back. Both faces let out a long sigh.

After getting dressed, Leon went downstairs. From the hall he saw Veronica and Lester dancing Mod-style to '60s music emanating from a Bush radio on the kitchen work-top, apparently oblivious to the stocktake occurring behind them. Richard was going through cupboards. Most were empty or near empty, and the determined loon was making a list – on a page he'd torn out of Leon's new notebook!

Leon paused at the door, fuming silently; he'd already had enough of *It* for one day. Richard's head whipped round as Veronica called out: 'Morning, son. Want a cup of tea?' but Leon had already disappeared.

'Is that you, Leon?' shouted Richard into the hall, immediately rushing to follow it there. 'Running away again!'

Seconds later, he was blockading the front door and waving an extensive shopping list under Leon's nose.

'Here, we need these,' he ordered, shoving the torn page into Leon's hand, 'and we need them as soon as possible.'

'Some of us have to go out to work, you know,' Leon said, 'even on a Saturday.'

'It's Sunday, you idiot,' replied Richard.

'*I know*,' said Leon affecting the corresponding face. 'I meant . . . go for a *workout*.'

'Since when did you start working out?'

'I'm going for a long walk – that's a type of workout.'

'Great, you can get the stuff on your way back.'

Leon failed to find a quick enough reply.

'Now go on, piss off.'

'Actually, I might just *do that*, Richard. I might just *piss off* – as in leave and not come back.'

'What, again?' Richard laughed uproariously, which annoyed Leon.

'You might be surprised – one of these days you might be *very* surprised!' Cramming the page into a pocket, Leon pushed Richard aside and marched out.

'Yeah, right,' scoffed Richard from the door. 'Go on, *run away*. We both know you're coming back!'

Across the way, Vicky Marsden, skinny woman, harsh face, an excess of kids, supervised reluctant men unloading shabby furniture from an even shabbier van. Various well-worn household items and beat-up appliances cluttered the pavement. Denying the grumbling men an unearned smoke break she watched Leon, muttering to himself, walk up the street then turned to slap her children for locking two of the smaller kids inside the washing machine.

'What did I say about climbin' in there?' she screeched, serving up more slaps as she dragged them out. 'You'll break the fuckin' barrel.'

'Barrel?!' the other kids laughed in unison.

'Drum,' advised one of the men.

'Who gives a shit,' snapped Vicky. 'Just gerrit in the fuckin' house, will yer?'

Each pace put it all further behind but it wasn't yet far enough for Leon; Richard's voice still reached him: 'You have to acknowledge what's going on at some point, Leon! Until you do, things will only get worse!'

'Yeah, right,' yelled Leon. 'Like, I'm going to take advice from *you!*'

WE ARE THE DEAD?

Nobby was elated. Yes, Svetlana hadn't yet returned from nipping out for a burger over an hour ago, but Leon had just paid for enough shopping to pack four carrier bags and was now, once again (after he'd realised he still had money left) perusing DVDs.

The combined weight of the bagged goods pulled down on Leon's right arm, stretched it taut. Without a counterweight, the left shoulder, raised high, operated its limb like a crane, the hand riffling through upstanding rows of titles – stiff and awkward work but not putting down shopping was instinctual around here.

As he flipped through cases, he mumbled in a low voice, mocking Richard: ' "We *need* them. We need them *as soon as possible.*" Yeah? Well, you'll just have to wait. Not only that but I didn't refer to your scrawled inventory at all; not once. Yeah, that's right; *not once.* Ooh . . .'

Richard went away for a moment as *Brief Encounter* came to hand. Leon read the back cover then put it aside.

Thoughts of Richard returned with resumed riffling:

'And what did he mean? *Acknowledge what's going on. Until you do, things will only get—*'

Leon stopped, eyes locked to David Cronenberg's *Crash.*

The title's effect was pronounced. He blanched, became immobilised.

And what the fuck was that? Moving past the window!

Ashleigh! Pushing a small baby in an all-too-familiar buggy . . . and beside her; now walking – *Tyler!* The soft toy clown swung from his little fist.

But how?

It can't be!

Dumbfounded, Leon twisted his neck to watch the eerie threesome head for the precinct exit but quickly became aware of a gentle tugging.

Looking down he spotted a tiny hand pulling at his trouser leg . . .

Slanting his view, he saw the dirty hand extended from a thin, grimy, ragged shirt sleeve that poked out from under the DVD rack. Stooping, he found two sad, lost and lonely red eyes staring back; they belonged to what looked like a Dickensian street urchin. The boy appeared pathetic, haggard and malnourished.

The hand gave up its weak grip easily as Leon, facial features in chaos, instinctively backed away. He wasn't repelled by the abject unkempt appearance of the anaemic, neglected urchin; he was horrified that the boy was the spit and image – except for the beggar clothing – of him as a child.

A BRIDGE TOO FAR?

Leon didn't stop running (if, with so much shopping, you can call it *running*) until he had left the precinct far behind.

At some point he had equally distributed the carrier bags, two to each hand, and now, wheezing like busted bagpipes, he finally put them down.

Looking back and seeing nothing, he seized the opportunity to suck cool air into his hot lungs; the gasping and rasping sounded as fetching as it looked.

He studied the angry marks on his palms. Why had he bought so many tins? And why had he run *this* way?

In his blind panic he had exited the precinct, headed in completely the wrong direction: west, over the canal bridge on Sale Road; and kept on as far as the old swimming baths (a big, beautiful, Victorian building, now boarded-up, ringed by security fencing, made ugly by neglect, slowly being reclaimed by nature, and long since replaced by an insipid, generic Leisure Centre on the far side of town).

This meant he would have to return, go back over the bridge and take a left, north, up Stickleback Road. He would definitely not continue eastward, for that way lay the precinct with its possibilities of Ashleigh and Tyler and new addition, plus Church Street and the backbreaking climb.

No way, not with this much shopping and no mule to assist, he thought – although it would be nice to see all the flowers again.

When he'd passed earlier, the area around the letterbox had been awash with them; a sea of flowers rippling with colours and scents. Several candles burned in small glass jars. And soft toys sat against and upon the wall, tucked between railings. Perhaps next time he would stop and read the messages. He hadn't done that before because he knew beautiful, heart-felt, moving messages had the ability to make him cry and it didn't do to be seen weeping like a nancy in this neighbourhood. With his luck, Danny and Carl would drive past and bingo: whole new shit-storm.

Leon had recovered half the canal bridge when he was again compelled to set down the carrier bags; each now weighed over a hundredweight, it seemed, and his breathing – or rather his *lack* of breathing – had returned to dangerous levels.

As he took a moment, rasping, flexing dead fingers, and coming to terms with his latest sightings – wondering how he would phrase the new log entries: 'Woman and child +1/Ghosts? (Precinct) Hurrying for exit' perhaps; and, maybe: 'Street Urchin/*Me?* (Nobby's) *Pleading for help?*' – he heard the clatter of rattling chains and his face immediately registered the bitter pill of a new abomination:

Up ahead, towards the end of the single, narrow walkway (which ran on only one side of the bridge; the north side), a Cardinal in finest scarlet cape and mitre, was bent over the outer railings, upper body sticking out over the canal, cassock raised over a bare behind.

Not only that: the ecclesiastical official's plump posterior was being rudely violated by a shaven-headed prisoner in a red prison boiler suit; handcuffs and heavy leg-irons securely chained to a tight leather transport-belt around his waist.

For some reason, Leon thought it best to get moving, even though the decision would take him nearer to whatever this was. *Bishop buggery?*

As Leon moved within spitting distance, hoping to slip past and be quickly away, the prisoner broke, momentarily, from rhythmic grunting: 'You're next,' he said, pointing an inky finger at the bearer of the heavy shopping bags.

Leon swallowed hard; head spinning and his breathing in desperate need of an inhaler. There was a time when his visions had seemed almost funny and entertaining, playful even; now they were *far* from amusing. Not only was the frequency rocketing dramatically but they had become seriously disturbing and increasingly menacing.

Leon was now so close he could see sweat beads running over the homemade tattoos on the prisoner's neck; in its own way, this image, with its thrusting and snorting, was perhaps the most repugnant yet. 'Jesus, he's drier than an altar boy on the feast of Saint Stephen,' said the prisoner to Leon. Then, smacking the holy backside, he addressed the Cardinal: 'Do you know what I mean, Father?'

'I certainly do not,' insisted the Cardinal. He looked, imploringly to Leon: 'Honestly, I don't.'

This was making no sense: if these *were* nothing more than apparitions, why couldn't Leon make them disappear; *will* them away. He screwed his eyes, commanded them to be gone, and reopened – not a thing had changed. Despite recognising that what he was seeing couldn't possibly exist, not in actuality; the visions, he acknowledged, were just too intensely 'real' to be disregarded. With absolute certainty, he knew it would be impossible to ignore them; accepted he would just have to keep on avoiding them – no matter what. This in mind, he pushed forward; if he could only squeeze by, he might be able to slip, hopefully unnoticed, down the steps to the canal towpath and from there—

But the prisoner and his rigid out-there penis took a step back to block what little room there had been. Biting the bullet, Leon closed his eyes and walked forward – surely that would work – he'd walk blindly *through* them.

Leon felt the prisoner shove him, violently, and he reeled back, opening his eyes. *Jesus, they can touch me! They can make* actual *physical contact. How mental is that?* He withdrew several paces and for the first time in his life, as far as he could remember, he actually wanted to scream. And it didn't ease his sense of trepidation when the prisoner stooped, parted the Cardinal's bare arse cheeks, and spat a gobful between them.

'Oh, my God,' said Leon. 'What the fuck is going on?'

'Forgive him, my son,' said the Cardinal. 'For he knows not what he does.'

'Come now, your Eminence,' said the prisoner, working in some of the bountiful saliva, 'does it feel like I don't know what I'm doing?'

'Sweet Mother Mary,' said the Cardinal signing the cross, 'may the blessed saints preserve us.'

The prisoner laughed. 'I tell you what, after this, I'll let you kiss *my* holy ring.'

Leon's uneasiness quickly escalated to alarm and he scuttled away, back across the bridge, stuffed carrier bags bending his spine like Quasimodo. He glanced over a hunched shoulder in time to see the prisoner renew the brutal assault with a number of extra forceful lunges. 'Oh, that's much better,' declared the prisoner. Then he laughed like the devil himself.

'Oh, sweet Jesus,' cried the Cardinal.

'I'll second that,' said the prisoner. 'Now get ready to sing Hallelujah and Amen.'

No, no, no, thought Leon, this is *too* much – but there was more to come.

He hadn't got far, just past the middle of the span, when he suddenly stopped. Crossing the bridge, at the western end, was Axe Man, axe at the ready, head at an anticipatory angle, muscling forward, looking powerful and eager to engage. The only thing missing was 'Eye of the Tiger' by Survivor, but the hallucination was so vivid Leon imagined he *could* hear it – loud and clear (his delusions certainly didn't lack for detail).

Pegged to the spot, Leon watched the wound-up axe man move closer. Finally, Leon turned and headed back towards the eastern side of the bridge but the prisoner, now finished with the Cardinal, was ready for a fresh victim – he slapped a *Thanks for that* on the Cardinal's arse, pointed at Leon, pantomimed an excited lick of the lips, then, chains rattling, shuffled forward with a gruffly 'Come on, you own a purse – I'd bet you'd *love* to play Altar Boy.'

Leon reversed, turned again but the other route hadn't improved: close now, Axe Man swung the axe in vicious circles; a taste of what was in store for Leon, Leon presumed.

A check back to the right: the prisoner, closing in . . .

Again, to Leon's left: Axe Man, moving forward, axe held high.

'*Oh, come on!*' wailed Leon, sounding much like he did every time he'd suffered death at the hands of a zombie horde whilst playing Left 4 Dead.

Right, left, right, left; it was no use, he couldn't go either way.

With only one option available and the antagonists very nearly upon him, Leon clambered onto the side of the bridge. Deep in a trouser pocket, his mobile rang.

'Oh, fuck off, Richard,' said Leon – then he jumped.

THAT SINKING FEELING

Holding on to the bags, Leon had fallen towards the dark water with the sound of metal on metal (axe on bridge) ringing in his ears. Inevitably, he'd plunged into the canal, the impact forcing a mighty splash and ripping apart carrier bags, exploding groceries across the water. A jar of coffee had tumbled towards the canal bottom, bounced off a reedy shopping cart and slumped into thick mud.

Now, he hung motionless underwater like a discarded marionette, strings cut, all animation gone. Groceries, toilet rolls and gutted carrier bags, drifted over and around him like flotsam or jetsam; some clinging to the surface, some slowly sinking. Semi conscious, suspended in the murky green-grey water, Leon sensed what was happening above:

Up on the bridge, the prisoner and Cardinal hurried to join Axe Man. Pogo appeared from somewhere, too – had he been keeping watch from nearby? – and together they looked over, to the canal below where ripples still chopped at the banks as packets of food and sodden toilet rolls bobbed up and down on the surface. Leon pictured the painted smile but sensed Pogo was far from satisfied; knew the angry clown would feel he had *got away* – and this was *not* over. And he thought he heard Pogo (or imagined he heard Pogo) berating the inept axe man. Would no one rid him of this self-centred, self-indulgent brat?

Slowly, Leon began to sink deeper. Light grew weaker as he dropped into the watery shadows. He heard a muffled *sploosh* above his head then saw the axe narrowly miss his left arm as it plunged towards the murky depths.

For some reason, Leon thought of Mr Crawley. Perhaps because he had bumped into Creepy a few weeks ago in the changing room of the Leisure Centre's swimming pool; the teacher unselfishly spent a lot of his free time at the pool, dedicated as he was to swimming, life-saving, and the fitness of young boys. A healthy body, he would say, is as important as an inquisitive mind. He also told Leon that he should in no way worry about the prom-night taunts from the kids and Mr Brawn (History) about having a below-average sized penis. He even joked, rather unnecessarily Leon felt, that he knew some handy enlargement exercises.

Mr Crawley was always cracking what he reckoned were hilarious and in no-way offensive or inappropriate comments like that. He once told a first-year pupil: 'That's right, lad, go on; now clamp your lips down hard and give him a good hard blow.' Even the CPR dummy looked uncomfortable. *So* Mr Crawley: *so wrong* in so many ways.

And if regular exercise was supposed to keep you in a healthy condition, why did he often sound so breathy around the boys? Another teacher Leon wouldn't miss. Except that Mr Crawley was unavoidable. Whichever night of the week or day of the weekend Leon chose there was Creepy in super-tight Speedos and mirror-goggles giving it endless underwater lengths. Is that why Mr Crawley sounded breathy out of water; because he had gills?

After two hours of breaststroke and seeing Mr Crawley constantly slide underneath, face up, like some kind of villainous Aquaman, Leon had had enough.

Climbing out mid-pool, Creepy surfacing behind him, Leon pictured a scene which involved the release of a giant man-eating squid in the shallow end, a great white shark in the deep, and every boy from Year 7 to Sixth-Form patrolling the edge of the pool with baseball bats and long poles.

The image wasn't pretty, an exhibition of carnage, lots of splashing and pleading and squealing and bleeding, but Leon felt no guilt for imagining such a lurid spectacle, he thought the wanker had it coming.

He also thought his old teacher out of order to insist he have a shower when he was no longer in Mr Crawley's class – or even attending school now, for that matter.

'Back off, Creepy,' mumbled Leon walking away. 'You can't tell me what to do anymore.' Though he also wondered if, actually, he *should* have a shower – wash off all that chlorine. As Mr Crawley had often explained to his charges: 'You can never be too careful with chlorine, it can make delicate young skin dry and itchy; so use lots of soap, boys – lots and lots of soap.'

Lots and lots of soap was his Shower Rule #1.

There were other shower rules: unwritten, possibly unauthorised, but disregarded at your peril. Like Rule #3: 'Costumes off, please; it's a shower, not a laundry.'

Leon could remember a time in Year 8 when Moss had lathered up as instructed (after Mr Crawley had dutifully looked in, reminded, and subsequently monitored) but then skipped Rule #4: 'Keep it nice, shampoo twice' when the teacher's ever-watchful eye was diverted to Aaron Spencer, a gentle but clumsy boy, who, to his credit, was complying with Rule #2: 'Dropped soap is a hazard – always pick it up *immediately.*'

By the next day, Moss's hair had turned green and for the rest of that week other boys ribbed him for looking like an Oompa-Loompa. The following weekend, Moss hacked off his previously-blond once-lovely locks with nail-scissors. His mother was mortified; a very sad day in the Kemp household – *very* sad. So let's ease up on Mr Crawley's officiousness and give the guy a little credit for passing on some sterling advice.

And, for the record, Mr Crawley has always strenuously denied any involvement in Leon's alleged prom-night depantsing.

What was that? Leon had heard something. He was sure of it. Something he'd heard before. Yes, somewhere in the darkness: that otherworldly, high-frequency noise returning; dampened by the muddy canal depths but still sounding heavenly and pure. And now, the familiar lights, like tiny stars: flickering with life, they sparkled and glowed, their bright friendly ethereal colours pushing back the gloom. As the glimmering lights moved towards him, they multiplied rapidly. In no time at all, countless thousands, perhaps *tens* of thousands, were swirling around his dormant body. He so wanted to touch them but his arms failed to respond. No matter; they appeared to be slightly beyond his reach, anyway.

A vague notion of not breathing came and went – that, too, no longer mattered.

At peace, he watched as some of the most radiant stars now broke away, inwardly, from their orbits. These gathered, dancing joyfully, it seemed, just inches from his heart. Then, as if simultaneously commanded, all the stars immediately ceased moving, except to commence a slow rise for the surface, the nearest casting a warm radiance upon his cold, inert face as they passed.

Inside, Leon was smiling.

He could feel *she* was coming . . .

* * *

Leon sat up, felt the chilly dankness of wet clothes, and looked around through dripping hair and a dazed expression. A faint aroma hung in the air: rainforest, cinnamon and oranges. He was by the canal, and under a bridge. Not *Sale Road* Bridge, though. Above was *Broad Street* Bridge (a swing bridge that hasn't swung since 1998), north of, and a good distance from, the bridge by the shopping precinct. At his side, torn carrier bags, now refilled with wet groceries and swollen toilet rolls, rested in strange puddles by his feet; strange because he had never known puddles to form *under* this bridge.

Standing at his side with a quizzical pout, Moss studied his friend, who was now staring intently into the canal water. 'And you just fell in?' he said, failing to mask a degree of scepticism.

Leon didn't explain. Not because he didn't want to but because he didn't have the words. Not right now. And anyway, he was feeling drained.

In the silence Moss rolled a spliff and wondered how to tell his best mate, life-long buddy, friends-forever, that he had, as promised, been thinking about things (the move, in particular) and had now decided he would *not* be going to Wales. He *loved* the countryside but the truth was: he loved getting stoned or trippy more. And he liked to get trippy or stoned whenever he felt like it – which was regular and often. And that might not be so easy in the middle of nowhere; which was, unfortunately, how he had come to think of the place Leon was always banging on about.

No, it might be right for his friend, probably was, but it wasn't right for *him*. He liked the 'attractions' of the city too much. And how easily accessible they were.

Moss didn't spell out any of this as they walked side by side, back down the waterway – both supporting armfuls of mushy groceries tentatively held together by split carrier bags – towards the steps that lead up to Stickleback Road.

Instead, he managed to blurt out his decision, without really going into detail why, by saying something vague but true about how it *wasn't right for him* and quickly adding that this shouldn't stop Leon. *He* should still go if that's what he wanted.

Leon said Moss should at least give it a go, maybe come for a weekend; try it on for size as it were.

The suggestion was gently and apologetically declined.

On hearing this, Leon – despite the weighty mass of water-logged provisions carried awkwardly in his arms – began to walk more briskly.

Moss, trailing, stopped to pick up a tin of tuna that had fallen from Leon's cargo. 'I did think about it,' he said loudly. 'It's just not for me.' Then, moving quicker to catch up, he called out: 'I'm sorry, Leon.'

Halting suddenly, Leon turned. 'Of course it's for you. I can't believe you can't see that.' Moss glanced down at a box of crackers thrown out by Leon's abrupt turn. Should he get that? He was already carrying a lot and this stuff was heavy, man. The pair stood looking at each other for a moment, neither speaking, both unsure what to say next.

'Why don't we sit on the steps and have a spliff,' suggested Moss.

Before Leon could reply two girls reeled noisily down the concrete steps on tall, chunky heels; skinny legs dangling from skirts so ridiculously short their g-stringed nether regions appeared to wink. Leon had seen the girls before but couldn't recall where . . . having staggered to the water's edge, the least drunk, Leon supposed, supported the more ill of the two as she vomited into the canal.

'Do you really want to stay here with all this?' asked Leon, nodding towards the girls.

The least drunk heard this slight, resented it, and was about to kick off big time (as she might have put it) when she was forced to comfort her friend, now suffering dry heaves. 'Go on, Kazza,' she encouraged, 'gerrit up, girl.'

276

Leon had seen enough. 'You coming?' he asked, inching towards the steps; his legs, back, and arms showing the strain.

'What? No. I'm, uh . . . going to the shops,' replied Moss falteringly. He nodded down the tow-path, in the direction of the precinct.

'Right, fine; I'll see you later, then,' sighed Leon taking the first step and then a second. 'But, Moss, have another think, eh?' he called over his shoulder.

'Wait!' shouted Moss.

'Yeah, what?' said Leon, performing a quick, hopeful turn. Had the hippie changed his mind?

Moss scuttled back and added the groceries he'd been carrying to his friend's burden, now a teetering heap of soggy commodities. Leon attempted to assert some degree of control by clamping his chin over the top of the pile.

'Right, see ya—oh wait, I meant to ask: can you lend me some cash?' Moss unfurled an I-hate-to-ask smile. 'Say twenty quid?'

Leon held back, suspicion adding weight to his already heavy load. The sound of empty gagging came from behind Moss's shoulder.

'It's my mum's birthday,' Moss said.

'Is it?'

'Yeah, I need to buy her a present. Don't worry, I'll pay you back.'

Between vociferous gags, Kazza requested: ' 'Old me fags, Sarah.' A packet of Silk Cut was exchanged. 'Don't let 'em . . . fall in't canal.'

Trying his best to ignore the side-show, Leon, somewhat reluctantly, pushed a hip-pocket forward. Moss felt inside and obtained Leon's wallet. He edged out a twenty. Then, looking at Leon, edged out another. 'Make it forty, eh? I'd like to get her something nice.'

'Right, just make sure you don't go buying any . . .' Leon raised cautionary eyebrows. 'I'm not lending it for—'

'As if; what do you take me for?' Moss replaced the wallet. 'Okay; better get moving,' he said already moving.

Having watched Moss scurry happily up the tow-path, Leon turned back to the concrete stairwell where he set about taking one, heavy, tottering step at a time. He had only managed a few miserable steps when Moss shouted from the tow-path: 'Hey, Leon, had any more weird visions?!'

Upon hearing this, Sarah eyeballed Leon in a way that said: And *you* looked down your nose at *us*, you nutter.

As Moss disappeared, not waiting for a reply, Kazza finally found the second batch she'd been searching for and with a loud '*HUUUUURP*' dispatched it vigorously into the canal.

'That's it,' praised Sarah, 'gerrit all up, girl.' Leon doubted that disgorging could ever be made to sound ladylike and was pleased that Kazza didn't bother to try.

Peggy, a portly woman with bad skin, several chins, and a Myra Hindley haircut (not something you see every day) was chatting to new neighbour, Vicky, when Leon approached his drive, his whole body fit to burst, grumbling quietly. The women fell silent, watched him enter the house – still mumbling – saw the front door kicked shut, and heard the sound of watery commodities crash to the floor.

Vicky nodded towards the house. 'What's with him?'

'Poor Leon,' Peggy scrunched her face sympathetically, 'the lad hasn't been the same since his parents died.'

'Oh, right. That's a shame. When did they die?'

'Last year.'

'*Both* of them?'

Peggy nodded.

Vicky's eyes widened. '*Same year?*' she asked.

'Same year – same car crash,' said Peggy, 'a year to the day, in fact. I remember because it was the day I went in for my hysterectomy . . .'

'Jesus.'

'It wasn't that bad. I was out in—'

'No, I meant him.'

'Oh yeah Leon . . .' Peggy sighed. '*He* was driving, bless him.'

'Fuck.'

'Exactly.'

CHAPTER SIXTEEN

It's a New Dawn

I'LL TELL YOU WHAT'S UP

Veronica washed dishes at the kitchen sink, hips swaying slightly out of time to 'Daydream Believer' by The Monkees on the Bush radio. Lester was at the table reading a football annual from the Sixties. Leon, forehead resting on the table, sat opposite.

'How was work today?' asked Veronica over a shoulder.

'I wasn't in work today, Ma.' Leon's voice was flat, tired.

'Oh dear, not feeling well?'

'It's Sunday, Ma.'

'Well, how was work yesterday, then?'

'Same old same old.'

Lester put down the annual and regarded the top of Leon's head as if he knew exactly what was wrong.

'You can't wait for others, son. Life's too short.'

'If you're not careful,' Veronica chipped in, 'you'll get stuck here.'

'Stuck in that job.'

'Stuck in this house.'

'You mustn't be afraid of the outside world, son.'

'Afraid?' said Leon without looking up. 'It's not *me* that's—'

'And do you really want to be repairing shoes forever?'

'Someone's changed their tune,' Leon mumbled into the table.

'Look at your hands.' Lester touched a few of the many small scars and fresh nicks on the back of Leon's hands. 'Imagine doing that for the rest of your life.'

Leon raised his head and spoke again. Lester twiddled a dial on his hearing aid, signed for Leon to reiterate (a V-sign rotated thrice). 'Say again,' he said in the unavoidable tone of someone with a profound hearing problem.

'I said: *It's not me—*'

Lester raised a hand to stop Leon then applied another tweak inside his ear. 'You know, it's not Moss that needs to get away – it's you.' A loud whistle filled the room. Lester removed his hearing aid, tapped it. 'What *is* up with this thing?'

'I can't just leave him, dad.'

Lester whacked the hearing aid against the table, popped it back in, and stared blankly at Leon.

The whistle grew louder and more high-pitched.

'I said: *I can't just leave him!*'

'Alright, no need to shout, I can hear you,' shouted Lester over the whistle. 'And course, you can. You're not kids any more. Forget Moss; you can't help him. It's time for you to move on.'

'And what about you guys?'

'Oh, don't be worrying about us.' Veronica placed the last soapy plate in the draining rack.

The marks on the back of Leon's hands disappeared under Lester's big goalkeeper-hands. 'Seriously, son, if you don't get away soon, you might never get away.'

'I don't know,' said Leon, his voice cracking. 'I really don't know.'

'You Really Got Me' by The Kinks came on the wireless.

'Ooh, it's our song,' Veronica cried, rubbing her hands together. For a moment, she sounded like a teenager. She pulled Lester to his feet and the pair danced, happily singing along. As Leon watched them, a sad, broken smile on his face, the whistle turned into a deafening shriek . . . the kettle was wailing like a banshee.

'Who fancies a cuppa?' asked Veronica still boogieing.

Something inside Leon snapped. 'Will you stop asking that! You're *always* asking. *"Do you want a cuppa? Cup of tea, Leon? Who's for a cup of tea?"* It's non-stop. *Tea* this, *tea* that. It's driving me up the wall!'

'Come on now, son, you know she can't help it.'

'Why can't she be like she was?' Leon cried. 'Why can't you *both* be like you were? It's not fair, Dad, it's not fair. Not fair at all!'

Richard entered from the hall and stood by the table, eyes drilling into Leon. 'What *are* you doing?' he asked.

'What do you mean?' yelled Leon over the screaming blare of the kettle.

'Who were you shouting at?'

Leon looked to where Veronica and Lester had been dancing. They were not there. He scanned the room. He had been alone. His face a crisis, he put eyes back to Richard, and within the screech of the kettle he heard an ill-fated squeal of tyres; the type of noise that invariably brings hands to faces and always ends in a violent crash.

Betty travels the empty road, headlights emphasising an expanse of driving rain. In the back, Veronica and Lester harmonise playfully to 'their song'. Leon, at the wheel, joins in; everyone now singing along to 'You Really Got Me' through enthusiastic grins.

Around the next corner – boosted by beers and Gangsta Rap, urged on by Carl – Danny hits the accelerator pedal with unrelenting commitment. The BMW, blacker than the night, drifts around the corner at high speed but fails to stay in lane and heads straight for the unprepared Beetle.

Blinded by the oncoming headlights, Leon swerves to avoid a collision but loses control. The car flips and heads side-on for the letterbox, Betty's headlights illuminating a pregnant woman and a child in a buggy. Pushing the buggy out of the way, she turns and dives behind the letterbox. The Beetle misses by a whisper. As she lands, the car smashes into the wall.

The Beamer screeches to an eventual stop. Danny jumps out and gawks back. The wrecked Beetle rolls over broken glass onto its back, wheezing oily smoke.

A small fire ignites.

Carl steps out. 'What the fuck are you doing? Get back in the car! Come on, let's go! Let's get the fuck out of here!'

The distraught woman, frantically removing fragments of glass from the buggy, examines her child.

Seconds later, Danny's BMW races over the hill; Ronnie, taking a leak in the bus shelter, swivels his head.

Back at the bottom of the hill, satisfied her child is okay, the young woman's attention now turns to the smoking, inverted Beetle. She pulls out a mobile phone and taps 999.

Lester and Veronica's contorted bodies lie slumped in the roof space under the upturned back seat in a spreading pool of blood – both very dead.

Leon, bleeding and covered in glass shards, hangs upside-down in the driver's seat, held by a safety-belt. In the rear-view mirror, he catches a glimpse of his mother's body lying motionless behind his head.

'Are you okay, Ma?' he coughs. 'Ma? Speak to me, Ma.'

No reply.

Searching with the mirror but unable to find Veronica's face, Leon, grimacing from pains laying siege to his neck, now angles the mirror towards the roof upholstery on the passenger side; finds Lester's legs, and then – on its own, no longer attached – Lester's head.

Leon lets out a long, painful wail: 'FAAAAAATHERRR-RRRRR!'

Leon was now on the sofa, Richard and clouds of fag smoke looming over him, kettle shriek persisting in the kitchen.

'You look peculiar,' Richard said. 'What's up?'

'*What's up?* Are you serious?'

Richard shrugged.

'I'll tell you what's up, shall I? Mum and Dad are dead, Richard. THEY'RE DEAD!'

'I know. They've been dead for a year.' Richard inhaled deeply, exhaled calm as you like.

'My God, you're so cold. Where's your compassion?'

'People have their own ways of dealing with grief. We're not so different.'

'Don't accuse me of being like you. You don't care about anyone but yourself.'

'Balls; of course I care. I worry about you, don't I?'

'Oh stop pretending you have a heart, Richard. You feel nothing.'

'Don't judge *me*, you little upstart. I'm not the crazy one here.'

Leon's eyes widened. 'Excuse me?'

'Well, I'm not the one talking to myself in empty rooms, am I?' He leaned in for emphasis. 'I hate to be the one to tell you, old chap, but one of us is seeing things – and it isn't me.' His head snapped towards the door. 'Jesus, that fucking kettle!'

The kettle was now whining like a siren gone mental. Richard, however, made no move to go and stop it.

Leon curled up into the foetal position and pulled a cushion over his head.

IT'S A NEW DAY

'Having another word with him won't help. That loser's never going to budge.'

'I think he'll come round.'

'What, that lazy bastard?' The stubby cigarette clenched between Richard's teeth made him sound like an amateur ventriloquist. Naked apart from Veronica's apron, he stood by the cooker, bare bottom to the room, frying an egg.

Leon had been at the table for ten minutes, arms folded, silently staring at Veronica's biscuit tin, before he'd finally poured out its contents: a pile of old photographs. Now, he studied a colour Polaroid of him and Moss, as children, on their bikes. This picture had always been his favourite.

'Get some protein inside you,' the egg-fryer said over his shoulder. 'That's what you need. Start the day right.'

'Why are you being nice all of a sudden?'

Richard spat his fag end at the sink. The stub landed in a bowl of dirty dishes surrounded by scummy water and instantly fizzed to death. 'And I've phoned in sick for you.'

'What?'

'You need a break. Take the rest of the week off.'

'What's your game?'

'No game. Egg's nearly ready.'

Despite his suspicion Leon conceded: 'I suppose I *could* do with a day or two off, after . . .'

'That's the spirit.' Eyes on Leon, Richard blindly flipped the flapping egg.

And with that, Leon began arranging photographs into small chronological piles: a group of monochromes with Mod stuff: Lester and Veronica with the Lambretta; sitting on it, standing next to it, cleaning it; some riding with other Mods on scooters (Lester and Veronica leading the pack on

283

a couple); some in Brighton and other places – various Parka-clad individuals smiling, posing or making rude gestures. One, taken after the scooter accident, showed Lester in a wheelchair, leg in plaster, Veronica pushing.

Another bunch ran a football theme: Lester in goal; blurry action shots; Veronica serving halftime tea and fags.

The 'Oh, it's a Boy!' pile (some Polaroid, some not), had: Veronica pregnant; Lester decorating the baby's room pink; Lester repainting the room blue; baby Leon in his inaugural bath; the first Christmas; and one of Lester and Veronica witnessing their boy's first steps in the back garden.

A huge heap contained family-holiday snaps: camping in Cornwall, the Blank's tent in the background; a wooden cabin at CenterParcs; on the rides at Blackpool; Butlin's Pwllheli, other places in Wales – and *loads* in Llanidloes.

Another set featured Moss, growing with Leon through the various stages of youth: infant, toddler, kid, schoolboy, teenager, young adult; summers, Christmases, each batch of snaps capturing another year – another year of age, another year of friendship.

As Richard's concentration returned to overcooking the egg, Leon, perhaps inevitably, went back to re-examining his favourite photo – happy times that now made him feel both happy and sad.

'That idle work-shy won't move,' said Richard, as if he knew what Leon was thinking. 'Not in a million years. And neither should you.'

'It'd be crazy to leave him here with Danny and Carl. I know how *that* would end. Hang on, that's a bit rich coming from you, isn't it? *Idle work-shy?* What have *you* ever done?'

'How dare you. Do you think I enjoy having a condition that keeps me housebound?' Sidling over, Richard brandished the sizzling pan close to Leon's head.

In the interest of safety, Leon leaned away.

'When it suits,' he mumbled.

'I cooked you an egg,' barked Richard as if this feat alone underlined his trustworthy character.

Slipped from fatty spatula, the oily monstrosity exposed an inedible blackened body and shrivelled yolk.

'That's all there is,' said Richard, throwing the cruddy pan into the sink without moving from the table.

The egg gradually slid to a stop. Leon looked up.

'Don't look at me like that. I haven't had an egg. Here, put some sauce on it.' Richard shifted a sauce bottle, plunked it down hard on a photo of Moss; scraped back a chair, parked his bare backside and lit a fresh cigarette.

Leon moved the bottle back to the small open space it had come from, at the corner of the table.

'I'll tell you what your problem is,' said Richard, blowing smoke in Leon's face. 'You want to move but you're too terrified to go on your own. And don't pretend it isn't true because we both know it is. I'm an expert on being stuck; I can spot a barnacle a mile away. I've said it before and I'll say it again – that's what you are: *a barnacle.*'

'Just because—'

'You won't move on your own, you haven't got the balls. And no-one's going with you, not him or anyone else, so get used to it, *Barnacle Brat.*'

'I'm not a brat.'

'We could debate *brat*, but you *are* a barnacle. *Stuck* and going nowhere; Lionel the lethargic limpet . . . Marco the moody mollusc . . .'

'Moody mollusc,' scoffed Leon.

Richard extinguished his cigarette in Leon's charred egg, his bare bottom squeaking against the vinyl of the chair as he did so. Leaning back he put his hands behind his head, and delivered his verdict: 'Laugh all you want but you, young fellow my lad, are stuck here with me.'

Leon's face was blank for a while but then it changed.

And if an expression can, Leon's suggested there may yet be a possible challenge to this notion.

AT THE CANAL

Moss leafed through the photographs, studied some of Lester and Veronica. 'You know, that's the first time you've spoken about them since . . .'

'I know,' said Leon, gazing deep into the canal. 'My head's been all over the place.

Leon faced Moss, earnestly. 'Feel like I'm pulling myself together now, though. You know, trying to look forward.'

'I'm sure that's why you were having all those crazy-arse visions. I did try to tell you.' Moss happened upon Leon's favourite. 'Oh wow, I remember this one. I *loved* that bike.'

All went quiet as Moss explored the photograph and the memories it stirred; the only sound, the occasional car passing on the road above.

'Keep it,' said Leon at last, pushing out a smile.

'For real? Oh thanks, man. I will.' Something about the gesture, or Leon's melancholy face, roused something in Moss. 'You know what,' he said, 'I'm going to have another think about moving. I am – seriously.'

'Really? That's great.'

'Yeah, I'm starting to think you might be right. All that fresh air and trees and stuff; might even get me off my backside, eh?'

'Exactly; a spiritual person, someone at one with nature, like you, *should* be living in the country. *Not the city.* Hey, maybe you could even get a job – something outdoors.'

'I will pay you that money back.'

'What? No, I didn't mean . . .'

'Hey, maybe I could work on a wind-farm. How cool would that be?'

Leon laughed then Moss, twigging, joined in. The pair sat there chortling like silly schoolboys for several minutes and when a brightly-painted narrowboat slowly chugged past the abandoned sofa they were sitting on, Leon took it is a good omen: he was getting there – slowly.

'Wonder why they didn't throw this straight into the canal,' said Moss, pondering the geography of the tired, dubiously-stained, but surprisingly comfy sofa.

'Dunno,' replied Leon. 'Maybe it's *dry-clean* only.'

They both pulled a face at that but laughed anyway.

Half an hour later, the guys were in Kath's Kaff having coffee and cream cakes. Leon had suggested it and said he'd pay; Moss didn't have any money on him. They had been talking about Wales since they'd arrived, at least, Leon had; trying to reinforce the notion of moving. As Jenny wasn't working today (evidently) Leon had been able to remain focused. And he was still going, hard-sell style: 'Lots of artists live there, you know: writers, *musicians* . . .'

'Musicians, eh?'

Leon imagined Moss was visualising strumming his guitar under a sunlit oak tree surrounded by hippie chicks and didn't speak lest he interrupt the musing. And when Moss absentmindedly produced a ready-rolled spliff, he still said nothing.

'Yeah but isn't it a bit dead?' Moss said at last.

'Are you kidding? There's loads of stuff. Kayaking, quad biking, abseiling, hang gliding . . .'

'Sounds intense, man. Not sure I'd have the energy for all that.'

'You might if you laid off the dope.'

Conversation halted as they slipped under Olive's shadow. 'I hope you're not thinking of smoking that weedy thing in here,' she said, folding her tattooed arms under her ample bosom.

'Oh no, yeah, sorry, man; it's cool.' Moss removed the spliff from sight.

Olive leaned on the table and spoke conspiratorially:

'Now, if you boys would like to try something *really* interesting, meet me round the back in ten minutes.'

Leon could have done without the interruption and didn't want to go but because Moss did, he felt obliged to join him; he was, after all, still working on persuading Moss to move.

On the quiet service road, behind the café, between bins and recycling bags, Olive blazed a carrot-shaped spliff, took a hit and handed it on. Moss had a deep draw, exhaled slowly. 'That's proper nice,' he said, his voice catching.

'Northern Lights, baby,' Olive said, 'Northern Lights.'

Moss handed the 'carrot' to Leon. Not wanting to appear uncool he took a blast, coughed a little. Strong shit indeed. Olive laughed and took another turn.

After a few minutes, she was clucking heartily, deep and bass and resonant, like Barry White on sulfur-hexafluoride. The extremely low-pitched chuckling made Leon and Moss howl with laughter which led to more booming baritone convulsions and so on and so on – a vicious hilarious circle.

By the time they were passing around the last of the spliff, all three were leaning against a skip, as high as Red Kites . . . and one of them was about to swoop.

'Have you guys ever had a threesome?' asked Olive.

Leon almost burned a lip on the roach. Moss, perhaps too spaced, didn't react; commandeering the roach, he managed one final blast before the huge waitress pulled both boys in, one braced inside each beefy arm. 'You know,' she looked from one to the other, 'one girl and two guys?'

Smiling, Moss puffed smoke from his nostrils. Maybe he thought she was joking. More likely, it was dopamine flooding his brain.

'It's fun,' said Olive. 'You should try it. Well, I've already tried it. But you guys should try it with me – the three of us.' Her hands, not exactly goalkeeper-size but close, dropped to the boys' bottoms. Biting down on her bottom lip, she turned to Leon, squeezed his left cheek in her left hand. He swallowed; his face unable to find a suitable expression. Olive turned to Moss, scrunched his right buttock in her right hand. His bloodshot eyes bulged.

'What do you think; are you up for it?' she asked. 'Yeah, come on; let's go to my place.'

Leon had thought for a moment Olive intended to have the threesome right there, next to the refuse; amongst the pungent aromas of uneaten plate scrapings, sour milk, and out-of-date produce – relocation offered little comfort.

The arse-locked paws pulled the boys in even closer and Leon got a close-up view of face jewellery as the waitress rammed her pierced tongue deep into the hippie's mouth.

Moss didn't pull away and a 'washing machine' kiss ensued – their tongues swirling like eels, all pink and wet, the barbell in Olive's tongue winking silver.

Although uncommonly high – a state that felt really pleasant – Leon didn't fancy *this* at all. In fact, watching the pair French-kissing made him feel bilious. *They* seemed keen though; perhaps he just wasn't as high as them yet.

When Olive finally extracted her cow-like tongue, she turned her meaty head towards contestant number two.

Wiping saliva from his chin, Moss squinted, eyes watering. 'What do you think, Leon?' he asked.

288

In a way, Leon was happy Moss had the kind of personality that could be swayed, although he recognised, even in his similar state, the dopamine's influencing role.

'What do *I* think?'

'Yeah, what do you think, Handsome? You up for an Olive sandwich?'

The question became moot as Leon up-chucked into the waitress's cleavage.

'Oh, you dirty bastard!' wailed Olive, bending forward to scoop matter from between her enormous boobs.

Leon wasn't sure if it had been the smell of the bins, the Northern Lights hashish, Olive's churning tongue, or the large Cream Horn he'd had with his coffee – but he felt a shade better now.

'Don't worry, man, it'll wash out,' Moss said.

He tried to assist in the clean-up but lack of coordination somehow resulted in both his hands becoming wedged, back-to-back, between Olive's breasts.

(Needless to say they were quickly wrenched out and slapped aside – the hands, not the breasts.)

'Dirty fucking bastards,' Olive said, holding the neck of her top away from her body as she bulldozed past and disappeared into the café.

When Leon called out an apology – something along the lines of 'Sorry, Olly; I think it was the horn!' – Moss keeled over, snickering, into a heap of bin bags.

EARLY NEXT MORNING

Leon looked in on his way to work. Janis, always up with the proverbial lark, told him to go up. Moss was fast asleep until Leon, snapping open a curtain, said: 'I really think we should do it.'

The bearded dreamer squinted bleary eyes against the morning light. 'If this is about last night . . .'

'Huh? No. What we were saying about getting away.'

'Oh, that.' Still wearing his Inca hat, strings of matted hair drooping over his ashen face, Moss reached into a drawer and pulled out a small spliff.

'*Already?*'

'Relax, man. It's just a mild one. Straighten me out a bit.'

Spotting the Polaroid on the floor, Leon picked it up and propped it against the lava lamp as his friend lit up. Moss coughed, leaned against the headboard. Morning had brought no obvious improvement. He still looked wasted.

'Look at yourself, Moss. You don't want to spend the rest of your life living like this, do you?'

'I'm alright, man.' Moss wiped his nose. 'Got my bed; my music; my PS3 – got my Doobie.'

'You could have all that in Wales,' said Leon, 'and *a lot more* besides.'

Moss exhaled. 'Yeah?'

Last night Leon decided to capitalise on Moss's Achilles heel; now he played what he hoped would be a trump card: 'Word is the Welsh government is about to legalise weed.'

Moss licked dry lips, scratched an ear.

The statement wasn't exactly true, of course. Leon had read somewhere that The Legalise Cannabis Alliance was planning to open a 'branch' in South Wales with the aim of lobbying The Welsh Assembly about decriminalising the smoking of pot as part of a Social Welfare charter, but for the sake of this conversation he'd convinced himself that any change in the law, no matter how inconceivable and remote, was a possibility worthy of Moss's consideration.

As Moss processed this early-morning information, Leon decided not to further burden him with the fact that even if the Assembly did go all 'Amsterdam', they would still need to get approval from Westminster.

'Wouldn't make any difference,' said Moss, rubbing an eye. 'People will still blaze. And in a way it's kind of cooler if it's *not* legal. You know, sticking it to the man.'

'I know but if they did go ahead, it would bring the price *right down*. They'd be almost giving it away.'

'Wouldn't they stick loads of tax on it?'

'Some. But it would still be dirt cheap because they'd be producing by the ton, in hundreds of government-run cannabis farms.'

Somewhere behind his pink eyes, Moss got to thinking.

In the silence, Leon knew he'd won him over, at least for the time being. Now, if he could just get him out there . . .

Moss took another drag, blew smoke circles.

'Is it really as good as you make out?'

'Give it a try,' suggested Leon. 'That's all I ask. Let's go for a couple of days and you can see what it's like.'

Moss offered the spliff. 'How much does it cost, though; train and everything – I'm a bit . . .'

'Listen, don't worry about that; I'll pay.'

'No, mate, I can't—'

'Course you can.' Wallet already out, 'Here take this,' Leon pushed a batch of notes into Moss's hand.

Fingers closed slowly around the money, accepting it.

'We'll go on Friday. You get the tickets and I'll meet you on the platform after work.'

Moss nodded. 'Okay, man,' he said. 'Let's do it.'

FRIDAY ON MY MIND

The night before last – All Hallows' Evening – had proved a nightmare. Leon had wanted to ignore the continual door knockings, pretend to be out, but Richard insisted on answering. A typical exchange went like this:

'Listen up, you little bastards,' Richard told them – mostly young teenagers, hands outstretched – 'there are no treats here, so you might as well piss off.'

'Give us the money and we'll buy our own.'

'You haven't even bothered to dress up. If you're going to demand money with menaces you could at least—'

'Quid for the guy, then.'

'What guy?'

'Just give us some money, you tight-arsed cunt.'

This got the door and yesterday morning Leon discovered the consequences of failing to embrace the festive spirit: toilet-papered house and trees, egged windows, pumpkin guts smeared upon garage doors and a mishmash of shits on the doorstep.

Let it go, thought Leon as he checked a new zip he'd just finished stitching into an old boot; all that would soon be a thing of the past. He felt sure Llani kids would celebrate Halloween by genuinely seeking a few candy treats and not using the night simply as a means to extort cash in exchange for withholding seasonal property damage.

The zip ran up and down, smooth as you like. The action and noise reminded Leon of opening and closing tent doors. Job done, he looked to the clock. Only fifteen minutes to go. He smiled at the thought of his rucksack, waiting patiently in the stock room.

At the other end of the counter, Reg was talking to a customer using his overly-accommodating voice:

'We *are* open Saturdays, yes. Of course we can do that. No problem at all, sir. They'll be done during the day and ready for collection by five.'

'Guaranteed?' asked the customer.

'Guaranteed, or my name's not Reginald Trimble.'

'Grand. I'll drop th'rest off in't mornin', then.'

As the Lancastrian departed, Leon got an impending sense of certain calamity.

'Right, Leon, you probably caught that,' said Reg sliding a box of trophies along the counter. 'I'm going to need you in tomorrow; sort out some engravings – these and a few others being dropped off in the morning. I know it's meant to be your Saturday off but needs must. It's an emergency job and I've promised to have them ready.'

'Oh come on, Boss; can't *you* . . .'

'I'm sure I don't have to remind you that we have a backlog of watch repairs that need doing. Not helped by the fact that you were off sick at the beginning of the week.'

Leon couldn't help it; he rolled his eyes.

'And one of the repairs might be *very tricky* as a matter of fact. An antique pocket watch; extremely expensive – might need a full overhaul. Not just a clean and refurbish. It calls for an experienced hand.'

'Like yours.'

'Exactly, like mine. Otherwise, naturally, I'd do the trophies myself.'

'Naturally.'

'Right, enough chit chat, final job for today, sweep the back yard. I'll be locking up shortly, so chop-chop.'

✶ ✶ ✶

In the walled yard, one hand on a brush, one on his mobile, Leon lamented, furtively, into the phone: 'Yes, I know but I've got to work now.' He swung a hard kick at a flimsy-looking box only to find it had all the mobility of a large anvil. 'What the fuck!' Clutching his screaming foot, Leon hopped for a while, then leaned against the white-washed wall, removed a shoe and rubbed his screaming toes.

Foot still throbbing, he ripped open the taped lid . . . the box contained the new anvil Reg had ordered.

'For fuck's sake,' griped Leon. 'Shouldn't there be some kind of warning label? *"Caution! Box contains rock-hard anvil. Do not kick."* In big red—*oh shit.*'

He'd glimpsed the tops of Pogo's clumped balloons on the other side of the wall, protruding above the capstones.

Crouching, he lowered his voice: 'I don't know; some bloody convention in Blackpool. I've got a shed load of trophies to engrave. Where are you now; at the station?'

Moss was in bed. The call had wakened him. Sitting up, he rubbed his eyes. 'Yeah, man, I'm at the station.'

He looked outside but there was no station, only chimneys and satellite dishes.

'Really?' whispered Leon's voice from the phone. 'It sounds pretty quiet.'

'Uh, yeah, the place is pretty dead, man.'

He surveyed the room as if it might really be the station. 'I thought it would be way busier than this.'

'Have you got the tickets?' the phone asked.

Moss looked to Leon's money beside the bed. 'Not yet.'

'Right, hang on to the cash,' the voice continued. 'We'll go tomorrow; half five. Reg said I can leave early.'

Moss threw back the covers, reached inside his trousers and scratched his sweaty balls. Why had he slept in his clothes again? He couldn't remember.

'Moss?' the phone quietly barked. 'Are you there?'

'Wait, did you say *tomorrow*?'

'Yes.'

'*Saturday*,' Moss sighed. 'Is it worth it?'

'Course it is. We'll have Saturday night and nearly all of Sunday. Right, gotta go. See you there. Don't be late.'

The call clicked off.

Although his system was by no means substance-free, Moss was no longer high, mellow or chilled. He didn't like that. The bedside drawer slid open. Devoid of what he sought, his eyes drifted to Leon's cash, an inner struggle with temptation written all over his face.

HELEN BLACK

Saturday brought heavy showers to the high street. Gusts of wind had thrown rain against the glass fronts of Keys-n-Stuff for most of the morning and early afternoon.

By the time the sun finally sent them packing it was fast approaching twenty to five.

Seema hung up a pair of corduroy trousers – having just successfully completed, by hand, the removal of a strange blotch on the crotch – and made a start on her paperwork.

Leon had just finished engraving the last of the trophies and now awaited Reg's final approval – if only he'd get off the phone. He was talking to Sherry, *again*. (Leon and Seema knew it had to be Sherry from the way their boss arched, conspiratorially, over the handset and whispered into the mouthpiece.)

Reg's wife was a 'shut-in' thanks to him; morbidly obese, with large rolls of fat covering her huge body. She had a reinforced bed and read Jeffrey Archer novels all day.

Seema knew all about Sherry, passed it on to Leon; what she hadn't been able to say was how many years it had been since Sherry had last been able to leave her bedroom. Reg, you see, was a compulsive Feeder[7]; *Sherry's* feeder – and with Reg's help, Sherry now weighed over sixty stone.

'What do you mean, *Stuck*?' asked Reg. 'How can you be stuck? Just tell me slowly. What happened?' (Leon and Seema exchanged a look.) 'Reaching for what? – Okay, keep calm, you'll be fine – No, I can't come now but don't worry, sugar dumpling, Daddy will be home soon.'

---

[7] Feeder: Male (virtually always) who draws sexual gratification from weight gained as a result of (over)feeding his female (again, practically always) partner: the Feedee. These actions usually have no limits and continue until the Feedee dies of health complications brought on from over-eating or they simply burst.

Seema widened her eyes and mouthed: *Dumpling?*

Leon made a similar face and mouthed: *Daddy?*

Both knew they shouldn't laugh – Sherry was probably on the floor, drowning under her own flesh – but they couldn't help themselves, and each progressively made the other worse until they ended up reeling and rocking, snickering silently; their antics like a baffling mime performance. Then, after two long minutes of disorderly eye-watering side-clutching back-slapping staggering around, the pair recovered in an instant: they'd both noticed Helen Black, observing them from the door.

She'd brought the rain back and scared away the sun. Thunder and lightning would surely follow any second.

Ms Black, Area Manager for the whole of Greater Manchester, late twenties: there was ambition and no nonsense here; inky power suit, severely tied-back hair and minimum make-up; Teflon briefcase gripped in one vice-like fist, a dripping black brolly clutched like a much-used sword in the other.

As Leon quickly got busy on something that didn't need doing at all, Helen exchanged a brief tepid smile with Seema then set to glaring at Reg's back, still hunched over the phone.

Sensing the Ice Queen's dark presence, Reg slowly straightened up, self-conscious and awkward then turned to face her. Eyes fixed on Helen, he spoke into the phone: 'Uh, yes, we can definitely repair those for you, Madam. Just drop them off anytime.' Reg attempted a face he hoped would express: *Sorry about this, Helen, but it's a customer; Nearly done.* 'Not at all, thank *you* for calling.'

'Reginald? Reginald!' the mouthpiece wailed, the telephone heading for its base. Reg grinned at his Area Manager, hoping she hadn't heard Sherry's panicked plea.

'This is an unexpected surprise, Helen,' said Reg in his sycophantic voice, 'how lovely to see you again.'

Helen clattered her briefcase onto the counter.

'How are things at Head Office?' asked Reg. 'Things have been a bit quiet here lately but we're definitely getting busier now.' Reg sought support from his staff: 'Aren't we?'

Seema threw Reg a bone: a half-hearted nod.

'That must be why you haven't had time to clean your windows.' Helen's voice was as harsh as her appearance.

Motoring on with 'Right, listen up, this is important; it could affect all of you,' Helen popped open her briefcase catches and took out three memos.

Leon snatched a glance at the clock. He did not need this. If Helen wasn't quick—

Tring-tring.

Leon and Seema looked to each other, then Reg.

Tring-tring.

Reg picked up the phone as if it might explode, inching the handset towards an ear. He swallowed, no doubt willing this not to be Sherry, and sighed: 'Hello, Keys—'

The tip of the wet umbrella cut off the call. 'I'm sure whoever it is will call back,' said Helen, eyes drilling into Reg. As the brolly withdrew, leaving drips on the handset, he replaced the receiver.

'Now, as you know, the company have made—'

Tring-tring.

Reg snapped out the connection lead.

Helen dumped her wet brolly on the counter, the tip close to Reg's tummy. 'As I was saying . . .'

Reg, one finger on the tip, gently pushed the umbrella back a few centimetres; Helen, eyes on Reg, deliberately pushed the brolly forward again – and a bit more besides. The tip now touched Reg's midriff. He left it there.

'*As I was saying* . . . the company have made some significant cuts over the last few months.' Helen handed out memos. 'And they might be about to make some more.'

Reg runs – if you can call it running – along the roof of the Piccadilly Hotel, rips off his warehouse coat as he barrels past Leon, and swallow dives, head first over the edge.

Leon watches as Reg, screaming, falls towards the busy city centre street below.

As Helen snapped her briefcase shut, Reg discovered he was dabbing his sweaty head with a hankie and Leon was watching him do it (neither Reg nor Leon would ever know if they had just imagined the same thing).

'And I want those changes implementing immediately,' said Helen, wrenching her briefcase and umbrella away from the counter.

'I'm sure you know best, Helen.' Seema smiled but it lacked conviction.

Helen said, 'I've already lost two branches in my area, Seema, I don't want to lose any more.'

Reg smiled, momentarily reassured.

'—It affects my bonus.'

Reg arrived at the door ahead of Helen, held it open for her. 'Think on, Reg; we need those sales figures if this branch is to survive.' And with that she was gone.

Reg remained at the door studying the memo.

Leon looked to the clock. 'Reg, is it okay if I get off now? I finished all the—'

'Right, you two, from now on, we push, push, push.' Reg used his 'inspirational' voice. 'I want everybody to treat the customers like royalty and push for those extra sales. Do that and we *will* save this branch. Do you hear me?'

'Yeah, push, push, push; first thing Monday morning.' Leon pointed at the clock. 'But right now I've got a train—'

'You heard what Helen said. We need to pull out all the stops if we're going to survive. You'll have to work until five thirty as usual.'

Leon's shoulders sank.

'Come on, it's only thirty minutes. Enough time to give the windows another clean. And do them right this time.'

'I wasn't even meant to be in today,' grumbled Leon.

By the time Leon had finished the windows to Reg's satisfaction, persuaded the boss to let him leave a few precious minutes early, and sprinted to Piccadilly, it was, according to the station clock: 17:28.

The train was in and most passengers had already boarded, just one or two stragglers stretching-out goodbyes to friends and family.

Leon was soon pacing beside the carriages, scanning the area. But Moss was nowhere to be seen. He hit redial (he'd already phoned twice: the first call went to voice mail; the second went dead). This one went dead, too.

A man raced up the platform scrutinising his watch. He stopped at the train door, threw a large hold-all aboard, and followed it.

Leon checked the station clock – it updated to 17:29.

Much more than a minute from Piccadilly – even as the fastest of crows fly – Moss wandered aimlessly around his bedroom, muttering, on a trip of his own, interacting with things only he could see; arms outstretched, eyes wide, his steps ungainly. He had the look of a zombie seeking a door in an unlighted, windowless cellar.

Plodding by the unmade bed, his knee caught the bedside unit, almost toppling the Polaroid, now encased in a simple wooden frame his mother had provided.

The boyhood pals looked out from behind thin glass, sealed in innocent times, oblivious to the blotter-sheet of Daffy Duck LSD tabs under the wheels of their bikes.

Leon climbed, reluctantly, onto the train, took a seat by the window. Outside, a guard waved a signal over her head and blew a high-pitched whistle. Leon stared up the platform, half expecting to see Moss turn up a moment too late. What he actually saw was Pogo rushing down steps.

The persistent clown, carrying his big yellow shoes, motioned behind him, urging an unseen accomplice to hurry. Leon strained to see who the accessory might be but the angle played against him.

As the train pulled out, Pogo threw his shoes down hard, one after the other before complaining angrily, his gloves in tight fists, to whoever was following. Even with head pressed hard against the window, Leon still couldn't see who Pogo was berating. Then someone, or some*thing*, came into view. Leon squinted, but it was too late; the train left everything behind: the station, Pogo, Pogo's accomplice – and, for whatever reason: Moss.

Leon settled back into his seat. He normally felt happy when he took the train to Wales but today, he didn't. Perhaps it was the rushing or Pogo showing up; more likely, Moss not turning up and not answering his phone – or perhaps it was because he knew he'd be coming back.

CHAPTER SEVENTEEN

Llanidloes

THE FIRST TOWN ON THE SEVERN

Dark hills underscored a black, star-filled sky, and way off, a flickering fire illuminated a small tent. Had it been daytime, the place would be recognisable as Leon's favourite camping spot, the one he had so enjoyed with his parents in the Eighties and Nineties.

Leon sat in the mouth of the tent, feeling the fire's heat on his face, new pocket-torch clenched between teeth, writing in his notebook. In the zone, words poured from his pen, adding sentence upon sentence. He was rewriting 'The Geisha and the Samurai' and at this rate he'd easily have a substantial first-draft to take back. As his subconscious beavered away, he was mildly aware that his *conscious* mind was looking forward to watching Poppy read the finished version. This surprised him . . . rather pleasantly.

There came then an *unpleasant* surprise: Leon's mobile rang, interrupting the flow; he'd left it on in case Moss called. He checked the caller: *Richard*; switched off, tossed the phone to the back of the tent and returned to writing.

During the outbound train journey, Leon had convinced himself that Moss, if he could just see what Wales was like, what it had to offer, would definitely want to move. He decided he'd make videos and take photos on his phone, lots of them, and show the no-doubt impressive results to Moss upon his return. He felt sure this plan would work. How could it fail? Happy with his decision, he had settled back to try *Aurora Leigh and Other Poems* by Elizabeth Barrett Browning; a paperback someone had left on the train. He hadn't expected to enjoy a story written in verse rather than prose, but he had – very much.

At 3:25 a.m. Leon finally stopped writing. This is because (a) he was falling asleep and (b) he felt he had got his story back to where it was before Carl stole the previous notebook; the rat! Again, the material would need further drafts and lots of polishing but overall he was elated. So elated, he decided he wouldn't head back later tonight as he'd originally planned but leave it until Monday morning.

Catching the 6 a.m. train would make him a little late for work (Leon reckoned Reg owed him one) but give him the whole of Sunday. One full day to indulge the sights and history he so enjoyed. One day to capture enough material to convince Moss to weigh anchor. Plus a load of extra hours away from *It*.

Further, he decided, there would be no more uncertainty, no more thinking and no more worrying. And no more writing, either – not a word. *People need breaks, Leon.* Yes, it was settled. After he'd slept, he would spend the rest of the day pottering around the area – then he'd go back fresh on Monday morning. He also made a vow: that he'd work ceaselessly on his story until it was finished; he would reread what he had on the return journey, edit where necessary, type everything into the computer when he got home from work and print out a hard copy, then start composing a second draft on Tuesday evening – writing until he fell asleep.

'I *will* turn this into a novella, even if it kills me!' he announced valiantly. Then he turned to a fresh page, recorded the vow, underlined it, and after some thought added another: to bravely hide the notebook down his undercrackers before the train reached Piccadilly, lest he bump into any nescient undesirables between the station and Norris Avenue.

Putting the notebook away he zipped up the tent and settled into his sleeping bag. Lit by the last of the fire, the tent glowed, a faint orange blush. As he gazed at the warm canvas and listened to crackling embers punctuated by a perched owl's intermittent calls, he again imagined showing the completed story to Poppy. And her being impressed – he hoped.

Leon had been thinking of Poppy more and more of late. Maybe she was growing on him. People do that sometimes. Had he been missing a trick? Could they, he wondered, become *more* than friends? Was that possible? The whole transformation, the sequence in which two people transcend from being just friends to becoming boyfriend/ girlfriend, dating, and so forth, was an enormous mystery to Leon, but he imagined Poppy would know. Girls understand these things. Yes, when he went back he would find some *courage*, as she had put it; he would grow some balls – he would ask Poppy out! Perhaps to the cinema and a meal afterwards; explain how he kept thinking about her; had started to miss her when she wasn't around. And then he would take it from there. Why not? He believed *she* liked *him*. Perhaps he could be her paramour.

Paramour? Don't make me laugh. I know you're sexually frustrated–

'Am not.'

–but you couldn't find a blowjob in Mandy's Megastars.

'Shut it, you!'

So what makes you think you're going to find lurve? That's how he heard Richard pronounce it: *LURVE.*

'I'm not listening. You're not even here.' Leon pulled the sleeping bag over his head and pretended he couldn't hear Richard's laughing. Which clearly did the trick because Richard pissed off fairly quickly (still laughing) leaving behind the blissful sounds of the countryside – that and nothing more.

A little later, drifting off towards sleep, another thought occurred to Leon: if *Moss* didn't fancy Wales – perhaps Poppy *would*.

✶ ✶ ✶

Leon was awake early; early enough to catch a breath-taking sunrise. The sun lit a blanket of thin mist that drifted gently between the surrounding hills, shrouding the ground. He took out his mobile and captured the first image of the day. A great start, he thought.

The rest of the day went equally well. The Welsh countryside revealed many wonderful spectacles and tableau: beautiful scenery, of course; a hill-top wind-farm; an art exhibition (at the side of a country lane) by a couple of local painters; the Yurt they lived in (also by the side of the lane); a pair of Red Kites riding rising thermals, chestnut plumage and deeply forked tails catching the sun as they soared; some modern-day beatnik-types camping in a flowery camper van; and a magnificent sun-speckled lake held back by a long curving dam. Leon captured them all.

And that was just the morning.

Leon entered the town of Llanidloes as the Town Hall clock struck eleven. He walked around taking photos of people, streets and buildings: the Old Market Hall; Great Oak street with its vegetarian café (Moss would love that), organic whole-food shops (ditto), and magnificent old bookshop (not so much); the river Severn; Short Bridge; Long Bridge; St. Idloes (a venerable medieval church) and all five of the town's 19th century chapels: Baptist Chapel; Wesleyan Methodist Chapel; Capel Bethel (once attended by Welsh Calvinistic Methodists, now an ironmongers); Welsh Presbyterian Chapel; and Trinity church (a union of Zion United Reform Church and English Presbyterian). Moss wasn't actively religious – he was an idle Buddhist – but Leon thought he'd find the architecture interesting.

Also snapped: the Town Hall: a grand stone-fronted Jacobean-style construction with a series of columned-arches surrounding a ground floor area (used today by market traders) and a high apex roof speared by a central clock tower.

(Sorry, forgot to say: *philistines may wish to get back in the cupboard, momentarily.*)

Leon knew from his museum visits that the Town Hall was originally constructed (1905-1908) as a Temperance building, a gift of the Davies family of Plas Dinam who were concerned with the drunkenness prevalent in the town (here, farmers could strike market day deals in full sobriety without being diverted by the intemperance of the many public houses; the museum curator once told Leon that Llanidloes had over twenty Inns at the turn of the last century, far more than would be reasonably expected for such a small market town with a then population of around 5000).

As Leon photographed the town's nine surviving pubs, it occurred to him that every era, wherever the place, would probably always have some individuals with a drug dependency problem – be it narcotics or alcohol.

Now, having ordered a meal in The Royal Head pub, Leon looked through snaps of the Trewythen Arms, scene of the famous Chartist riot of 1839 and pictured the past:

Chartists meet in The Red Lion, knock back ales, argue about how working people have 'a rough deal' and make uppity noises about getting better treatment for working folk everywhere; a vote for every man ('Forget the women, Lewis; one thing at a time, eh?') to be held by *secret* ballot, and no property qualification for members of Parliament.

'That's how all these rich house-owning landed-gentry types (toffee-nosed bastards for short) are keeping power, isn't it,' someone says, banging fist on table and gaining applause. Another beer then off to the Trewythen Arms for more loud reform talk.

Unfortunately, when Lord John Russell, English Whig and then Home Secretary, gets to hear about the unrest, he sends three London Peelers to quell the trouble-makers.

But news of southern Bobbies arresting local Chartists quickly spreads through the town and an angry crowd surround the place. There is much hurling of abuse and throwing of stone. Windows are smashed; doors bashed.

Far from restoring order, the Home Secretary's actions have kick-started a revolt. The rebellion doesn't last long, though; the Chartists run away when the military are sent to restore order.

Leon was about to visualise some serious Cavalry on Chartist head-bashing when his food and a second pint of Ramblers Ruin arrived.

The Chartist riot was not a booze-fuelled uprising, as the museum curator had been keen to point out, but Leon's imagination, for the purposes of his own entertainment, had made it so. And why not, they can't deport you for it.

Not like they did with many of those involved; the ringleaders were transported to Australia.

Abraham Owen (weaver), John Ingram (labourer) and Lewis Humphreys (shoemaker) were sentenced to seven years apiece. James Morris (weaver) was controversially banished for *fifteen* years . . . He was nineteen.

Leon decided to revisit the museum. Not to review the Chartist exhibition, but to have another look at the two-headed lamb. He was a bit odd like that.

(Oh and the uncultured may now release themselves from self-induced limbo. And don't worry, that's *absolutely* and *categorically* it so far as historical edification is concerned. Honest.)

638 AND MISSY

Late afternoon found Leon sitting on a stone wall close to where he'd pitched his tent, scanning the area.

Behind him, a backdrop of rolling hills. To one side, the copse trees in their early November colours. And ahead: fields, sheep (funny how they never stop eating), and the town in the valley below. He closed his eyes and absorbed the peaceful tranquillity: gentle quiet, so different to the city; only birdsong, stridulating grasshoppers (or crickets), the gurgling stream, an occasional *baa,* and now, the soft beat of a passing heron's wings. As he inhaled the oxygen-heavy exhaust-free air (laced with the scent of inoffensive day-old cow pats) and enjoyed the sun's gentle autumnal heat warming his cheeks, it suddenly dawned on him: he had never experienced a single weird vision in Wales.

Not one.

Regular-weird: slightly oddball farmers, unconventional beatniks, but nothing *crazy*-weird; nothing comparable to that time he discovered a giant red-chilli-pepper sleeping in his bed or the Virgin Airlines Flight Attendant being spit-roasted by two Santas (in the middle of the supermarket; up the aisle with the nuts and nibbles, if you please!) or Pogo, or Adolf, or—

Leon jumped as his phone rang. (Must have left it on, he realised, after snapping the Welsh lamb he had for tea.)

'Hey, buddy, how's it going?' asked Leon. 'Can you hear me okay—the signal's a bit—hello?—hello?'

Moss's disembodied voice: 'I can hear you, man; Jesus, calm down. I was just asking what you were up to.'

'Just chilling really. The view is amazing. It's so peaceful and quiet. Honestly, Moss, you are going to love it here.'

'Yeah, about that . . .'

'Sounds ominous, what's up? Is it something to do with why you missed the train? I did phone but—'

'No, listen, man . . .'

'Go on.' Leon noticed a sheep close to the wall, staring up at him. In her left ear, the ewe had a bright orange tag; it read: UK 0 532627 00638. The phone was silent. 'Moss?'

'Not sure how to say this . . .'

Leon smiled at the sheep. 'If it's about missing the train, don't worry about it. We can rearrange for—'

'I'm not going to do it, man.'

'But you said you'd have a look . . . *then* decide.'

'It's not happening, Leon. Sorry, I know you must be—'

'*You said* you'd come for a visit.'

'Yeah, I know.'

'I distinctly remember you saying you'd give it a try. *Fresh air, trees and stuff*, that's what you said. Getting off your backside, remember? *The wind-farm?* We laughed.'

'I know.'

'That's why I gave you the train fare.'

'Yeah, about the money . . .'

'You said you'd like to get a job.'

'I know.'

'Give up the weed and the Lucy.'

'Never said that.'

'Okay, maybe you didn't say that, but if you moved . . .'

'About the money—'

'It's not about the money, Moss.' Leon, getting wound up, took a breath, hoping to find neutral. 'It's about starting a new life.'

'Leon, you're not listening . . .'

'There are loads of hippie chicks out here,' interrupted Leon with a mildly desperate chortle. 'Go into town and it's like the Sixties. Wait till you see all the photos I've taken for you. I'm telling you, Moss, you will *love* it. Just give it a chance. What was it John Lennon said?'

'Sorry, man.' The phone went dead.

'Moss? You there, Moss? *MOSS!*' Leon growled; felt like throwing his phone against the wall and running around the field yelling 'you stupid, stupid fucker!'

'638' shook her woolly head. Others might have missed this slight but Leon didn't. 'No, *you're* losing the plot!' he snarled. The ewe got daggers. Then he turned, arms wide to chide the flock: 'Look at you all. Stupid woolly things! And what's with the freaky doleful eyes and following each other about and constant chomping? Grass, weeds, thistles, gates; you'll eat anything, won't you? *Nom-nom-nom-nom.*'

638 said nothing. What could she say; it was all true — except for the bit about gates.

'Oh, and by the way,' complained Leon, 'your field stinks of cattle's business!'

'Whoa,' Leon protested, 'calm down.' This anger was, he realised, merely due to the disappointing phone call.

'Let it go,' he said quietly – Moss *would* feel differently when he saw the photos.

But what if he didn't?

Leon remembered instantly: he would sound out Poppy – this had become official Plan B; perhaps a promotion to Plan A was already in order. Aloud he said: 'Sorry, Moss, but if you will insist on being a barnacle, that's how it goes.'

'Why don't you just piss off back to Manchester,' said a fuzzy voice. 'We don't want your type here.'

Leon blinked, raised a hand to the sun. 638 was walking away, taking her mucky backside with her. She'd left something behind, though – a pile of fresh sheep shit (picture muddy figs). She looked back, as if to say: *That's for you.* Then, finding a clump of grass a tiny bit taller than the grass around it, she set to munching.

There came now a new sound, unpleasant and rasping; something alien and inappropriate; yet, at the same time not. The noise was loud and getting louder.

'Oh shit, that's all I need,' said Leon, looking down the field. Richard was heading this way on a bright red quad bike, bumping over the rough terrain, parting sheep before him. A pair of crows were sent flapping.

Presently, the quad bike slid to a stop inches from Leon's legs. Richard killed the engine.

'Richard, what the fuck are you doing out here?' Leon jumped down from the wall, eyes now fixed on a crumpled plastic sheet which covered something bulky on the back of

306

the bike. 'Long way from the house, aren't you? You know, for an agoraphobic.'

'Wales isn't just for you, Leon.' Richard raised mud-spattered goggles onto his forehead. 'It's for everybody.'

A voice mumbled under the plastic cover. Leon's eyes widened. 'Ignore that,' said Richard, taking out a cigarette.

'Oh God, please tell me you haven't . . .'

Leon attacked the binding around the groaning package with both hands . . . and after a mere three minutes (and two slightly sprained wrists) the thin, wet string snapped.

The heavy plastic fell open to reveal shocking content: a young woman, mouth gagged, limbs restrained.

'Jesus, Richard!' barked Leon, stepping back.

The girl's eyes bulged, silently screaming for help. She was naked, lying on her stomach, head up, wrists tightly bound to ankles with black duct tape behind her back, in what appeared to be a kinky fusion of yoga and bondage. The image didn't look feasible yet there it remained: a terrified female trussed like a sacrificial turkey on the back of a quad bike driven by Richard – who was *here*, in an open field more than a hundred miles from Manchester.

'What do you think; not bad, eh?' asked Richard. 'Found her in the village at the bottom of the hill.'

'And what, you thought you'd just help yourself?'

'Why not? Besides, I think she's the village idiot. They'll probably be glad to be rid of it.'

Leon attacked the sticky black tape between the girl's ankles and wrists, straining . . . twisting . . . labouring for a break. She yelped, wet and muffled, under her gag, tears streaming from her inflated eyes. Richard watched the hopelessly poor attempt at emancipation (tricky stuff, duct tape) puffing on his cigarette, unconcerned.

'She hardly put up any kind of struggle. I think she's actually quite happy on there.' Richard blew smoke in the air, patted the captive's head. 'Aren't you, darling?'

'Mumhfhh!' was the hoarse reply.

'Right, so you don't think we should, I don't know, maybe get her back *BEFORE SHE'S MISSED!*' Leon looked around, fully-expecting to see hordes of villagers with pitch-forks and farmers with industrial tools swarming from all points of the compass, closing in on the kidnapping-outsiders, hell-bent on releasing the distraught hostage. 'A little help here,' he suggested.

'Balls; I intend to take her home, smother her little arse in baby oil, and beat it blue with a table tennis bat.'

'Mumhfhh!'

'But first there's a horse I want to check out in the next field.'

'You have to be kidding me.'

'Do I look like I'm joking?'

Richard revved up the bike. 'Ready to go, Missy?'

'Mumhfhhhhh!'

Leon tried to lift 'Missy' from the bike and might have succeeded, despite a twinge in a lower vertebra, if she hadn't been tied to the carry-bars with baling-twine. He quickly switched to where the twine was knotted: a double Constrictor Hitch-Knot; tighter than any gnat's chuff.

'Oh, and keep your phone on, Leon. I know you've got it with you.' Richard tossed his cigarette away with zero regard for the countryside or the potential combustibility of sheep. Whipping out a hankie, he collected some of the copious drool hanging from the girl's chin, pulled down his grimy goggles and gave them a wipe. 'That's better,' he said. 'Nothing beats slobber for a good clean up; if you catch my drift.' To Missy he said, 'Right, hang on, darling.'

Sheep scattered as Richard hit the throttle and drove away, spraying mud. Leon gave chase but quickly realised the hopelessness of his endeavour. Helpless, he watched the quad bike disappear down the hill; Richard bouncing on the seat, the open plastic flapping ridiculously, the girl screeching like a terror-stricken monkey; and given the restrictions of her soggy gag it was an excellent scream – worthy of any horror movie.

Leon paced a short line up and down the field, back and forth, fingers rubbing hard rings into the temples of his troubled head whilst repeating 'This *cannot* be happening' over and over again.

Ewes congregated around Leon's track, letting out *bahs* and *mehs*.

'Shut up; let me think!'

After a bout of mumbling and concern, Leon stopped pacing. 'Come on, get a grip,' he said quietly, 'let's work this out logically. Richard might venture to the bottom of the garden to watch a neighbour shower, sure, but he'd never come out *this far*. And even *Richard* wouldn't *actually kidnap* a girl. Not even to . . . you know, what he said; I'm sure most of you heard.'

Rows of sheep's slot-like pupils remained unblinking and unmoved.

'Oh come on. I ask you . . . would he? *Really?*'

The huddled assembly, now over twenty and still swelling, gave no reply; except for 591, she tilted her head fractionally – it didn't go unnoticed:

'And how would you know?' asked Leon. 'You don't know him.'

Someone at the back let out a long *bah* which Leon took to be a sign of sheep solidarity; a backing of 591's inferred allegation. 'Okay, he might kidnap a girl, *maybe*, but wouldn't he do it nearer to home? I mean, not close enough to the house for suspicion to fall on him but near enough to get back if his agoraphobia suddenly got worse; so within a few miles – a bus ride at most. He doesn't drive, you see.'

A sheep coughed. They do that sometimes.

'I know you saw him on a quad bike, 610, but that doesn't count; that's not *proper* driving. He hasn't even got a licence. So, I think we can all agree, can we not, that he would *never* come to Wales?'

No reply.

So what *had* happened? Leon looked for an explanation that made sense. The bottom field, where Richard vanished from sight just moments ago, now contained no sheep at all; every ewe in the area, about forty, had flocked around the speaker . . . Leon investigated the tight, gathered circle and its unbroken ring of lined-up eyes – apart from a trace of mild curiosity, every eyeball was completely vacant.

'Come on, there has to be a simple explanation. What about you, 647 – any ideas?'

Silence.

'512, any suggestions?'

Still nothing.

'*Anybody?*' A slow, full circle . . .

'Give me a break; *somebody* here must—' Leon slapped his forehead. 'I know what it is!' He addressed 638 directly: 'I'm cursed by an overactive imagination, that's all.' And to the entire crowd he explained: 'It's like before; Richard wasn't *here*. Not *really*. I just *imagined* he was.'

Blank faces were studied.

'Like I imagined you lot were actually taking this in.'

Leon took on the air of a sergeant major performing parade inspection.

'Look at you. None of you would last five minutes in Manchester. They would chew you up and spit you out. You have to be tough to survive where I'm from. *Hard*, like me.'

If the ewes believed him they gave no indication.

'You don't have a clue where Manchester is, do you? Do you even know *this*,' Leon rotated, hands outstretched, 'is Wales? . . . Seriously, do you have any conception of where you are right now?'

If the sheep still present (most were now walking away) had any idea they were standing on a heavily-grazed hill in Wales, in a marshy field dotted with their own droppings, ignoring a crazy Manc rambling on about another crazy Manc who may or may not have kidnapped a 'local' for something involving baby oil and table tennis bats, they weren't letting on. Leon looked around: perhaps fifteen woolly heads left and not a thought at the top of them.

'No, not a clue,' he said, answering his own question. 'You're just a bunch of empty-headed sheep.' The sun had vanished behind thick cloud and a chill wind had arrived.

'And yet here am *I*, standing in a swampy poo-strewn field addressing *you*. I must be *really* losing the plot.'

Shaking his head, he walked away, ignored by the five remaining sheep – three of which had gone back to dispassionate chewing.

'*Meh*,' said 638. Leon recognised her voice.

✳ ✳ ✳

The last photo Leon took that day was of a deep-black night sprayed with glittering stars, background to a watery moon that hovered above the hill, misty and far away.

Settling down to sleep he reasoned, reasonably he felt, that if Moss didn't love the photos, Poppy *surely* would.

Then he wondered if a sheep could ever be agoraphobic.

Be kind of tough if they were, he thought. What could they do; stay near a wall?

WEALLY, WEALLY?

'Oh come on, you *must* like that one.'

'A disused lead mine?'

'Exactly,' enthused Leon. He tabbed to the next photo. Moss stared blankly at an image of a wind-farm.

'And it's much bigger than it looks on here . . . I mean, huge . . . No? Not feeling it? Okay, what about this one?'

'A field?'

'Fine, not that one . . . *There*.'

'Sheep?'

'Still nothing? . . . How about . . . Ta-da! . . . Well?'

'Well, what?'

'Have you ever seen a night sky like that? Look at the moon, the stars, how they shine. Help me out here. The hill tops all . . .'

'I'm not being funny, man, but it doesn't look any different to how it looks here.' Moss leaned back on the bed putting distance between himself and Leon's photos.

'Okay, maybe the photo hasn't captured it properly but trust me everything in a Welsh night sky is clearer. No car exhaust and sodium street-lighting blocking it all out, and *the sounds*, you can actually hear—'

'I'm just not feeling it, man. Sorry.'

'Let me show you the Town Hall again. It used to be—'

'I know, you showed me; *a Temperance building* – whatever *that* was.'

'Someone hasn't been listening. Let me recap. Imagine a giant pub, but without a bar . . .'

'Leon, it's a *Town Hall*. A place for corrupt councillors and bent—'

'How about these?' Leon held the phone close to Moss's face. 'A church; a rather fetching barn conversion; a Belgian hiker – Eddie something – friendly guy, travelling around Europe; a chapel, not to be confused with a church; the Welsh Oggie I had for lunch – it's like a giant Cornish Pastie but tastier and, well, bigger. Did I tell you about Oggies?'

'Yes, twice.' Moss had nothing more to say. You don't have to be a body-language expert to know the folding of arms, pinching of lips and shaking of head means *I'm done. Next subject, please.* Surely, only a fool would press on under these circumstances.

'What about this one?'

Moss sighed. '*A tractor?*'

'Moving a bale,' Leon enthused.

'Sorry, man, it's just not for me.'

'But we agreed. You said you loved the countryside.'

'I know – *I do.* But city life's good, too, clubs and shops and that, different people buzzing about.'

'*Shops?* Well, that's the first time I've heard that.' Leon sat back, deflated for the moment. A hush fell upon the room and its occupants, the only sound, the shower running in the bathroom across the landing, beyond Moss's open door.

'Your mum's taking a long time in the shower, Moss.'

'No, she isn't.'

'I think you'll find she is. We've been going through the photos for, what, twenty minutes?'

'Seems longer.'

'And she's been in there the whole time. Correct me if I'm wrong but Janis is normally a once-a-month, in-and-out kind of person. You know, conserve water and all that.'

'Yeah, she is but . . .'

The shower stopped and they faced each other through the silence that followed. Even Leon, with his poor recognition of non-verbal communication could see Moss looked uncomfortable. He suddenly felt the need to fill the dead-air with words:

'Not that I keep tabs on your mum's showering habits, you understand.'

'No, man – course not.'

'Why would I?'

'Exactly.'

'That's the last thing I'd keep in my notebook.'

One of Moss's eyebrows adopted a quizzical stance.

'So I don't,' added Leon.

'That's good.'

'Shouldn't she be at Yoga by now? She's going to be late.'

The bathroom door opened, sending a surge of steam over the landing. The woman appearing through the mist, wrapped in a fluffy pink towel and dabbing her hair with a smaller blue towel, was not Janis . . . but Poppy. She brought a smile into Moss's room. 'Hello, Leon.'

'Hi.' After a slightly awkward beat Leon said, 'I didn't know you two knew each other.'

'We met a couple of days ago,' said Poppy. 'In the precinct.'

'She writes beautiful poetry, Leon. You should hear some of it.'

'We had a deal, Moss. We shook hands.'

'We didn't shake hands.'

'Not physically, but we did mentally. That's a deal in my book.'

'Sorry, man.'

'Come on, Leon, don't be such a grouch,' said Poppy. 'We can all be friends.' She sat on the bed, tousled Leon's hair. 'Might be kind of fun.'

Moss said, 'You're not suggesting we . . .'

'No,' said Poppy.

Leon went with: 'You don't mean . . .'

'Again, no. Honestly, what are boys like? I just mean . . . I don't know . . . we could be like Bonnie and Clyde . . . with an extra Clyde.'

'Right.'

'Gotcha.'

Another hush fell upon the room and it was Poppy, after wrapping the blue towel around her head, who eventually broke it: '*Would* you have, though?'

'Would we what?' Moss flicked a piece of imaginary fluff from his sleeve.

'Now, see here, young lady.' For some reason Leon had adopted an upper-crust accent. 'I'm not sure what you're inferring . . .'

Poppy shuffled backwards, sat between them.

'I mean I couldn't blame you – a gorgeous girl like me, sitting here nearly naked, all warm and wet after a steamy shower.' She laid a hand on each nearest male thigh. Again silence. Gazing out through damp tendrils of hair she moved her big green eyes from one to the other.

The boys didn't seem to know where to look.

'Oh calm down, I'm just joshing with you.' She snorted that snorty-laugh of hers then brayed like a donkey.

As the hee-hawing continued, Leon saw that Moss's eyes had widened.

'Didn't know about that, did you?' said Leon.

'Not a clue,' Moss replied.

Poppy laughed so hard the pink towel began to unravel about her boobs. This didn't stop the gleeful guffawing; if anything it fired up the donkey even more. And laughter, no matter how odd it sounds – perhaps more so because of it – is, as everyone knows, deeply infectious. Before long, all three were laughing uncontrollably.

A few minutes later, after much rolling around and cracking-up and squealing and tears of joy and side-holding and playful pushing and yet more cracking-up – just before the hilarity had died down completely – Leon had an idea and announced it thusly: 'Hey, hey, guys, I've got an idea.'

Moss, clutching his side, couldn't draw enough breath to ask.

'Oh this is genius.' Leon was beaming. 'You're going to love this.'

'What is it?' asked Poppy, wiping away tears. 'And it better not be anything pervy, Leon, or the only thing saying hello to your dangly bits will be my knee.'

'Poppy, how do you fancy taking a really big–'

'Leon!' barked Poppy (a change from braying, at least).

'–leap of faith. Just leave everything behind and come to Wales with us.'

'That *is* genius. And that's why I shouted *Leon!* just now. Not because I thought you were going to suggest something pervy, but because it is – what you said – genius.'

'I know, right?'

'Hold on, man.'

'We could get an old camper van and travel around in it. Or rent a log cabin. Or a Yurt! Moss said he could live in a Yurt.'

'A Yurt's like a tent, right?' asked Poppy.

'A portable home,' said Leon.

'See, that still sounds like a tent to me.'

'Definitely not a tent,' insisted Leon. 'They've got wooden frames and thick walls.'

'They are pretty cool as it goes. Mongolian Nomads use them.'

'That's right, you tell her, Moss.'

'There's not a lot to tell. The nomads move their sheep and goats around . . .'

'Looking for new places to graze them,' added Leon.

'And the Yurts are carried around on the backs of yaks.'

'Yaks? Yuk.'

'Or camels,' said Leon.

'Yaks. Camels. Sounds enchanting.'

'It does, doesn't it? And the rent on a Yurt can't be much. Three people sharing the rent would be easy. We all get along so why not? It would be fun; an adventure – like you said, Bonnie and Clyde and Clyde.'

'I'm sure it would be lovely,' said Poppy. 'But . . .'

'Moss could write songs. You could write your poetry. I could—'

'It's a lovely thought, Leon, but I've got my job; my family – all my friends. And to be honest, I'm really more of a city girl.'

'Yeah, me too,' said Moss; adding: 'I mean city *guy*.'

'Aw bless. That's so sweet.' Poppy and Moss rubbed noses and as if by magic, Leon, if he wasn't already, became a gooseberry; a big fat official green one.

When Poppy eventually noticed that Leon's spirit had drained from his face, she gave him an understanding smile. 'Don't get me wrong, Leon, I love the countryside, nature, trees and everything; nice for breaks and holidays – I just don't really see myself *living* there.'

'Exactly,' said Moss. 'I couldn't have put that better myself. You definitely have a way with words.'

'Again; sweet – thanks. Besides, I don't really know either of you yet. I only met Moss on, when was it . . . Saturday?'

'Was it only Saturday? Yeah, it was.'

'Feels like longer, right?' Poppy smiled at Moss. 'But that's all it was, Leon. Two days.'

'And yet here you are sitting on his bed wearing just a towel.'

'Whoa, easy, man.'

'And what, that makes me some kind of slut?'

'Not a slut, exactly.'

'Oh not exactly. What *exactly*, then? A slag?'

'No.'

'A tart?'

'No.'

'So, what: a harlot; a hussy; a hooker; a whore?'

'God no, not a whore.'

'A floozy, then? A jezebel, perhaps; a strumpet; a trollop; a slapper; a loose, skanky-bitch-Ho?'

'Not to be picky but I think Ho and Whore are technically the same.'

'Still an impressive list though, Poppy. You're like a sexy, walking thesaurus.'

'Shut up, you.'

'Will do.'

'If you must know, Leon, I fell in the canal. Why do you think my clothes are on the radiator?'

'You fell in the canal?'

Moss gestured for Leon not to ask but, of course, it was already too late. 'I'm sure Poppy doesn't want to—'

'Yes, I fell in the canal – or should I say I was *bumped* into the canal – because clumsy-arse here is incapable of looking where he's walking.'

'Bit harsh. It only happened the once.' Moss got up, went over to the radiator.

'What happened? Or shouldn't I ask?'

'Well, I'll tell you . . .'

'Your clothes are dry, Poppy.'

'We were walking along the canal tow-path, all very nice. I'd stopped to throw a coin into a lock to make a wish.

316

People say it's lucky if you do it when the lock is full. Well they obviously hadn't accounted for *Moss* being around.'

Poppy stared at Moss, forcing him to accept the figurative story-baton.

'Yeah, we were walking by the canal when I heard my phone ring. But it wasn't in my pocket, it was on the ground.' He pulled out the pocket, showed a hole. 'I stepped over, picked it up, and it was Janis.'

'He calls his mum *Janis*.'

'Yeah, I know,' said Leon.

'That's her name,' Moss said, as if everyone should call their mums by their first names. 'Anyway, I was talking—'

'To Janis.'

'To Janis – and I'm not sure what happened but I turned round and must have caught my foot or tripped or something and kind of bumped into Poppy a little bit.'

Not for the first time that day he offered her an apologetic face. 'I could have sworn I wasn't that close.'

'And I fell in, arse over tit, like a proper Mary.'

'Into the canal,' said Leon.

'Exactly,' Poppy replied.

'And I take it that's not what you wished for?'

'Yes, that's what I wished for, Leon; to be pitched head-first into a filthy canal.'

Poppy noticed the flicker of a smile on Leon's face.

'It's not funny. I lost a shoe.'

But Leon couldn't help it; he laughed . . . it didn't take long for Poppy to crack, and Moss swiftly followed.

When the laughing finally fizzled out, Leon had another question: 'So what *did* you wish for?'

'I can't tell you that, if I did it wouldn't come true. Let's just say it wasn't me that was falling, but it might have been me they were falling for.'

'Aw that's beautiful, man. You definitely have a way with words. Doesn't she have a way with words, Leon?'

'Oh yes. I particularly enjoyed the "arse over tit" reference.'

Moss and Poppy got all smoochy-smoochy again and as the bed wasn't the biggest, Leon was obliged to tolerate episodes of inadvertent squishing by the doting duo.

'Do you really think I have a way with words, Moss?' asked Poppy.

'Definitely,' said Moss.

'Weally, weally?'

'Weally, weally.'

After a prolonged series of *Weally-weallys* Poppy said: 'We're doing baby talk, Leon.'

'Yeah, I got that.'

The gooseberry's eyes went to the top of the room where they studied the blue sky and fluffy white clouds Janis had painted on the ceiling over twenty years ago. She'd also depicted the ends of leafy tree branches at the edges of all four sides. The mural gave the impression you were standing in the middle of an English wood, looking up.

Leon thought the paint could do with touching up now (Moss's persistent smoking had rather dulled the summer's day effect; tobacco and weed staining having given rise to a more autumnal, and currently topical, feel) but felt it still looked good, considering.

Janis had always possessed an artistic bent; wonder why she never moved to Wales, he wondered.

'Weally, weally, weally?'

'Weally, weally, weally, weally.'

'Okay, you're back in the good books.'

'Weally?'

'Oh for God's sake.'

'What?' the enamoured twosome said in unison.

'Get a room.'

'This *is* my room.'

'Fair point.' Leon ignored the continuous giggling and occasional bump, and looked around the various ceiling-branches until he noticed, for the first time; a tiny robin perched on a twig. *I wouldn't stay there too long if I were you. Not if Dylan's around.* 'He might pounce on you and rip out your feathers.'

'He might what?' said the Poppy-Moss combo.

'Nothing.' Leon coughed unnecessarily. 'So, Poppy, did you *see* anything in the canal?'

'Yeah, lots of scummy water, and what looked like an old sofa.'

'Nothing weird?'

'Actually, yes, now that you mention it; it looked like somebody had thrown a load of groceries in there – tins and jars and bottles and that. All *full*, not empties.'

'Wish we could bottle *you*,' said Moss and another cuddle ensued. Leon had seen enough.

'Oh, don't go, Leon,' said Poppy. 'You've only just got here. Sit down and I'll get dressed. My clothes are dry now. Like I said, I do know how uncomfortable boys can get being round half-naked beauties like myself.'

She laughed and patted the bed.

'Come on, stay and have a coffee. Moss will make it.'

'Yeah, right; that's *woman's* work.'

Poppy jokily punched Moss's thin bicep *really* hard.

'Ouch! I was only kidding.' Moss rubbed his arm. 'That really hurt.'

'Aw, diddums.' Poppy stuck out her bottom lip and a play fight ensued. Moss jumped wholeheartedly into some serious tickling manoeuvres. Poppy squealed; one arm locked around her bath towel, one arm 'fighting' back, her bare legs thrashing around like Riverdance on steroids.

When Leon accidentally caught sight of *punani*, he knew it was time to leave.

Leon opened the front door to the sound of fireworks, here and there; bangs and pops and fizzes and whooshes and screeches and crackles. Rockets climbed and exploded beyond roof tops. The acrid smell of cordite filled the air.

Bonfire Night.

Ignoring the light-show for a moment, Leon stepped carefully over Dylan, currently encamped on the WELCOME, FRIEND mat, and got a fare-thee-well of:

'That's right, piss off. Nothing for *you* here.'

Leon was at the gate before Poppy had gathered enough breath to shout, 'You should ask that girl out!'

Because of the fireworks, Leon didn't hear her.

'What girl?' Moss asked.

'Never you mind,' said Poppy.

'Oh, Lord,' said Leon aloud. She was walking towards him. Norris Avenue – No bra!

Should I speak to her? Leon wondered. This would be the complete opposite of what he would normally do.

His mind replied: *No, stick to the usual plan, it's safer.*

But his mind had been wrong about so much, it seemed, of late. Maybe he *should* do the opposite and say hello. What harm could it do, really?

She doesn't look happy, though. Why doesn't she look happy? Is she pissed off with *me*? No, it *can't* be; I'm not sure she even knows who I am. And I'm not looking at her tits – even though I *can* see them, *indirectly*, jiggling away.

Jesus, it is *me!*

No, it isn't – she's just had a bad day. Perhaps a warm smile and a '*Hi, Kelly, how are you?*' might be just what she needs right now.

Go on. Do it.

Oh god, should I?

It would really put Richard's nose out of joint.

It would, wouldn't it?

Yes, so do it, you wuss!

'Hi, Kelly.' Leon smiled his best smile. 'My name's—'

'Fuck off.'

'How are y— Excuse me?' An image of Wayne, rejected and moving on, flashed into his brain.

Kelly – who had passed – now stopped and turned.

'What are you, some kind of pervert?'

'Come again?'

'Do you think I haven't seen you – watching from the window?'

'I might have just happened to see you passing once or twice but I'm pretty sure that doesn't make me—'

'A pervert? A *dirty* pervert?'

'I'm not a pervert.'

'Then, what's with the binoculars?'

'What?' The penny dropped immediately. 'No, that's not me.'

'And I suppose it wasn't you I saw on the tram.'

'On the tram?'

'Yes, on the tram – yelling at an empty platform. How fucking weird is that?'

'No, I can explain all that.'

'Really? Go on then.'

'Well, it's a bit complicated.'

'I'm listening.' Kelly folded her arms.

Leon couldn't help glimpsing how her soft boobs rested gently upon— *Leon, focus!*

'Okay . . . Well, I'm not sure I fully understand it all *myself*, yet . . . but with my parents . . . after the whole . . .'

Kelly's stance softened a little. 'Look, Lionel . . .'

'Leon.'

'I heard about what happened to your parents . . . and you . . . and I'm sorry about that. But that's no excuse to go around spying on girls with binoculars.'

'No, no, Kelly, that wasn't me.'

'Yeah, right,' said Kelly. 'At least have the balls to—'

'You might have *thought* it was me–'

Jesus, look at her nipples, Leon. You don't need binoculars to see those beauties. They're like bullets. Then in a rhapsodic, almost sing-song voice: *I think she's getting turned on!*

'–but it wasn't.'

Ask her to lift her top.

Kelly shook her head. 'Right, whatever.'

She turned and marched away, breasts leading her home and no doubt dancing all the way.

'Honestly, it wasn't!' yelled Leon. 'IT WASN'T ME!'

Kelly gave him the middle finger and without looking back shouted, 'I saw you!'

'NO – THAT WAS RICHARD!'

Don't tell her it was me, you fucking weasel.

Leon cast his eyes homeward. Surprise, surprise; there was Richard, at the landing window, binoculars hanging from a strap around his neck. He made an O shape of his mouth, held his hands under imaginary boobs and made them bounce.

CHAPTER EIGHTEEN

Confronting Demons

WIKIPEDIA

'Why else would they be standing out like bullets?' asked Richard.

'I told you. I don't want to talk about Kelly. I need to read up on what's going on with my head. How can I explain to her, or anyone else, if *I* don't know what the fuck is going on? Why isn't that on yet?'

'It's booting up. Give it a minute.' Richard, cigarette perched on his lip, spun around in the computer chair, watched as Leon paced up and down the room waving away smoke.

'I'm really more of a city guy,' mimicked Leon. 'Weally, weally?' he mocked. 'Yes, weally, weally.'

Richard chain-lit a fresh cigarette. 'I told you he wasn't going anywhere.'

'I really think he would have gone. At least he would if—'

'If he hadn't met the tart?'

'Poppy isn't a tart.'

'Whatever, Moss is currently gaga so that's him well and truly out of the picture. Even you, Mr Losing-A-Grip-On-Reality, can no longer deny this to be fact.'

'Oh shut up, Richard. You don't know everything.' Leon plonked down onto the sofa. 'And isn't it about time you washed that horrible dressing gown?'

'No it isn't. It's about time you stopped trying to change the subject. So get your notebook out and cross Moss's name off your list – and Poppy's.'

'What list?'

'Your *Oh-Please*-Come-To-Wales-With-Me list.'

'I haven't got a list. Not for that.'

'Well, if you haven't, and we both know you have, it's only because two items – in this case, names – does not a real list make.' Richard swivelled back to the computer screen. 'And now you haven't even got those – You're fucked, matey.'

As Richard clicked around the Web, Leon quietly slipped out his notebook and crossed out MOSS and POPPY – the only names written on his MOVE TO WALES list.

After Richard had visited and read aloud (Leon listening intently) from *Mental-health.info*, *Wikipedia.org*, *Whats-wrong-with-me.co.uk*, and various other random 'medical' sites – which may or may not have been bona fide – he visited *Fucked-in-the-head.com* (which turned out to be a hard-to-close-down porn site where he was forced to endure over twenty minutes of various filthy videos that he accidentally kept clicking on before he finally managed to inadvertently shut down the site).

'Hey, you!' blurted Leon. 'What happened to the girl?'

'If you're referring to that last video . . .'

'I'm referring to the girl on the quad bike. The one trussed up like a sacrificial turkey.'

'There was no girl.'

'Don't give me that.'

'And no quad bike.'

'Bollocks. I saw you. And you still haven't explained what you were doing in Wales. And let me add,' he pointed an accusatory finger, 'agoraphobic my arse!'

'There was no girl. No quad bike. No me. I wasn't there.'

'I saw you, remember. We spoke.'

'What, like you saw a singing tomato and half a dozen zombie pensioners?'

'*Chelsea* zombie pensioners.'

Richard moved to the sofa, put an arm awkwardly around Leon's shoulder and said, 'Leon, you simply *imagined* I was there.'

'Actually, I'd thought the same thing.'

Leon's eyes were watering, and not just from smoke.

'But why would I do that?'

'Because you're not well. And that's why you need to forget about moving. You need to concentrate on staying here and getting better.'

'You really think so?'

'Absolutely. You can't possibly think about leaving in your condition. Come, look, I've found a really good site: *Think-you-might-be-a-mentalist dot net.*'

Richard helped Leon stand and led him to the computer as if guiding a sleepwalker back to bed. As Leon sat, light from the monitor reflected in his moistened eyes. Richard pointed to a block of text and after allowing time for the initial sentences to be absorbed, he patted Leon's head and said, 'I'm afraid you really are quite mad.'

About twenty minutes later, after Richard had made coffee (for one), Leon said, 'Can this be right?'

'The Internet is never wrong, Leon.' Richard spoke from the sofa where he'd just lit up yet another Marlboro. 'The Internet is Truth; the ultimate pool of all human knowledge.'

'Okay, well, it says here, and I'm quoting: "In almost every situation, it is advisable to confront your demons".'

'Does it? Then ignore the bollocks.'

Leon swivelled to face Richard.

'But you said I should avoid the visions at all costs. *Run away*, you said. *Get back here pronto.* You said if I confronted them, it could be – how did you put it? . . .'

'A disaster; an unmitigated disaster – and it would be, trust me.'

'That's what *you* say. But according to this: "Exposure is a really effective form of Therapy". *Cognitive Behavioural Therapy* they call it. I used the Chat Window; have you ever known a more helpful thing? Had a good chat with Steve—'

'Yeah, right – *Steve.* He's probably a *Saahir* or a *Ragesh*, lives in New Delhi or Calcutta.'

'Steve, a very friendly guy, I have to say, reckons my problems were probably brought on by the shock of losing both parents so suddenly and unexpectedly.'

'No shit, Sherlock.' Richard blew a cloud of smoke across the room.

'According to Steve—' Leon read from the Chat Window: '—"Psychotic episodes often include not only hallucinations but delusions and paranoia as well". Jeez. That's quite a package, isn't it?'

'You can't believe everything you read, Leon; especially on the Internet.'

'He says: "Exposure Therapy is based on the concept of habituation; a psychological process that involves a decrease in response over a period of time". They call it "getting used to" or "growing accustomed to".'

'Sounds like a lot of tosh to me. I bet *Steve* doesn't even work there. He's probably the tea-boy – an office-wallah at best.'

'Richard!'

'Well . . .' said Richard, dragging the word out.

'Steve—'

'Cha-wallah.'

'*Steve* – the live chat assistant at – where are we? – *Let-us-be-helping-you dot com* – says: "E.T. patients who stand up to their manifestations will become so accustomed to them and their unwanted pathological reactions, that they will lose their intensity, become manageable, and eventually disappear".'

'Sorry, what will disappear – the manifestations, the fear or the patient? Oh dear, I'm getting one of my headaches.' Richard rubbed a temple. 'Do we have Aspirin?'

'*Stand up to.*' Leon repeated the phrase a couple of times. 'Steve's saying the same thing: *confront your demons.*' He spun back to Richard, dread on his face.

'But I hate confrontation; especially with strangers – especially *weird, possibly-imaginary* strangers.'

'For once, I agree with you. Turn that thing off.'

The computer made a gentle *boop* sound.

'Wait, he's typed something else: "But first, and this is most important, the sufferer has to acknowledge the root of their individual problem".'

Leon turned, brow furrowed. 'But I've acknowledged mum and dad are dead . . . so why hasn't it stopped?'

'Beats me. Why don't you nip out for a takeaway? I'm sure some Peking Duck would make us feel better.'

'I'll ask Steve.' Leon swivelled back to the screen, started to type. The monitor died and the computer made a *dooooom* noise as it lost power. He turned to find Richard with an unplugged power cord in his hand.

325

'What did you do that for?'

'It's for your own good, Leon. You need to stop reading that shit. It's all bollocks on the Internet, everybody knows that.'

'I don't know – maybe Steve's right. Maybe I do need to confront my demons . . . look my monsters in the face.'

'You've known *Steve* (Richard placed the name in air-quotes) for what, ten minutes? I think I know you better than he does. Mark my words, Leon; on no account should you ever confront your demons.'

Leon appeared deep in thought, mainly because he was.

'Hello, Earth calling Leon.'

'Hey, maybe Steve could help you with your *agoraphobia*.' Leon put the doubted disorder in air-quotes.

'Don't you dare air-quote my disorder.' Richard stubbed out his cigarette. 'And don't you think if I could be helped it would have happened by now? We just have to admit the truth – agoraphobia is for life. And whatever *you've* got is probably incurable, too. We are both chronic and without hope.' He flopped onto the sofa and curled up. As Leon scrutinised, Richard donned the pathetic air of someone who must never be abandoned. 'I'm not feeling well, Leon.'

'Really? You wanted Peking Duck a minute ago.'

'You're not the only one who's suffering, you know!' barked Richard. Then he sat up and in a smarmy voice said, 'This is your home. It's where you belong; with me.' He patted the sofa, his face breaking into a wretched fixed grin.

Leon said nothing. Somewhere in the middle of research or talking or thinking or chatting, he'd had an idea.

He had thought of someone else he could ask about moving to Wales.

CHICKEN NUGGETS

The big yellow chicken held out a flyer to a passer-by. The offer was ignored.

There were precious few people about and those that did pass within wing's reach seemed far from interested in ten percent off a Big Chicken Meal Bucket – with or without a free Big Chicken Beverage. The patch the chicken had been ordered to patrol and exploit was simply dead. Not surprising considering the only things here were a constantly vandalised bus stop, a dark foreboding church with a hole in the roof, and an extensive grave yard.

Chicken-Man strutted over, flyer at the ready, back to the bus shelter, to retry his luck with the two women there.

'Oh fuck off, will you,' said the one that looked like Myra Hindley. 'Yeah, fuck off,' added the child.

Before the second woman could chastise her prodigy, if indeed she was going to, a Number 41 pulled up and two old dears, each transporting a small bunch of flowers, alighted – the chicken followed them to the church entrance, volunteering a leaflet to the back of their old-lady hats as they scurried along. The dears maintained their indifference with each stone step climbed.

After he'd pantomimed kicking the old ladies up the arse, the chicken had a good scratch at his long-standing sweat rash. And that's when he spotted the young man staring at him from across the road.

The spectator was Leon.

'And you, big yellow chicken man – what kind of demon are you?' Leon asked quietly.

Having eyed the young man warily, the chicken edged towards two workmen now exiting the church. Stopping close to the gate, the men lit thin cigarettes and leaned against the wall. When the chicken caught their icy demeanour he decided to abort.

'Can they see you, you big yellow chicken?' wondered Leon in a low voice. 'They don't seem to.'

Vicky and Peggy gave Leon a wave from the bus stop but he didn't notice. They watched as he now crossed the road (funny, you'd think it would have been the chicken crossing the road, but no) and approached the big yellow chicken.

'Is there a problem?' asked the posh-sounding chicken. The face-holed mug was pink, puffy and clammy; with high forehead and bulbous eyes (made to appear extra globular by the magnifying properties of thick-lens glasses). Picture a sweaty, swotty strawberry of university age.

'Would you like a flyer?' A leaflet was offered: 'Ten percent off.'

'Confront your demons,' said Leon in a dull tone.

'Excuse me?'

Leon's eyes had a fixed, glassy look. 'Only by confronting our demons will they eventually disappear.'

Chicken-Man got as far as 'I' in what was to be a hesitant 'I see,' when he received a kick to one of his orange legs.

Flyers went everywhere as he hopped around clutching the assaulted limb squawking *Ohs* and *Ows* and *Oohs* and the like. Leon stepped back, startled. Clearly not the outcome he'd expected.

'What on earth did you do that for?' The chicken's snooty-sounding accent drew attention to a countrified air.

'Uh, not sure now,' said Leon. He tried: 'To make you disappear?'

'What? Are you mental?'

'Don't try and put this back on me, you, you, demon.'

'You need help, you really do,' said the bouncing pullet.

'Leon, what are you doing?' asked Peggy. 'What were you thinking?' added Vicky. They had hurried over from the bus shelter. The child seemed to be the only one to appreciate the comic value of it all; a cartoon without the need for a telly. The little tyke was laughing himself hoarse.

'He's an absolute nutter. Please, get him away from me.'

'Alright, mate, calm down, he's not going to do anything else,' said Peggy. 'You're not – are you, Leon.'

'Wait. You can see him?' asked Leon.

Peggy and Vicky looked to each other, baffled.

Leon turned to the workmen. 'Can *you* see him?'

The men laughed, nodded a *We should be getting back to work* to each other and scuttled off.

'This posh fuckwit?' said Vicky. 'Course we can.'

'Thanks for that. I am here, you know,' said the chicken, rubbing his shin. 'And the name's Nigel.'

'Kick him, kick him,' urged the tyke, swinging out a dinky trainer. Restrained by mother's hand his out-stretched leg couldn't quite reach the target.

'You can *all* see him,' said Leon, moving backwards.

Peggy made a calming gesture. 'Come on, Leon, take it easy.'

'Did the fuckwit *say* something?' asked Vicky.

'Again, right here.'

Leon reversed into a puddle of spilt flyers. 'This is *so* fucked up; *seriously* fucked up.'

'Come on, Leon,' said Peggy, 'it's alright now.'

'My shin's not alright.' The chicken pulled an orange legging above his calf and presented the limb for inspection. 'That'll be bruised for a week, I shouldn't wonder.'

'I know you've been through a lot, Leon,' Peggy continued, 'a hell of a lot – but try and keep it together, eh?'

But Leon wasn't keeping it together: he pulled out his notebook, opened it to the Sightings List, and shook it at the women in turn, laughing like a loon. 'Are *all* these real?'

'What's he going on about?' asked Vicky. 'You got any idea?' Peggy shook her head.

Leon continued to laugh, pointing at the page.

'Still think *I'm* the fuckwit?' asked the chicken.

'Leon, we're taking Ben to the hospital.' The child had a long, fresh graze on his forehead. 'Why don't you—'

'No, no, I hate hospitals.'

'Okay, well, how about—'

'No, I'm completely fine now; really. Thank you.'

There followed an awkward silence as Leon – who didn't *look* completely fine – put his notebook away.

'Sorry about your leg,' he said at last.

'Yes, well, let's just say it's a good job I didn't resort to my boxing skills, or you may have taken a beating.' Nigel stuttered forward, dukes up, jabbing the air, pretending he might really have some boxing skills, but made sure to keep the women between his ludicrously-thrusting wings and Leon – as if they might be holding him back.

Vicky and Peggy rolled their eyes at each other.

'Again, I'm really sorry. I don't know what happened. I thought you were . . .'

Leon had shut off, eyes staring through the church gates.

'Excuse me but I didn't quite catch that. You thought I was . . .' The chicken waited but got no reply.

The women followed Leon's gaze and saw nothing.

'Leon, what is it?' asked Peggy. 'What do you see?'

'Can't you see that?' barked Leon.

'See what?' Vicky asked.

Leon pointed. '*That!*'

There was much looking: up the steps, to each other, to Leon. Nothing. Whatever *that* was, only Leon could see it.

'Oh shit, it's coming!'

Aided by mild panic, Leon battled to skate across the strewn glossy flyers, now mimicking all the attributes of a frozen pond. For a moment it played like a scene from a Marx Brothers film, but once Leon had negotiated the slippery leaflet-slick, he was able to run off down the hill. And he did.

'Go on, run away, you – you – big yellow chicken!' the big yellow chicken shouted.

The women stared at him, shook their heads.

'What?' the chicken asked.

Just then, a Number 22 to the hospital soared past, dipped over the brow and travelled downhill.

Peggy and Vicky turned to each other, stone-faced.

'Never mind, ladies,' said Nigel cottoning on. 'I'm sure further transportation will be along in due course.'

'You're not from round here, are you?' said Peggy.

'Hardly,' scoffed the chicken. 'Hey; how about something to read whilst you wait?' He offered a flyer. 'You *can* read, can't you?' he laughed.

Peggy punched the chicken in the nuggets. Winded, he went to his knees, wheezing.

'Pathetic,' said Vicky, shoving him over with her foot. He rolled onto his back, legs bent double, clutching his eggs. The only thing missing was Sage & Onion.

'Kick him, kick him,' urged the tyke as he was led, reluctantly, back towards the bus stop.

Behind them, the chicken was heard to wheeze, 'Thank you, ladies.'

BACK TO THE PRECINCT

The argument Leon was having with himself – out loud – outside Pound Shop about the pros and cons of demon confrontation was not a pretty sight. The altercation was punctuated with wild gestures, frantic pacing and face slaps. Luckily, the precinct was having a quiet spell (a big United game about to kick off on TV) so there were few around to witness the unpleasant spectacle.

One idling shopkeeper, Mr Fassner, the Algerian who ran Pound Shop, *could see* but he had become accustomed to Leon and his ways; he was convinced it was Tourette's – either that or schizophrenia.

'Come on, come on, get a grip,' Leon said, still panicky and breathing hard from running.

'*Get a grip? Are you kidding me? It was your idea to confront—*'

'Balls!'

'*It bloody was!*'

'Okay, but you didn't have to kick him.'

'*What difference did that make?*'

'I don't know! Let me think, let me think.'

'*And what was that other thing? It looked like a—*'

Leon slapped his face.

'*What was that for?*'

'Don't say it.'

'*Okay, but stop slapping me.*'

'Will do. Sorry about that.' Leon leaned over, hands on knees.

'*Again with the hands on knees – Now, what's wrong?*'

'Still trying to get my breath back.'

'*It was your idea to run.*'

'Seemed like a good idea at the time.'

'*Bollocks, you just panicked.*'

'So did you.'

'*Did not.*'

'Did too.'

'*Okay, maybe I did a bit.*'

Leon looked up and made an exaggerated *Told you* face which the Pound Shop window reflected back.

'He's pulling his face like a stupid camel again now,' Mr Fassner said. 'Always the same with this boy; what is wrong with him? The face slapping is new; I'll give him that . . . but this constant talking to himself . . . it's unbelievable.'

The Algerian was alone in the shop.

'So what are we going to do? – I mean, next time.'

'Well, if we are *going to confront our "demons",'* – Leon made air quotes – '*I really think we have to stop running.*'

'You're right, no more running. No more running, and no more backing down.'

'*So we're agreed?*'

'Agreed.'

'*Good. Now let's get over there and grab the floozy.*'

'Jenny's not a floozy.'

'*She might be, if we're lucky.*'

'You be quiet now.' Leon made a mouth-zipping gesture. 'And remember, we need to stay calm.'

'See; unbelievable,' said Mr Fassner, still alone, watching Leon march off towards Kath's Kaff.

'Watch it, dickhead,' said Carl, deliberately bumping into Leon as he entered the café.

'Yeah, I will,' replied Leon.

Tell him to fuck off. Tell him to fuck RIGHT off.

'And maybe you should watch it, too,' added Leon.

Carl, laughing, turned to Danny and hitched a thumb over his shoulder. 'Did you hear that?'

Rather than put distance between them, Leon sat at the nearest empty table; one by the window.

He was feeling bullish.

And when Danny came over, planting big hairy knuckles on the plastic tablecloth, Leon looked him full in the face.

Punch him. It's the last thing he'll expect.

Danny chomped slow and noisy on a wad of gum.

Punch the fucker!

Olive sidled behind the counter and Leon wondered if she kept a Peacekeeper shotgun back there in case of trouble – like bartenders did in Westerns' saloons.

'Question for ya,' Danny said.

'Cup of tea and bun, please,' said Leon without missing a beat.

Okay, you're going for the condescending approach. I like it. Physically you're no match, of course – he could easily pull your head off – but intellectually you can wipe the floor was his ass. That's a proper phrase, right?

'Oh, this is fucking priceless,' said Carl, all excited.

'Cup of tea and bun?' repeated Danny.

'Yes, please; *iced* – the bun, not the tea.'

On the surface Leon was presenting well; calm and collected. But could he keep it up?

Danny scanned the café . . . most customers were openly minding their own business; those that weren't, now switched. Only Olive, refilling a sugar dispenser, kept both eyes on proceedings. There would be no trouble in here. She would see to it. Olive did not allow violence in Kath's Kaff and would happily beat the shit out of anyone to keep it that way. *Anyone*. And Danny knew it.

To Leon, in a restrained voice, Danny said: 'That wasn't my question.'

'Oh right, sorry. Well, could you spit it out? Only there's a bun with my name on it and my stomach thinks my throat's been cut.'

Nice one! Not sure I'd have mentioned throat-cutting.

'I'll cut your fucking throat for you,' mumbled Carl edging forward.

See . . . But never mind, you're doing really well. Now tell him to stick his question up his—

'I'll handle this,' said Danny sticking out a meaty paw that arrested Carl's progress.

'You're not going to let this Nancy Boy talk to you like that, are you?' asked Carl.

'I said I'd handle it,' the big guy repeated.

'He's mugging you off, mate; in front of *everyone* – mugging you *right off.*'

'Carl, shut the fuck up, will you?'

Carl buttoned it but appeared ready to unbutton at a moment's notice . . .

Olive slid the now-full sugar dispenser aside, prepared it seemed, to climb the counter and body-slam from great height, if necessary, anyone who went too far.

Danny turned back to Leon. 'Now, where was I?' he asked as if he'd been giving dictation.

'I believe you had an important question,' said Leon.

Danny removed his chewing gum and thumbed it into the plastic tablecloth with a wet squish.

'Have you been giving money to the hippie?'

'Really, after all that; that's your question?' said Leon.

'Well, have ya, punk?'

Danny looked back to Carl, perhaps expecting the kind of admiration Eastwood no doubt enjoys.

'Nice one,' said Carl between an approving nod for Danny, a sneer for Leon, and a quick glance to make sure Olive wasn't yet mounting the counter.

Leon sighed. 'Okay, I'm assuming – and please tell me if I'm incorrect – that if I was to point out that the *actual* line is "Well, *do* ya, punk?" not "Well, *have* ya, punk?" you would protest, understandably, and claim that you were simply paraphrasing for dramatic or comedic effect. Would that be an accurate assessment?' He smiled and waited.

Danny couldn't find the question, let alone the answer.

Straightening up, he spun to face Carl.

'WHAT THE FUCK IS HE . . .'

Danny caught sight of Olive readying her formidable frame, one knee on the counter. 'I mean,' he continued in a low voice, 'what is he talking about?'

'How the fuck do I know,' said Carl. 'He's a mentalist. Nothing he says makes sense.'

'No problem,' said Leon. 'How about we let that one slide on this occasion? But to return to your initial entreaty, I would say this: What if I *have* given a little financial assistance to the person in question?'

'Moss?' asked Danny.

'Exactly. Why is that a problem for you?'

'It's not a problem for me. In fact, it's the opposite of a problem,' Danny said trying to sound smart.

'Opposite of a problem,' echoed Carl. 'Good one.'

'No problem at all. Indeed, it's a good thing,' said Danny.

Although impressed with his use of the word *indeed*, Danny instantly recognised that he was starting to sound like his barrister.

Dropping all pretence, he leaned in close enough for Leon to smell cheese-toastie breath and whispered:

'Make sure you keep it up . . . *Leonard*.'

Leon let this go. *Leonard* was an improvement on *Fuckwit*, at least. And nowhere near as bad as *Lionel*.

'Give him as much as you can; the more the better. It's good for business.' Danny straightened up, drilled his eyes into Leon's. 'How's that for an *accurate assessment?*'

'Sound, mate, sound,' yapped Carl.

Danny scanned the room. 'Alright, everybody, show's over. You can get on with your meals now.'

'Yeah, and mind you don't choke,' added Carl.

'Sorry for the interruption, everyone; that's the right word, isn't it, Leonard . . . *interruption?*'

Danny patted Leon's back, *hard*. 'You can keep the gum, by the way.' He nodded for Carl to follow.

Olive's knee came down from the counter as the pair exited.

Watching the duo cross to the off-licence, she made for Leon's table, advising: 'Don't let them two bother you.'

Leon shrugged. 'Did I look bothered?'

'A bit, yeah.'

'Nah, not with my samurai training.'

'Don't you need a sword to be a samurai?'

'Good point.'

'Well, don't worry; they wouldn't dare touch you in here – they know I'd kick *both* their frickin' heads in.'

'That's probably what they need, a good kicking. Teach them violence is not the answer.'

'Of course if they decide to attack you on your way home, knife you, glass you, set you on fire . . .'

'That kind of thing.'

'Throw you under a train . . .'

'Under a train. Interesting.'

'There'd obviously be nothing I could do, then.'

'Obviously,' Leon agreed.

'Seriously though, Leon, watch out for that Carl. I think he's a bit crazy.'

'You think?'

'And not crazy good.'

'Crazy bad?'

'Crazy bad.'

'Thought so.'

'He'd as soon slice your face off as look at you.'

'Good to know. Thanks for the heads-up.'

'Yeah, Carl's a right twat. But Danny, I dunno . . . that *restrained* aggression . . . there's something really sexy about it. Like something inside is just waiting to explode.'

Leon gave her wide eyes. 'You find *aggression* sexy?'

'What can I say? Girls like a Bad Boy. Remember Amy?'

'Ah Amy . . . yes . . . thank you for reminding me.'

Olive went all moony and quiet; perhaps imagining being *under* Bad Boy Danny and finding it altogether agreeable. In her 'absence' Leon considered her face jewellery: piercings in brows, nose, lips, tongue and cheeks. *How can people do that?* Her pencil and notepad hovered in mid-air, suspended in time and space as her steamy subconscious took flight. Leon could have coughed, brought her back, but decided it was kinder not to. He understood the pleasure such meanderings can bring.

Besides, he didn't want Olive taking his order. Not when he'd just spotted Jenny slipping on an apron in the kitchen.

'Hey, Leon, I forgot to ask . . .' Carl at the door. 'How are the folks?' An evil grin broke out across his ratty face.

'Why don't you piss off, Carl,' said Leon calmly.

Carl raised an invisible handbag to his chin and emitted a camp *Oooh* (get you) noise, inferring Leon was having a Hissy Fit. He blew Leon a kiss then added, ominously, as he closed the door: 'See you later . . . *mate*.'

Olive's mind finally came back to earth. She touched pen to pad and asked: 'Now, what can I get you?'

Leon picked up a menu. 'Can you give me a minute?'

'Sure,' she said.

'Two Belly-Busters,' grunted a male voice from the kitchen. The cook, a man as oily as the fare he fries, placed the plated heaps of cholesterol in the serving window and returned to his blackened pans, spitting eggs and greasy spatulas.

As Olive headed off, Leon heard distinct tapping on the window behind his shoulder. What awful apparition would be there to torment him now: Carl dressed as the Joker; winged Leviathans, prancing vicars in pink leotards; hunchbacks on stilts; a Cyclops?

Leon shifted to see but immediately wished he hadn't. The sight was none of the above; though it was, arguably, a

336

one-eyed monster – and it *was* Carl: pants dropped, bare backside pressed against the glass.

'Oh, that's lovely,' said Leon. 'Really nice.'

Turning back and resolutely ignoring the spotty arse mashing by his head, he focused strictly on Jenny, now waiting on the other side of the room at a table occupied by a group of Sixth-Formers who were, apparently, unable to decide what to have. Jenny made suggestions, pointed to their menus, but they continued to dither.

Leon took out his notebook, opened it to a page dominated by a JENNY!!! doodle; the kind of thing you might see in an infatuated child's school exercise book. Her name vibrated in big, colourful bubble letters surrounded by loops and flowers and shooting stars and hearts and little birds. He started on another flourish: a miniature ice cream sundae (which, to be honest, it didn't really need).

As he topped the tiny dessert with a miniscule cherry, Richard's disparaging voice rang out in Leon's head:

How pathetic. You're twenty-four and you're doodling like a pubescent teenager.

'It's not pathetic, it's lovely,' muttered Leon in a barely audible voice.

You're not going to ask her out, are you? Please tell me you're not.

Leon flicked to his MOVE TO WALES list. Below ~~MOSS~~ and ~~POPPY~~, he'd already added JENNY. He circled the new name and looked over to where the waitress was still on hold for the Sixth-Formers . . .

'Hey, Jenny, how would you feel about moving to Wales?' he whispered.

You're not going anywhere, Barnacle Brat, Richard chimed in.

'We'll see about that,' Leon mumbled, underlining JENNY as if to make a point.

'Hi. What you doing?' asked Jenny.

'Not doing anything–Nope–Nothing at all.' Leon quickly pointed. 'What's that behind you?' As Jenny looked, he snapped shut the notebook, yanked a menu over it.

'It's the Specials board,' she said turning back.

'No – I mean – what *is* that?'

'What, Cottage Pie?'

'Yep.'

'Well . . . it's basically mashed potato on top of minced beef. Or *here*, what *passes* for beef. And you didn't hear that from me.'

'Mum's the word.' *Oh shit, what was in that lasagne!*

'Whatever you do, don't have the *Shepherd's* Pie. The chef uses what passes for—'

'Lamb?'

'Mutton.'

'He uses what *passes* for *mutton*?'

'Hey, what can I tell you? If you want to play safe, have the soup.'

'What is it?'

'Campbell's Condensed Catering Cans.'

'Nice alliteration.' *Dad would have loved that.*

'Cock-a-Leekie,' added the waitress with a big grin. They laughed and Jenny looked back, perhaps to check if the Sixth-Formers were ready to order. Leon ran a finger over the laminated menu and both eyes over Jenny.

'What are you doing?' complained a voice from an adjacent table.

'I wasn't,' barked Leon, a little too quickly, and aloud.

'Get a move on,' the dad on the next table said to his teenage son. 'The game'll be over at this rate.'

Yet another fucker stalling, said Richard's voice.

Jenny's full attention came back to Leon. 'Seen anything you fancy yet?' she asked.

Just you came out as 'Jush . . . uh . . .'

Leon heard Poppy's voice say, *Ask her, Leon, ask her. Maybe that's what she's waiting for. Faint heart never won fair lady, you know.*

Yes, and look out how that turned out for me with Kelly, thought Leon. 'I'm just, you know,' he said, 'deciding what to do.'

You can't include Kelly Buxton, said Richard. *She's just a prick-teasing whor—*

'Sorry – not what to *do* – I mean, what to *have* . . .'

'No problem,' Jenny said dispensing a knowing smile. 'Can I make a suggestion?'

338

BRIEF ENCOUNTER

'*How many?*' the woman in the ticket kiosk asked.

'Two,' Leon repeated.

The woman still looked uncertain. She was a dead ringer for Margaret Rutherford, which Leon thought kind of appropriate because this compact old cinema was almost a carbon copy of the Flea-Pit in *The Smallest Show on Earth*. The foyer, kiosk, stairs and refreshment counter of this 'Bijou' were pure 1940s (maybe even earlier). The place was so old and faded it was nearly in black and white, or to be more exact: shades of grey.

Leon seemed to be bestowing Peace on 'Margaret' as he held two fingers to the kiosk glass. He said, 'Two adults, upper circle,' slowly and distinctly, then, leaning close to Jenny, added: 'I think she's a bit deaf.'

'Let's get treats.' Jenny nodded towards the refreshment counter.

As she decided *which* treats, Leon took great delight in Jenny's hair: no longer tied up for hygiene reasons, it hung down, long and dark, rich with big captivating curls (someone, thought Leon, has been on the curling tongues).

A few minutes later, settled into front row balcony seats, Leon and Jenny smiled to each other under the dusty, silvery light of the projector's beam. A whistling steam train cleared the way for the opening titles of *Brief Encounter* and the sound of Poppets boxes being ripped open.

Eighty-six glorious minutes later, film over, the house lights came up. A woman passed in front and headed for the exit. Jenny and Leon were in no rush to leave.

They had held hands and shared Poppets (they may even have had a little kiss but Leon wasn't certain he hadn't just imagined that); Jenny had quietly fumed when Dolly Messiter crashed into the famous Parting Scene; and Leon accidentally shed a tear when, in the same scene, Dr. Alec Harvey placed a hand so movingly on Laura Jesson's shoulder. Touched by its simple, beautiful understatement, he wondered why he had never watched the film before. And having thoroughly relished the heart-warming melancholy, the pair now wanted to bask in its afterglow.

Jenny leaned forward, peered over the balcony, and soaked up the small-scale magnificence of the auditorium: the cute little screen bordered by velvet curtains, now closing, and the empty rows of curved-back seats, split down the middle by a deep maroon carpet.

'I feel awfully grand perched up here,' Jenny said, easily acquiring the posh, cut-glass English accent portrayed by Celia Johnson. 'It was very extravagant of you.'

'What kind of man would I be if I couldn't lash out on a couple of one-and-nine-pennies?' said Leon, getting into the role of Trevor Howard's character.

'A rather silly one, I'd wager,' Celia/Laura/Jenny said.

They laughed, and even this sounded frightfully posh.

'Listen, Jenny,' said Trevor/Alec/Leon, his voice cinematically dramatic. 'I'm going away . . .'

'I see . . .'

'But not quite yet.'

'Please, not quite yet.'

They embraced theatrically then laughed again.

Outside, a thick darkness had settled upon the shoulders of the street lamps and luminescent buildings of city-centre Manchester; light from shops, restaurants, offices and bars, pooled around the street. By a flowing stream of traffic, amidst a host of shifting, chattering voices, Jenny and Leon, waiting at a bus stop, were deep in conversation:

'No way,' Leon said.

'Yeah way,' Jenny replied.

'You're not just pulling my leg?'

'I'm serious. I've always fancied living in the country.'

'So you might . . .'

'Easy, Tiger,' said Jenny, stepping in for a hug. She whispered into his ear: 'Let's just say I'm open to the idea. Why don't you ask me after a couple more dates?' All too soon she stepped back.

Leon, flagging down her bus, switched back to British Cinema's finest 1940s aristocratic English accent: 'Can't you stay?'

'It's frightful of me I know,' Jenny said, instinctively joining in, 'but I have a rather pressing prior engagement.'

The bus pulled up and she stepped inside.

'Until Friday then,' Leon said.

'Until Friday,' she replied.

As Jenny took a seat, the driver stared at Leon.

'Aren't you getting on?' he asked.

'Afraid not, old chap,' came the reply.

The driver grumbled, shook his head, but Leon didn't care; he'd just noticed who was sitting behind Jenny . . .

Richard nodded, gestured that he was keeping his eyes on Jenny (now waving).

Unsettled and mystified, Leon, hand frozen mid-wave, watched the bus drive away.

Forty minutes later, Leon had walked most of the way home (he didn't like night buses; not since the unfortunate incident involving a Knackwurst sausage and a surprisingly aggressive Morris Dancer – don't ask). He was passing the east entrance to the park, when he was grabbed by Richard and pulled by a sleeve towards the open gates.

'What the hell are you up to?' asked Leon.

'I'm helping you,' Richard replied.

'How is this helping, exactly?' Leon tried to plant his heels but Richard had momentum.

'Do you want to know what her prior engagement was?'

'Whose?' Leon was now inside park grounds, skidding under propulsion across the car park towards a lone car parked beside a clump of dense bushes.

'Jenny, of course,' said Richard.

Metres before they reached the vehicle, Leon managed to break free. But he didn't head back; he stood, rooted in the deserted, dimly lit car park listening to a string of passionate, sexual gasps emanating from within.

'No, it can't be,' Leon insisted.

'Oh it be. Come see.' Richard crept to within touching distance of the steamed windows, pushed his nose close to the glass. 'Oh, look; she's got a little birthmark on her—'

'No! She told me about a birthmark.' Leon pointed to his Mons Pubis. 'Is it – here?'

'Yes, but don't panic, it's nice. It's in the shape of a crescent moon.' He waved Leon in.

Frozen to the spot, Leon shook his head.

'No? Well, don't worry it's all on here.' Richard whipped out a camcorder from inside his overcoat. 'Most of it anyway; bloody memory card's full.'

Grunts in the car got rhythmic, quicker. Richard's head spun so fast, something cricked. Rubbing neck, he checked the latest in-car gymnastics. 'Damn, such a shame. She's shaved and *very* slutty; the perfect combination.' Richard sighed, turned to Leon. 'I don't suppose you've got one?'

'Yes, of course. I always carry a spare memory card around for exactly this kind of situation. Now, where did I put it?' Leon patted pockets.

'No need for sarcasm.'

'Yes, like I'm the one in the wrong here. And can you please come away from the car. In fact, why am I still here?'

Leon moved away but Richard jumped in front.

'Here, you might as well take this.' With a seedy grin Richard offered the camcorder as if presenting an award.

Leon pushed away the accursed thing and its latent toxicity. 'Do you really think I'd ever want to watch my girlfriend dogging in some stranger's car?'

'*Girlfriend?* You had one date.'

'Sometimes, that's all it takes.'

'Oh really?'

'Yes, really.'

'Then why is your *girlfriend* currently squatting on Danny's Holden's face?'

'Danny? . . . Danny Holden? . . . That's *his* BMW?'

Richard nodded. 'And FYI, he's got a *massive* cock.'

'Oh fuck off, Richard. Just fuck off.'

But it was Leon who fucked off . . . for the exit.

Unmoved, Richard slithered back to the window.

'Hey, Leon!' he shouted. 'Good news!'

Leon turned on his heel, took a hopeful step forward.

'It's not her?'

'Of course it's her.' Richard held something aloft. 'Found another memory card in my pocket.'

'That's great, Richard. No, really, thanks for that.'

As Leon resumed his retreat, Richard got busy by the car – Russ Meyer in overdrive.

342

CHAPTER NINETEEN

Here They Come (Like the Video Films he'd seen)

DIRTY HARRY MEETS *MISERY*

Everything had turned to crap and Leon gave great thought to the two remaining Mad Hatters now perched on his fingertips.

'Oh fuck it,' he said at last.

He placed both Hatters under his tongue, turned off the TV, lay back on the duvet, and when his eyes had adjusted to the dark, gazed at the movie posters clinging to the wall.

A few minutes later he chewed the tabs and swallowed them. Fifteen minutes after that he was either tripping or had accidentally fallen asleep and entered a Mad Hatter nightmare (it was actually the former – it's hard to fall asleep on acid – but the trip would have several of the hallmarks that make for a superior nightmare).

The journey starts on a school bus; one of those yellow, American jobs – a space-suited astronaut at the wheel, visor up: Leon, but he'd give anything not to be there. He shifts uncomfortably on the seat, checks over his shoulder. Behind him, Richard barks menacingly at the passengers: three girls, four boys. He looks like the *Dirty Harry* villain: 'Scorpio' – wild hair, plaster over the nose, nasty red mark on the forehead, and the vicious attitude of an evil fuck.

'Come on, sing,' Scorpio/Richard urges. The children are extremely hesitant. '*Row, row, row your boat*,' he marks the beat with an insistent hand, '*gently down the stream.* Come on, sing!'

The children cooperate, nervously: '*Merrily, merrily, merrily, merrily, life is but a dream.*'

Only Astronaut/Leon is not singing; his visor has dropped, the helmet now full of dank water. He gasps for air, trying to keep the bus on the road, away from the barrier-free cliff edge.

343

The boy nearest the back frantically waves a raised hand. 'Where are we going?' he asks. 'This isn't the way we're supposed to be going.'

'We're going to the ice cream factory, see how ice cream's made,' Scorpio/Richard tells them. 'Now anybody who doesn't want to go can get off right here.'

Two more boys hoist a hand. The shorter boy says, 'I want to go home to my mother.'

'*What!*'

'I want to go home to my mother,' he repeats.

'You want to go home to see what!' Scorpio/Richard slaps the boy's face hard; a real stinger.

'Alright, sing. Sing!' He prowls the aisle like a savage animal. '*Row, row, row your boat, gently . . .*'

A boy in a blue shirt receives a harsh whack to the head.

'Sing! Sing! What's the matter with you, why don't you sing?'

Instinct or terror or both motivates the kids. '*Row, row, row your boat,*' they sing, '*gently down the stream . . .*' but it's spiritless and tame. School choir this is not.

Scorpio/Richard senses their lack of enthusiasm and isn't best pleased.

'Are you sick?! What is it?! *Row, row—* All your mothers are going to die if you don't start singing,' he yells.

Astronaut/Leon finally snaps open his helmet visor. A surge of mucous slime drenches his space-suit. His lungs suck in oxygen as, over his shoulder, Scorpio/Richard winds up for another assault: '*Row, row—*'

'Why don't you get the fuck out of here, Richard,' Leon screams.

The children cower as Scorpio/Richard stalks the passageway. The singing fades, turns into sobbing. Leon hears their cries but can no longer see. He's on the roof now, naked, spread-eagled, fingertips clinging, the bus veering side to side. Pieces of rock spray over the cliff edge.

Richard can't drive! Who the fuck is driving? A kid?

The road narrows to hardly a road at all. A little girl with pig-tails jumps from the emergency exit (or is thrown) and rag-dolls into oblivion. Leon howls but the howl is lost in a sudden fall of cold heavy snow. Legions of fire-ants crawl up his arms. Increasing speed begins to melt hair and teeth and skin. Using the last of his eyes, Leon looks ahead, but the road has ended; as if a mountain bridge and the mountain beyond had been erased. Only clouds remain.

Eyes and road now gone, Leon can only *feel* the fall: the rush of air between his ribs, the splatter of icy snow on his heart and a whistle inside his skull.

Time can stretch. Time can shorten. Time can stand still and Time can flow. As a measurement, Time is sometimes deceptive. Under acid, Time can become even stranger – and also meaningless. Time can distort: moments can become eternities; hours can seem like minutes.

Leon sat up, sweating profusely; late night had become early morning – weak dawn light all around – but it felt like no time at all. Though his body was all there (he checked) a sense of mild panic also remained. He scanned the room but found no signs of Richard or Scorpio or terrified children. Familiarity settled him. His breathing eased and he laid back, rested his head on the pillow; a moment of calm . . . then Dylan came to the open window and stuck his cat face inside.

Leon blinked as spiteful feline eyes bore down.

'*It* was right,' said Dylan. 'You *are* fucked, matey.'

Before Leon could reply, an axe head ripped into the door. He eyed the razor-sharp chunk of metal poking through splintered door-panel, unsure for a moment what to make of it. Was it still the acid; another hallucination; or had Carl broken in, seeking revenge?

The axe withdrew taking shards of door with it. An eye came to the gap; blinked, focused on Leon, blinked again then vanished. Leon felt a sudden deluge of leadenness fill his body as the axe crashed back into the door. The process repeated; the axe smashing and splintering until a face-sized hole had been made. Leon's mouth flapped open, shaped for a sound of some kind but none came.

Richard stuck his crazed face into the ragged hole; stared in like a madman, eyes wide open, teeth bared.

'Here's Richard!' he intoned.

'Well and truly fucked,' said Dylan, grinning and making no move to leave.

Richard opened the door, strolled over. A *thump* as he placed the axe at the foot of the bed.

Leon, turned to stone, could only watch and wait.

Richard whipped away the duvet.

'*What the fuck are these!*' said Leon – his chest, hips, thighs and shins held down by straps and ropes tied around the bed.

'Last night it came so clear,' said Richard. 'I realise you just need more time. Eventually, you'll come to accept the idea of being here.'

With Annie-Wilkes-like calmness, he reached down, out of sight, and came up holding a 16-inch block of 4x4 wood.

'Richard, what's going on? Is this some kind of sick joke?'

Richard wedged the 4x4 firmly between Leon's legs, just above the ankles, secured it and adjusted Leon's feet.

'Now don't fuss, Leon.'

As Richard grabbed the shaft and lifted not an axe but a fucking sledgehammer, Leon screamed: 'Richard, have you been watching my films!'

Richard's expression said: *Really – is that your biggest concern right now?*

'Because if you have, it's fine,' said Leon. 'In fact, there's one in my sock drawer . . .'

Richard positioned himself next to Leon's left ankle.

'Shush, darling, trust me. It's for the best.'

He pulled the sledgehammer back, took aim.

'Richard, for God's sake – please.'

Swung, the sledgehammer made contact with the ankle, breaking it with a sharp crack, and Leon shrieked in agony.

Richard moved to the other side of the bed.

'Almost done,' he said, his voice calm, 'just one more.'

When Leon sat up, he yanked away the duvet and was relieved to find both feet intact. The door, too, was untouched. He let out a long breath and laughed a little – until he noticed the rest of the room was trashed:

TV overturned, broken action figures scattered to all corners (The Dark Knight back on the desk but missing his head); movie posters torn down; books and DVDs everywhere; and all Leon's boyhood games, models, and toys, spread around as if relocated by mini-tornado.

Leon gnashed his teeth, snarled quietly: '*Richard*...'

As he surveyed the damage, he noticed his cork-board map; it hung down at one side, the pins in Wales now rearranged to spell: C.R.A.Z.Y.

'*Crazy!?* You do this and then have the nerve to call *me* crazy? You complete and UTTER SHIT!' Climbing out of bed he yelled: 'RICHARD! WHERE THE FUCK ARE YOU!'

Richard was fast asleep in grubby underpants on the sofa.

Leon stood over him, shaking his head. Richard looked like Withnail on a bad day; a *really* bad day – cold, grey and spectral. Leon was surprised not to find him covered in Deep Heat and up against a radiator.

After a slow stroll into the kitchen, Leon returned with a pan of cold water. He held it over the ashen monstrosity and poured. Richard squealed like a razored piglet.

'Why the fuck did you trash my room?' asked Leon sedately. The calmness he portrayed made him look oddly sinister.

Richard planted his feet on the floor, mopped his chest with a cushion. 'What are you talking about?'

'Why did you trash my room?' Leon repeated.

'It wasn't me, you nutter. It was you.'

'Oh that's a good one. And I suppose that's Jenny, is it?'

Leon nodded to the TV where a woman's face, made green and ghostly by night-vision recording – and filmed in such extreme close-up that it appeared to mush against the television screen – belted out spasmodic encouragement as it squished back and forth ... *Olive's* face. Or, to be more exact: Olive's *sex*-face – piercings and all.

Leon pointed at Richard and yelled, 'Liar!'

Richard watched the screen: the view, pulled out now, showed Olive, contorted face squashing in instalments on the car window, face-jewellery tapping rhythmically on the glass, noisily encouraging Danny, behind her, to go harder.

'Camcorder night-vision is notoriously unreliable, Leon. It distorts. That's why, in Dogging trials, in matters of identification, the police are unable to rely solely—'

347

'Oh, no, no, no, no, Richard, please . . . correct me if I'm wrong . . .' said Leon, sounding like a barrister. 'But this contorted face, squashing by instalments on the car window, its face-jewellery tapping rhythmically on the glass . . . belongs, not to *Jenny* . . . but to *Olive!*'

Richard squinted at the TV. 'Looks like Jenny to me.'

'No way – that's fucking Olive.'

'I think someone here is in denial. *That*, Leon . . . is Jenny.'

From the television, Danny's voice panted: 'Is this why . . . they call you Bulldog . . . Olive? . . . Coz you like it . . . doggy?' Olive's nose flattened against the window and she began a series of rough dog-like growls, slobber running down her chops. 'Take it, Olive. Take it. That's a good girl,' grunted Danny, pumping hard. 'Who's your daddy, Olive? Who's your daddy!'

'Okay, might be Olive,' said Richard as Leon knocked off the sound.

'Hallefuckinlujah,' Leon sang.

'But what difference does it make? Olive, Jenny – Jenny, Olive – they're all cunts.'

'What!'

Richard shrugged into his dressing gown.

'She's a cunt. They're *all* cunts. Forget her.'

Leon's face registered the familiar toll of a distant bell – and something was starting to seriously concern him.

'Just stick with what you know and you'll be fine,' said Richard pulling Leon in for a hug.

But the squeeze was cold and insincere and Leon wasn't buying it. He pushed Richard away.

A minute later, Leon was pounding up the drive.

Richard came to the front door.

'Okay, it wasn't her but it might as well have been.'

Leon clanged the gate behind him and didn't look back.

'And you saw what she was doing! That's what they're *all* doing! *With every Tom, Dick and Harry!*'

Richard ferreted a packet of Marlboro from his dressing gown. 'Just not with us,' he mumbled cheerlessly.

Cigarette lit, he watched Leon stomp as far as the maple tree, stop and make an immediate return.

'I *really* have to stop doing that,' grumbled Leon. 'Why didn't you tell me I only had my underpants on?'
He pushed past and re-entered the house.
'Crazy kid,' said Richard, blowing out smoke.

AMERICAN BEAUTY AND ZULU

Whatever was bothering Leon an hour ago was still on his mind now as he filed a key and did his best to ignore the group of cheerleaders rustling pompoms by his head.

Bouncing about in red-and-silver uniforms they chanted (in twangy American accents): 'Give us an *L*; give us an *E*; give us an *O*; give us an *N*. What have you got? *Leee-on!* Yay!'

Leon continued to deliberate, working the rasp ever louder as the girls performed high-kicking dance routines.

Seema looked over, saw Leon, filing frantically.

'You okay, Leon?' she asked.

Leon nodded but he didn't look okay. He wasn't feeling okay, either; his hands, he thought, had become far too big and the file kept 'rippling'. Note to self, he determined: Google the possible effects of *two* LSD tabs and how long they might last[8].

The cheerleaders surrounded him, filling the air with encouragement and hearty cheers, such as: 'Lee-on will file that key.' (Rapid claps.) 'Clap your hands if you agree!'

Leon filed, hard and fast, but the rasps failed to mask the girls' vociferous excitement. Oddly, he was now starting to *see* music and *hear* colours.

They kept it up all day; Leon hardly able to think straight. And he was mortified when, at the end of the working day, the cheerleaders got between him and Seema as they said their goodbyes, then followed him out of the shop.

All the way along the canal the girls jittered around him belting out a variety of short, animated ditties; each

---

[8] Some 'Acid' users have reported having weird experiences for weeks, even months, after a bad trip. You might want to look up HPPD: Hallucinogen Persisting Perceptive Disorder.

invariably opening with 'Hey, Leon; hey, Leon!' and ending with 'Go, Leon; go, Leon!' He detoured through the park but still they trailed, like a high-school sports entourage, performing express tumbles and high-flying splits. (Should all this go in the notebook as *one* sighting? he wondered; this unremitting persistence was something new.)

Whilst still in the park, when the cheerleaders formed what seemed an *impromptu* human pyramid, Leon tried to disappear into the Gents. But the shortest, skinniest cheerleader (the one on top) spotted the escape attempt and informed her supporters. The girls pursued Leon into the dingy brick building and parked themselves around the urinal, jiggling pom-poms in his face and at his member, chanting his name (for the zillionth time) and singing about how he was so fine he blew their minds.

(Were it not for the concern of appearing a bit pervy, Leon might have confessed to finding this small part of the whole annoying-cheerleader-experience a bit of a weird turn-on. *A little bit.* Oh shut up, give the guy a break.)

As the circus headed towards the precinct, along Stickleback Road (Leon had doubled back in a vain attempt to shake off his retinue) there followed yet more incessantly infuriating cheering and dancing and pumping of crowds – for 'crowds' read: odd passers-by who failed to notice anything beyond Leon's unfathomable irritation and distress. In the precinct the girls were joined by a beefy guy in a tight leotard who proceeded to throw the short, skinny cheerleader around as if she were a baton. He held her up on one hand and flung her, spinning, high into the air, catching her just inches from the concrete. It was during these shenanigans that Leon was finally able to slip away unnoticed – into the Newsagents.

From behind the DVD rack, Leon watched as the extended cheerleader troop realised he was missing. He instinctively ducked when they probed for signs of his whereabouts. The skinny girl threw her pom-poms to the ground, jumped up and down on them. The others backed towards the exit, waved for her to come along. She ran after them and they departed the precinct en masse.

Leon now resurfaced above the DVDs, moved to the window and scanned outside; craning his neck to make sure they hadn't circled round to the other entrance.

Finding the precinct cheerleader-free he did a little celebration dance of his own . . .

'Give us an *L*,' he sang, 'give us an *E*, give us—'

The chant went unfinished as he started an unnecessary coughing fit; he had spotted Nobby watching from the counter and panicked.

'Bit of cheese,' said Leon, pointing to his windpipe. 'Fine now, though. How are you?' Nobby said nothing. After a final throat-clearing bark Leon returned to the DVDs, picked one at random and pretended to read the back.

Nobby continued his silent vigil.

'I'll probably be buying another of these today,' said Leon, 'maybe two.' A stiff, awkward, self-conscious smile was finally relieved when Nobby was collared by a middle-aged woman wishing to purchase a heap of scratchcards.

But Leon's mind wasn't on DVDs for long, if it had been at all; he'd spotted Jenny in the café, standing by a table talking to three Butlins Redcoats: a man and woman sitting couple-close, and a spare bloke, handsome and cocky, blue eyes and white teeth beaming up at the attentive waitress.

To Leon's great surprise, Mr Confident suddenly pulled Jenny onto his lap.

Leon's eyes narrowed.

The Redcoat couple fell in with the frivolity, teasing playfully. Jenny took it in good spirit but quickly freed herself – more with a wriggle than a struggle. As she chided the saucy scamp, he apologised with those big blue eyes.

Leon looked ready to pop. Then, suddenly, he felt something. He looked down:

The Urchin was back, pulling at his trouser leg. Leon stepped back . . . the pitiful boy gazed up, jabbed a finger at the exit. Leon's eyes followed the course directed.

Five British colonial soldiers double-timed through the door: a sergeant, sword in hand, and four privates, Martini-Henry rifles at the ready. All were kitted out in white helmets, red tunics and navy trousers as per the Battle of Rorke's Drift (Anglo-Zulu war 1879).

351

'Come on, you 'orrible lot, form a line!' the sergeant bellowed.

Leon backed up against a chiller-cabinet.

The privates shuffled around, elbowed each other, organised themselves.

A batch of DVDs slid from Leon's hand and clattered on the floor. The titles included *A Beautiful Mind*, *Donnie Darko*, and *Shutter Island*. The sound alerted Nobby and he wondered if the time had come to throw Leon out.

The sergeant raised his sword.

'Front rank, take aim,' he bawled. (Leon wasn't sure why he'd said *'front* rank' when there was only *one* rank but decided that wasn't important right now.)

As the privates took aim, Leon made a break for the exit.

What happened to not running away? – asked a voice in Leon's head. *What about standing your ground?*

'Fuck that,' squealed Leon. 'They've got guns.'

No, they haven't, the voice said.

'Fire!' yelled the sergeant.

Propelled by a volley of rifle fire, Leon burst through the door, landed on all fours, and found himself surrounded by a jumble of startled shoppers. He heard Jenny's voice shouting to him. Saw her being encouraged by the handsome Redcoat to come back into the café – as if the situation might be hazardous to her health.

Under protest, Jenny went back inside.

Leon sensed the privates piling out of the Newsagents; heard the sergeant, behind them, shout:

'Fire at will!'

TEXAS CHAINSAW MASSACRE VS GOOD WILL HUNTING

Leon, up in a flash, zigzagged through shifting clusters of shoppers and sprinted for the nearest precinct exit.

By the time he couldn't run another stride, he'd got as far as the private taxi hire shop on the corner of Stickleback Road and Broad Street. He leaned on the window, head down, tight chest burning and seriously out of breath.

When he eventually looked up, he found, to his amazement, the shop interior full of crystal-clear liquid and the water-nymph at the glass. Leon smelled oranges and cinnamon again (at least, he imagined he did).

The angelic mermaid smiled and using one hand, signed: in the first gesture, her hand extended, the index finger pointing towards Leon. This was quickly followed by the hand, held open, running a short distance down her chest. Next, her hand, again with index finger extended, moved across her body, touched her chin, and then moved forward. Finally, she waved goodbye.

Leon imitated the signs, perhaps trying to memorise them but a loud, revving engine disturbed him. He turned to find Pogo on a powerful motorbike, and, in an attached side-car, packed in tight, a stocky man in a blooded apron over a shirt and tie, holding a chainsaw, his face hidden behind a mask made from stitched pieces of human skin.

He looked exactly like 'Leatherface' from *The Texas Chainsaw Massacre*.

After a bout of inelegant squirming and awkward levering, Leatherface finally managed to squeeze free from the side-car and step out. He cranked the pull-cord, started the chainsaw, and lurched forward.

Despite his legs and lungs not having fully recovered from the previous extrication, Leon ran like he had never run before. Norris Avenue would have been the nearest but sadly in his blind panic he had headed back towards the precinct. Luckily though, he got a good head start as Leatherface proved even less efficient at climbing *into* the side-car than he had getting *out* – a fuming Pogo effing and blinding with screamed commands the whole while; things like: '*Move it, Motherfucker! Jesus, look at you! Come on, you stupid bastard, he's getting away!*'

Longstanding asthma problems aside, Leon had always been a good runner (well, a *fast* runner; as long it wasn't over *too* long a distance) and now was no different – by the time he heard the motorbike engine finally get back into gear, he was almost parallel with the skateboarding park.

Back in the precinct, Leon stopped outside the charity shop and looked around, hands on knees, shins on fire, panting hard; seconds later, Pogo and Leatherface cruised the motorbike through a sea of shoppers. As Leon backed inside the charity shop, a hand grabbed his shoulder and made him jump. He turned to find a friendly face:

'What is it?' asked Poppy. 'What's wrong?'

'Oh hi,' gasped Leon. 'How's Moss?'

'Don't worry about Moss, he's fine. And if he stops being fine, I'll bloody well sort him out. But what's with you?'

The familiar rumble of motorbike engine grew nearer.

'Leon, what is it?' repeated Poppy.

But Leon had no explanation. Where could he start?

Poppy pulled him in, locked the door and led him into the back. The shop was closed; just a couple of ancient volunteers sifting through bags of old clothes.

'We're just sorting stuff for tomorrow,' she said.

Inside the changing cubicle Poppy sat Leon down, said something he didn't catch then left.

He listened to the motorbike engine as it passed, diminished, then expanded and passed again.

Poppy returned with two mugs of coffee.

'You know your problem,' she said, stepping inside the cubicle. 'You keep it all inside.' She handed Leon a mug. 'You should let it out, talk to someone.'

And with that, she snapped the privacy curtain shut and adopted a firm but matronly air.

It was time for her and Leon to have a heart-to-heart.

An hour later, outside the charity shop, Poppy said, 'Okay, so you're going to stick with your new plan, yes?'

'Are you sure it's a good idea?' asked Leon. 'My ideas aren't always—'

'Yes, definitely – now go.'

'Maybe I should have another cup of coffee, first?'

'Maybe I should give you a kick up the arse, Bishop Brennan style.'

Leon laughed.

'That's better,' said Poppy. 'Now, remember . . . it wasn't your fault.'

'Don't start that again,' said Leon, smiling.

Inside the charity shop's changing room, Poppy had finally got Leon to speak at length about the accident. Moss

354

had told her all about it; Leon had never said a word. She had begun by saying, simply: 'It wasn't your fault.'

'Oh, I know,' Leon had said nonchalantly.

'It wasn't your fault,' Poppy had repeated.

'I know,' Leon said, smiling.

'It wasn't your fault.'

'I know.'

'It wasn't your fault.'

'I know,' said Leon, dead serious.

'No,' insisted Poppy, 'It wasn't your fault.'

'What is this – *Good Will Hunting?*'

Poppy moved in really close. 'Leon, it wasn't your fault.'

Leon said 'I know.' Tears started.

'It wasn't—'

'I know, I know.'

And with that, Poppy had taken Leon, sobbing now, in her arms and held him like a child; gave him a prolonged, beautiful, tight, desperately-needed, achingly-reassuring hug and listened intently, deeply moved, as he opened up.

And once he'd started it all came out – *everything.*

Leon described the special evening he'd arranged for his parents' Ruby Wedding Anniversary; and how it had ended with a car heading straight for them; how he had inadvertently rolled Betty as he'd tried to avoid a collision; the Beetle sliding; the slow-motion details of the crash; Mary Magdalene; the football boots; the mother and child; the toy clown; the clunk of his head hitting something hard and the deal he had made with Lord Archibald.

The dummy had said someone always has to die and Leon had asked that it not be him. But before Leon could think it through, before he was ready, they had shaken hands on a deal. Even so, for some reason, Leon had assumed Lord Archibald meant the strangers would have to die. The woman and, *Oh God, I'm so sorry,* the child.

Leon felt deep guilt for that but it had been an intuitive reaction; he had instinctively wanted his *own* family to survive. However, his foggy, post-crash, no-doubt unconscious mind had not been specific; had not expressly asked Archie to spare Lester and Veronica by name.

He should have *named* them; been exact and explicit.

355

'Why,' Leon wailed, '*didn't I ask that my parents be included in the deal?*' He'd broken down again, bawling and weeping like a distressed infant.

Poppy had pushed him back gently, held him by the shoulders, looked him full in the face and speaking softly but sternly said:

'There was no dummy, Leon. No Lord Archibald. That simply did not happen. So there couldn't have been a deal.'

She spoke into his eyes: 'It wasn't your fault.'

For the rest of their hour Leon had spoken at length about how he'd only recently accepted that his parents were really dead, how he had imagined his parents visiting him during his coma (not that he remembered actually being in a coma), how they'd later watched home movies together, how he had interacted with them on a regular basis (up until the 28th), how he loved them and missed them.

Poppy had listened and comforted and listened some more; then she'd stepped back, opened the curtain, given him another long hug, then held him once more by the shoulders and reminded him of what he himself had decided; what he'd said, just minutes ago, that he had to do . . . what he *needed* to do.

Now, outside the shop, Leon filled his lungs as if preparing to jump in the sea from a great height.

Poppy made a fist. 'Ready?'

Leon nodded. 'Ready.' And he did look ready; psyched – somehow primed for action. He made a fist and playfully imitated Poppy. She smiled, kissed him on the cheek, then gave him a little shove and watched him walk away.

Poppy shouted, 'Remember, Leon: COURAGE!'

As Leon exited the precinct, Poppy muttered, 'Oh shit, this is never going to work.'

✳ ✳ ✳

Throughout his journey home Leon had scanned ahead and behind but saw nothing unusual; not a thing.

Presently, as he turned onto Norris Avenue, the street where he lived – had *always* lived – he stuck out his chest, adopted the countenance of someone willing and wired, and strode on.

'Maybe Poppy was right,' he said. 'Maybe this *will* work.'
No way, said a familiar negative voice.
'And you can piss off for a start,' said Leon.
Never going to happen.
'It will, it will. Stay positive.'
Balls, you're fucked, matey.

THE WILD ONE/DAWN OF THE DEAD DOUBLE FEATURE

The end of an unseasonably warm day was turning into a balmy evening. Peggy and Vicky, reclined on plastic chairs in Peggy's front garden, had spent the afternoon there, drinking beers, smoking fags, and putting the world to rights. It was Vicky, halfway through a sustained fanny-scratch, who first spotted Leon striding up the pavement on their side of the street.

Leon's voice of doom had not remained silent; it had chipped and chimed tirelessly all the way from the precinct. But he had ignored it, refused to get into conversation. This was no time for negativity, he'd determined. If he was to see both parts of this thing through he would have to be positive and strong. *Positive* for the first part; ready for whenever it happened – if it did happen . . .

Oh, it'll happen again. Bound to.

Maybe it won't, Leon thought. Not now.

It will, insisted the negative voice. *And even if you do get through it – which I doubt – the other thing will be even harder. Maybe impossible.*

'Yes, there we agree. But I am going to do it,' said Leon aloud. '*I will—*'

'Yoo-hoo, Leon!' yelled Vicky, waving.

'What are you up to?' asked Peggy.

'Feeling a bit horny,' slurred Vicky. 'You feeling horny?'

'What, with my guts?' Peggy shifted uncomfortably, flicked away her cigarette end. 'Anyway, he's a bit young, isn't he? Even for you.'

'Cheeky cow,' laughed Vicky, slurping her can. 'Anyway, I like 'em younger. They need a bit of trainin' but they've usually got loads of stamina.'

'Yeah, I'm sure he needs *you* after all he's been through.'

'I might be just what he needs.' Vicky batted eyebrows at Peggy and the pair cackled like drunken witches. They had come to know each other well on this day of many cans.

Peggy grimaced, let out an extended belch.

'Sorry about that, vicar,' she said.

By now, Leon had stopped a few doors down.

'Leon, what are you doing?' shouted Vicky. 'Come and have a beer.'

But Leon didn't respond; he was just standing there, staring towards his house . . . to where Pogo and Leatherface were waiting at his gate, the motorbike and sidecar parked on the drive.

Told you – quick, run round the back.

'No – no more running away. It's time to face up to the fuckers; time for my resolve to be tested.'

Oh shit.

'Get that thing off my drive,' Leon shouted.

'Why don't you make us, *Brat*.' said Pogo, elbowing his accomplice.

Leatherface removed his jacket, reached over the gate and lifted the chainsaw from the sidecar. He advanced straight for Leon dragging the machine along the tarmac; saw-teeth scraping and screeching.

Leon moved forward until they were toe to toe – a Sergio Leone moment – a showdown that cried out for the music of Ennio Morricone.

In silence, Vicky and Peggy watched Leon, standing stock still, alone, in the middle of the road.

Leatherface's beady eyes twitched as Leon stared deep into the jagged eye-holes of the mask of stitched human skin.

'I know you're not here,' Leon said.

Leatherface's fat tongue slid a wet trail along his bottom lip. He cackled, barely containing his excitement as a large group of zombie Chelsea Pensioners drove down the avenue. The zombies had formed a motorbike gang; about twenty strong: *The Wild One* meets *Dawn of the Dead*.

They rode muscular Nortons, Triumph Bonnevilles and BSAs; wore tall boots, motorcycle leathers and goggles – each with a bright red bandana tied tightly around the lower half of their face. Those with surviving hair had styled what remained with Brylcreem into exaggerated pompadour styles. The decomposing Rockers pulled up, ringed the combatants, revved their powerful engines and howled like wild animals. But Leon ignored them; kept his focus on Leatherface's eyes.

'Do it,' shouted Pogo. 'Do it.'

Leatherface pull-started the chainsaw; the engine jumped to life, buzzing and throbbing. Snatching at the throttle trigger, he made it growl like a wild thing as he swung it around. Leon heard it snarl overhead, filling the air with its cacophonous whine.

'I *know* you're not here!' shouted Leon above the din.

The zombies laughed uproariously as Leatherface hopped from foot to foot, evil anticipation twitching every sinew.

See Leon's eyes.

See Leatherface's eye-holes.

See Pogo's twisted white face. 'Do it!' he urged.

The undead took up the chant: '*Do it! Do it!*'

The chainsaw roared; the Doppler Effect shifting the frequencies as Leatherface waved the machine in arcs over Leon's head.

Peggy and Vicky turned to each other and frowned.

Leon and Leatherface leaned in, eyeball to eye-hole; centimetres apart. Without blinking, not even once, Leon cut through the building tension and said, serenely:

'I'm going to close my eyes, then start a count to three. And when I look again, I'll find there's only me. For you must all be gone, no more will you I see.'

Leon heard Pogo laugh. 'What a pile of shit!' yelled the clown. 'Who wrote that bollocks – you or Poppy?'

The remark stung, briefly, but Leon quickly gathered his thoughts; relaxed, and let the calmness really settle in.

'Now!' shouted Pogo. 'Fuck him up!'

Leatherface stepped back, swung the roaring chainsaw.

Zombie pensioners nudged each other.

Leon's eyes closed and he settled into the darkness; darkness filled with the explosive sound of angry, revving chainsaw.

'One,' announced Leon.

Turbulent, horrendous noise of vicious chained saw-teeth sliced the air, this way and that.

'Two . . .'

Leon smelled burning motor oil as the uproarious racket continued, blaring and ripping, a fizzing maelstrom assaulting his ears. Painfully close. So close, he felt hot exhaust blast his hair and face.

'Three.'

The heat ended. The smell went away. The chainsaw had fallen silent.

Leon blinked open his eyes and scanned. Norris Avenue was free of Leatherface, zombies, motorbikes – and Pogo.

He was completely alone.

Well, almost . . . Vicky and Peggy were looking over, concern etched all over their faces. 'Are you alright, Leon?' asked Peggy, her voice hesitant and a tad wary.

Leon smiled in reply.

Suddenly, a new sound: loud, racing, and dangerously close as Danny's BMW appeared at speed from nowhere.

Leon dived and only just avoided being hit.

'Jesus! The fucking idiots,' shrieked Vicky.

Leon heard Danny and Carl laughing as the car raced away.

The women rushed over, helped Leon to his feet.

'That Danny's going to kill someone one day,' said Peggy.

AWAKENINGS

'Please tell me you're not still translating signs.' Richard wiped away eye-muck after a heavy sofa-nap.

'Signs?' Leon spun from the computer, faced a yawning, stretching heap. 'What do you know about signs?'

'Was this it?' Richard repeated the Nymph signings.

'Yes, but . . .'

Leon's interrogation was held at bay as Richard retrieved a packet of Marlboro Reds from his dressing gown pocket, removed the one and only cigarette, lit up then made a show of scrunching the empty packet.

'It means,' said Richard, after a puff and a cough, '*You should go home. I looked it up.*'

'*When* did you look it up?' asked Leon, doubting every word.

'It's good advice, you should heed it. It's what *I* said before.' Richard's head went into search mode. 'Where's the ashtray?'

'No, you're wrong. It isn't that.'

'What is it, then?'

'It's . . .' Leon double checked the monitor. '*You need to say goodbye.*'

'Same thing,' said Richard, still searching.

'Oh my God, it's exactly what I said to Poppy.'

'Where *is* the fucking ashtray? I *must* have an ashtray.'

Leon pointed. 'There, behind you.'

'It's full,' said Richard, his voice as pathetic as his demeanour.

'Then empty it, you lazy—' A knock at the door startled Leon; uninvited possibilities. He looked at Richard.

'Pizza; can you get it? I'm a bit short at the moment. We'll settle up later.'

Leon opened the front door to Chicken-Man and what had become a cold night. The familiar pullet, costume now pinched by a fuzzy money-belt, was surrounded by a pack of dogs that sniffed at legs and cargo: a large pizza box, chicken-wing sides, various dips, ice cream and a two litre bottle of Pepsi.

Outstretching an orange leg, the chicken tried to push back what appeared to be the Alpha dog (half Staffordshire Terrier, half Hell Hound) but the creature, size of a small pony, would not be budged. Leon registered its stubborn disapproving growl as the other dogs – smaller, but only slightly less vicious-looking – shuffled and bounced under what Leon somehow sensed would be a Meat Feast, Large.

'Big Chicken delivery,' said Nigel from his feathery port-hole. He proffered the goods over the swirl of monster mutt and mixed mongrels.

Taking possession, Leon raised the food to what he hoped would be a *safe* height.

'Do I know you?' asked the chicken.

361

'No.' Leon had remembered their previous encounter but hoped Nigel wouldn't.

'You look familiar.'

'I get that a lot.'

'Hmm . . . I don't normally forget a fa—*argh!*'

Alpha Dog, snarling and slobbering, had locked fangs onto Nigel's tail. As Chicken-Nigel made a futile attempt to break free, Leon went into hurry-up mode: struggling to balance the large order on one arm, he rooted a pocket, and after some fumbling, produced a twenty.

'Not sure I've got change.' Nigel fought to maintain equilibrium as he checked inside his fluffy money-belt.

Leon hooked the door with his foot. 'Keep it, Nige.'

'Oh, cheers. *Get off!* But how did you—'

Nigel's tip-joy was short-lived as Alpha Dog, still locked onto tail feathers, put a growl into second gear and shook his massive head, slobber shooting out in all directions.

The lesser dogs were getting feisty, too: showing teeth, going up on hind legs, gnarling and snapping, barking and the like – two got so excited they started having sex.

Leon's leg swung the door shut.

'Go away, bad dogs, shoo, shoo,' fussed Chicken-Nigel flapping his wings at the frenzied pack. But Alpha Dog, growling deeply, was about to advance, in one rapid move, from costume tail feathers to *actual backside.*

Leon didn't witness this savage escalation but heard the scream as he turned off the hall light. Mental images: a gazelle, its hindquarters snared by pouncing lioness; a wolf, hard-shaking a limp rabbit; and a young wildebeest, seized by a river crocodile, sprang into his mind's eye. He would not be opening the door. If Nigel couldn't hack it, he should get another job. Sorry, but that's how it is, Leon thought.

Welcome to the city.

As Leon re-entered the living room, feathers and a costume chicken-head flew past the window. Richard hijacked the food and replanted his arse in the sofa. Leon drew the curtains.

'I got extra Pepperoni. I know how much you like it.' Richard rammed in a Meat Feast wedge and spoke through a mouth full of toppings and dough: 'Not sitting?' Then he poured Pepsi down his gullet until the plastic creaked and Che Guevara took a soaking.

'Do you *ever* change your clothes?' asked Leon. 'You've been wearing that T-shirt for as long as I can remember. And I'm sorry but that dressing gown . . .'

'What about it?' A chunk of half-chewed Pepsi-soaked pizza fell from Richard's mouth to the carpet.

'It smells something chronic.'

'Balls, it's perfectly fine. It's no worse than yours.'

Richard scooped up the fallen lump of pizza, shoved it back in. 'Did you pick up more cigarettes?'

Leon fished a pocket, caught a pack of Marlboro Reds; held them out.

'Put them in the drawer, will you?' Richard took another slurp of pop.

Leon opened a drawer in the computer desk . . . and another . . . and another . . .

Each drawer was stuffed full of Marlboro Reds.

Leon sat down hard on the computer chair.

'What the fuck?' Shovelling a heap of packs, he turned, brandishing the discovery in Richard's direction – Exhibit A for the prosecution.

'Oh, those,' said Richard. 'I'd forgotten about—'

'*Forgotten?* Look at them.' Leon scooped out packet after packet, tossed them into the air. 'So much for: *I haven't got any cigarettes. I must have some cigarettes. Leon, I'll simply die if I don't get some cigarettes.*'

'I just meant . . .'

'Liar!'

'How dare you. I didn't know—'

'Sure. Like you didn't know the difference between Olive and Jenny?'

'An easy mistake to make,' said Richard, ripping the lid from a dipping sauce. 'Damn; thought this was barbecue.'

Back in the drawers, rummaging had turned up something even more interesting . . . a large bag of weed.

Leon touched the bag, hoping it wasn't really there.

And that's when he noticed his *saffron-coloured fingers.*

Under appalled eyes he sniffed. 'Fuck,' he blurted.

'What is it now?' asked Richard.

363

'My fingers!'

'What about them?' Richard held out Pizza. 'Here, try some Meat Feast.'

'They're *yellow*, Richard. *They're fucking yellow!*'

'So? My fingers are yellow, too. See. It's what comes of being a slave to the old weed.'

'But I don't smoke.'

'Balls, you don't.'

'Okay, yes, I sometimes have the odd one – when I'm stressed – but never more than one a day. Ten a week, tops – *maybe* – on a *bad* week. And that's not smoking. Not really. That's not . . . *this*.'

'*One a day?* Do me a favour. The only thing you do once a day is take a dump. And, for the record, that's *your* weed – not mine.'

'Richard, please! Stop talking shit.'

'Don't get uppity with me, you flaky fuck . . . I'm on *your* side.' Richard's features slowly shuffled from peeved to pastoral to philanthropic. 'If you don't want pizza, have some Häagen-Dazs. Maybe it'll cheer you up.'

He held out the tub of ice cream. 'It's Cookie Dough.'

Leon studied the dreadful image: mangled greasy hair; grey unshaven face; soiled and stained T-shirt; painful grin packed with Meat Feast; stained fingers; tired, smelly dressing gown; lost, watery eyes. And he came to realise (as the more astute no doubt realised long ago) that the wretch on the sofa – the pitiable wreck known as 'Richard' – was just another vision; an aberration of Leon's disturbed mind. Richard belonged in the notebook with all the others.

'Fuck no,' said Leon. 'It can't be.'

Richard had nothing more to say – for now.

Leon held his troubled head in his hands, his mind flashing backwards.

To the bathroom:

It's as if Leon is actually there, everything sharp and bright; the smell of dry soap, spilt toothpaste and unflushed toilet; there's a cloud of steam and . . . what's that . . . the bitter smell of tobacco? Sure, but the sweet odour of cannabis, too. And not *steam* hanging in the air: *smoke*. He feels a chill in the room. The bath is full, though the water is stone cold, and occupied by a gaunt, angular figure reclining within the grey scum, smoking a spliff.

Onlooker Leon approaches slowly, tentatively, until he encounters the face: a face belonging to a partial doppelganger; a version of himself he can't recall seeing before. Not in any mirror or reflection. This, whatever it is, half-Leon/half-Richard hybrid, clearly hasn't eaten or slept properly for a long time. The eyes are dark and lost, the head tilted to one side as if contemplating a world beyond this one; the only nod to being here, the suck of the spliff and a shiver it seems not to notice.

The onlooker slumps, puzzled and disorientated, against the sink – but confusion gradually gains a faint sense of clarity lazily approaching. Motionless and silent, he watches his ashen semi-clone take a final drag and extinguish the roach in the grimy water (the surface teems with phlegm and scores of diffused stubs) before reaching for a Marlboro chaser. Then the spectre stands, steps out, shuffles, dripping, to the toilet and squats. Onlooker Leon's epiphany finally barges in when the hybrid speaks:

'The only sustenance I've had in the last twenty-four hours is a thin rasher and a single slice of Farmhouse.' The voice is more Leon than Richard, but only just.

In nothing flat, the surroundings transform effortlessly from interior to exterior, from bathroom to back garden:

The hybrid is now robed in dressing gown and Che Guevara T-shirt. 'I'll be back in a second,' it says, scurrying for the house. 'Shout me if she heads south of the equator.'

Onlooker Leon observes the hybrid break into a short run and launch Dylan with his foot. The cat's scream arcs over the fence. 'No wonder that cat hates me,' says the onlooker. But his words are lost. Anne, shrieking, has opened her bathroom window, wide; clouds of steam issue forth into the night sky and her big oily breasts heave with each screech as she points at the hybrid.

The onlooker notices the binoculars in the hybrid's fist – *his* fist. 'Oh shit,' he says thickly.

The shrieking continues in the kitchen:

The kettle is blaring, the last of its steam now mixing with dark smoke and the smell of burning. Onlooker Leon experiences this from the living room where, at the same time, he witnesses the hybrid – this blurred, psychotic facsimile of what he, Leon, once was; the deranged creature he had turned into over the last twelve months – address the empty sofa: 'I hate to be the one to tell you, old chap,' it says, to a space between cushions, 'but one of us is seeing things – and it isn't me. *Jesus, that fucking kettle!*'

The hybrid storms out of the room. Seconds later, the high-pitched screech fades and dies. A short hiss as the kettle is given the cold tap.

Leon lifted his troubled head from shaking hands; the flashbacks over. Richard had opened the Häagen-Dazs and was now shovelling in spoonfuls of Cookie Dough.

'*Why?* Why would I imagine *you*?' asked Leon. 'Who the fuck *are* you, anyway? I don't even know who you are.'

'Of course you do,' said Richard. And somehow, his manic smile, teeth coated in Cookie Dough ice cream, inferred: *I am you, one and the same.*

'No, I'm not having that,' said Leon. 'I'm not . . . You're just—' He needed to sit down . . .

The sofa too far for jelly legs, he made do with the floor.

'It can't be. I mean . . . what the fuck?'

'Oh well, at least you know now – *that's something.* Just think of me as Mr Pickles; grown up but without the strings. Hey, want to see me dance?'

Richard held up a bag of LSD tabs.

'And after that, we can *paaaar-tay!*'

Loud rave music on, he shed the grubby dressing gown, filthy T-shirt, scummy pyjama bottoms and stained slippers, and danced naked.

Now at close-quarters with the carpet, from a slanted view and with unfocused vision, Leon watched Richard's legs gyrate and twirl. As Leon slipped into what would be his last ever blackout, he felt Richard toe-poke him and then, getting no response, party on.

The following year, Leon would write (in a new note-book; a birthday present from Jayne Angel – the *real* Jayne Angel) about his annus horribilis in this way:

I'm still not really sure what it was all about — that night, after a miserable, crazy year of voices and visions and losing myself. After a long twelve months of not accepting the truth of my parents' deaths and my psychological refusal to move on, the whole thing felt a bit like—

Here he'd pause to find the right words.

—a bit like the twisted relief you feel when you finally receive long-expected bad news . . . REALLY bad news . . . Grave news.

Another pause, then:

So Richard, possibly the strangest apparition of them all — what in the world was going on there?
Perhaps in some strange way, having Richard around gave me strength; the strength to cope — a bit like a child retreating into the comfort of an imaginary friend.
Or maybe he was a warning; a glimpse of the future; my future.

And here, Leon's writing would get shaky:

But at least on that night, just over a year after the awful, fatal crash, the nightmare was finally coming to an end.

Then he'd add:

Well, almost. There was still something I had to do.
No, make that a couple of things . . .

Leon would write more on the subject, but enough of that for now.

CHAPTER TWENTY

Onwards and Upwards

MORNING AFTER

As the night (a night Leon would come to refer to as Meat Feast Night, then later, unhappy with that, Epiphany Night) had delivered simple clarity to that which had been super confused, the morning, too, brought something: a sense of completion (or perhaps more accurately, a sense of *near*-completion).

Leon awoke to find his room disgusting but not trashed. Not a thing in its right place, everything seriously untidy, but nothing *wrecked*. Batman still had his head on, for example. And his bed wasn't in need of repair as he'd first thought. But it *was* foul; truly revolting – and he meditated on when he'd last washed the pillowcases and bedding.

By the open window he noticed the scattering of seeds; they waited there still with no sign of a red-breasted visitor.

As Leon questioned if *Robin* had been real it suddenly occurred to him that all his visions had had something *red*: red nose; red armband, a gore-stained apron; lumberjack jacket, boxing gloves, Guevara T-shirt, bandana, et cetera.

And not always items of clothing; sometimes just lips or eyes, he recalled. For a time, Leon couldn't think why that might be . . . then he thought of the Royal Mail letterbox, freshly painted, standing like a marker at the scene of the crash. He figured it must be that.

He did not consider the obvious connection: *blood.*

If Leon thought the bedroom and bathroom were bad, downstairs was even worse: the kitchen sink was piled high with unwashed plates and congealed pans, counter tops were riddled with mouldy lumps of God-knows-what, and the cooker was greasy and blackened beyond recognition; the living room, littered with the remnants of Meat Feast Night and all the nights that had preceded it, looked like a bomb-site and stunk to high heaven.

Leon phoned work and asked if he could take a day or two off even though it was short notice. Reg was out of the shop but Seema said it would be fine and not to worry; told him it was about time he used some of his holiday entitlement. Did he want to take longer? No? Sure? Okay, she would see him on Monday.

For the next three days Leon cleaned the house from top to bottom. He tidied up, washed clothes, changed bedding, vacuumed carpets, scrubbed and disinfected the toilet (you don't want to know what *that* was like), dusted surfaces, and mopped floors. Chewed pizza crusts, the empty boxes they came in, ice cream tubs, chicken-wing bones, and squashed Pepsi-bottles, along with the rotting contents of the fridge, out-of-date freezer meals, scores of Marlboro packs (both empty and full) and stinky ashtrays, were consigned to the wheelie bin. He wiped mirrors and skirting boards and sills, scoured sinks, washed dishes, purged the microwave, cleaned the inside of every window, swabbed the bath, cleared out the box room, emptied wastepaper baskets, scrubbed the windows on the outside, and generally cleaned and tidied until his back ached. And throughout the 'spring clean', Richard remained, as they say, *conspicuous by his absence*.

On the fourth day, Leon moved on to the garden to tackle the weeds and overgrown 'lawns'. The grass hadn't been cut for over a year and took some shifting. He hacked and carried, mowed and trimmed, all the time being careful not to look towards Anne's place. He did accidentally catch a glimpse of her bathroom window at one point and noticed the glass was frosted. Was that new? He wasn't sure. Anyway, it mattered no longer. He'd been happy to assume that particular night might not have happened at all and had got on with mowing, sweeping the drive, disposing of various dog shits, and collecting discarded fag ends.

Finally, he spent the remainder of Sunday evening, having first had a long overdue soak in a hot bath (the first in eleven days; could be worse, Leon's record for 'forgetting' to take a bath or shower was four weeks!), eating Chinese take-away, reading quietly, feeling *normal*, and considering his future.

✶ ✶ ✶

Now, early Monday morning, as he made a full English breakfast for one, Leon was happily surprised to find himself whistling – like his dad used to do.

The radio predicted favourable weather and followed it with '*I Can See Clearly Now*' by Johnny Nash.

Leon thought this quite a coincidence.

'That would explain a lot,' said Poppy, getting off the tram. 'You do look much better now.'

'Thanks, I *feel* better.'

Leon was feeling happy, too; happy he'd found no weirdly-unusual passengers in the carriage; only the usual, and the usual unusual – commonplace to all cities.

'And no offence, but you *smell* better, too.' Moss was really starting to grow on Poppy but she had to be honest with herself; Leon would have been her first choice.

'I know. Turns out I'm not allergic to soap and water after all.'

'*Mmm*, you can't beat a nice deep, hot, soapy bath . . .'

Poppy's eyes stayed on Leon but her mind wandered.

Leon gave her a second then cleared his throat.

'Sorry, where was I?' asked Poppy.

'Not sure; something about a deep, hot . . .'

'Really? Did I say that out loud?'

Leon nodded and there followed an ever-so-slightly awkward beat. Both parties silently acknowledged it was funny but that they should move on.

'So . . . no more visions, then?'

'Nope. Touch wood.' Leon tapped his head.

'Fantastic. *And?* . . .'

'I'm going today, after work.'

Poppy smiled, adding a nod when Leon motioned that he needed to get cracking.

They hugged – then Poppy watched him go.

'Girls like flowers, Leon!' Poppy shouted.

Lunchtime ended Leon's unremarkable and rather typical morning: some key-cutting, a few engravings and several shoe repairs; the odd finger cut and a hammer bruise.

In the back room, he binned an empty triangular sandwich carton then opened a bottle of water.

Seema, eating from a salad bowl, nibbled up a piece of limp lettuce hanging from her mouth.

'Is it good?' Leon asked.

'Oh yeah, delicious,' Seema replied with due sarcasm. A stick of celery vanished in stages as she munched it, rabbit-fashion. Leon twisted the top back onto his bottled water.

'Not going out for a smoke?' Seema asked.

'What?' asked Leon confused for a second. 'Oh no, I've given up.'

'Good for you.'

At this moment, Reg stuck his head in just long enough to say, 'Right, you two, a minute please.'

Seema and Leon followed. They found a tray filled with cream cakes on the counter and Reg pouring a bottle of something fizzy into three glasses.

'And what are we celebrating, Reg?' asked Seema, her tone a little suspicious.

'I've just had a phone call from Helen.' Reg handed out glasses. 'And it's good news.'

'They're closing us down,' said Leon.

'Not us,' Reg replied. 'The Cross Street branch.'

'Oh what a shame,' said Seema. 'That's Alan Boardman's shop. He's been there ages, poor thing.'

Reg raised his glass. 'And Helen said no further cutbacks are planned. That's it.'

'That's what they said last time,' Seema whispered.

'So, here's to *another* twenty years.' Reg hoisted his glass higher, willing his staff on.

Leon checked the label on the bottle as Seema took a hesitant, unpleasant sip. Reg knocked back a gulp and quietly slid the cakes towards Seema.

Leon took a long look at Reg then put his glass down.

'No, I can't,' said Leon. 'I don't want to do this anymore. Keys, and cobbling, and cat's collars . . .'

Reg said, 'Are you mad? You've probably got a job here for life now.'

'Yeah, that's what bothers me.'

'You won't find another job like this one.'

'Good.'

'So what, you're quitting?' asked Reg.

Leon nodded.

'Well I don't know, there's nowt so queer as folk, as my mother used to say.' Reg took another gulp then drifted off, presumably down memory lane.

'Ain't that the truth,' mumbled Seema, sniffing the contents of her glass.

She made a face to Leon that said: *What is this crap?*

'I don't know,' Leon said quietly, 'but it tastes like sh—'

'Champers!' exclaimed Reg, back in the room. 'Not proper Champagne believe it or not but it *is* nice, isn't it?'

Raising the bottle, he went on the attack.

'Come on, shame to waste it; more Bubbly, everyone.'

Ignoring the sounds of the unwilling, he squeezed a few more drops into their glasses, refilled his own.

'By the way, Leon, for the record, I've never liked you.'

'Reg!' barked Seema.

'And you've got enough outstanding holidays to cover your notice so you might as well go now.'

'*Reg!*'

'I'll have somebody in to cover before you can say "Now, piss off".' Reg raised his glass. 'Cheers, everybody!'

As Reg necked his drink, he pushed the cream cakes directly in front of Seema.

And fuck you, too, Reg, Leon nearly said. He didn't, because for some reason, he felt he didn't need to.

* * *

Outside the shop, Leon handed over his divested tabard.

'Ignore Reg,' said Seema. 'He's an idiot.'

'I know,' Leon replied.

'Can't take his drink either.'

Leon's nod carried the weight of impending sorrow; that of parting with a true friend. Seema gave him a long, dazzling smile. 'Well, if it's alright with you,' she said, 'I'd like to give you a traditional Indian farewell.'

'It doesn't involve getting me naked, covering me in coloured paint powder, and throwing me in the Manchester Ship Canal, does it?' asked Leon.

'No; it's not *Holi Day*. And stop being rude, this is a very sad moment for me. I'm going to miss having you in the shop.'

'Sorry.'

'Not to mention having to deal with Reg on my own.'

'Yeah, I feel bad about that.'

'Don't worry; I'll give him a slap if he gets out of order. Did you see him push those lovely cream cakes in front of me? Bloody cheek! And I'm so hungry after that rubbishy little salad. Honestly, Leon, I felt like grabbing that chocolate éclair and shoving it right up his you know what.'

'His arse?'

'Yes, exactly,' laughed Seema, 'his big fat arse!'

'I'd liked to have seen that.' Leon smiled but it was a sad smile.

'Sorry, where were we? Oh yes, traditional goodbye.'

Seema cleared her throat then held Leon by his shoulders (he seemed to be getting a lot of that recently).

'Until we meet again, may the Great Spirit make sunrise in your heart. And may your moccasins make tracks in many snows yet to come.'

Leon's brow furrowed.

'What? Okay, it's not *British-Asian* Indian; more *Native-American* Indian, but it's still beautiful, right?'

'Right. Thank you.'

They hugged. 'Look after yourself, Leon.'

'I will.'

'And don't be a stranger.'

'Okay.'

'And if you do start seeing crazy things again, seek qualified medical assistance.'

'Okay.'

'I don't just mean Googling the Internet.'

'Okay.'

'Leon . . .'

'Are you about to say: *And stop saying* okay, *okay*?'

'No. Why?'

'No reason.'

'Go now. And don't look back.'

'Okay.'

They hugged again – for the longest time – and then Leon walked away. After about ten paces he turned round and headed back. 'Sorry,' he said, pointing to the florist's shop next door, 'I meant to go in there first.'

Seated on the tram, Manchester city centre slipping by the windows, Leon looked around the carriage.

He was alone; just him and two bouquets of flowers: one of yellow sunflowers, one of white orchids.

Upper Church Street: Leon stood before the entrance to St. Mary's church; stone arch above, open iron-gate ahead – everything solid and calm.

Flowers gripped, Leon waited a spell then entered.

ORCHIDS

Leon fluffed the orchids a little, crouched, and then gently placed them by the headstone. The epitaph read:

IN LOVING MEMORY OF LESTER & VERONICA BLANK,
TRAGICALLY TAKEN, GREATLY MISSED.

After a few minutes of silent contemplation, he rose, brushed all traces of dust and grit from the top of the stone then sat, a few yards away, cross-legged, like a primary school child posing for a class photo.

He put the sunflowers to one side, took out his notebook, opened to a clean page, and wrote:

Mum and Dad,

First of all, please forgive me for taking so long to come and see you. A year is much too long. I'm sorry.

I've missed you. I missed you both so much that I got myself into a bit of a mess. You're not to worry, though; I think I'm okay, now.

Don't even know why I'm telling you this; I'm sure you already know.

374

Having immediately regretted the last sentence – of course, this needed saying – Leon crossed it out.

He resumed with:

Mum,

How I wish we could hug again. Those warm soft cuddles of yours always made things right, always made me feel better. That big contagious smile of yours and the way you used to call me 'little soldier' when I cut an elbow or grazed a knee.

I miss your cooking, Ma — especially the homemade chicken broth, the ribs and cabbage, and Lancashire Hot Pots. Mmm.

I loved the sound of your voice. And when you laughed, it was so sweet I could cry; tears of joy though, Ma, tears of joy.

Thank you for being there, Ma. Thank you for being my mum.

Leon turned the page, continued on the reverse:

Dad,

I was finally able to go in there. The garage had felt so empty and wrong without you inside, working on something or other; the back garden, too: all those hours we spent, me in goal, you taking penalties. Even with your bad leg, child-size goals, and trying hard to make it easy for me, you still scored more than I saved. I would never have made a great keeper like you were. Unlike me, you were a natural. It's such a shame things didn't work out for you, Dad. You would have been BETTER than Stepney!

Thank you for the fishing trips and teaching me to juggle and amazing summer holidays and all those Saturday afternoons in the Stretford End. Watching football is not the same without you, hearing you cheer or boo, encouraging players, or berating them, and telling the Ref or Linesman what you thought of their decisions. But most of all, I will miss our chats — chats about everything, chats about nothing.

I will always miss you, Dad.

Look after Mum for me. I hear her laughing, even now.

Leon contemplated the voids in every direction: spaces through overhanging branches; the brief lulls in road traffic; cracks in the old church wall and stone slab path; gaps between headstones, the short-lived intervals that divided four joyless bell tolls as St. Mary's marked the passing of time; and for a while – the hole, no, the chasm, in his life.

But then he pushed the emptiness aside, filled it with his mother's sweet laughter and his dad's reassuring voice; pulled in the memories, all the happy times; moments to be held on to and cherished: Lester and Veronica; Mum and Dad . . . onwards and upwards.

Leon spoke into the air: 'I hear you clearly, dad; as if you're right here beside me.' He closed his eyes and drew in a long breath; perceived the sun's mild warmth on his eyelids and felt his dad speak to him. The oh so familiar voice, voice of his father, so like his own, echoed inside – as if the sound vibrated through his core, through the very DNA they shared.

Their common voice said, 'What have we learned?'

Leon thought for a while, considered late-afternoon sky and the crooked spire that eventually pointed to high clouds, sensed a light breeze pass over his skin, caught the orchids' scent and heard a bird chirrup in a tree by the church wall. He sat there for a good ten minutes then wrote:

I have learned that life is about learning to let go. Parents must one day let go of their children, and so, in turn, must the children let go of their parents. It's not easy, how could it be? But it's something, at some point, everyone has to do.

Leon welled up – but he didn't cry, not in a sobbing, uncontrollable way, just watery eyes and a lumped throat.

Once the flow of emotion had ebbed, his pen moved again:

And like you always said, Dad: Onwards and upwards; onwards and upwards . . .

Then he wrote:

I LOVE YOU BOTH.

Leon signed his name, drew kisses and tore out the page. Then he stood and walked back to the headstone.

'Mum . . . Dad . . .' He spoke as if addressing all that he could see and all that he could not. 'It was a nightmare twelve months. You were there yet you weren't there. But what's *really* odd . . . is that now I've accepted you not being here, I feel that you *are*. Does that make sense?'

Leon laughed. 'Listen to me. How ridiculous am I? Like there was ever anything you didn't know before me. You always were the ones that knew.' And you probably know this, too, but I'm going to say it anyway . . .'

'Know that I will *always* love you, and I shall think of you both, often and fondly.'

He folded the torn-out page and placed it under a child's-fist-sized rock at the bottom of the headstone. The action felt Jewish – like he'd seen on *Schindler's List* – but his action wasn't religious or symbolic, he just didn't want the note to blow away. Maybe that's how the whole deposit-a-small-rock thing started, he thought.

He kissed the headstone, simply because it felt right and then stepped back.

Picking up the sunflowers, Leon noticed an elderly lady, close by, kneeling before a parlour-polished headstone.

Mrs Perkins (Leon assumed her surname matched DEAR DEPARTED HUSBAND, ARTHUR H. PERKINS who was now, according to the etched stone: ONLY SLEEPING) had also placed flowers.

Wiping her eyes with a tissue, Mrs Perkins smiled at the young man. The old lady had heard and understood and was moved and didn't think it at all odd to be talking to the dead – it was something she had been doing for the last three weeks.

'Don't believe Elton John,' Mrs Perkins said.

'Excuse me?' Leon replied.

Mrs Perkins dabbed the tissue against her nose.

'*Sorry* isn't the hardest word.'

'I see,' Leon said, not seeing at all.

'*Goodbye* is the hardest word,' explained Mr Perkins' widow.

Leon nodded; advanced one of those *I understand* funeral-service smiles.

'Arthur just told me that.'

'Did he? It's very astute. Was he a big Elton fan?'

'Oh God, no. He hated Gays.'

'Right. Bit harsh.'

'With a vengeance.'

'Did he? That's a shame. What about you?'

'What about me? I don't like Lady Bits if that's what you're implying.'

'No, no, sorry, I was just . . .'

'Never let it be said that Deirdre Perkins drank from the furry—'

'No, no, please, I wasn't inferring . . .'

'That whole thing with Reeny Reynolds was just a simple misunderstanding.'

'I'm sure it was.'

'Innocent camping-trip high-jinks – and nothing was ever proved.'

'Exactly.'

'And that was all such a long time ago. No need to dredge up ancient history.'

'People should just move on, I say. Put it behind them and . . . let's all just move on, shall we?'

'Wonder what Reeny's doing now?' said Mrs Perkins, misty-eyed all of a sudden. 'I haven't seen her since that summer. Father said we couldn't. Not after . . .'

Deirdre's voice trailed away and her face went blank; her mind perhaps considering a wasted life with Arthur *Homophobe* Perkins – possibly revisiting summer-camp dalliances and girly sleeping-bag fumblings with Reeny '*Go on, you know you want to*' Reynolds and thoughts of what-might-have-been had times been different . . . or maybe that was just Leon, projecting. He did that sometimes.

Deirdre Perkins showed no sign of returning so Leon cleared his throat. She blinked and came back.

'Speaking of lyrics,' he said, 'I heard an old Johhny Nash song on the radio this morning – "*I Can See Clearly Now*".'

'And?'

'And I thought it might be, you know, *significant*.'

Deirdre put out a big old shrug. She might have been thinking: *You ripped me away from Reeny to tell me that* – Leon wasn't sure. The moment was becoming awkward. How did he get into this conversation? The only way out he could see was to push on.

'He said he could see clearly now the rain had gone.' The way Leon spoke made it sound like a question.

Mrs Perkins squinted, tilted her head, slightly confused.

'He could see all obstacles in his way.' Again, upwards inflection at the end of the sentence; I must stop doing that, he thought. He was starting to feel ridiculous. And why am I quoting song lyrics to a widowed dyke-in-denial, anyway?

Deirdre arched her grey eyebrows.

'There was that rainbow he'd been praying for.'

Deirdre's features contorted into a mélange of what-the-fuck-are-you-talking-about?

What's her problem? Leon wondered. Maybe she's questioning what I'm doing with these sunflowers. Maybe she thinks I nicked them from somebody's grave. *Explain!* No, it's nothing to do with her. He pushed on:

'He said it was going to be a bright bright bright bright bright sun-shiny day.' Leon was immediately unsure about the number of 'brights'. He may have used too many.

'So?' The old woman sounded like a stroppy fifteen-year-old.

'So . . . I thought it was, you know, like I said, kind of significant. At last I have my eyes open. Like the song, I, too, can see clearly now.'

Deirdre Perkins grimaced.

'Too cheesy?' asked Leon.

'Johnny Nash?'

'I believe so.'

'Arthur didn't like Blacks,' said Deirdre.

379

Leon had walked away without looking back, but if he *had* looked back he might have seen the two robins (one considerably larger than the other) that landed on his parents' headstone – coincidence, no doubt.

He stood now under the stone archway staring off into the distance, contemplating his next move and he remembered, not for the first time, something Poppy had told him in the café; part of that whole pep talk chat about courage and writing and hopes and dreams. Felt like ages ago now but he knew it verbatim:

'There are many possible futures,' she had said, 'but it's about choosing the one we want . . . and going for it.'

No doubt about it, he mused, the girl is good with words.

'And you know what, Leon,' he told himself, 'When you're right, you're right.'

And with that, he set forth; next stop, Kath's Kaff.

SUNFLOWERS

Leon entered with sunflowers, a courter come to call, but Jenny was nowhere to be seen. Several customers put eyes on the chump with the bouquet but Leon wasn't fazed.

Retaining a confident air, he approached Olive.

'Are those for me?' she joked.

'Hi. Can I have a word with Jenny, please?'

'Who?'

'Jenny. The other waitress.'

'I'm the only waitress works here, love. Why do you think the service is so slow?'

A customer – sixties, flat cap, bad eye – respectfully raised a finger.

Olive waved a hand. 'Yes, in a minute,' she groaned.

'You *must* know Jenny,' Leon insisted. 'She's got a tattoo on her back.'

Olive exhibited the ugly Bulldog on her bicep.

'Like this?'

'*Christ, no.* But very nice by the way. No, this is a sunflower.' Leon pointed to his lower back as if that might jog her memory.

380

Olive's perplexed head showed no sign of remembering.

'Perhaps she's in the kitchen,' suggested Leon. 'Or working a different shift . . .'

'Look, Leon, I'm not being funny but—'

'Oh no,' said Leon.

'What?' Olive asked.

Leon realised instantly, or more like he already knew: *Jenny wasn't real.*

'Not again,' he said, through an insightful smile.

Knowing for certain, and immediately resigned to the fact, Leon laughed long and hard.

—And whilst laughing his mind zipped back:

Upper Church Street, one year ago: outside the church, in a white shirt, dark jacket and black tie; features burdened, sad and lost (not unlike the Urchin that had reached out from beneath the DVD section in Nobby's Newsagents); breathing wrong, more in than out, and feeling stuffy, like he was dressed backwards; heavy, too, awash with emotion, submerged in it, yet empty, detached, dislocated from the moment; deserted; abandoned – and refusing to get out of the car.

This is when he had first seen 'Jenny' . . . through the funeral car window, walking by on the far side of the street. Moving like a gazelle; gliding like a model.

His eyes, dull one minute, shining the next, had followed her. But, of course, the street was empty. He saw that now. She was *never* there. He absolutely knew it to be true.

There had never been an *actual* 'Jennysis'; only an *imagined* one.

Leon, not laughing now but still smiling decided it *was* kind of hilarious; pathetic, sure, but funny. Thank God for a sense of humour, he thought.

And then he remembered *here*, in the café, the place packed and him running around tables pretending to be King Kong, grunting and growling as he chased his invisible prey – the 'Jenny' that no-one else could see.

He thought of all the mystified customers who had watched his strange behaviour: the young mum who swept

381

up her child and rushed for the exit, her friend holding the door open, urging them to hurry; the old man who applauded and stomped his feet; and the two nut-loaf eating do-gooders who agreed how marvellous the Care In The Community program was then audibly shat their pants when Leon had jumped on their table, beat his chest and roared.

Leon grinned at the thought of that. The image was mad; comical.

'Are you okay, Leon?' Olive put a hand on his shoulder.

Leon nodded.

'You sure?' she asked.

'Yeah, I'm sure.'

'Excuse me, waitress?' asked Flat Cap/Bad Eye, politely.

(Leon thought Flat Cap might have been the same man who stomped and clapped his King Kong but wasn't sure.)

Before Leon left, he gave the sunflowers to a bemused black guy sitting by the door. He was fifties and wore a bus driver's uniform. Leon secretly hoped the guy was gay and that Arthur Perkins would be spinning in his grave.

'Aw,' purred Olive. 'Why doesn't anyone ever give me flowers?'

'Excuse me . . .' a friendly reminder from you know who.

'Fucking hell, what?!' barked Olive.

Minutes later, Leon and a plastic bottle passed under the low-slung bridge; one, purposeful and intent on the tow path, advancing all roused and peppy; the other, top on, body-cracked, neck full of trapped rank air, shoulders suspended above the surface, drifting aimless in the canal.

A single stone was kicked. A depleted splash replaced a muffled thunk and a triumphant fist punched the shaded light.

'He shoots, he scores, and the crowd go wild,' exclaimed Leon, turning slow, arms wide like Cantona, nodding contentedly to the crowds gathered under the bridge.

CHAPTER TWENTY-ONE

Speed of Life

RUN, LOLA, RUN

For several days and nights, between the meals he remembered to eat, Leon had sat on his bed reading various drafts of 'The Geisha and the Samurai' – turning pages, engrossed, lost in the world of his own creation.

Despite regular cacophonies of ugly sounds beyond his window – dogs that woofed, and front doors and car doors that slammed, and shouts that called or answered or threatened or cursed, and cats that mewled, and cars that raced, and sirens that chased and an unattended alarm that rang on and on and on – he made changes, gave the story a new, 'more suitable' ending, removed material ultimately deemed 'superfluous', polished every remaining sentence, paragraph and page until it shone, typed it all back into the computer and reprinted. He had come up with what he believed was a final draft so strong; he wouldn't be able to improve on it further. To do more would spoil it; the story, he felt, was now 'finished'.

He studied the last page, still warm from the printer:

The final words spoke of Nathan and Ramona; of how they upped ropes, pushed away from the coastal quayside mooring and set off in a small boat, without maps, unsure of the tides or winds, and lacking even a rudimentary knowledge of how to sail – armed only with a few provisions and a sense of being underway.

And sou'-sou'-west of bold or foolhardy adventure Leon wrote: *THE END*.

Stubbornly ignoring the swelling internal voices of self-doubt, he allowed himself an unmeasured moment of satisfaction and achievement. Soon after, he set down the manuscript, picked up the remote and put eyes on his TV.

About to press Play, he finally noticed the exterior noise.

Shit, I must have found the Hole without even realising it, he mused. 'Nice one,' he said aloud. Then he closed the window, spun up a DVD, and hiked the volume.

The soundtrack was powerful, liberating and free, and Lola was running, running, running.

ONE WAY TICKET

No-one had seen Leon for three weeks; it was now early December, and Vicky and Peggy were getting a little concerned. They had wondered if they should contact Social Services or knock on Leon's door, check he was okay, but decided not to; he had acted *very* weird before he'd 'disappeared' – besides people around here tended to mind their own business unless something directly impacted *their* lives. Instead, they gossiped idly about a *different* neighbour and all the loud rowing and door slamming late last night. But as the women nudged and insinuated, they suffered an interruption: strange clunking noises from over the road, behind the doors of Leon's garage.

Tittle-tattle on hold, they listened to the harsh sound of objects being dragged and placed then shifted and rearranged; a long silence – then more, softer, shuffling and moving-about noises.

The women, curious, looked to each other then refocused on the garage, for there came now a new sound: a 200cc engine, low and throaty.

Moments later, the doors burst open to reveal a dark and dusty interior.

Again, the women eyed each other before returning their gaze to the garage – to where Leon was easing out of the gloom; rolling out on Lester's 1966 Lambretta SX 200.

The scooter was immaculate, polished to showroom quality, covered in mirrors and horns, and still with its original 'LB' decals. Only the tall aerial's original Target flag was missing. A helmet hung from the handlebars.

Leon advanced slowly up the drive – all fine and dandy – to the open gate where he stopped and sat for a moment, surveying the area, proud as a popinjay.

Slack-jawed, Vicky and Peggy watched in silence.

Leon, dressed in Lester's Parka, handsome mohair suit and thin tie, with a pair of his own black, matt-leather lace-up Weaver shoes (he had found and tried on dad's Winkle-pickers, but two sizes too big would have put the journey at serious risk of shoe-slippage) took a long, long look at the house and then – rebelliously refusing to don the helmet – drove away.

The women, faces like netted cod, said nothing.

As Leon drove by his grandparents' house he glanced over. Bill and Norma were in the front room. Bill, naked apart from a black cape and vampire teeth, chased Norma, also naked (and wearing a long blonde wig for some reason), around the sofa.

By the time Leon had passed the barren maple tree, he was being trailed by several small kids who shouted infantile abuse: 'Get off and fucking milk it!'; 'What the fuck is that?'; 'Sounds like a fucking hair-dryer!'; 'Fucking wanker!' and other fucking variations. One shouted, 'Go on, run away again, Leon, you fucking wuss!'

'This isn't running away, you little shit,' exclaimed Leon, 'this is leaving in style!' And with that he gave the little bastards the middle finger. Deeply angered they gave chase with great intent but eventually fell behind.

As Leon drove down Stickleback Road, he spotted Reg struggling home, weighed down by several bulging carrier bags; packed, Leon assumed, with high-calorie food for Sherry. Reg looked to the fine scooter, seemed to get confused by who the rider was, then toppled sideways as one of the carrier bags burst.

A little farther on, in front of the precinct, Leon pulled up beside Poppy and Moss, sharing an ice cream. Poppy raised eyebrows, gave a thumbs-up for the scooter and the apparel. Leon echoed the gesture. She made a bee-line and apprehended him in a mad squeeze. (Poppy was wearing a black-and-white mod dress with high Mary Quant 'Daddy-Long-Legs' boots – something Twiggy might have worn – which Leon thought uncannily coincidental, what with him being on a 1960s scooter and all. She would have looked great on the back of the Lambretta but oh well.) The three conversed for a while, mostly Leon filling them in on the events of the last fortnight or so. There followed approving noises and rounds of sad but happy *Goodbyes* (and *Must keep in touch* and *Look after yourself* and *Definitely visit* and *Take care* and the like). Then Leon and Moss long-hugged with firm pats like old mates do – especially when one is leaving town – and finally it was time to separate; Leon riding off, Poppy and Moss staying behind.

Everybody waved until Leon turned the corner at the bottom of Lower Church Street and there was nothing left to wave to. He'd been gone only seconds when a familiar BMW pulled up. Carl got out, rodent features leading the way. He approached Moss but Poppy stepped in his way.

'What's your problem, bitch?' Carl said.

'He doesn't need anything, thanks.' Poppy's voice was polite but stern (like everyone else, she knew all about the gruesome twosome). *Courage, Poppy, courage – but don't kick him in the balls unless you really have to.*

Carl squared up and looked ready to slap her.

'I know what you need,' he said through a ratty smirk.

'Maybe you're right,' said Poppy. 'But I doubt you're the one that can sort it.' She leaned in, close to his ear. 'You know why?' If Carl knew, he didn't say.

'Because I can guess what you're angry about. What you're *really* angry about.' She pulled her face back and looked him full in the eyes, allowing time for the statement to reach in and find the nerve. Carl's ratty face twitched a bit but still he said nothing. He appeared a stage actor unsure of his next line (had this been theatre, the front row audience would now cough and fidget uncomfortably).

Danny didn't appear uncomfortable at all; he seemed to be *enjoying* the standoff – he had got out of the car and taken a ringside seat, resting his cocksure backside against the front wheel arch.

Though it was probably too late, Carl did now act. He sucked his teeth and gurned an over-egged expression of stupefaction, but the pause and lack of immediate vocal denial had added gravitas to Poppy's unspoken but not altogether ambiguous suggestion.

A growing certainty filled the air and everyone felt it. Carl laughed, unconvincingly, and his bony hand batted away the ridiculous accusation; this nasty bitch and her sad muppet boyfriend weren't worth his time.

'Come on, let's go,' Carl said to Danny. 'This loser's lost his fucking balls.' He disengaged and got back in the car.

'Bollocks! Takes a man with real fucking balls to come off weed,' said Poppy. 'You . . . you . . . mother-flipper.'

'Fuck you,' barked Carl. 'You coming, Danny, or what?'

Danny scrutinised Poppy and she was ready to take him on too, if he fancied it. But Danny didn't – if anything, he seemed to respect her courage. 'That's some woman you got there, Moss,' he said. 'You look after her.'

'Let's go!' yelled Carl from inside the car.

Danny winked at Poppy, climbed back in the BMW and drove Carl's ugly mug away.

'Wow, man, you really told him.'

'I know, and did you hear my bad-ass street lingo?'

'I did,' said Moss kissing her cheek. 'It was kinda sexy.'

Poppy decided he deserved to share another ice cream.

SOMETHING IN THE AIR

Around the corner, as Poppy was setting Carl straight, Leon stopped by the letterbox. Removing his backpack he took out an A4 envelope. Package bulk suggested a manuscript of one hundred pages; around 25,000 words – a good-sized novella. Addressed to a publishing house, the envelope was marked for the attention of an agent Leon had found on the Internet. The agent stated on her website that she was 'always on the lookout for exciting new projects and liked the quirky, the unconventional, and above all, a challenge!'

Leon hoped his unconventional and quirky story would fit the bill. He kissed the package for luck and dropped it into the letterbox. Then he put his helmet on – he'd proved his rebellious side for long enough (besides he didn't want to get a ticket) – and drove off.

At the top of the hill, passing the church, tooting playfully to the spirit of his parents, Leon noticed a damaged and despondent Chicken-Man sitting in the bus shelter. Clutching a handful of screwed-up flyers, he didn't acknowledge the shiny Lambretta as it whizzed by.

THE GOOD, THE BAD, AND THE UGLY

Hours later, daylight and Chicken-Man long gone, it sleeted a cold, soft snowy rain. In the bus shelter, Ronnie, mumbling, saluted something or someone only he could see. He sucked on a can but it instantly ran dry. Cursing the lack of another, he muttered something about arseholes.

A car pulled up on the far side of the road. The driver's window slid down part way.

'Hey, Ronnie, you mad Marine,' shouted Danny. 'Come here.'

Ronnie gazed over but didn't move.

Carl lowered his head so Ronnie could see him.

'He said *here*, piss-head – y' deaf?!'

Ronnie made them wait a moment then blundered out into the road and weather. A lopsided walk weaved to the car. The feathery sleet mottled his back as he bent to the gap in Danny's window.

'What do *you* want?' Ronnie said, pulling up his coat collar.

The window scooched all the way down.

'We just wanted to say well done on keeping quiet all this time, Ronnie. Must be what . . . a year now?'

'Yeah, and to celebrate,' added Carl affecting nonchalant conviviality, 'we've got you some of your favourite: White Lightning.' He held out a four-pack, and Ronnie gave them the once over. 'Not that anyone would believe you now, Ronnie. But make sure you keep it up anyway, yeah?'

The ciders floated at Danny's window but Ronnie didn't accept. Danny offered an incentive: he lifted his shirt, revealed the Glock 17 tucked into his pants.

'We're not going to start having a problem with you, are we, Ronnie?'

Still Ronnie did nothing – apart from get wetter.

'Go on, take 'em,' said Carl. 'You don't wanna offend us.'

'Trust me, that's the last thing you should do,' added Danny.

'Take 'em!' Carl shoved the cider cans forward.

'I don't want anything from punks like you. I know the kind of crap you sell to the kids round here.'

'They only take what they want, Ron; no different to you and your booze. Now hurry up, you're getting my car wet.'

'They're just kids,' said Ronnie, 'kids who don't know any better.'

'What; like Moss?' asked Carl with a sneer. 'Like your fucked-in-the-head nephew?'

Ronnie's bloodshot eyes fired a piercing beam at Carl. A stare-off was underway . . .

Carl spoke first: 'You better stand down, Major,' he said. 'Or should I say, *ex-Major?*'

But Ronnie didn't stand down, and the stare-off gained intensity with no sign of either party backing off. The only thing missing was the theme tune from *The Good, the Bad, and the Ugly* (how apt) playing on Danny's sound system.

Anyway, after however long the standoff lasted – hard to judge these things – Ronnie moved: he lurched forward, reached for the gun and *BANG*, shot Danny in the crotch.

Despite the trouser-holing and instantaneous blood, Danny, for some reason, mustered only a whimper.

Ronnie, who had kept his unblinking eyes on Carl the whole time, now grinned, slowly, enjoying the moment and the weight of the smoking gun in his hand . . . Carl was next, no doubt, and Ronnie wanted him to suffer the absolute certainty of knowing exactly what was coming.

'Oh my God, he's shot me in the balls,' complained Danny looking down for the first time.

'If you think that's bad, wait till you see what I'm going to do to Rat Boy here.' Ronnie winked. 'Ready, Rat Boy?'

But Carl turned into Johnny Ringo. He whipped out his Heckler P30 and *BLAM*. Ronnie toppled back clutching a bleeding chest and collapsed out of sight.

'When you have to shoot – shoot – don't talk,' said Carl adopting a truly terrible Mexican-Bandit accent.

'Film quotes – *now* – really? He shot me in the balls!'

Carl's look suggested Danny had missed the *most* important fact here: 'I shot a fucking Marine,' Carl said.

'*Ex*-Marine,' Danny whined.

'It's still a fucking Marine. It counts.'

Danny raised his top and pulled out the waistband of his blood-soaked pants but his vision was already turning dark.

'Is it bad?' asked Danny. 'Take a look. Is my cock still there?'

'What? No way. Anyway, I don't need to – look at all the claret.'

'*Claret?* What are you, a fucking cockney gangster now?'

'Whatever. That's a fatal wound right there. Believe it.'

'Fuck off, it won't be fatal. I might have lost a bollock at the most; two, tops. Here, call me an ambulance.'

Danny tossed his mobile then shoved a hand tight against his groin, trying but failing to stem the flow.

'Carl, what the fuck are you waiting for? Call a shitting ambulance.'

'You mad? I've just killed a war hero. I can't call Five-O.'

'Fuck's sake, Carl.'

Carl shrugged.

'Give me the fucking phone, I'll call it myself.'

'Sorry, mate.'

Danny was now sitting in a rapidly deepening pool of blood. 'Carl, you fucking bastard,' he groaned, his voice weakening.

'They won't be here in time. What's the point?'

'I fucking knew it.' Danny's voice trailed away then he passed out – or died, who knows.

Carl's ratty, feral eyes did a hurried three-sixty, found the coast clear. His slippery streetwise brain shot into overdrive and an idea was instant.

Moving quickly, he wiped his Heckler with an old Big Chicken paper napkin from the glove-box, and set the Marine-murdering gun in Danny's hand, pressing the limp bloody fingers against the weapon's grip and trigger.

Then, taking care to avoid the *claret*, he removed drugs secreted under the driver's seat, and a fat roll of bank notes from inside Danny's blood-spattered jacket.

Finally, out in the now heavy wintry mix, Carl confirmed that Danny's crotch-shooting Glock was still gripped within the cold meaty fingers of Ronnie's tattooed hand.

The rat would have liked to set the car on fire but figured he couldn't risk spending more time at the crime scene. He ran off, down the hill – in the same direction the snowy rain was slowly shifting Ronnie's blood.

CHAPTER TWENTY-TWO

A Tale of Two Summers

WISHFUL BEGINNINGS

The following summer, at a window table in The Red Dragon Café, Leon wrote at length . . . reaching the end of a page, he turned over, and continued.

He was working on a new project: *Extra Time* – a novel.

Having heard back from the agent, it seems he *had* missed the window on 'medium-length' pieces. Nobody bought 25,000 word novellas anymore; it was either *small*: short stories (1000-7500 words); *very* small: Micro- or Flash Fiction (up to 100 or 1000 words respectively); or traditional 'good-sized' novels (between 80- and 140,000 words).

Poppy had been right.

The agent said she liked his work, though; encouraged him to send more – but of a length people were currently buying. Leon sent her the finished version of 'Dark Horse' and a batch of other short stories, including a new piece called 'The Snowman and the Scarecrow'. He was waiting to hear back. In the meantime he would work on the novel.

Leon had kept himself extremely busy in Wales and no longer maintained an Oddity Log; he'd seen nothing 'odd' since leaving Manchester.

Presently, a pretty brunette waitress weaved between tables towards him. She brought over a smile, a cup of tea and her name-badge. Jayne, twenty-two, spoke with a beautiful Welsh accent:

'There you go. Sorry it took so long. We've had a bit of a rush on.'

Leon smiled; there were only four customers.

'No, that's great. Thank you, Jayne.'

He sipped his tea and she showed no hurry to leave. The pair had taken an instant liking and both sensed it.

'*Mm*, nice,' he said with arguably too much enthusiasm.

'Goodness,' Jayne said, 'I don't think I've ever seen anyone so pleased just to get a cup of tea.'

Leon beamed like The Cheshire Cat, went a little pink in the cheeks. She had the nicest smile he had ever seen; genuine and friendly – the expression suited her.

'So how come I haven't seen you before?' he asked.

'Been travelling; New Zealand, Australia, Thailand, India. Lovely it was . . .'

Jayne's mind had wandered, Leon presumed back to her travels, and he watched her for a good twenty seconds, an *excellent* twenty seconds, until she returned.

'Oh sorry, I forgot your meringue; back in a minute.'

She tootled off.

Nice walk, Leon thought, watching her shapely backside shimmy under her skirt. He wondered if 'forgetting' was just an excuse for two trips. He hoped it was.

As Jayne disappeared from sight, something outside caught his attention: a dishevelled-looking Father Christmas, one eye notably bigger than the other, looking in at the window. Leon felt an instant biliousness rise in his stomach and a wave of panic sweep through him.

His concern increased when Cleopatra, a small band of pirates, two nuns, and a teenage pilot all walked past in quick succession. And there were others, all moving or talking or entering shops or coming out of shops.

Here are some of the others Leon saw: a ninja, a Mexican with an over-sized sombrero, a white rabbit constantly checking his watch, a woman on stilts, someone dressed as Wally from *Where's Wally?* (Leon found him easily), a robot (made from cardboard boxes covered in kitchen foil), Death (with a large sickle), a tipsy Mr Blobby, an M&M (green), and Dorothy and the Tin Man (who walked, stridently, arm-in-arm, towards China Street).

There were also people in groups: a brass band (playing something vibrant and booming) marched past the café followed by four bananas, several young jockeys, a group of native Americans in ceremonial gear, a few relatively-short Na'vi (blue aliens from Avatar), a flock of human sheep, and a banner of Camelot knights clapping coconuts as they 'rode' invisible horses.

Not all moved on foot; some drove past in vehicles. One, a dark blue Mitsubishi *Outlander* driven by a Minotaur, had an Imperial Storm Trooper riding shotgun and two small Hobbits in the back; the Minotaur parped his horn at Beetlejuice and Elvira who turned and waved to the mythological Greek creature and his entourage.

A flat-bed truck shipping a splash of waving mermaids with beauteous faces and beatific smiles came next but Leon's goggle-eyes were now pulled down the street, to near where the Lambretta was parked:

A large mustard tube and a big round Marmite jar, both on colour-coordinated legs, had got into a tummy-bumping competition. The strange, almost-cartoonish pair bumped and jumped in a friendly but challenging contest of hot condiment versus that yeasty love-it-or-hate-it stuff.

'Who's your money on, then – Marmite or mustard?'

Leon turned sharply. 'What?'

'Marmite or mustard?' asked Jayne. 'Or Win and Dai Evans as they're known round here.' Jayne placed a dish of Lemon Meringue on the table. 'I don't know; fancy wearing the same costumes every year. I couldn't do that.'

'Every year?'

'Fancy Dress Day.'

'Fancy Dress Day?' parroted Leon.

'Llani Fancy Dress. Our carnival Day. Quite famous it is.'

Leon looked nonplussed.

'You've not heard of it, then?'

Leon shook his head.

'That's amazing. Been going for years it has, annual like. Since the Sixties, I heard. Whole town turns out, just about. Starts in the afternoon and goes on all through the evening. Pubs do a roaring trade.' Jayne laughed. 'Well, it's a chance for us to let our hair down and have a bit of fun, isn't it?'

'Right, of course, Llani Fancy Dress Day,' said Leon.

Outside, the man-sized condiments, an ancient, twisted mug in each face-hole, were intensifying their argy-bargy.

'Funny pair, aren't they? Look at them, pushing and shoving. You think they'd know better at their age.'

Jayne and Leon watched what appeared to be a cross between bad amateur wrestling and a slow waltz: a metre

393

this way, a metre that way. Then Marmite fell on his back, stuck like an upturned tortoise. Mustard jumped on top, well, more like *flopped* on top, pinning Marmite down. The pair flapped around in an orgy of flavouring.

'What's their problem?' asked Leon.

'They both want to be Mustard.'

'Why?'

'Both hate Marmite, they say. Don't know why; I love it.'

'Yeah, same here,' said Leon. 'Wouldn't want to dress up as it, though; not with my legs.'

'Funny guy,' said Jayne, giving him a playful shove.

'So, you see all these?' asked Leon. 'The two punk rockers over there; Marilyn Monroe; that band of Roman centurions . . .'

'Yes, of course. Even without my glasses. Why?'

'No reason. One second.' Leon stood, addressed the other customers, now six in number:

'Excuse me, everybody, sorry; just a quick question. Do you all see Jayne – this fine-looking waitress, here?'

Jayne gave him an abashed nudge with her elbow.

Three customers looked confused but two nodded and one said, 'Yes, why?'

'Good, because I want you to know: she's the best waitress I've ever had.'

'No, I'm not.' Jayne pushed Leon down, onto his chair.

'Sorry?'

'Silly me, I forgot your serviette; back in a tick.'

She tootled and shimmied again.

There came then a hard knock on the window.

Leon jumped. *Fuck! Is that Pogo?* No, just a clown; a regular, clown – freaky, but *ordinary* – and he's not coming in, Leon realised, relieved; he's just walking by.

Idiot wants to stop knocking on windows, though; you can give somebody a heart-attack doing—Jesus!

Another knock, even harder, found Molly dressed as an angel; a grandiose version of the doll in her hand. Her flamboyant twirl followed by a combination of elaborate ballet moves got a thumbs-up, and then it dawned on Leon:

He had never been to a Fancy Dress.

Molly's mother, in a cowgirl outfit, now walked past the window and beckoned for Molly to come along. Both angels curtsied then hurried to catch up.

Leon smiled and got to thinking:

He thought he'd done the right thing. Yes, he was *sure* he had. He'd made the break. And it was all good now, as Moss might say. The novel was going well, he felt, and he was happy to have a list of ideas for more – and he'd only been in Llanidloes seven months. Maybe Poppy was right; it had just needed some courage.

As Jayne returned, a large group of Mods led by a smiling couple, vaguely reminiscent of a young Lester and Veronica, drove past on scooters. Leon wasn't sure if he was projecting – but he took the chimera, if indeed it was, as a good sign.

Jayne placed the napkin on the table. 'So, would you like anything else?' she asked, her eyes fixed on Leon's.

The question felt loaded, loaded in his favour, and he thought she had, as some say, a certain sparkle in her eye.

'Yes,' replied Leon. 'I was wondering if I could take you out later.'

'Well, let's see . . .' she said, pausing to think and tease. 'I've got to pick up my costume from my sister's . . .'

'What are you going as?'

'Little Red Riding Hood.'

'Nice.'

'Grown up, kind of sexy version – you know: white stockings, bodice, little red cape . . .'

'*Very* nice.'

'Perhaps you could be a big, bad wolf?'

Before Leon could think of a reply, clever or otherwise, Jayne leaned over and wrote her phone number in his notebook.

'See you later, then,' she said through a big smile.

Then she walked away leaving him a backward glance – one of those little looks that only women can do.

As Leon watched her clear plates from a table near the kitchen, he noticed something on her back: a yellow Sunflower tattoo.

And his mind drifted . . .

THE GEISHA AND THE SAMURAI

In the middle of a forest, surrounded by tall fir trees, a Geisha and a Samurai are making love. Light summer breezes caress the pine cones; below, ladybirds and butterflies frisk and gambol about swaying foxgloves and magenta bells – and all around, unseen birds sing. The scene is beautiful; *looks* beautiful and *feels* beautiful.

Inside his elaborate, crested helmet, the samurai's face beams with euphoria. A happy delirium sweeps through him – as if he were spinning, riding a whirlpool; exquisitely inside her, yet beside himself – outside the sublime intimate pairing, beyond the physical, able to look in at the radiant courtesan, orbit around her, to see her far away but at the same time focus on detail – taking in her exquisiteness: her flowing kimono, her full white face make-up, and her traditional Shimada hairstyle – tied up and decorated with ornate hair-combs and -pins.

He is a happy samurai.

The geisha, for her part, has the air of the queen of all the woodlands, sitting astride, as she is, her man. Her face, softly convoluted in divine ecstasy, gazes down at her samurai: he is adorned in full, ceremonial battledress armour and looks magnificent.

At this precise moment, the geisha feels like a goddess, a woman of celestial divinity; she is in Heaven, Shangri-La, Zion, Utopia, and Paradise – a place of bliss, intoxication, rhapsody, and delight. And she is making the noises any samurai worth his katana would want to hear: *Mmms* and *Oohs* and *Aahs*. And so on.

She is a very content geisha.

Her sounds lilt gently like soft music in the air. If this were a film there would be a song: something like 'One Love' by The Stone Roses – forceful and moving, passionate and romantic.

A musical soundtrack might have been absent but the air is filled with scents and sounds, both sweet and musty: violas, pine, pansies, moss, ferns, late bluebells; grasshoppers, crickets, woodpigeons, pheasants, bees, dragonflies . . . all the natural noises and aromas of the forest. And, of course, its new incumbents: fooling around, making love . . . fornicating.

The geisha and the samurai look stunning but from a distance it would be hard to tell their identities. An observer, had one been there, might have thought he was witnessing a mystical mirage, a harmonious marriage of aesthetic beauty and magical rapture. He might have found it hard to tell if the couple were real – or not real.

After all, it's not every day you see something like that – if ever.

Later, beyond the edge of trees, after the resplendent geisha and proud samurai had exited the forest and the samurai had removed his lacquered, metal-plated kabuto helmet and held it under his arm, Leon said:

'Well, I've not done that before.'

Play-punching, Jayne said, 'You say that every time.'

Leon laughed. 'But you were right; it *is* nice in the woods.'

'And to think, you once thought it might be weird. Honestly, you city boys think you know everything, but us country girls . . .'

'Yeah – I'm not sure I'm your *typical* city boy.'

'Well, stick with me, kid, you might learn something.'

'Already have,' said Leon, grinning from ear to ear. 'Still, I wasn't expecting all those *yee-haws*.'

'What? I never . . .' She realised he was kidding and whacked him with her fan. He reached out to her but pretending to be riled she walked off towards the scooter.

He knew she was pretending.

Jayne stopped by the Lambretta and brushed her geisha robe.

As she checked her make-up and hair, sunlight caught the mirrors and it made Leon think of a home movie he had watched in the past.

He studied Jayne for a moment, admired how she looked, the elegant way she held herself – and it wasn't just because of what she was wearing – then he put his helmet back on, shouted 'Banzai!' and ran towards her.

397

The samurai grabbed the geisha. They embraced, kissed passionately, then mounted the Lambretta, laughing.

'Come on, Leon-san,' Jayne said, 'the carnival will be starting soon.'

As they drove away, a new flag, attached to the scooter aerial, fluttered – it read COURAGE in Japanese symbols.

Scooting along a country lane, the geisha's arms entwined around the samurai's middle, reflections of passing hedgerows smearing across their visors (they'd donned crash helmets when forest dirt-track had met traditional road surface), their fancy-dress costumes – reminiscent of a 16th century samurai and an 18th century geisha (sandwiched between 21st century crash helmets and a 20th century scooter) – fluttered enthusiastically as the wonderfully timeless Welsh countryside slipped by.

Above the scooter's raspy engine, the pair whooped, happy and free.

Before they had travelled a full mile, there came a great noise: a deep, resonant whir; it murmured, powerful and low – its rhythmic pulse beating the air. And within the vibrant hum, Leon heard a familiar voice:

Leon! You selfish evil tosser!

Leon shouted over his shoulder: 'Jayne, can you hear that?'

'No!' replied Jayne.

'Me neither,' yelled Leon.

'Yee-haw!' shrieked Jayne.

They laughed and Jayne held tight as Leon hit the throttle.

As they drove away from that which had only just swelled into view – a wide expanse of hillside spiked with tall, white turbines; giant rotor blades atop tubular steel towers, swishing and spinning, chopping through the air – the huge wind-farm now appeared to push the hill farther and farther away . . .

Had you been standing on that hill, you would have seen the scooter and riders head for the horizon, shrink to a speck on the landscape, and gradually fade into the distance.

EPILOGUE

Extra Time

By the way, before I start this bit, can I just say to any grouchy malcontents who thought the ending a trifle hackneyed or cliché: I'm sorry – but that's what happened!

And would you really have wanted to see a tragic ending after all that Leon had been through – perhaps falling into farming machinery or being carried off by a giant buzzard?

Well, would you? Hmm? Just saying.

Okay, now I've got that off my chest, we can get on with the epilogue:

Two years later, Leon completed his novel: *Extra Time*, a quirky dark comedy with several twists and turns – the tale told of Stan, an elderly retired referee, who had just been informed, on his birthday of all things, that he was terminally ill and had only a few weeks to live. The old man, an inveterate gambler, refused to believe the prognosis and placed a large bet that he would still be alive on his *next* birthday.

The problem was: the independent bookies Stan used (the only gambling establishment in the neighbourhood that *hadn't* been firebombed), belonged to Maggy McCulloch, the hardest bitch in Glasgow – a domineering gorgon with a suspected history of violence that most Weegies[9] dared not even whisper about. Maggy was perfectly happy to *accept* big money bets but wasn't so keen on making big money pay outs.

And so, one year later – when Stan, despite his fatal illness, looked like he was actually going to reach his birthday – it was perhaps inevitable that the ruthless battle-axe would decide it was time to act.

---

[9] Weegie: Noun. Scottish slang for a resident of the city of Glasgow. (Also used as an adjective. Example: 'How ya doin, ya weegie bastard!') Really, you couldn't have got that one on your own? The clue was in the sentence.

Plan A was to offer the widower a series of increasingly dangerous 'proposition bets' – and if those failed – well . . . Stan would just have to meet with a slightly fatal 'accident', wouldn't he?

Unfortunately for Maggy, Stan seemed to have the luck of the devil.

Unfortunately for Stan, his time *really was* running out – the final whistle getting closer and closer . . .

Leon had sent the novel to several agents and publishers and was waiting to hear back (sadly, the original agent – who, by the way, had *loved* Leon's short stories – was 'taking a break' from the business for a while. She had written to Leon to explain as much from HM Prison Holloway where she was now 'on holiday' for tax fraud).

If Leon couldn't find another interested party (either agent or publisher) he would, he'd decided, put the novel up for sale as a download and print-on-demand on Amazon and elsewhere, and count on favourable blog reviews and Twitter to spread the good word.

He hoped his books (he'd already started writing another, a kind of, as he'd come to think of it: Billy Liar meets Donnie Darko – to be loosely based on his own experiences) would make enough money for him and Jayne to rent a small house in Llanidloes.

But if not, the caravan would do just fine.

A NOTE ON THE AUTHOR

Adrian Baldwin is a Mancunian now living and working in Wales. Back in the Nineties, he wrote for various TV shows/personalities: Hale & Pace, Clive Anderson, Brian Conley, Paul McKenna, Smith & Jones, Rory Bremner (and a few others). Wooo, get him.

Since then, he has written three screenplays, one of which received generous financial backing from the Film Agency for Wales. Then along came the global recession to kick the UK Film industry in the nuts. What a bummer!

Not to be outdone, he turned to novel writing – which had always been his *real* dream – and, in particular, a genre he feels is often overlooked; a genre he has always been a fan of: *Dark Comedy*.

Barnacle Brat (a dark comedy for grown-ups) is his first novel.

He is currently working on two more novels to complete what will be his 'Let's all Laugh at Death' trilogy; three separate stories loosely linked by theme.

A second trilogy: 'Let's all Snigger about Sex' has been proposed as a follow-up. If it happens, it will no doubt be an orgy of filth and depravity and far-fetched characters (perverts, most likely!) all smothered in copious amounts of distasteful black humour. If that's the kind of thing that appeals to you, you sicko, you're probably just the type of reader he's looking for.

For more information, check out: **adrianbaldwin.info**

The author invites readers to e-mail him at:

adrian@adrianbaldwin.info

Follow him on Twitter **@AdrianBaldwin**

and on Facebook at **Facebook.com/AdrianBaldwinAuthor**

*A photo of me and my dad. (Please note the lack of an imaginary friend!)

A few final thanks need go to the following:

Film-maker/photographer/artist, Marco Zaffino: his beautiful shading work was gratefully incorporated into the front cover design.

Christopher Hansen, who gave kind permission to use his wonderful font, *Carnivalee Freakshow*, throughout **BARNACLE BRAT**

(A note on Leon's handwriting: Despite more than twenty-odd minutes of research I couldn't find a font that I felt reflected Leon's 'style' so in the end I created one based on my own dreadful scrawl. My thanks to MyScriptFont.com for making this possible and my apologies to any readers whose discerning eye I offended.)

And last, but certainly not least:

I'd like to sincerely thank all my Left 4 Dead gaming comrades for their online-support and encouragement over the last couple of years; especially:

Swampbeetle, FecKiT, Matt, Boudicca, Rossi, Danbarino, Scooper, Izzy, Shane, Lulu, Midge, Metzi, Ronnie, Zobble, Hazz, Con-Angel, and yes, even Adski – plus all the other (far too many to mention) members of the Twisted Fire-$tarters Clan.

Here's to our battle cry: *'I've got a Molly and I know how to use it!!'*

Front Cover Art/Design by Adrian Baldwin & Marco Zaffino
Rear Cover, Spine & Frontispiece Art/Design by Adrian Baldwin

Author photo by James Alan Baldwin

Photo of James Alan Baldwin and the author by Ken Baldwin
(by kind permission of Ken's family: Ruth, Lynne, Julie and Christine)

Lightning Source UK Ltd.
Milton Keynes UK
UKOW04f0003141213

223000UK00001B/11/P